Mistletoe
BRIDES

Mistletoe BRIDES

SARAH MORGAN
LIZ FIELDING
JAN COLLEY

MILLS & BOON

Published in Great Britain 2015
by Mills & Boon, an imprint of Harlequin (UK) Limited,
Eton House, 18-24 Paradise Road, Richmond, Surrey, TW9 1SR

MISTLETOE BRIDES © 2015 Harlequin Books S.A.

Italian Doctor, Sleigh-Bell Bride © 2008 Sarah Morgan
Christmas Angel for the Billionaire © 2009 Liz Fielding
His Vienna Christmas Bride © 2009 Jan Colley

ISBN: 978-0-263-91796-3

012-1115

Harlequin (UK) Limited's policy is to use papers that are natural, renewable and recyclable products and made from wood grown in sustainable forests. The logging and manufacturing processes conform to the legal environmental regulations of the country of origin.

Printed and bound in Spain
by CPI, Barcelona

ITALIAN DOCTOR, SLEIGH-BELL BRIDE
SARAH MORGAN

USA Today bestselling author **Sarah Morgan** writes contemporary romance and her trademark humour and sensuality have gained her fans across the globe. She has been nominated four years in a row for the prestigious RITA® Award from the Romance Writers of America and has won the award twice.

Sarah lives near London with her family. When she isn't writing, she loves spending time outdoors. Visit her website at www.sarahmorgan.com.

CHAPTER ONE

'I'M ABSOLUTELY not getting married again. Not ever. Not in a million years. Don't even suggest it. Once was more than enough.' Liv closed the drug cupboard and stared at the bunch of glittering silver tinsel attached to the door. 'That can't stay there, Anna.'

'Of course it can. It's Christmas. I hung mistletoe there to begin with, until I realised that the only male I'm ever alone in this room with is the chief pharmacist.' Her colleague gave an expressive shudder. 'Now, stop changing the subject. You have to forget that you've been married before. Everyone's allowed one mistake in life.'

'Well, Jack was certainly that. A mistake disguised as a smooth-talking, good-looking man. On the outside he seemed entirely normal.' Liv glanced at her friend and gave a little shrug. 'Actually that's not true. His disguise was a bit thin in places. There *were* clues, it's just that I missed them. Which is the other reason I wouldn't dare to get involved with anyone again. Obviously I just see what I want to see.'

Anna frowned. 'You're *so* hard on yourself.'

'Well, that tends to happen when you've deluded yourself once.'

'It wasn't delusion,' Anna said firmly, 'it was trust. You trusted him. And he let you down.'

'It was delusion,' Liv said calmly, checking the stock of antibiotics. 'All the signs were there, but I ignored them because I just didn't want to see them. Even when Jack walked out of the delivery room saying "I can't do this", I told myself he was just talking about the stress of seeing his beloved wife in labour, whereas what he was *trying* to say was that he just couldn't "do" responsibility. He didn't want to be a father. And he didn't want to be married to me. It's just a pity for Max that he didn't make that decision a little bit sooner.' She put the boxes back on the shelf. 'Actually I don't mean that because then I wouldn't have Max and he's the best thing that has ever happened to me.'

'You're a wonderful mother and Max is a lucky boy.'

Is he?

Liv pushed through the guilt that was always pressing in on her. 'Well, I've learned to kick a football, if that's what you're saying, and I know the difference between a Lamborghini and a Ferrari but that doesn't make up for the fact that Max has a mother who works and no man in his life.'

Anna beamed at her. 'So use those tickets you won to the Snowflake Ball!'

'I'm not using the tickets.'

'Liv, it's Christmas! Time to let your hair down and party. This is a fabulous opportunity to meet someone. For goodness' sake, those tickets are like gold dust. Michelle on Paediatrics was offered a thousand pounds for hers but she refused to sell.'

'You're kidding! Who on earth was stupid enough to offer her that much money?' Liv's jaw dropped. 'Did she make a note of the name? I could sell my tickets and replace my car.'

'Why must you always be so practical?'

'Because I'm a single mother with a child of seven and responsibilities.' Liv checked the expiry date on a tube of eye ointment. 'If I'm not practical, we don't eat.'

'Has your car actually died?'

'Not yet. It likes to keep me in suspense.'

Anna waved a hand dismissively. 'Forget the car. This is London—you can always get the train. Keep the tickets and go to the ball, Cinderella.'

'Given the meagre contents of my wardrobe, that's not a bad analogy. I certainly have plenty of rags to choose from.'

Anna stood back and narrowed her eyes. 'I'd offer to lend you a dress but you're actually quite— Your boobs are—'

'Big,' Liv slotted in wryly. 'I am aware of that, actually, having had them stuck to the front of my chest for the past twenty-eight years.'

'You were born with those?' Anna started to laugh and Liv rolled her eyes.

'How did we start this conversation? It isn't as if we're not busy. There's ice on the roads and we've had three road traffic accidents in so far today. Last time I looked the waiting room was busier than the shops. *Stop* interfering in my life and go and heal the sick.'

'Only if you promise me that your New Year's resolution is to start seeing men. You don't actually have to get married—'

'That's a relief.'

'But at least go on a date. I'm worried about you. I mean…' Anna looked despairing. 'Aren't you lonely? When did you last have sex?'

'For crying out loud, Anna!' Mortified, Liv glanced over her shoulder to check that they were still the only two people in the tiny room.

'The fact that the mere *word* is enough to embarrass you tells me it's been far too long. You've been divorced for four years. It's time to get out there again,' Anna said firmly. 'If you're scared of a relationship then just have a one-night stand.'

'No way!' The thought horrified Liv. 'I hate the idea of waking up next to a man I don't know and don't care about. That just leads to misery.'

'There are two solutions to that. You can either kick him out of bed before he falls asleep or you could find a man you *do* know and *do* care about.'

'That just leads to misery, too. And anyway, I don't have the courage to take my clothes off in front of anyone.' Liv shuddered at the thought. 'And anyway, it isn't just about me. I have a little boy of seven. I don't want to trail a series of different men through his life. That's not how I want him to grow up.'

'You should be showing him that relationships are part of life, Liv. Yes, sometimes they go wrong. But sometimes they work. What message are you giving him? That love isn't worth taking a risk for?'

Engulfed by a tide of guilt and anxiety, Liv stared at her. 'You think I'm putting Max off relationships?'

'No, but I think you're so afraid of being hurt you just won't even give it a try, which is ridiculous because you're incredibly pretty and you have huge—'

'Anna!'

'Sorry. I just don't think you have any idea how gorgeous you are. Do you know what the men call you behind your back? Luscious Liv.'

'That's because they only ever see me with my clothes on. If they saw me naked, they'd be calling me Lumpy Liv.'

'You're ridiculous, do you know that? You have a fabulous figure.' Anna leaned forward and gave her a swift hug, her voice husky. 'I don't mean to nag or upset you but you're my best friend and I want you to meet someone nice. You *deserve* to meet someone nice. I wish I could buy you a night of hot sex for Christmas.'

'I don't want pity sex. I'd rather have bubble bath! It would be less embarrassing.' But Liv hugged her back, allowing herself an indulgent moment of female solidarity.

'Am I interrupting something?' A deep male voice came from behind them and Anna gave a strangled gasp and jumped back, her face scarlet.

'Mr Lucarelli! I mean—Stefano—' She cleared her throat, acting more like a student nurse than a senior sister with years of experience. 'We were just—we were…' Too embarrassed to speak coherently, she waved a hand helplessly and Liv sighed and took over.

'We were hugging,' she said calmly, desperately hoping that he hadn't overheard the conversation. 'Did you need something?'

Dark, challenging eyes settled on her face and Liv wished she hadn't drawn attention to herself.

Forcing herself to meet his gaze calmly, she tried not to notice his glossy black hair, his superb bone structure or the sensual curve of his mouth. He was indecently, impossibly handsome and Liv wondered idly how many female hearts *he'd* broken since he'd reached adolescence. They could probably be laid end to end across Europe. From the width of his shoulders to the blue-shadowed jaw, he epitomised all that it meant to be masculine.

He stood at least six feet two and the blue scrub suit encased a body that was hard and powerful. 'I came to tell you that we have transferred the patient to ICU,' he said in a cool tone. 'And I wanted to talk to you about Rachel.'

Anna immediately snapped back into her role as Sister. 'Is there a problem?'

'*Sì*, there is a problem,' he said impatiently, his eyes still on Liv. 'I don't want her working with me in Resus again.'

Anna frowned. 'She's a very good nurse and—'

'She can work with the others, but not me. She's nervous of me…' angling his arrogant dark head, he transferred the full force of his gaze to Anna '…and her nerves make her dangerous. Her hands were shaking, she dropped sterile instruments and every time I spoke to her, she jumped.'

Anna sighed. 'She's very young. You probably scared her.'

Bold brows came together in a frown. 'I didn't once raise my voice.'

'You don't need to. You're—' Anna broke off, clearly searching for a way to say what she wanted to say in the most tactful way. 'You're the senior consultant and obviously some of the more junior staff might find you…intimidating.'

'Then find me someone who isn't intimidated.' His voice was hard and tightly controlled. 'When I'm in Resus I don't want to have to be thinking about anyone other than the patient. I want the equipment in my hand, not on the floor and I expect the team around me to be completely focused and to anticipate everything.'

Anna's mouth tightened. 'So basically you want the people you work with to be able to read your mind.'

A sardonic smile touched his firm, male mouth. 'Precisely. That skill is essential to the smooth running of any emergency department. And now that we've cleared that up I'll leave you to your…' his gaze swept them both '…hug.'

Anna watched as he strolled back down the corridor towards his office. 'Great. Now he thinks we're lesbians.'

Liv let out a breath. '*Please* tell me he wasn't standing

there when you were talking about the size of my boobs and when I last had sex. Do you think he heard you saying that you wanted to buy me a night of hot sex for Christmas?'

'I'm not sure. Possibly.' Anna covered her mouth with her hand to smother the laughter and Liv gave a groan.

'OK, that's it. I resign. But only after I've killed you. I won't be able to look him in the face again.'

'I can't *stop* looking him in the face. I'm probably worse than Rachel. And you can't resign. You need the money. But remind me not to hug you in public again.' Anna frowned. 'Now he'll think I'm unavailable.'

'You are unavailable! You're happily married.'

'I know, but don't you just look at the man and think "sex"?'

'I look at him and think "trouble".' Liv pinned the keys into her pocket, trying to erase a disturbing image of shimmering dark eyes and bold male arrogance.

'I wouldn't mind getting into trouble with him. He certainly isn't afraid to speak his mind.'

'He has high standards,' Liv said firmly, 'and that's a good thing. He just won't accept anything less than the best and I like that. If I were to crash my car, he's the one I'd want treating me.'

'Now that is a terrifying thought.' Anna's expression was comical. 'Imagine, all your colleagues would see your underwear. Just for the record, if I'm ever brought in here and you have to cut my clothes from my body, I want you to make sure I'm wearing silk designer knickers and not chain-store cotton.'

'I think if you'd reached the point of needing to have your clothes cut off, the label on your knickers is going to be the least of your problems. Do you want me to check before or after I save your life?'

'You can joke, but I just know that Stefano Lucarelli dates women who wear matching silk underwear.'

'That doesn't mean he expects the same high standards from his patients,' Liv said dryly. 'Now, are you going to talk to Rachel or am I? His comment is justified, by the way. She's dreamy and needs to sharpen up.'

'Poor Rachel. He obviously chewed her up and spat her out. I'd better go and give her some sympathy.'

'She doesn't need sympathy, she needs a wake-up call,' Liv said briskly. 'She developed a crush on our Italian consultant from the moment he drove his Ferrari into the car park. If she stopped staring at him and concentrated on her work, she wouldn't drop things.'

'He *is* a little scary.'

'He is clever and efficient.'

'I'm glad you think so. Given that you respect him so much and you're indifferent to his charms, you can work with him in Resus so that solves one problem. Now, what was our other problem? Oh yes, what to do with your tickets to the Snowflake Ball.'

'I'm selling them. I have no man, no dress, no babysitter and no inclination to go to the ball. Nor do I have stepsisters, ugly or otherwise.'

'Invite Stefano Lucarelli.'

'Oh please! If I want public humiliation, I'll just strip naked. I have no intention of embarrassing both of us by issuing an invitation he will certainly reject.'

'He might not. He was looking at you.'

'He was probably wondering why someone with hips like mine hasn't gone on a diet.'

'You don't need to diet!' Anna looked at her thoughtfully. 'He noticed you, Liv.'

'Anna, he walked in while we were hugging and talking about sex,' Liv reminded her wearily. 'Of course he noticed me. It probably classes as one of the most embarrassing moments of my career.'

Anna ignored her. 'He's single at the moment, can you believe that? I don't get it. I mean, he's super-wealthy. His family owns some enormous construction business in Italy. There's no justice in the world, is there? Rich and good-looking is very unfair.'

'Anna, you're a married woman with two children.'

Anna ignored that, too. 'Apparently he was dating some glossy Italian actress but rumour has it that he ditched her because she was insisting on moving in with him. He's only been in the country for a month. He might be glad of a night out before Christmas.'

'He certainly strikes me as a man who needs help finding women.' Her tone sarcastic, Liv lifted a hand. 'Enough. End of subject. Do you and Dave want the tickets, or do I sell them?'

Rachel appeared in the doorway, her face pale. 'Ambulance Control just called and they're bringing in a man who was kicked on the rugby field. If you don't mind, I'd rather not work in Resus again today.' Her voice was high-pitched and decidedly wobbly. 'Dr Lucarelli was a bit…sharp.'

Anna straightened. 'Injuries?'

Rachel looked at her blankly. 'None. Except my pride, I suppose. I mean he was really—'

'The patient,' Anna interrupted her wearily. 'What are the *patient's* injuries, Rachel? And it's *Mr* Lucarelli, not "Dr". He's a trained surgeon. Surgeons are "Mr", remember?'

'Oh. Right.' Rachel cleared her throat. 'That patient was kicked.'

'Yes, but *where*?'

'He has breathing problems,' Rachel said vaguely and Liv gritted her teeth and handed Anna the keys to the drug cupboard.

'I'll take this one. Call the trauma team and ask Mr Lucarelli to come to Resus.'

'I'll send Sue to help you,' Anna muttered. 'Rachel, you and I need to have a chat.'

Leaving Anna to deal with the hapless Rachel, Liv pushed open the doors that led to the high-tech resuscitation room.

Always prepared for an emergency, the room was kept stocked and ready for patients and Liv was pulling on an apron and a pair of gloves when Stefano Lucarelli strode into the room.

He looked straight at her and for one brief, disturbing moment, neither of them spoke.

For sheer raw impact, she'd never met a man like him. Neither had she ever experienced the blaze of sexual awareness that suddenly flooded her body.

Mortified, she turned away quickly, her heart pounding and her face scarlet, just *furious* with herself for being so predictable. The man must be so tired of women staring at him. *It was just that stupid conversation with Anna*, she told herself crossly, pulling open a cupboard and removing the sterile pack she thought they might need.

Talking about sex had made her think about sex, and thinking about sex had made her—

Oh for crying out loud!

'Apparently the paramedics reported that the patient has some respiratory problems,' she said crisply, keeping her head in the cupboard for slightly longer than was necessary to give the colour in her cheeks time to fade, 'so I thought it might be wise to have a thoracotomy pack ready.'

'Good.' But there was a sharp edge to his voice that made her wonder whether she was about to become another casualty of his legendary high standards.

The doors to Resus flew open and the patient arrived along with the rest of the trauma team.

Swiftly and smoothly they transferred the patient onto the trolley and Stefano Lucarelli took charge, demanding silence from the entire team with a single sweeping glance.

He had presence, Liv admitted to herself, as each person around the trolley quietly busied themselves with their allotted tasks, while listening to the paramedic's handover. He was confident, but he didn't swagger like Greg Hampton, one of the more junior doctors. But neither was he as approachable like Phil, the other casualty officer who was currently looking for a vein in the patient's arm.

Working on automatic, Liv attached BP, cardiac and oximetry monitors to the patient and the paramedic collected his own equipment and left the room.

Stefano glanced at the monitor, a frown on his handsome face as he swiftly assessed the readings. 'Phil, put in two lines and send blood for immediate cross-matching. I want all clothes covering the front and sides of the chest removed.' He had an unmistakable air of authority that communicated itself to all the staff in the room and Liv cut through the man's clothing and reached for warm blankets to prevent him developing hypothermia.

'His respiratory rate is thirty-eight and it's very shallow.'

'He's in respiratory distress.' Stefano examined the man's chest and Liv noticed that Phil was watching out of the corner of his eye. Although he'd only been working in the emergency department for a few months, Phil soaked up information and never missed an opportunity to learn.

And there would be plenty to learn from Stefano, Liv thought, watching the way he examined the patient.

'There's a great deal of bruising,' she murmured, looking at the purplish marks on the man's ribs and Stefano looped the stethoscope round his neck.

'He has diminished breath sounds and decreased chest expansion.' Working with a cool, calm sense of purpose, he finished examining the man's chest. 'He has a clinically significant haemothorax. Call the trauma surgeon and ring the operating theatre co-ordinator and warn them. He might need a thoracotomy to drain it. Let's do a chest X-ray.'

The radiographer responded immediately. Like a carefully choreographed ballet, everyone worked simultaneously, carrying out his or her own clearly delineated roles.

'I need a hand here, Liv.' Phil was struggling to find a vein and Liv stepped forward to help. The more junior doctor slid the cannula into the vein and breathed an audible sigh of relief. 'OK, I'm in. Let's tape this, before we lose it.' Beads of sweat had formed on his forehead and his gaze flickered to Stefano. 'Wouldn't he have distension of the neck veins or raised jugular venous pressure if he had a haemothorax?'

'He's hypovolaemic.' Stefano's eyes stayed on the monitor. 'If you look closely at the patient, you'll see that there is a degree of tracheal deviation. Do we have two lines in, yet?'

'One. I'm just sending blood for cross-matching.'

'Get that second line in now. I need two lines before I put in a chest drain.'

Phil handed the bottle to Liv and then turned back to the patient to deal with the second IV.

'His veins are terrible,' he muttered after a few minutes. 'The first one was fine, but I've failed twice so far on this side. Do you want to have a go?'

Stefano stepped towards him. 'Turn his arm over. *Bene*. Cannula.' He held out a lean, strong hand and Liv passed him the equipment he needed, watching in silent admiration as the consultant slid the needle into the vein with no apparent effort.

He made the seemingly impossible look easy, she thought wistfully and clearly Phil thought the same thing because he shot her a rueful glance.

'The X-ray is up,' the radiographer said and they all turned to study the screen.

'There's no visible fluid level,' Phil murmured and Stefano's eyes narrowed, his gaze fixed intently on the screen.

'Because with the patient in the supine position the blood collects *under* the affected lung. If you look, you can see blurring of the hemidiaphragm contour. I'm ready to put in the chest drain.' He turned towards her. 'Liv?'

He knew her name?

Liv taped the cannula to make sure they didn't lose the second line. *Did he also know that she hadn't had sex for four years?* 'Sue will assist you with the drain.' Her hands occupied, she glanced towards her colleague. 'There's a sterile pack behind you. I got it out earlier.' Then she turned back to Phil. 'That blood needs to be given through the rapid infuser,' she reminded him. 'It needs to be warmed.'

'Sue can help Phil. I want you to assist me.' The sudden bite in his tone left no room for argument so Liv simply stepped aside so that Sue could take her place, quietly instructed her to call the operating theatre and the trauma consultant and then opened the sterile pack herself.

Suddenly she found that her hands were shaking and she shook her head, exasperated with herself. All right, so he'd already demolished Rachel—he obviously had high standards, but so did she! She had no reason to be nervous.

Working quickly, Liv opened the cannula that she knew he'd need, but he was already one step ahead, his movements so swift that it required all her concentration to keep up.

For a terrifying moment she almost lost her nerve. She'd never worked with anyone quite as talented as him before and the sheer speed and skill of his fingers left her dragging behind. Fortunately her own natural ability asserted itself.

Don't think about him, she told herself firmly. *Think about the job*.

She kept her gaze fixed on those long, bronzed fingers, every nerve and muscle in her body tense as she focused on what he was doing.

Not once did he hesitate or pause. His fingers were precise and steady as he cleaned the skin, injected local anaesthetic and then aspirated the syringe to confirm the presence of blood.

It was no wonder he demanded the best from those around him, Liv thought as she handed him the scalpel and watched him incise the skin down to the rib with astonishing speed and precision. He was a master, and it was obvious that he wasn't satisfied with anything less than accuracy.

His handsome face blank of expression, he slid a gloved finger into the pleural cavity, checking the position of the incision. 'I'll want a 36F tube. Have it ready.'

'Roberts forceps.' Without being asked, Liv handed him the instrument she knew he'd need next and watched as he slid the drain into position through the track he'd made. Then he attached the tube to an underwater seal drainage system.

'That's a large tube he's used,' Phil muttered and Liv glanced at him briefly.

'It has to be of sufficient calibre to drain the haemothorax without clotting. And if the haemothorax doesn't drain, there's a risk of infection.' Her attention back on Stefano, she reached for the suture. 'Zero gauge suture.' She held it out to him and he took it immediately, their movements smooth and synchronised even though they'd never worked together in Resus before.

He inserted a purse-string suture to secure the drain and then glanced at the monitors again.

'I want another chest X-ray so that I can check the position of the drain.'

The radiographer hurried over and as they shifted the patient and took the X-ray, Phil glanced at the drain.

'He's losing a lot of blood. Should we clamp the tube?'

Stefano shook his head. 'Clamping the tube has no effect on the amount of haemorrhage—the blood just collects in the chest and further compromises respiratory function.'

'Mr Lucarelli? The X-ray is up on the screen,' the radiographer said and Liv glanced up as the door suddenly opened and Anna walked into the room.

'His wife's arrived. I've put her in the relatives' room,' she said. 'Can someone find a moment to talk to her?'

Liv glanced towards Stefano Lucarelli but the consultant was staring at the X-ray, his handsome face unsmiling and his concentration absolute. *He's young*, she thought, looking at his masculine profile and dark glossy hair. *Young to be in such a responsible position*. His strong legs were planted firmly apart, the thin cotton of the scrub suit skimming wide, muscular shoulders, his dark head tilted slightly as he studied the screen. He was staggeringly good-looking, confident and very much in control.

Realising that she was staring, Liv looked away quickly and caught Anna's speculative glance.

Her friend gave her a wide smile. 'I can see everything is going well in here.'

Liv glared at her. 'We'll talk to his wife in a minute, Anna.'

Stefano turned. 'We're waiting for the trauma surgeon.

When the patient is stable and they've decided on the next step, I'll talk to his wife.'

Phil studied the drain again. 'He's drained 1000 mils.'

'The initial volume of blood drained is not as important as ongoing bleeding.' Stefano looked up as the trauma surgeon strode into the room.

The two men conferred although Liv could see that the entire conversation was driven by Stefano Lucarelli.

Clearly his reputation was as formidable as his clinical skills because the senior trauma surgeon seemed only too happy to listen to his advice.

'I don't want to perform a thoracotomy unnecessarily.'

'I've used a large enough tube and it's positioned well.' Stefano glanced at the drain as if daring it to misbehave. 'It will drain the haemothorax. Admit him for observation, monitor the drainage output over the next four to five hours. If he loses more than 200 to 250 mils of blood per hour, take him to Theatre. I'm going to talk to his wife. Liv, come with me.'

Liv blinked. 'I— Yes, of course.'

She was about to make a mild comment about his dictatorial style when he looked at her, his gaze frank and direct. 'You're an excellent nurse. When I'm in Resus, I want you with me.'

'Oh…' The compliment was so unexpected that hot colour flooded her cheeks but she was saved the bother of replying because they'd reached the door of the relatives' room.

Without pausing, Stefano opened the door and strode into the room, leaving Liv to follow. She closed the door behind her, braced for him to open his mouth, put his foot in it and then walk out leaving the patient's relative distraught, a scenario she'd witnessed on all too many occasions with other doctors.

But instead of fumbling for words and making the quickest possible exit, he walked across to the patient's wife and sat down next to her. 'I am Stefano Lucarelli, the consultant. I've been looking after your husband.' He held out his hand and the woman shook it and gave a wobbly smile.

'I'm Helen Myers.'

'This has been a shock for you, I know.' He spoke in a deep, velvety voice that held equal amounts of confidence and sympathy. 'I am sorry I couldn't speak to you earlier, but your husband was my priority.'

'Of course—I understand.' The woman was white with shock, her eyes pink from crying. 'Is he—is he going to be all right?'

'He was kicked in the ribs and that kick has damaged his lung.' In simple, easy-to-understand terms, Stefano gave her the facts, explaining what had happened and the treatment he'd given so far. He kept it short and non-technical. 'Tim has been transferred to Intensive Care. They are going to monitor him and, if necessary, they will take him to Theatre and drain the blood clot.'

Tim? Liv blinked. She hadn't realised that he even knew the patient's name.

'Oh God, I can't believe this is happening. I saw him at lunch-time and we were making plans for Christmas. We were going to take our two girls to Lapland to see Santa Claus.' The woman sat still for a moment and then her face crumpled and she started to cry. 'I'm sorry, I'm really sorry, it's just that it's such a shock.'

Reaching for a box of tissues, Liv sat down on the other side of the woman and waited for Stefano to leave so that she could offer whatever comfort she could. But instead of leaving the room as fast as possible as most of his colleagues would have done, Stefano leaned across and took a tissue from the box.

'Don't apologise. It is hard for you, I know. Here.' He handed the woman the tissue. 'You mentioned that you have daughters? So who is looking after them now?'

'My mother.' Helen blew her nose hard. 'I called her as soon as I got the news. I didn't want to bring the children here. I'm sorry. You don't want to listen to this. I know how busy you must be. You have much more important things to do than talk to me.'

'At the moment, talking to you is the most important thing,' Stefano said calmly, his gaze not shifting from her face. 'Is there anything else you want to ask me?'

Helen gave a choked laugh. 'I want to ask you if he's going to be all right, but you can't tell me that, can you?'

'Not at this stage,' Stefano said honestly. 'The consultant in Intensive Care will be able to give you a better idea in a few hours.'

He was good, Liv thought to herself. Really, really good. He was honest, didn't give false hope and didn't try and escape from the emotions in front of him. And despite the workload pressing down on him, he seemed to really care.

'Liv will stay with you for a few minutes,' Stefano said, 'and then she will ring ICU.'

Liv gave an inward smile. *He was also controlling.* 'Once they have him settled, I'll take you up there,' she assured Helen and the woman blew her nose again.

'Thanks. You've been incredibly kind, both of you.' Tucking her handkerchief up her sleeve, she tried to smile. 'Men. Why must they play these dangerous sports?'

Stefano rose to his feet, a sardonic smile touching his mouth. 'We are incomprehensible, no? Blame it on testosterone.' Suddenly he sounded very Italian and Liv felt her insides tingle.

She found herself wondering if some glamorous, skinny woman was at that moment lying naked in his enormous bed, waiting for his return.

Horrified by the direction of her thoughts, she rose to her

feet. 'I'll make you a cup of tea, Helen,' she said quickly. 'And then I'll find out what's happening in ICU.' And while she was at it, she was going to bang her head against the wall a few times to try and reprogramme her thoughts back to the place they'd been before the conversation with Anna.

Why on earth was she envying a woman she hadn't even met for having something that she didn't even want?

She was definitely losing her grip.

CHAPTER TWO

'MUMMY, can we have a *really* big Christmas tree this year? Up to the roof?'

'Absolutely.' Liv tried not to dwell on just how much 'really big' was going to cost. Maybe if she waited until Christmas Eve she could negotiate a bargain. 'How was school today?'

'Fine. I want to get our tree at the weekend.' Max scrambled onto a chair and spread his toy dinosaurs over the kitchen table. 'Then we can enjoy it for ages and ages.'

'It's only December the first. 'If we buy it on Saturday it will have no needles by Christmas.'

'If we don't buy our tree till Christmas Eve we won't have time to have fun with it. Sam is getting his tree next weekend. Can we? *Please?*' Max looked up at her hopefully and Liv felt something shift inside her.

'We'll see,' she said gruffly, promising herself that she'd sit down with a pen and paper once he was asleep and take a serious look at her budget. 'I love you. Have I told you that, lately?'

'Every day. You're always telling me that.'

'Are you complaining?'

'Nope.' Max picked up a plastic tyrannosaurus. 'I love you, too. It snowed again today, but not much. I want there to be piles and piles. Wouldn't that be great?'

Seeing the sparkle in her son's eyes, Liv forgot about the havoc that snow always caused. 'Fantastic.'

'Ben broke his leg yesterday.' Lower lip between his teeth, Max crashed the tyrannosaurus into a less superior species and sent it flying. 'He went to the hospital and they gave him crotches.'

Liv hid a smile. 'Crutches,' she said, spreading creamy butter onto crusty bread, 'it's crutches.'

'That's what I said. I told him my mum works in the hospital, but he said he didn't see you there. You won't work on Christmas Day, will you?'

Liv felt her heart flip. Every year she faced this dilemma. The money was good and in her situation that was incredibly tempting, but working Christmas meant not being with Max.

'I'm not working,' she said firmly, putting the plate on the table next to Max. It didn't matter how tight her finances were, nothing would make up for not spending Christmas Day with her son. 'I've saved up my holiday. I have a whole week off. I might work on New Year's Eve, but not until you're in bed.'

'So I'll do a sleepover with Sam?'

'Maybe. I'll have to speak to Anna.' Liv filled the kettle, wondering what she'd do if her friend and colleague hadn't had a child the same age as hers.

'Cool. I love sleeping over with Sam.' He looked at her, his eyes sparkling. 'Do you know what the best thing is about his house?'

No, but she could guess. Liv's heart plummeted as she thought of Sam's house, with its five large bedrooms, three bathrooms and huge garden. Then her eyes scanned the tiny living room of her cramped flat. If she stood in the middle, she could almost touch all four walls. And although she had two bedrooms, one of them was so small it would barely accommodate a single bed. And when the train went past the entire flat shook…

Aware that Max was looking at her, she braced herself. 'So what's the best thing about Sam's house?'

'Their guinea pig. It's called Rambo and it's *so* cute.'

Liv laughed and then impulsively she bent down and kissed her son, *the son who had noticed the guinea pig instead of the huge bedrooms or the soft white sofas and wall-to-wall luxury.*

'You're a nice person,' she said gruffly, but her eyes were drawn to the patch of damp on the wall. She'd painted over it repeatedly but it always came through again and now that the weather had turned cold…

Suddenly she wished she could wave a magic wand and make the world perfect for her son. Why was it that no one told you that parenthood came with non-stop guilt and anxiety? Especially *single* parenthood.

Telling herself that she was doing all right, Liv watched as her son played a make-believe game with his toys. He was bright, happy and well adjusted. She worried too much.

Everything was fine.

Max lifted his head and looked at her wistfully. 'And Sam's dad's buying him a goal for Christmas so he can practise. You should see it, Mum. It's just *awesome*. It's huge, with a big white net—I've seen the picture. Could we have a goal?'

'Not in a fourth-floor flat,' Liv said dryly, squashing down the guilt that swamped her once again. He was a little boy. He needed a garden. Somewhere he could kick a ball when she was too tired to take him to the park.

'If we had loads of money, would we buy a house? I heard you telling Anna that if you had a bathroom like hers, you'd lie in it all day. Why don't you lie in ours all day?'

Because of the chipped tiles, the draught from the window and the stubborn black mould that refused to die. 'Because I have to work. I've explained that to you. I work to make the money we need.' Liv lifted an onion out of the vegetable basket. 'Now, enough of this conversation. If I don't get on with the supper it will be bedtime.'

The tyrannosaurus attacked again, scattering other dinosaurs over the kitchen floor. 'You could do the lottery or something.'

'It's a waste of money. We wouldn't win.'

'You could get married. Emma's mum got married again and now they're really rich because her new dad is *loaded*!'

Liv gasped. 'Where did you hear that expression?'

'Emma told me.' Max stopped playing and looked at her anxiously. 'Is it swearing?'

'No, but it's not very polite.' Her mind slid back to the conversation she'd had with Anna earlier that day and she frowned, pushing away thoughts of Stefano Lucarelli. 'And it isn't how much money someone has that counts, it's whether you like them or not that matters.'

'Well, Emma's mum has been married twice now, and you've only been married once.'

'It isn't a competition, sweetheart.'

'Why did you stop being married?'

Liv closed her eyes briefly. Why did the hardest questions always come when she was tired? 'We've talked about this before, Max.' She peeled the onion. 'Sometimes these things just don't work out. And when that happens, it's no one's fault.' Yes it was. It was her fault. She hadn't been exciting enough for Jack. Her eyes suddenly started pricking and she told herself it was just the onion.

'You should definitely try being married again,' Max said

sagely. 'You're always telling me I have to keep trying things. You always say you can't tell if you like something if you've only tried it once.'

'That's food,' Liv said dryly, reaching for a chopping board. 'Marriage isn't like broccoli. Marriage is a very big thing. You have to really, really love someone to do that. And they have to love you, too. They have to think you're special.'

'You *are* special, Mum.' Max looked at her, his eyes huge. 'I don't know any other girls who love football and cars and *no one* makes pizza like you do. All my friends think you're cool.'

'Well, maybe I am cool to a bunch of seven-year-olds.' But bigger boys wanted something very different. They wanted someone sexy and she was—

Ordinary.

Liv stood for a moment, distracted by her own thoughts. Across the road she could see lights from the other flats and in one window she could see a man and a woman sitting down to eat with two lively, excited children.

Then she glanced at Max. Her little boy, his face a mask of concentration as he lined up his dinosaurs. She paused for a moment, swamped by a feeling of such intense love and anxiety that she almost couldn't breathe.

He deserved so much more. He deserved a loving father who would kick a football with him.

Damn Jack. Damn Jack and his slick, womanising ways.

She put the onion on the chopping board and stabbed the knife through it.

Why should Max suffer because his father hadn't been adult enough to face up to his responsibilities?

'Mummy, you're chopping that onion like you *hate* it or something.'

Liv's gaze slid from the blade in her hand to the minute

slices of onion that now lay on the chopping board. Pulverised. She gave a weak smile. 'I'm making supper.' *There was no point in regretting the past.* 'We can play football together this weekend, if you like.'

'Cool. I've been picked for the match on Friday. I was a reserve but now Ben can't play so I'm in the team.'

Liv's face lit up. 'That's fantastic! Why didn't you tell me before?'

'It's only the second team, not the first.' He looked at her and his little shoulders lifted in a tiny shrug. 'And I knew you wouldn't be able to come. You'll be working.'

Liv swallowed. 'Max—'

'It's OK,' he said firmly. 'It isn't your fault. We're a team, isn't that what you always say? You go to work, I go to school.'

'Actually I'm not working on Friday,' Liv said brightly. 'I—I have the afternoon off.'

'Really?'

No. 'Yes.' Somehow, whatever it took, she was going to make it happen. She was going to her son's football match. 'What time is kick-off?'

'Two o'clock.'

'I'll be there.' How, she didn't know. But she was going to be standing on that school field even if it meant changing her job.

Exhaustion washed over her making her head foggy. As usual her day had started before five and one glance at the washing, ironing and the pile of Max's toys in the living room was enough to tell her that she wouldn't be in bed before midnight.

She envied mothers who could be at home for their children. Yes, she loved her work but the constant pressure of trying to be in two places at once was grinding her down.

Welcome to single parenthood.

Max scrambled off the chair and hugged her tightly, his arms round her legs, his head pressed against her stomach. 'You're the best mum in the world. I know it's hard for you because you have to work. That would be one of the good things about having a dad. He could do the work bit and you could just come and watch me.'

Liv felt a lump in her throat. 'There's more to being a dad than signing cheques, Max.' *And some men didn't even manage that bit*, she thought wearily as she bent to kiss the top of his head. He smelled of shampoo. 'Spaghetti bolognese all right for supper?'

'Yum.'

Dismissing fantasies of herself standing on the school field, while someone else worried about the family finances, Liv squashed down the guilt, gave him a quick kiss and released him. *Reality*, she reminded herself. That was what she had to concentrate on. 'So what was the funniest thing that happened to you today?' Taking the lid off a can of tomatoes, she emptied it into the pan. 'Make me laugh.'

'Sam told me a great joke.'

'Go on.'

'What's the best thing to give a seasick elephant?'

'I don't know. What is the best thing to give a seasick elephant?'

'Plenty of room.'

'Max!'

The following morning brought a flutter of snow and a sharp drop in the temperature.

'Isabella? *Tutto bene?*' Stefano brought the Ferrari to a smooth halt, his attention on the phone call. Snow dusted the pavements and the roads were slick with ice. It was going to be a busy day in the emergency department and he knew this would be his only chance to make this call. 'You called me?'

'Every day for the past two weeks!' His sister exploded into Italian. 'Where have you been? You don't call—you don't come home! Have you forgotten your family? Don't we matter to you any more? *You don't have a heart, Stefano!*'

'That's the sort of comment I expect from my girlfriend, not my little sister.' Stefano sprang from the car, his long, black, cashmere coat swirling around his strong legs as he strode across the consultants' car park. Knowing *exactly* which buttons to press to annoy her, he smiled wickedly. 'Why are you at home? You should be taking your children to school.'

Ever predictable, Isabella bristled with indignation. 'I dropped them at school and now I'm on the way to the office. Remember the family business, Stefano? The business you turned your back on? Well I am here, keeping our father happy while you stroke your ego by playing doctors and dating actresses with bodies as thin as spaghetti and brains as soft as ravioli.'

Already bored with the conversation, Stefano pushed his way through the swing doors that led to the emergency department. 'Are you ringing me to nag me about my choice of career or my choice of women?'

'I'm ringing you because despite your many faults, you're still my brother and like all men you need reminding about family responsibility. When did you last call Papa?'

Stefano strode along the corridor, oblivious to the sideways glances he received from the female nurses. 'I don't have any news.'

'News? What is "news"?' Isabella didn't bother hiding her exasperation. 'He just wants to hear your voice, Stefano!'

'Talking about nothing because you enjoy the sound of your own voice is more of a girl thing than a man thing,' Stefano drawled. 'And I've been busy. I'm working.'

'Well, find the time to call. And make sure you come home for Christmas. We'll all be in Cortina from the twenty-third of December.'

Stefano was well able to picture the scene: a noisy group of family and old friends descending on the enormous family chalet in the exclusive mountain resort of Cortina D'Ampezzo, in the Italian Dolomites.

'Isabella—'

'I know you're busy, but this is family time, Stefano. Be there.'

'I will be there, but I don't know when or for how long.' *Or how much of his well-meaning, interfering family he'd be able to stand.*

'All the cousins will be there—' it was Isabella's turn to tease '—including the lovely Donatella. She's still single, Stefano.'

'Fortunately for both of us, my taste in women doesn't run to children,' Stefano said wryly and Isabella giggled.

'She's twenty-one, Stefano, hardly a child. And she's been trying to remind you of that fact for a few years now. Surely you haven't forgotten last Christmas? The push-up bra and the low-cut top? I thought Papa was going to have a stroke. Anyway, she wants to sit by you for Christmas Eve dinner.'

'Donatella finds me so intimidating that she can barely speak in my company,' Stefano reminded her in an acid tone. 'If you throw her in my way at Christmas it would be cruel to both of us. Isabella, drop this subject.'

'She'd be a traditional Italian wife, Stefano.' Isabella was clearly enjoying herself. 'She would stay at home and cook you pasta.'

'Unfortunately for Donatella one of my requirements in a life partner is that they're able to sustain an intelligent conversation for at least eight seconds. Sadly, she can't. Or at least, she can't when she's with me.'

Isabella snorted with laughter. 'You're so harsh. Frankly I can't see why she's so crazy about you. I mean, I know you're filthy rich and good-looking but you're *unbearable* to people who aren't as bright as you are and when you're *really* bored, which usually takes far less than eight seconds by the way, you can be horribly cutting.'

Taken aback by that blunt assessment of his attributes, Stefano was about to answer when his sister made an impatient sound.

'Anyway, it's nonsense to say you need a woman with a brain. According to that actress of yours, you don't waste any time talking to women.'

Stefano glanced at his watch. 'I'm a busy man, Isabella. Was there something else you wanted to say?'

'She gave *such* an embarrassing interview to all the papers. What did you ever see in her? No—don't answer that, it's obvious. *Why* are men so shallow?'

Stefano gave a deadly smile. 'Because women wear push-up bras and we are easily distracted,' he purred. 'I'm so pleased you called me. Your conversation is always so…intellectual.'

'Don't try and intimidate me.' But Isabella was laughing. 'I rang you for a chat because I love you, even though you sometimes forget that you have a family and you're basically horrible. I'll see you at Christmas, Stefano. I'm sure Donatella is already choosing her dress.'

Stefano closed his eyes briefly. '*Maledizione—*'

'Don't swear in front of your sister!'

There was a sharp rap on the door and Stefano looked up

with a frown, irritated by the interruption. Greg Hampton, one of the casualty officers, stood in the doorway and Stefano's mouth tightened. Unlike Phil who had managed to impress him, this particular junior doctor's attitude was far too casual for his liking. 'I've got to go. *Ciao*.' He terminated the call and dropped his phone into his pocket. '*Sì?* There is a problem?'

'Can you check an X-ray for me before you get dragged into Resus? Everyone else is still tied up with the RTA that came in an hour ago.'

Stefano slung his coat over the back of the chair, ignored the mound of paperwork on his desk and strode towards the door. 'Who is the patient?'

'That's the bad news.' Greg pulled a face. 'A screaming, un-cooperative kid with a bruised finger. I sent her for an X-ray.'

Stefano dealt him a measuring glance, less than impressed by the younger doctor's dismissive tone.

They arrived at the main area and Stefano automatically glanced at the computer screen on the wall. It listed every patient in the department and enabled the staff to track their progress. That one glance was enough to tell him that he was in for a busy morning despite the fact it was barely light.

His mind still half on the conversation with his sister, his gaze shifted to the smaller computer next to the screen that was displaying an X-ray of a finger. He hit a button, zoomed in closer and stared at the image. *Why did his family see the need to interfere with his life?* If it wasn't his love life, it was his profession. 'No fracture. How was the finger on examination?'

Greg shrugged. 'I haven't examined her yet.'

'You sent her for X-ray without examination?' Stefano transferred his gaze from the X-ray to the doctor and Greg frowned slightly.

'The child was really difficult. Didn't seem to want to be

distracted by anything. Trust me—no one could have done anything with this kid, and as for the mother...' with an exaggerated shudder, he picked up the notes '...she was your average nightmare. Reminded me why I didn't do paediatrics. Caring for kids is all about the mothers, isn't it? What's the point of seven years' training if I have to waste my skills on a load of hysterical women?'

'What skills?' Stefano spoke softly and Greg's smile lost a fraction of its arrogance.

'What do you mean?'

'You told me that you don't want to waste your skills,' Stefano said silkily, 'but I am still waiting to see a demonstration of these skills in which you have so much pride and which you seem so reluctant to waste in my department, Dr Hampton. They weren't in evidence when you needed to examine the child.'

Greg cleared his throat. 'I didn't manage to examine the child.'

'Precisely.' Stefano watched with cold detachment as the less experienced doctor flushed to the roots of his hair, suddenly a great deal less sure of himself.

'The kid was freaking out.'

'Then it is your job to "un"-freak them,' Stefano advised helpfully. 'After all, what is the point of seven years of training if you cannot get close enough to your patient to carry out an examination?'

'I ordered an X-ray,' Greg said stiffly, and Stefano raised an eyebrow.

'So you sent her to X-Ray with no examination and you were planning to discharge her without examination? You have good medical defence insurance, I hope? A skilled lawyer? Because if that is the way you practise medicine, you will need both.'

Greg's face was scarlet. 'I assumed that the X-ray would tell me what I needed to know.'

'An X-ray is simply one part of the overall picture. Never again even consider discharging a patient without carrying out the appropriate examination. You are a doctor, not a car mechanic. The decisions you make affect people's lives.' Stefano let the doctor squirm for a few more moments and then he flicked off the X-ray.

'Mr Lucarelli—'

'One more thing.' Stefano's icy tone cut through the doctor's feeble attempt to redeem himself. 'In this department, if a mother tells you that she has a bad feeling about her child, you will listen to what she has to say with both ears open and your mouth closed. Understood?'

Greg stared at him. 'Yes.'

'Good.' Stefano watched him with cool appraisal. 'Most mothers are uncannily accurate when it comes to assessing the health of their children. Remember that. They sense things that we doctors, even with years of training, can take longer to detect. Now, given that you have been unable to examine the patient, show me where she is and I will do it for you.'

Stiff and defensive, the casualty officer led the way down the corridor and into one of the small cubicles.

Prepared to deal with a very distressed child, Stefano stopped dead in the doorway, astonished to see the little girl laughing and smiling.

Liv was kneeling on the floor, chatting away happily and the child sat listening, clearly absorbed by the conversation. Her eyes were fixed on the nurse in fascination and Stefano found himself reacting in much the same way.

From his vantage point in the doorway, his gaze was drawn to the curve of her soft mouth and suddenly he found himself comparing the sweetness of her smile to Francine's sexy scarlet pout.

Surprised by the direction of his thoughts, Stefano wondered why he was comparing two women who were so blatantly unalike.

Francine was an actress and a model—her looks were part of her job. Whereas Liv—well, she was entirely different. She wasn't beautiful in the conventional sense. Her mouth was too wide and she had a pronounced dimple in her left cheek when she smiled, but there was something about her face that made it difficult to look away. Her eyes were bright and intelligent, and she radiated warmth and good humour as she talked to the child.

Stefano's gaze swept her body in an instinctive male appraisal.

Her uniform wasn't tight, but there was no missing her enticing curves and he felt the immediate and powerful response of his body. As irritated by his reaction as he was surprised, he turned his attention back to the child, assuming that it was just that ridiculous conversation with his sister that was suddenly turning his thoughts to sex in the middle of his working day.

'So you sit next to Annabel.' Liv spoke in a calm, gentle voice that removed all the stress from the room and smoothed Stefano's frayed nerves like the stroke of a velvet glove. 'And who is your teacher?'

'Miss Grant.' The little girl smiled at her. 'She has her hair in a ponytail, like you.'

'Well, that's the best way to wear it for work, especially if it's curly because it can get in your eyes. So how did you fall on your finger?'

Aware that Greg Hampton was about to speak, Stefano

silenced him with a lift of his hand and a searing glance, intensely irritated that the man would even *consider* intervening when the nurse clearly had full control of the situation.

Fortunately the child hadn't even noticed their presence. 'I did it yesterday. We were practising the nativity play,' she was saying, 'and I tripped over a sheep. I mean, not a real sheep, actually it was Gareth, dressed as a sheep. But I fell on my finger, I mean like *all* my weight was on my finger.'

Stefano watched as Liv listened attentively to the child's story and then carefully examined the child's finger.

Her hair was the rich brown of a conker and it gleamed and shone under the harsh emergency room lights. Although it had been pulled back into a ponytail, several curls had escaped and now drifted around her face. Having not looked twice at a woman for months, Stefano found himself staring. She wasn't wearing a trace of make-up and yet her lashes were thick and dark and her cheeks had a healthy glow. But what really drew his attention was her absolute focus on the little girl.

She wasn't thinking about herself or her appearance. She hadn't even noticed that he was standing in the doorway.

Suddenly his mind drifted back to the conversation he'd overheard the day before.

Why did Anna want to buy her hot sex for Christmas?

Stefano dismissed the question instantly as one of those things that women laugh about and men are better off not knowing.

But his eyes trailed back to her mouth and lower.

She didn't look like a woman who needed someone else to find her hot sex.

Why had Anna been hugging her? Had something happened? Was there something wrong in her life?

'Ouch. That's the bit that really hurts.' The little girl winced as Liv gently manipulated her fingers.

'It's bound to hurt because it's really bruised, can you see? It's just a bit black there—over the joint. I think you're incredibly brave.'

The little girl looked doubtful. 'I *was* crying.'

'I'm not surprised.' Liv's tone suggested that anything less would have been unthinkable. 'If it were my finger, I would have cried, too. I think you've been amazing. But what we need to do now is fix it so that it doesn't hurt so much. What were you in the nativity play?'

'A star. Is it broken?'

'Well, I'm going to take a look at your X-ray and then have a chat with the doctor.'

'Not the same doctor as before?' The child shrank slightly. 'He was really angry with me—' Suddenly noticing Greg in the doorway, she snatched her hand back. *'He's not going to touch me.'*

The atmosphere altered in the blink of an eye.

Deciding that swift intervention was called for if he wasn't to lose all chances of examining the child himself, Stefano cast a meaningful glance towards his less experienced colleague and strolled into the room.

'Ciao, cucciola mia.' He addressed the little girl directly but her eyes were fixed on Greg in horror.

'I don't want him to be my doctor.'

'He isn't your doctor.'

'So why is he here?'

'Because he works with me.' Well aware that his height and physique could make him intimidating, Stefano dropped into a crouch so that he was at the same level as the child. 'So you fell off a stage, is that right?'

'Yes.' Finally the little girl looked at him and her expression was curious. 'Why do you speak with a funny accent?'

Stefano smiled. 'Because I'm from Italy.'

'Like pizza? I love pizza.'

'Just like pizza. So tell me…' Stefano gently took her hand in his and examined her fingers '…what is your favourite pizza?'

'Margarita, but not too cheesy and no lumps of tomatoes.'

'Obviously you are a woman who knows what she wants.' Amused, Stefano turned the child's hand over. 'Show me how you fell on your hand.'

'I fell all on one finger, like this…' The little girl pretended to stab the ground and Stefano pulled a face.

'Well, that is why your finger is hurting. You are supposed to walk on your feet, not your finger.' Gently he manipulated the finger. 'Does this hurt? This? Can you squeeze—make a fist?'

As he examined the dark bruising over the back of the finger, he was acutely conscious of Liv next to him. He allowed himself one sideways glance, but she wasn't even looking at him. All her attention was still focused on her little patient.

'I thought it was probably a volar plate injury,' she murmured and Stefano silently compared her calm efficiency with Greg's ineffectual arrogance.

'I agree.' Impressed, he gave her a rare smile but she didn't even seem to notice.

She didn't blush, stare or send him a subtly flirtatious look. In fact she didn't look at him at all. Instead, she rose to her feet, her eyes still on the little girl. 'You'll have to be careful with that finger for a few weeks, Bella.'

Stefano was so accustomed to being cautious in his inter-action with women that for a moment he was taken aback by her apparent indifference to him.

For a brief moment in Resus yesterday he'd felt a powerful explosion of chemistry and he was sure that she'd felt it too. But clearly it had been his imagination.

He almost laughed at himself. Had he really grown so arrogant that he expected every woman to look at him?

Unfortunately the child's mother *was* looking at him with what she obviously believed to be feminine allure.

'You're the consultant?' She scanned Stefano's face and her eyes widened slightly. 'What's a volar plate? I've never heard of it.'

Stefano ignored the look in her eyes and kept his response cool and professional. 'Your finger joints are like a hinge, yes? They must bend and straighten. The bones are connected together by tough bands of tissue called ligaments. In this joint—we call it the PIP—the strongest ligament is the volar plate.'

The mother studied his face a little more intently than was necessary. 'So she's pulled a ligament? Like a sprain, you mean?'

Instinctively adjusting his body language to create distance, Stefano stepped back. 'This particular ligament connects the proximal phalanx to the middle phalanx on the palm side of the joint.'

'These two joints,' Liv said quickly, demonstrating on her own hand and Stefano gave a faint smile because he realised that he'd made his explanation far too complicated, which was unlike him.

But he'd been extricating himself from the flirtatious glances of the mother.

Forcing his mind back onto his work, he tried again. 'The ligament tightens as the joint is straightened and keeps the joint from hyper-extending—bending too far back, in other words. But if you do overextend this joint, the volar plate can be damaged.'

The little girl's face drooped with disappointment. 'So does that mean I can't be a star in the nativity?'

Unusually for him, Stefano found himself at a loss. 'What exactly does a star do?'

'I dance a bit and then I stand still while the shepherds walk towards me.'

'That will be fine,' Stefano assured her. 'Just be careful not to fall over any more sheep.'

'Is it broken?'

'Not exactly broken, just damaged. And we're going to have to give it some help to make it better.'

'Will I have a plaster that everyone in my class can sign?'

'No. We're going to give it a buddy to hold onto. This finger next to it—it will support your bad finger until it is healed. Your good finger will help your injured finger. Like a friend.' Stefano glanced at Liv. 'Can you arrange that for me?'

'Of course. And I expect you want her to go back to the hand clinic in ten days, to check that Bella has full movement in that finger.' She scribbled on a form and signed it. 'Now, if you just wait there, I'll strap that finger for you.'

'I know who you are.' The little girl's eyes narrowed. 'You're Max's mum, aren't you? You're called Liv.'

In the process of writing the notes, Stefano's hand stilled. *She had a child?*

He didn't know which surprised him most, the fact that she was some child's mother when she really didn't look old enough, or his own thunderous disappointment that she belonged to another man.

If she was married, why had Anna been offering to buy her hot sex for Christmas?

Seriously concerned by the alarming direction of his own thoughts, he scrawled in the notes and strode to the door. 'If you need anything else, call me,' he said in a cool tone but Liv didn't appear any more disconcerted by the chill than she'd been impressed by the smile. Instead she simply concentrated on applying Elastoplast strapping to the child's finger.

As they walked out of the door, Greg cleared his throat. 'Is everything all right, Mr Lucarelli?'

'That nurse is obviously very experienced,' Stefano said smoothly. 'My advice is to watch and learn. Next time you run into trouble with a child, ask for her help.'

Why did he care whether she was married?

What difference did it make to him?

He glanced over his shoulder just as Liv lifted her left hand to remove a piece of strapping. And Stefano noticed one more thing about her.

Her finger was bare. She wasn't wearing a wedding ring.

CHAPTER THREE

HER heart thudding frantically in her chest, Liv finished strapping Bella's finger and gave the mother a set of instructions.

It had proved really, really hard to work shoulder to shoulder with Stefano Lucarelli without once looking at him, but somehow she'd managed it.

Not that her display of willpower had done anything to reduce the effect he had on her. Whenever he was in the room, her body felt oddly lethargic, her skin tingled and there was a tiny thrill in her stomach that took her breath away.

Chemistry.

No, not chemistry. That implied something shared and there was no way he would feel the same way about her. Which meant that what she was feeling was…lust. Good old-fashioned lust.

Well, whatever it was called it was extremely irritating and inconvenient, she thought to herself crossly, as she directed mother and child back towards the exit. It had been the same the previous day in Resus. One glance was all it had taken. The look itself had probably lasted for less than a second, but the aftershocks had been with her all day and the depth of her reaction shocked her because she'd had no idea she was even *capable* of experiencing that sudden fiery burn of sexual awareness.

It was all Anna's fault. If they hadn't had that ridiculous conversation about sex, Liv wouldn't have noticed Stefano Lucarelli.

Or maybe she would.

With an exasperated sigh, Liv dried her hands and forced herself to think about Jack, something she usually avoided at all costs. But desperate times called for desperate measures. *If she thought about Jack, she'd remember why she was single.*

Having thoroughly depressed herself, she was just about to call her next patient when Anna slid into the room, her eyes gleaming wickedly.

'You'll never guess what.'

Liv slipped her scissors back into her pocket. 'No, I probably wouldn't but I'm glad you're here, because I need to ask a favour.'

'Anything.' Anna waved her hand airily. 'Since our irascible consultant has taken a shine to you, you're my best asset. But if it's a pay rise, forget it.'

'Can I work a split shift on Friday? Max has been picked for the football team.'

'Really?' Anna's face brightened. 'That's fantastic. Yes, work a split. I'll juggle the rota if I have to. Why don't you let me pick him up from school afterwards and he can do a sleepover with Sam.'

'I can't ask you to do that—'

'You'd be doing me a favour. If the boys are playing, I can write my Christmas cards. They've been glaring at me from inside their packaging for the past two weeks.'

Liv smiled. 'All right. Thanks so much.' It would save her having to beg yet another favour, this time from the childminder.

'It's the least I can do for Super-Nurse. Our cool, hard-to-please consultant is sending shivers of terror throughout the department but apparently *you* make the grade.' Anna's smile was wicked. 'He strode up to me this morning and said in his most commanding voice, *"When I am in Resus, I want Leev with me."* The way he says your name is incredibly sexy.'

Liv tried to ignore the bump of her heart. 'You need to work on your Italian accent. That was a terrible imitation.'

'What exactly did you do to him in Resus to make him love you so much? I really want to know. I'm trying not to be offended by the fact he clearly thinks the rest of us are rubbish.'

'We just worked well together.'

Anna gave a slow smile. 'Obviously you make a lovely couple. Have you invited him to the Snowflake Ball yet?'

'No, I haven't invited him to the Snowflake Ball, because I'm not going.'

'You should invite him. At least then you'll have something to tell your grandchildren.' Anna glanced over her shoulder to check they were alone and then whipped a piece of paper out of her pocket. 'One of the nurses in fracture clinic looked Sexy Stefano up on the internet and came across an interview with his ex—some gorgeous blonde Italian actress.' She unfolded the paper. 'Listen to this—*"One of the drawbacks of Italian men is that they're extremely macho and dominating."*' Anna glanced up. 'Is that a drawback? I'd give anything for David to ignore the fact that I'm loading the dishwasher and just throw me down onto the sofa for a bit of wild sex.'

'Anna, for goodness' sake—'

'You haven't heard anything yet.' Anna cleared her throat. '*"Stefano was so hot tempered and passionate that our entire relationship sometimes felt like one long blazing series of rows and reconciliation."*'

Unsettled by the conversation, Liv concentrated on putting the dressings away. 'That doesn't sound very relaxing. I'm not surprised they broke up.'

'Hold on, I'm just coming to the best bit—"*Maybe it's because he's a doctor, but he knew exactly what to do to my body. He was so skilled in bed and so demanding that for six months I was too tired to get up in the morning. My career almost fell apart. Two words come to mind when I think of Stefano and they are sex and stamina.*" All right, now I'm jealous.' Anna scrunched the paper up and threw it in the bin in disgust. 'I can't remember the last time I was kept awake by a man's ravenous libido.'

'This is too much information.' Liv covered her ears. 'I really like your husband.'

'I like him too, and it's as much my fault as his. Life is so exhausting that when I see my bed I just want to sleep in it, not set fire to the sheets. I wish I hadn't read that article. I was relatively happy with my life until I realised that I could be having hot sex all night with a luscious trauma surgeon who knows exactly what to do with my body. I mean, can you imagine waking up in the morning next to Stefano Lucarelli?'

'No, I can't imagine it because it would be too terrible for words.' Liv shuddered. 'It would be daylight and I would never have the confidence to show my body to anyone in daylight. He'd probably be sick.'

Anna gaped at her. 'You have absolutely no idea how lovely you are.'

'Oh yes.' Liv gave a mocking a smile. 'So lovely that Jack could barely drag himself away from me to sleep with other women.'

'Jack was just a—' Anna used a word that made Liv blink.

'I can't believe you just said that. Wash your mouth out.'

'I just hate the way he's made you feel about yourself,' Anna said simply. 'Because of him, you have no self-confidence. Just do me a favour—try smouldering at Stefano and see what happens.'

'He'd probably throw a bucket of water over me and I wouldn't blame him.'

'He's seriously rich, gorgeous and single. If you're not even prepared to flirt with him then you need therapy,' Anna said and Liv smiled.

'Anna, darling, one of us definitely needs therapy, but I don't think it's me.'

'Are you telling me that you can look him in the eye and not think of sex?'

'*Stop talking about sex!*' The words came out louder than she'd intended and Liv slammed a hand over her mouth and giggled in disbelief. 'For crying out loud, Anna, what is the matter with you? Go to lunch, or go and have a cold shower or—something.'

'"Or something" sounds good but unfortunately I'll have to settle for lunch.' Anna handed her the keys to the drug cupboard. 'You're in charge. Hire and fire at will. Try not to get up to anything while I'm gone.' She walked briskly out of the room and Liv pinned the keys in her pocket with hands that weren't quite steady.

All this talk of sex was starting to unsettle her.

Her eyes slid to the article in the bin.

Did he know what to do with his hands? Well, of course he did. He was a good-looking, confident, experienced man. He didn't fumble in Resus and she didn't for a moment expect him to fumble in the bedroom. He just wasn't that type of guy.

She gave a sigh of exasperation. Pretending that she hadn't noticed him or that he wasn't attractive was just silly. Who was she kidding? Everyone had noticed him and with good reason.

Wealthy, good-looking doctors weren't exactly a common species. Most of the doctors she worked with were pale-skinned and out of shape, like plants that had been deprived of sunlight. Stefano's bronzed skin and Mediterranean good looks made him stand out like a bold sunflower in a field of withered dandelions.

But what really stayed in her mind was his skill as a doctor. He was breathtakingly skilled and ruthless in his demands for perfection, and yet at the same time he'd shown himself capable of displaying a surprising degree of compassion when it was required. He was gorgeous.

Seriously worried by her own thoughts, she gave herself a sharp talking to. *Enough!* Even *thinking* of him in that way was embarrassing. He was smooth, sophisticated and stunning whereas she was—she was…

Delusional, Liv thought, exasperated with herself. Delusional, for thinking that a man like him might be interested in someone like her.

Ordinary, wasn't that what Jack had called her?

Ordinary. Dependable.

She was a good nurse, a loving mother and a caring friend. But she wasn't sexy or glamorous.

And she wasn't the sort of woman that a man like Stefano Lucarelli would ever notice.

She needed to stop thinking about sex and get on with her life.

'Down the wing, Max, *down the wing*!'

Two days later Liv stood on edge of the school field with a row of parents. Several of the men had obviously taken the afternoon off from work to cheer the children on in their football match.

And it was cold. Really cold. Liv had wrapped a scarf

around her neck but her breath clouded the freezing air and her fingers were numb.

'Hi, Liv. You've met my husband, Simon, haven't you?' The mother of a boy in Max's class was standing huddled next to a stocky, cheerful-looking man whose polished shoes looked out of place on the school playing field. A toddler slept in a pushchair next to her and every now and then she jiggled the handle to keep him asleep. Even under the large winter coat, it was obvious that she was very pregnant.

'Hi, Simon.' Liv smiled. 'How are you, Claire? When's the baby due?'

'Christmas Day.' Claire cast a teasing glance towards her husband. 'You'll be cooking the turkey, sunshine. Better start practising.'

'Ah—I had something to tell you about that.' Simon was concentrating hard on the game, his eyes following the ball. 'I've invited my mother to stay at Christmas. It seemed like a good idea. *Go on, James!*'

'You've invited your mother? Are you kidding?!' Claire's mouth dropped open but Simon was urging the team on and didn't respond. Claire glanced at Liv and rolled her eyes. 'Men! At the first hint of domestic work, they ring their mothers.'

Simon dragged his eyes from the pitch for half a second. 'Did you really want to eat my turkey?'

Claire glared at him. 'So you're going to be on the sofa watching the TV?'

His eyes were back on the pitch. 'I do my bit.'

'Oh, really?'

'Yes, really! I'm the one that's been coaching James on his football skills. And just look at him go!' Simon gazed at his son proudly and Liv felt something uncurl inside her. *Something uncomfortable that made her feel slightly sick.*

She looked away quickly, reminding herself that she could kick a football with her son, too. *But it wasn't the same, was it?* Sometimes she just ached when she saw the way Max stared longingly at the fathers playing with their sons in the park. She'd seen the way he sidled up to the fringes of other male groups, hoping to be included.

The truth was that there was no male influence in his life and he needed one. If she had the money she would have given him football coaching for his Christmas present but that was out of the question.

She was his football coach. She was everything.

Liv turned her attention back to the football match, shocked by the thick sludge of jealousy that surged through her veins.

Hating herself for feeling that way, she gritted her teeth. It wasn't like her. She was incredibly lucky. She had a son she adored and a job she loved—a good life.

Her eyes slid back towards Claire and Simon who were still sharing a laugh together at the prospect of their crazy, noisy Christmas.

But she didn't have anyone to share her life with, did she?

Perhaps Anna was right. Perhaps it was time she thought about dating again. But she really didn't think she had the courage. Perhaps if she used the internet and said *SINGLE MOTHER WITH CHILD*, at least that would warn people that she wasn't a supermodel. But she had to put something nice about herself. *Can make pizza, kick a football and read bedtime stories?* What sort of person would that attract?

The truth was that the mere thought of internet dating, horrified her. What if someone met her in the flesh and thought, Yuck?

Shrinking at the thought, Liv concentrated on the game. She watched as Max sped down the field, a determined look on his face as he chased the ball. His little legs were bruised and muddy and his football shirt was so long it looked as though he wasn't wearing any shorts, but he was trying so hard that he was almost bursting. *He looked so small and vulnerable*, Liv thought to herself, wondering whether parenthood affected everyone like this.

When she looked at him she just ached, wanting everything to be all right for him.

Dating when she was single had been hard enough. Dating with a child didn't bear thinking about. This time it wasn't just her who would be hurt when it all went wrong.

Conscious of Claire's husband yelling at his son, she wrapped her arms around herself and tried to subdue the envy. There *were* men out there prepared to shoulder the responsibility of family. It was just that she hadn't found one. Maybe she would, one day. Someone who wouldn't think Yuck when he saw her. Someone who would see past the fact that she wasn't sexy and value her other qualities.

She watched as Max's foot made contact with the ball and it flew into the goal. Max yelled triumphantly and all his teammates jumped on him, barely able to contain their excitement.

Liv clapped her hands and Claire and Simon gave a little whoop.

'Did you see me, Mum?' He came running over; her little boy with shining eyes and cheeks pink from the cold. 'Did you see me?'

'I saw you.' She bent and hugged him, loving the fact that he still wanted her to do that, despite the presence of his friends. 'You were brilliant.'

'I love football, Mum. I love it.'

'I know you do.' Liv hugged him tightly, breathing in the smell of little boy and muddy field.

'Are you going to work now?'

'Yes. And you're going home with Anna and Sam. Be good. I'll pick you up tomorrow morning.'

'Great, bye Mum.' He turned and sped across the field to join his friends who were making their way back towards the school.

Swallowing down the lump in her throat, Liv said a quick goodbye to Claire and Simon and walked towards her car. Having taken a few hours off in the middle of the day, she was due back at the hospital. No time to mope or feel sorry for herself. The reality of her life. Work. If she didn't work, there was no money.

The moment she walked through the doors, Stefano Lucarelli strode up to her. '*Where* have you been?' His raw masculinity took her breath away and Liv felt the instantaneous reaction of her body. Her heart pounded, her knees weakened and she felt horribly light-headed. To make matters worse, the interview with the actress was fresh in her mind and suddenly she had a disturbingly vivid image of him sliding those strong, confident hands over the pliant shivering body of a sickeningly slender woman.

Flustered, she unwrapped the scarf from around her neck. 'I had a few hours off this afternoon.'

'In the middle of your shift?' He stood in front of her, legs spread in a confrontational stance, blocking her path. For a moment she couldn't speak. Sexual awareness burned hot and dangerous and every thought was blown from her head except one. *He'd noticed that she hadn't been working.* For a reason that she didn't want to examine, she felt like singing and dancing, but somehow she managed to keep her feet still.

'You were looking for me?'

Maybe the feelings weren't all on her side.

'*Sì*, I was looking for you. We had a very distressed child with a fractured tibia,' he growled. 'I *needed* you.'

A distressed child.

Liv returned to reality with such a bump that every part of her felt bruised even though she hadn't moved a muscle. Disappointment swamped her like a flutter of freezing snow. He'd needed her. *At work*. Of course, at work. 'There are other nurses.'

'I was given other nurses. And they were slow. I had to *ask* for the instruments I needed,' he said scathingly, 'and they had *no* idea how to comfort the child. *Where were you?*'

Liv didn't know whether to laugh or cry.

She should be grateful to him, she told herself. It was just the wake-up call she needed. She wasn't the sort of woman a man turned to when he needed hot sex, she was the sort of woman a man turned to when he needed something done. 'I'm working a split shift, today. I went to watch my son play football.'

The thunderous expression on his face vanished and his mouth curved into an unexpected smile. 'He plays football? Did he score?'

Transfixed by that smile and the sudden change in him, Liv blinked. 'Y-yes, actually,' she stammered finally. 'He did. He was thrilled.' *And he wanted to be picked for the first team but she had no idea how to coach him properly*.

His eyes lingered on her face for a long, unsettling moment. 'So why are you looking so worried?'

'Worried?' She was so astonished that he'd noticed that the word came out like a squeak and she almost laughed at herself. *Talk about unsophisticated*. Anna would have thought of something flirtatious and clever to say, but she couldn't even hold a conversation with the man without her tongue tying itself into a knot. 'I'm not worried.'

'But something is wrong.' His eyes didn't shift from her face. 'Tell me.'

She stared up into the dark glitter of his eyes and felt her stomach flip. Oh boy. *My son needs a father, I need a make-over, I'm broke and it's Christmas in three weeks.*

Liv gave a laugh, trying to imagine his face if she spilled out her problems. 'Nothing is wrong. I'd better go.' Before her thoughts and her words became mixed up. 'I'll be back in the department in a minute, Mr Lucarelli.'

And by then she would have pulled herself together.

She needed to stop dreaming, before she embarrassed herself. *What was the matter with her?* Normally, she was realistic and practical. Even if she were single with no responsibilities, she wouldn't have allowed herself to be tempted by this man.

His life was so far removed from hers, it was laughable.

She could just imagine his reaction if she were to invite him to the ball. His polite refusal would no doubt become her second most embarrassing moment ever, after being overheard discussing sex with Anna.

'I'll see you in a minute, Mr Lucarelli.' She lifted the bag that had slipped off her shoulder and his eyes narrowed.

'*Stefano,*' he purred in a disturbingly male voice. 'My name is Stefano. Why does everyone keep calling me Mr Lucarelli? The emergency department is a very informal place to work.'

'Well, you're extremely senior and you're also relatively new so I suppose people are wary about being too familiar, and some people find you—' She broke off and backed towards the staffroom. 'I really need to change.'

'Wait.' His fingers closed over her arm. 'You didn't finish your sentence. Some people find me…?'

She hesitated. 'Intimidating. Just a little.'

'Intimidating? Me?' His dark eyes were lazily amused. 'I'm a pussycat.'

'Technically, so is a tiger,' Liv said dryly and he laughed.

'Providing people do their jobs correctly, I promise to keep my claws sheathed.' His gaze lingered on her face. 'You say "some people". Not you?'

Did he know that he was still holding her arm? 'I like the fact you have high standards. It means you're one less thing I have to worry about when I'm in Resus. I'm a control freak.'

He laughed. 'Likewise.'

'Two control freaks working in the same room could be a disaster.'

His eyes narrowed thoughtfully. 'Not if they were working towards the same objective. That would make them a powerful team, I think.' He sounded impossibly Italian and she sucked in a breath and eased her arm away from his grip.

'I'd better get changed or they'll be wondering where I am.'

Liv took refuge in the staffroom, slung her bag in the locker, quickly changed into her uniform and stared at herself in the mirror.

Her heart was thumping and her arm was tingling where he'd touched her.

Take a look at yourself, she told herself, standing square to the mirror. *Remember who you are*. Twenty-eight-year-old single mother. Nothing special. Now remember who he is. Extremely good-looking rich guy with a taste for skinny actresses.

Get a grip, Liv.

CHAPTER FOUR

IT WAS past ten o'clock before Stefano was finally able to leave the emergency department.

It had been a chaotic evening, with two serious car accidents in quick succession placing enormous demands on the already overstretched staff.

Fortunately for him, Liv had been working in Resus with him and things had run amazingly smoothly.

As he walked across the car park, the ground sparkled with frost and the sky was clear enough to warn him that it was going to be another cold night. Mentally he braced himself for a spate of accidents in the morning as drivers hit black ice.

From across the car park came the splutter and cough of an engine that didn't want to start and he saw Liv sitting in a small car, her scarf wrapped tightly around her neck, her breath forming clouds in the cold air.

Stefano tensed, instinctively suspicious.

On at least two occasions in the past, women had faked car problems in order to wangle a lift home with him.

He took a closer look at the car and decided that this particular bout of engine trouble couldn't possibly be anything but genuine. The car was ancient and there was a significant amount of rust at the base of the door. He wasn't surprised that it wouldn't start. What surprised him was that she'd managed to drive it to the hospital in the first place.

Stefano strode across to her and pulled open the door, amazed that it didn't come off in his hand. 'Problems?' He waited for her to give a sigh of relief and ask him for a lift, but instead she just shook her head.

'I'm fine,' she said firmly. 'But thanks for asking. Have a good evening, Mr Lucarelli. See you tomorrow.'

Fine? See you tomorrow? Astounded by her reaction, Stefano rested an arm on the top of the driver's door and leaned down so that he could talk to her properly. 'That engine doesn't sound fine to me.'

He should walk away. She was encouraging him to walk away.

So why didn't he do just that?

'It's a little temperamental, that's all. It likes to keep me guessing.' With a determined look on her face, she turned the key in the ignition again. The car gave a feeble cough and then there was nothing.

'Liv, there's temperamental and there's dead. Your engine is dead.'

'It can't be.' She slumped in her seat, a desperate look in her eyes. 'It just hates cold weather, that's all. If I leave it for a moment, it will start.'

Her teeth were chattering, her lips had a bluish tinge and Stefano reached into the car and gently removed the keys from her frozen fingers. 'This car is *not* going to start. I'll give you a lift wherever you want to go.' He wondered what it was about this particular woman that made him say things he wouldn't normally dream of saying.

But instead of accepting his offer with relief and gratitude, she shook her head firmly.

'Absolutely not.' She gathered her things together. 'I'll be fine, Mr Lucarelli, honestly. But thanks for checking on me. I'm sure you have somewhere you need to be. Please don't hang around on my account.'

She was refusing his offer of help?

Finding himself in completely unknown territory, Stefano didn't know whether to be amused or exasperated. 'And what do you plan to do? Sleep here until your next shift?'

'I'll take the underground. The train runs very close to my house.'

Her black coat was at least two sizes too big, but he caught a glimpse of slim legs in black tights and black boots. She looked more like a teenager than a mother with a young child. 'You're not taking the train.' The thought of her travelling on the underground horrified him. 'I'm giving you a lift.' He leaned across her, swiftly undid her seat belt and gently tugged her out of the car.

'Mr Lucarelli, I really don't—'

'It's Stefano.' He locked her car, not because he thought anyone was likely to steal it—*no one would be that desperate*—but out of consideration for her feelings. 'And you may think you're controlling, but you can't be as controlling as me. If I don't get my own way, I'm unbearable. Ask my sister if you don't believe me. Leave the car. Your garage can sort it out.'

'I don't think so.' Her expression was one of utter desolation and he frowned.

'It's just a car, Liv.'

For a moment she didn't answer and then she looked up at him, her smile just a little too bright. 'Yes, I know. Absolutely. And thanks for the offer of a lift, but I'll be fine on the train.' She eased her arm away from his and he felt a flash of exasperation.

'Do you always refuse help?'

'I'm never usually offered help. I'm used to doing things on my own. Taking care of myself. I suppose I feel…awkward. I don't want to put you out.'

He wondered why she was so suddenly so lacking in confidence when an hour earlier she'd been saving a life. 'So let me get this straight. You would rather skid along an icy pavement in freezing conditions and then wait on a draughty platform for a dark smelly underground train than have a lift to your door in my warm car. I confess I'm not flattered by your choice. Am I really that intimidating?'

Liv's glance was self-conscious. 'You can't possibly want to give me a lift home.'

Faced with the unusual situation of having to persuade a woman into his car, Stefano applied the full force of his personality. 'Just get in the car, Liv, and stop arguing.'

'You're right, you are controlling.'

'In this weather, it's an advantage. *Accidenti*, we're both going to freeze.' He took her hand and led her across the car park, noticing that her fingers were very slim and very cold. 'You should wear gloves.'

'I lost them.' She snatched her hand away from his as if she had only just realised that he was holding her. Immediately she slipped on the ice and would have crashed to the ground if he hadn't caught her. 'Oops! Oh my goodness!' Her legs slithered and he held her firmly, gritting his teeth as he felt the brush of her body against his.

Liv started to giggle and her laughter was so infectious that he found himself smiling, too.

'Stefano.' He held her firmly as she struggled to regain her footing on the icy surface. 'My name is Stefano. Start using it or I'll drop you.'

'If you drop me, you'll end up fixing the damage. You can let go of me now, I'm fine.' Gingerly her fingers released their grip on the front of his coat. 'Thank you.'

He tried to ignore the scent of her hair and the way her soft curves pressed against him, but the reaction of his body was instantaneous and he was experienced enough to know that the astonishing chemistry wasn't all on his side.

Her cheeks were pink and she was looking everywhere except at him.

Definitely not all on his side.

Wondering why she was so determined to get away from him when the attraction between them was so powerful, he reluctantly released her. 'Let's get in the car before we both develop hypothermia. Give me directions to your house.'

Her eyes slid over his car, the streamlined black Ferrari that had been his Christmas present to himself two years previously. 'All right, now I'm envious. Your car has no rust and I bet the engine starts first time.'

'Actually it doesn't.' Stefano opened the door. 'It hates the cold damp weather. I'm starting to think I should garage it over the winter and—' He had been about to say 'and use the other car' when he'd realised how insensitive that would be in the circumstances. 'Get in, Liv, before we both freeze.'

With obvious reluctance, she did as she was told and he strode round the car and settled himself in the driver's seat.

With an unconsciously sensual movement, she slid her hands slowly over the leather seats and her eyes flickered to the dashboard. 'Four point three litre engine,' she murmured, 'Naught to sixty in 3.9 seconds, F1 paddle shift transmission and carbon ceramic composite brakes.'

Stefano stared at her in incredulous disbelief and she smiled at him.

'Modified version of the 360s semi-space frame aluminium chassis. Capable of a top speed of 196 miles per hour.'

Stefano drew some much-needed air into his lungs. 'You're interested in cars?'

'Not in the slightest, but don't tell my little boy. He thinks I love cars.' Her eyes danced and her cheeks dimpled. 'I'm living proof that it's possible to sound knowledgeable about a subject without actually understanding anything. All I really know about your car is that it can go fast. Which isn't much use in London.'

Stefano started to laugh. 'You memorised all that?'

'Well, not intentionally. But Max doesn't like fairy-tales much. He prefers to read about engines and how things work. Anna's husband gave him a book on super-cars.'

'So you curl up in bed at night reading about Ferraris?'

'Gripping, don't you think? I can hardly wait to turn the page. Next week we should be moving on to Lamborghini. I particularly enjoyed November because that was Maserati.'

He loved her sense of humour but most of all he liked her smile. She was smiling at him now and it took all his will-power not to bring his mouth down on hers because the curve of her lips was so, so tempting.

But there was no sign of flirtation. Nothing to suggest she was even aware of her own appeal or the effect she was having on him.

'Your little boy is very lucky,' he said softly and her smile dimmed slightly.

'Not really. He's crazy about cars and football. I've done a great deal of homework on both subjects but it isn't really the same.' Staring at the monitors on the dashboard, she looked suddenly wistful. 'My own bedtime reading is a book on coaching football. Max is desperate to make the first team.'

He could imagine her studying the book, trying to help her little boy. 'He played today, so your coaching has obviously paid off.'

'I wish that were true, but I'm afraid it isn't. I think he has a natural talent but I have no idea how to foster that talent,' she admitted. 'I need to get some practical advice from somewhere. This afternoon all these fathers were yelling technical stuff to their boys and—' She broke off and shot him an apologetic glance. 'Sorry. This is very boring for you.'

He'd never been less bored by a woman in his life. 'I'm sure that the important thing for Max was that you were actually there, supporting him. Where is his father? Does he ever come and watch him?' He leaned across and fastened her seat belt, feeling her shrink against the seat as his hands brushed against her body.

She snuggled deeper inside the coat and he wondered why she was so self-conscious.

'I have no idea where his father is,' she croaked, her cheeks a little pinker than they had been a few moments before. 'Off enjoying himself somewhere, I should imagine. I'm not married, Mr Lucarelli. Nor do I want to be,' she said hastily and he hid a smile because she was obviously concerned that he might misinterpret her unguarded declaration.

He thought of Francine, who could have turned flirtation into an Olympic sport. Then he glanced at Liv's sweet profile and suddenly wanted to know more about her.

'You're not in touch with his father?'

'Jack was allergic to children. Unfortunately for Max, I didn't discover that until after I became pregnant.'

'He knew you were pregnant and he left you?' Unable to hide his disapproval, Stefano frowned and she cleared her throat.

'Not immediately. He hung around until Max was three. Sort of.'

'Sort of?' Uncomprehending, Stefano glanced at her but she was staring straight ahead.

'Well, we were married but not really…together. He had someone else, but I didn't find out for quite a while. Actually he had quite a few "someone elses" which doesn't do much for one's confidence, obviously. And I can't believe I'm telling you this.' She glanced at him, appalled. 'Why am I telling you this?'

'Because I asked.'

'Well that will teach you not to ask.' She looked away. 'It was all my fault, anyway.'

'*How* was it your fault?'

'I wasn't his type. I should have seen that right at the beginning,' she said quickly. 'Jack was handsome and clever.'

Not that clever, Stefano thought grimly, glancing at her profile and wondering if she realised just how much she'd revealed about herself with that simple statement. 'He wanted nothing to do with his son?'

It was a few seconds before she answered. 'No.'

'But he gives you financial help?'

Liv turned her head and stared out of the window. 'Do you think we should get going before the temperature drops any further? The roads will be lethal. I can't remember much about the Ferrari's performance on sheet ice.'

Stefano sat still for a moment, interpreting her answer.

So that was why she was so worried about her car.

It was obvious that she had no financial help and she was raising a child in an expensive city on a nurse's meagre salary. She was doing it all on her own. All of it.

But that didn't really explain why Anna had been talking about Liv's apparently non-existent sex life. Why wasn't she dating? Silently contemplating that issue, he started the engine and reversed out of his space. 'So who is looking after Max now? Do you have a nanny?'

'I use a childminder before and after school, but tonight he's doing a sleepover at Anna's. Max is best friends with her little boy.'

'So you're not rushing home to him?'

'No. Why?'

Making an instantaneous decision, Stefano steered the car down a series of back streets and then pulled in and parked. 'Because it means we have time to grab something to eat before I drop you home. Neither of us has eaten since lunchtime. You must be starving and there is an absolutely fantastic Italian restaurant here.'

'No!' Liv swivelled to face him, her expression horrified. 'It's incredibly kind of you, but I couldn't possibly do that.'

'Why not?'

'Because— No.' Her gaze slid from his. 'I'll make myself some toast before I go to bed.'

'Toast?' Having never eaten toast for dinner in his life, Stefano looked at her in amazement. 'I'm suggesting we go out to eat and you're choosing toast?'

'Yes.'

'Why?'

'Loads of reasons.' She fiddled with the strap of her handbag, her discomfort so acute that it was almost painful to watch. 'I'm not dressed for a fancy restaurant and I can't afford to eat out.'

The change in her was startling. Working with him in Resus she'd been a poised, confident professional, but faced with a trip to a restaurant she'd become a shy, awkward woman. And she wasn't even looking him in the eye.

Instinctively taking control, Stefano reached across and

undid her seat belt, noticing the way she flattened herself against the seat again. 'It isn't fancy and this is my treat. A thank-you for having made my life easier in the department.

'Mr Lucarelli, I really can't—'

'Liv, I'm buying you a bowl of spaghetti, that's all.' He'd never before had to persuade a woman to have dinner with him and she was obviously well aware of that fact because she shot him an agonised look.

'There must be someone else you can take!' Her tone bordered on the desperate and he gave a faint smile.

'You're not doing much for my ego. Is the thought of facing me across a bowl of spaghetti really that terrifying?'

'No! It isn't you, it's me. I'm just not—' She broke off, clearly finding the situation painfully awkward. 'I'm not very exciting company, that's all.'

Accustomed to being with women who were confident both socially and sexually, it took him a moment to adjust to the contrast.

He studied her face in silence, taking in the self-doubt in her eyes and the touch of colour in her cheeks. 'Liv, what is the matter with you? Do you really expect me to believe that you can handle the most demanding medical emergency with total confidence but can't wind spaghetti onto a fork and talk at the same time?'

She gave a reluctant laugh. 'I suppose it's all about practice. I'm more confident at Resus-speak than dinner-table-speak.'

'Fine, then we'll talk about pelvic fractures. Or we won't talk at all. I really don't care, just as long as I eat something in the next five minutes.' He extracted her from the car and propelled her, still protesting, through the door of the restaurant.

They were instantly enveloped by warmth and delicious

smells and Liv hesitated on the threshold, scanning the room like a gazelle sensing danger.

All evidence of the cool professional had left her and she looked so painfully unsure of herself that for a moment Stefano thought she might actually turn and run. He planted himself behind her, watching as she took in the cheerful red tablecloths, the enormous Christmas tree and the cosy, informality of the place.

Then she turned her head and gave him a hesitant smile. 'It's nice.'

'*Sì*, I know. Just wait until you taste the pasta. It's incredible.' Stefano tried to peel the coat from her shoulders, but she clutched at it self consciously.

'I'll keep it on. I'm not dressed to go out to dinner,' she muttered and he gently but firmly uncurled her fingers.

'You can't eat dinner in your coat. This is a very informal place.' He prised the coat from her grip and handed it to the waiter. 'No one dresses up to come here and anyway, you look fine.'

She looked a lot better than fine. Without the protection of the coat he could see that her legs went on for ever and the way that her skinny rib jumper clung to her gorgeous curves drew the attention of several men in the room, but he decided that to comment on her appearance would just make her even more uncomfortable.

She obviously had no idea how attractive she was.

Which made a refreshing change from the women he usually mixed with, he thought wryly, recalling Francine's endless preoccupation with her own reflection.

Not wanting to risk increasing Liv's anxiety levels by offering her a menu, he turned to the owner and spoke in rapid Italian, telling him where they wanted to sit and what they wanted to eat.

The owner led them to a quiet table by the window and Liv gave a soft gasp of delight.

'We're right next to the river here—I didn't realise. It's so pretty, especially in the dark when it's all lit up and you can't see the dirt.'

'This restaurant is a hidden gem. I discovered it on a trip to London a few years ago. Because you approach it via all the back streets, you don't realise that it's by the Thames. What can I get you to drink? Champagne?'

'Champagne?' Startled, she dragged her eyes away from the view and looked at him. 'No thanks, water will be fine.'

'Water?'

'I did warn you that I'm incredibly boring.' Reaching for her napkin, she spread it on her lap. 'Champagne is for women who don't have to get up at five in the morning.'

'You get up at five?'

'If I don't start then, I can't get everything done.'

A waiter placed two heaped bowls of spaghetti bolognese in front of them and Liv glanced at him in surprise. 'I didn't know you'd ordered.'

'This is the best thing on the menu and it's just what you need after a day on your feet. Eat.' He picked up his fork and then suddenly wondered if he'd ordered the wrong thing for her. 'Just leave the pasta and eat the sauce, if you prefer.'

This time she laughed, her green eyes sparkling in the candlelight. 'I think you're definitely confused about who you're having dinner with.' She spiralled pasta onto her fork like a professional. 'I'm a working mother, Stefano. If I don't eat carbohydrates, I collapse. Anyway, I'm starving and this smells delicious. I couldn't leave any of it if you paid me.'

Stefano watched her eat the first mouthful and felt an explosion of heat through his loins. 'You must have Italian genes.'

'No, I have a son who loves spaghetti. It's Max's second favourite gourmet treat.'

'His first being?'

'Pizza. He'd eat it every night if I let him. We make it together, from scratch. There's nothing quite like kneading dough to let off steam after a hard day.' Gradually she relaxed with him and he kept the conversation flowing, deriving immense satisfaction from the fact that she seemed to have lost her earlier awkwardness.

Soon she was telling him all the details of her life. They talked about work, about living in London and she mentioned Max a lot, recounting several anecdotes that made him laugh.

'It must be pretty tiring, working a full day and then going home and being a mum.' The amount she did in a day stunned him. 'I don't suppose you have much time to yourself.'

'I don't really want that,' she said simply. 'I love being with him. He's fun. We have a nice time together. And once he's asleep I have time to myself.'

And then she read books on coaching football.

'So you basically work all day and spend time with your seven-year-old.' *Was that why Anna had been offering to buy her hot sex for Christmas?* Stefano reached for some more bread. 'Do you ever go out?'

'Oh yes, we often go to one of the museums at the weekend and sometimes we'll go to the cinema for a treat. He loves it and so do I.'

That wasn't what he'd meant, but he didn't push her.

Clearly her life was her work and her child and Stefano finished his spaghetti and lounged in his chair, listening as she talked about her hectic life and her hopes for Max. He was intrigued by how happy she seemed. 'So is Max looking forward to Christmas?'

'Yes. Not that we do much. Turkey, presents, trip to the park…' She shrugged and added, 'Last year we went on a trip to the seaside and played on the beach. Freezing but fun. I try and do a special trip, to make up for the fact it's just the two of us.'

'You don't have family?'

'No.' She concentrated on her plate. 'I only have one aunt and she lives in Scotland so I never get to see her. What about you? Will you be spending Christmas with your family?'

'Yes. I have an interfering younger sister, an even more interfering father and at least eight first cousins.'

'Lucky you.' Her tone was wistful. 'I imagine there's nothing better than a noisy, chaotic Christmas when everyone is driving everyone else mad.'

'You think that's lucky?'

Liv reached for her water. 'I suppose that the fact they interfere at least means they care. And it's lovely to have someone who cares. The world can be a lonely, scary place.'

Did she find it scary? *Was she lonely?*

Sensing that to delve deeper into that comment might send her back into her shell, Stefano shifted the conversation. 'My sister has twin boys the same age as Max.'

'Really?' Her face brightened. 'That must be a handful. I can't imagine two.'

'She has a nanny. My sister works in the family business.'

Liv studied him across the table, her green eyes reflecting the flickering candlelight. 'And you disapprove of that?'

'The children need her. And she doesn't need to work.'

'I presume you mean financially. But maybe she needs to work for other reasons.'

'Let me ask you a question.' He wondered how he could ever have thought she wasn't beautiful. Her face had a pure, innocent quality but her mouth had been designed for seduction. 'If you had all the money you needed, would you still work?'

'I have no idea. I've never thought about it and I wouldn't allow myself to because it isn't an option for me. Happiness is being realistic, Stefano.'

Noticing that she was trying not to yawn, he caught the eye of the waiter. 'Time to get you home.'

'Sorry. It was a bit of an early start this morning.' Her attention was on a different part of the restaurant and when he followed her gaze he saw that a table of women were all watching him and laughing. They were obviously enjoying a girls' night out and one of them lifted her glass and sent a flirtatious look in his direction.

Stefano didn't react, but Liv's friendly, open chatter suddenly ceased and she returned to looking awkward and uncomfortable, her eyes on the view instead of him.

Why was she so self-conscious?

She'd retreated back into her shell and he knew that her reaction had something to do with the noisy group of women who were partying at the nearby table.

He was unable to retrieve the situation because the waiter arrived with the bill and stood hovering while Stefano produced his credit card.

'Tell me how much my half is,' Liv said huskily. 'I'll pay you back tomorrow. I'm so sorry I don't have enough money with me now.'

Amused, he glanced at her. 'When I buy a woman dinner, I don't expect her to pay.'

'Maybe not, but that's when you're on a date and this wasn't a date. This was just two colleagues sharing food. I'll pay you back tomorrow.'

The money was obviously an enormous issue for her and

he wondered how, if she was really so short of cash, she was ever going to get her car fixed. 'I don't want you to pay me back. I was hungry and there's nothing more grim than eating alone. You did me a favour.'

'Hardly. I talked far too much about really boring subjects.' Clearly in a hurry to leave, she rose to her feet and didn't speak again until they reached the car. 'Thank you, Stefano.'

'Give me directions to your flat.' He steered the conversation away from money. 'Have you worked in the emergency department for long?'

'The last few years. Before that I was on Paediatrics and sometimes when they're short staffed I still go and help there. What about you? Where did you work last?'

'In a trauma unit up in Scotland and before that Milan.'

'Milan.' She repeated the word with the same emphasis he'd used. 'That sounds exotic.'

Stefano laughed. 'If you think that, you have clearly never been to Milan.'

'I've never been anywhere. Take a left at the lights. And then it's straight on all the way to my flat. Just keep going. So what's Milan like?'

'It's a wonderful city, but I wouldn't describe it as exotic.'

'Why did you choose to come to frozen England?'

'I needed a change.' And this was certainly a change, he thought grimly, scanning the streets. As she directed him, the area he was driving through grew more and more rundown. There was litter on the streets, graffiti on the walls and gangs of teenagers wearing hoodies lurked on street corners.

'You were escaping from your interfering family?'

'Something like that.' His family and a clingy ex-girlfriend. A police car raced past them, light flashing, horn blaring, and Stefano felt the tension in his shoulders mount. He wouldn't want any of his family living in a place like this.

'We're here,' she said a few minutes later. 'If you pull in just past that lamppost, that's my flat. Thanks very much.' As the car drew to a halt, she reached for her bag. 'I really am grateful. The meal was delicious and you've been very kind. See you tomorrow.'

One glance at the area told him that she shouldn't be coming back here late at night on her own. 'Wait.' His hand on her arm prevented her leaving the car. 'I'll see you to your door.'

'There's really no need. I know it looks grim but I'm used to it.' Not looking at him, Liv produced her keys. 'I'll be fine.'

'You're very independent, aren't you?'

'I've had to be.' She glanced at him then and their eyes met and held. Then she gave a tiny frown and tore her gaze away from his. 'Goodnight, Mr Lucarelli. And thanks again.'

The chemistry was shimmering between them like an invisible force and yet her hand slid to the door.

'Invite me in for coffee.' His softly spoken command obviously surprised her and he watched with some satisfaction as the keys slipped from her fingers. It was nice to know she wasn't indifferent to him. Uncomfortable, yes. Shy, maybe. But indifferent? *Definitely not.* 'You've already told me that Max is at Anna's tonight, so you have no bedtime story to read.' He lounged in his seat, enjoying the effect he was having on her. She was delightfully transparent.

'You don't strike me as the sort of man who'd step out of his Ferrari to drink a cup of instant coffee in a damp flat that is probably smaller than your bathroom,' she said lightly and he gave a slow smile.

'I love instant coffee and I'm nervous in large spaces. I promise to give you a lesson on how to coach football.'

'Now you're being unfair.' She laughed. 'Mr Lucarelli—Stefano.' She stumbled over his name and stooped to retrieve her keys, 'That's a really tempting offer and I really am grateful for the lift, but I've already taken up enough of your Friday evening. I'm sure you have plenty more exciting ways to spend your time than drinking coffee with me.' And before he could answer, she slid out of his car and hurried across to her flat.

Stefano wondered why he was so desperate to follow her.

She had nothing, absolutely nothing, in common with the women he usually spent time with. Obviously her life revolved around her work and her son. It was almost as if she'd forgotten that she was a woman. Or maybe she just ignored that fact.

His eyes narrowed as he remembered the way she'd hung onto her coat in the restaurant. She was woman enough to care that she hadn't dressed to go to a restaurant.

He watched as she hurried up the steps to the front door of her flat, his eyes narrowed and his body aching with awareness. She moved with the grace of a dancer and flakes of snow settled on her dark hair as she fumbled to get her key into the lock.

As the door opened she paused and Stefano waited for her to look back and smile at him.

She was going to look back. He felt it.

She stood for a moment on the threshold and then stepped inside her flat and firmly closed the door behind her.

And she didn't look back.

Liv stood in the kitchen, willing herself not to run to the window and see if his car was still there.

Had she imagined it or had he really invited himself in for coffee?

And why had he done that?

Surely the time they'd spent together in the restaurant should have been enough to prove to him that she wasn't exactly stimulating company. She'd talked about work and Max.

Thinking about how much she'd talked and how boring she'd been, she covered her face with her hands and gave a groan of embarrassment. Not only had she been boring, she'd been wearing her most ancient skirt and jumper. A man like Stefano Lucarelli must be used to being with women who were groomed to within an inch of their lives. And on top of that, she'd cleared her plate. She'd eaten absolutely everything and his comment about just eating the sauce had made it perfectly obvious that he was used to stick-thin women who went to restaurants to be seen, rather than to eat.

He'd offered her champagne!

Thank goodness she'd had the sense to refuse, otherwise the evening would have been even more embarrassing. As it was, he was probably regretting ever offering her a lift. Because of her stupid car, he'd been stuck with her all evening.

And he'd been incredibly kind about it. So kind that for a short time she'd completely forgotten to be shy and awkward and had really enjoyed herself.

After a while she'd even managed to forget how impossibly good-looking he was and how he absolutely shouldn't be wasting an evening on her, and just concentrate on the conversation. And he'd been really, *really* good company. Although she knew it wasn't fashionable to admit it, she loved the fact that he'd just taken charge.

He was *so* sure of himself and confident and wasn't afraid to make decisions. Just having someone else make a decision for her had had the same effect as a month on a health farm.

It was just because she was a single mother, she thought wistfully. Every decision that needed to be made, she made it—by herself, with no help or input from anyone else and sometimes the unrelenting responsibility of her life was just *exhausting*. Yes, she was controlling, but only because she'd had to be. It was hardly surprising that when someone else did the thinking for five minutes, it had felt wonderful.

It had felt so incredibly indulgent to have a plate of food put in front of her that for a short time she'd relaxed and been herself with him. Only she'd talked far too much about her life—it was a wonder he hadn't fallen asleep in his spaghetti.

It was just as well she'd happened to notice the table of women near to them. Made up and dressed up, they'd obviously spent half the day getting ready for their night out and they had gazed at Stefano as though they'd wanted him for their main course.

At that point she'd remembered just who she was with and she'd returned to earth quickly, reminding herself that it wasn't a date.

He'd been with her because he was polite, not because he'd been attracted to her. For a moment in the car the atmosphere had been stretched and tight and she'd thought—she'd really thought that it was caused by mutual attraction and then she'd realised that the tension had simply been caused by him trying to find a tactful way of extracting her from his car.

Why would a man like him be interested in someone as ordinary as her? He just had well-developed social skills, that was all.

He'd only invited her to dinner because he'd been hungry and he'd been forced to give her a lift. It must have been a horribly awkward situation for him.

No wonder he'd suddenly asked for the bill, instead of lingering over dessert and coffee.

He'd obviously been desperate to escape as fast as possible.

And for her own sanity, she needed to remember that.

CHAPTER FIVE

'LIV, you're needed in Resus. We've just admitted a woman with chest pains. She had a Caesarean section seven days ago.' Anna removed the keys to the drug cupboard from her pocket. 'By the way, why was your car iced over in the car park this morning?'

'It didn't start last night. Did you say she has just had a baby?'

'That's right. Second baby, six-hour discharge, no problems. How did you get home if your car died?'

'I grabbed a lift.' Without elaborating, Liv hurried into Resus just as the paramedics left the room, pushing the empty stretcher.

'We're going to give you some oxygen to help you breathe, Michelle,' Stefano was saying and he glanced up as Liv joined him by the side of the trolley. For a brief moment his dark eyes lingered on hers and that one look was sufficient to trigger memories of the explicit dreams that had disturbed her sleep the night before.

Remembering just what he'd been doing to her in those dreams, colour flooded into her cheeks and he noted her response with a slight narrowing of his sexy eyes before shifting his gaze back to the radiographer who was hovering. 'We'll do a chest X-ray, although I'm not sure it's going to tell us much.'

'I can't breathe—I'm so worried...' The woman's lips were blue and Liv took her hand and gave it a gentle squeeze, trying to ignore the increase in her own heart rate.

It had just been a dream, for goodness' sake. A dream he knew nothing about. Unless he could read minds, he was never going to find out that she'd been having totally inappropriate fantasies about him.

Angry with herself, Liv checked the monitor. 'Pulse is a hundred and fifteen.'

It was totally ridiculous to feel like this. He'd given her a lift home, that was all. Trying to forget about the previous evening, she concentrated her attention on the patient. 'How are those pains, Michelle?'

Michelle closed her eyes. 'Worse when I breathe.'

Liv's immediate thought was that the woman had suffered a pulmonary embolus, a clot in her lung. She looked at Stefano and he gave a brief nod of agreement, clearly reading her mind.

At least in the emergency department they were completely in tune.

'You're in hospital now, so try to leave the worrying to us, Michelle.' Liv glanced over her shoulder to one of the other nurses. 'Alice? Can you call the obstetric unit and see if they can track down her notes, please?'

'I've left my husband with the kids.' Gasping for breath, the woman was clearly frantic with worry. 'The baby's only a week old and I'm breastfeeding. He's never going to cope.'

'Is he coming to the hospital?' Liv watched as Stefano prepared to take blood from the radial artery, his fingers swift and confident.

Michelle coughed feebly. 'He's supposed to be following in the car.'

'I'm just going to take some blood from your wrist, Michelle,' Stefano murmured. 'This might hurt a bit.'

'I'm worried that the baby is going to be starving.' Tears welled up in Michelle's eyes. 'She has no idea how to take a bottle. Ow.' She screwed up her face. 'You're right, that does hurt.'

'*Mi dispiace.* I'm sorry. I know it's uncomfortable.' Stefano straightened. 'I want her catheterised so that we can monitor her fluid output. Let's give her some high-flow oxygen and we need to get a line in. Phil, I want FBC, ESR and U&Es. She has pleuritic chest pain and a pleural rub.' He delivered a string of commands, his instructions succinct and fluent and Liv stood back for a moment so that the radiographer could do her job.

'We're just going to run a few tests on you, Michelle, and then I promise I'll go and talk to your husband. If necessary I can fetch someone from the obstetric unit to help with the baby.'

Michelle pressed a hand to her chest, her breath coming in shallow pants. 'I've never felt anything like this before. It feels as though I'm being stabbed.'

'The chest X-ray looks completely normal,' Phil muttered and Stefano's dark eyes flickered to the screen. For a brief moment all his attention was focused on the image and everyone in the room looked at him expectantly.

Liv glanced at the monitor again. 'Sats are dropping,' she murmured and reached for the ECG machine.

'The clinical signs are all consistent with a diagnosis of PE,' Stefano reached out a hand to take a set of results that one of the nurses was flourishing in his direction. He scanned them quickly and then put them on top of the notes. 'She's seven days post-Caesarean section, which is a major risk factor. Let's give her a dose of tinzaparin.'

Liv checked Michelle's blood pressure again. 'Her pulse is a hundred and ten and she's hypotensive.' She turned back to the patient. 'Michelle, I just want to do a trace of your heart so I'm going to undo your shirt and attach some wires to your chest.'

'Has my husband arrived?' Michelle's breathing was shallow and rapid. 'Could you find out? It's really worrying me.'

'Rachel?' Liv spoke over her shoulder. 'Can you go to the desk and ask them to tell us as soon as Michelle's family arrive? Put them in the relatives' room and make sure they have everything they need. I'll be with them as soon as I can.'

Michelle gave a strangled laugh. 'I can't be in hospital. I have a new baby and it's Christmas in a couple of weeks.'

'Don't worry about that, now,' Liv soothed, her eyes on the ECG. 'Stefano?'

'*Sì*, I am looking.' His eyes narrowed, he studied the trace. 'Get ICU on the phone for me. And I want 10 milligrams of alteplase as a starting dose. Let's arrange for a CT scan.'

It was another hour before Michelle was finally transferred to ICU and only then did Liv and Stefano go and talk to her husband.

They found him pacing the relatives' room, holding a bawling baby against his shoulder while a toddler clung to his leg.

'How is she? The other nurse said she was being transferred.' White-faced with anxiety, he stepped towards Stefano and the baby's screams intensified, as if the infant sensed that something important was happening. The father rubbed her back helplessly. 'Sorry. I'm so sorry. I don't know what to do with her. I think she's hungry and I can't get her to take the bottle. Michelle expressed some milk last night and left it in the fridge, so it isn't that it tastes different but I think she just isn't used to the teat, or something.'

'Why don't I have a try?' Liv held out her arms. 'Then you

can have a proper conversation with Mr Lucarelli. I'm sure there are lots of things you want to ask him.'

'Would you mind?' Gently and slightly clumsily he lifted the baby from his shoulder and handed her to Liv. 'You forget how tiny they are when they're first born. It's terrifying.'

Liv expertly snuggled the baby against her and reached for the bottle, leaving Stefano to update Nick on his wife's condition.

She sat down in the chair, settled the baby in the crook of her arm and drew the teat across her lips. 'You poor little thing,' she murmured softly. 'Are you starving?'

The baby was red-faced from crying and gave a little hiccough. Then she played with the teat for a moment before turning her head away in disgust.

'I know it feels a bit weird, but it tastes just the same. Trust me.' Liv squeezed a tiny bit of the milk onto the baby's lips and watched as her mouth moved hungrily. 'See? It tastes nice. We just need to teach you to suck.' She skilfully manoeuvred the teat into the baby's mouth and the infant lay still for a moment, and then gave a gulp and swallowed. Liv smiled. 'Good girl.'

'Oh thank goodness,' Nick muttered, watching from across the room. 'She's been crying for hours. I was at my wits' end. You are utterly, utterly amazing.'

Liv glanced up and met Stefano's eyes and there was something in his watchful gaze that made her shift awkwardly in her seat.

What was he thinking?

Probably that she was good with babies but hopeless at scintillating dinner conversation.

Still mortified that she'd gone on and on the night before, she dipped her head and concentrated on the baby. 'She's fine. She just needed a bit of help to suck from a teat. It's a different technique.'

Nick gave a helpless shrug. 'I don't suppose you fancy moving in with me for a week or so?'

Liv gently withdrew the bottle from the baby's mouth and lifted the baby against her shoulder. 'What about Grandma? Can she help?'

'She's great with this one…' Nick scooped the toddler onto his lap '…but the baby needs Michelle.'

Stefano rose to his feet. 'Let's see how she goes this morning. Once her condition is stabilised we may be able to transfer her to a ward and she can have the baby with her. We'll do everything we can to help, I assure you.'

'You've been very kind.'

The door opened and Anna put her head round the door. 'Liv? Can Rachel take over in there so that you can help me out here? Everyone is obviously bored with Christmas shopping so they've decided to spend the afternoon with us instead.'

'No problem.' Liv carefully handed the baby back to Nick and smiled at him. 'You can stay here for now. Once we have some news from ICU, you can go and see Michelle.'

She left the room and hurried after Anna but Stefano's fingers curled around her wrist and stopped her.

'Liv, wait.'

The touch of his hand turned her limbs to jelly and she took several deep breaths before turning to face him. This time she was *not* going to embarrass herself. 'Thank you for last night,' she said brightly, staring at a point in the middle of his chest. 'Best spaghetti I've ever eaten. Oh—here's the money I owe you.' She dug twenty pounds out of her pocket, trying not to think what that bowl of spaghetti had done to her budget.

'I don't want your money, Liv.' His voice was a deep, lazy

drawl and the breath stuck in her throat because he was so cool and in control and she felt so, so awkward.

'Please take it. Honestly. There's no reason why you should pay for me.' She risked a glance at him and then wished she hadn't because he was the sort of man you just couldn't look away from. He was impossibly, indecently handsome and his gaze held hers for a moment and then flickered to her mouth.

Liv stopped breathing and a slow, dangerous warmth spread through her body. For a wickedly delicious moment she thought he might actually be wondering what it would be like to kiss her.

And then she returned to reality.

Boring.

His eyes narrowed. 'What would be boring?'

Horrified, Liv stared at him. *Had she really spoken her thoughts aloud?* 'Nothing. Take the money.' She pushed it into his hand and started to back away. 'I really have to go. Anna needs me, and—'

'Liv, stop it.' His eyes were amused. 'Why are you so jumpy? Last night over dinner you managed to relax and be yourself. For the first time I actually had a glimpse of the real you.'

Liv almost groaned. 'Yes, I know,' she muttered, 'and I'm really, *really* sorry about that. I suppose it's because I don't often find myself in adult company, apart from with the patients and they don't count. I was a little carried away talking about my life. No wonder you only ordered one course.'

Surprise flickered in his eyes and he watched her for a moment, his expression thoughtful. 'I ordered one course because most of the women I take out to dinner don't eat anything,' he said softly and she gave a resigned smile.

If she'd needed a reminder that she bore no resemblance to the type of woman he usually dated, she had it now. 'Well, you only have to look at me to know that I'm not in that category—but then you weren't really taking me out to dinner, were you? It was more a question of me gatecrashing and—' she broke off and studied his face. 'Why are you smiling?'

'Because you fascinate me. In Resus you are always cool and in control. You are fast, bright and confident. And then we leave Resus and you are a nervous wreck. Why is that, I wonder?'

The way he was looking at her made her feel hot and shivery at the same time.

'I…really ought to go, because…' horribly out of her depth, she waved a hand vaguely. 'I…just really ought to go.' Why was he talking to her, anyway? Why was he bothering?

'Give me your car keys.'

'My—' She frowned. 'Why?'

'Because someone from my garage is coming to pick up your car in ten minutes.'

Liv stared at him in astonishment. 'Your garage? But they fix Ferraris.'

'They're skilled mechanics.' Stefano inclined his head as the neurology consultant wandered past and muttered a greeting. 'They can fix anything with an engine.'

'I'm not sure that mine even falls into that category,' Liv joked weakly, incredibly touched that he'd offered. *Why? Why had he offered?* 'I couldn't possibly say yes. Even if they could fix it, they'd charge a fortune. Garages take one look at me and rip me off.'

'All the more reason to let me sort this one out. Garages don't rip me off.' His tone was pleasant but there was a hard glint in his eyes that made her smile.

'I imagine they wouldn't dare.' Panic fluttered inside her when she thought about all the demands on her meagre salary. 'I suppose I could use the Christmas-tree money.' She murmured those words to herself and Stefano raised an eyebrow in question.

'The Christmas-tree money?'

Trying to work out how to find a Christmas tree that didn't cost anything, Liv felt her head start to throb. 'Look, I hadn't expected my car to die three weeks before Christmas, which obviously wasn't very sensible planning on my part, but there you are. I basically can't afford to get it fixed yet.' What was the point in pretending? It was obvious from the state of her car that she wasn't rolling in money. 'But thanks for offering.'

'How much is your budget?'

'A hundred pounds.' Saying it aloud, it sounded so ridiculous that Liv started to laugh. 'You see? It's hopeless. I doubt they'd even tow it away for that.'

'It might not be anything too serious. Let's wait and see what they say. My mechanic is cheap and reliable.' His eyes lingered on her face and she felt her insides heat.

'I don't know what to say.'

'You say yes.'

Faced with the tempting vision of a problem solved, Liv felt herself waver. 'If it's more than a hundred pounds—'

'Then I'll tell them not to do the work. Now give me the keys.' He held out his hand. 'Keys, Liv.'

She handed them over. 'I don't know why you're helping me.'

'I know you don't.' With that enigmatic comment, he strolled away from her, her car keys in his hand, leaving her staring after him in bemusement.

'I don't care how much it costs.' Stefano trawled through his emails as he made the call. 'I just want it fixed. Fast. And I want the bill to say £102.' He listened for a moment as the mechanic outlined the dire state of Liv's car. 'Yes, I know all

that. I have eyes… I don't care about that, either… A new
engine—yes, whatever, and there's one other thing.' He
frowned as he scanned the email from the chief executive demanding his presence at a meeting on cost-cutting. 'I want you
to deliver a hire car here this afternoon. A new, safe hatch-
back, nothing too flashy.' Having sorted out that problem, he
terminated the call and turned to the pile of letters on his desk,
but he was called to see a patient and then another and it was
several hours before he was finally able to return to the
mounting paperwork.

He was just trying to work up some enthusiasm for an extremely dry memo from the Department of Health when there
was a tap on the door.

Liv stood there, a set of keys in her hand. 'The garage delivered me a car,' she gasped. 'Did you arrange it?'

Stefano relaxed back in his chair, watching her. 'They
always give a complimentary car. Perhaps I forgot to
mention that.'

'When they're servicing your Ferrari, maybe, but *not* when
they're given an ancient rust bucket to resuscitate.'

'It's Christmas. I told them that you have a child and that
you work at the hospital. People are extra-kind to nurses and
rightly so. Just accept it, Liv.' His order was met by silence
and she simply stared at him. Then she gave a little sob and
suddenly burst into tears.

Appalled, Stefano rose to his feet. '*Accidenti*, who has
upset you? Tell me and I will sort it out right now!'

'No one. Nothing. I'm sorry.' She rubbed the palm of her
hand across one cheek and then the other, wiping away the
tears, visibly struggling to pull herself together. 'It's just that
I'm not used to—I usually have to sort out everything myself.
I'm not used to people being kind and—I can't believe you

persuaded them to lend me a car.' Her voice cracked. 'Thank you. Thank you so much.'

Frozen to the spot, Stefano watched her, uncertain how to respond. Usually female tears left him cold, but he'd never encountered the genuine article before. Neither had he ever been so profusely thanked for so small a gesture. He'd once given Francine a diamond necklace, but even that extravagant gift had merited little more than a loud squeal and a comment that matching earrings would have been nice.

'You're welcome,' he said softly and Liv gave him an embarrassed smile and pulled a tissue out of her pocket.

'I seem to make a habit of making a fool of myself in front of you.' She blew her nose hard. 'You're probably thinking I'm a complete psycho.'

He thought she was delightfully natural, refreshingly honest and achingly sexy. 'I think you're tired, and that is hardly surprising given how hard you work.'

'I like my work.'

And in her time off, she read to her child. Books on cars and football.

He'd never met anyone as selfless as her. Sensing that she was struggling for control, Stefano shifted the subject away from the personal. 'I just spoke to ICU. Michelle is stable.'

Liv's face brightened. 'That's good news. How's the baby?'

'Taking the bottle quite happily since the lesson you gave her.'

Liv laughed and he couldn't help comparing her confidence at work with her lack of confidence in her social life.

'Have dinner with me tonight.' He'd spoken those words on umpteen occasions in the past, but never before had he braced himself for rejection. Up until this point in his life it had been a foregone conclusion that the woman in question would just say yes.

As he'd anticipated, Liv instantly shook her head. 'I couldn't possibly. Why? Why would you want to?'

He was asking himself the same question. He'd never before dated a colleague or a single mother.

Neither had he found himself thinking about sex at inconvenient moments during his working day. 'I owe you dessert.'

Liv backed towards the door. 'You don't owe me anything.'

Unaccustomed to having to persuade a woman to join him for dinner, Stefano watched her for a moment, trying to read her mind. 'Is it a babysitting issue?'

'Yes.' She said the word quickly and then breathed out and shook her head. 'No, actually that's not true. It isn't just about the babysitting. It's about *me*. And you. I mean, you found out everything there is to know about me last night. You've already listened to my entire life history and I'm sure it bored you to death. I don't have anything else to say. I work, I spend time with my child. That's it. I'm just not interesting. You already know all there is to know.'

He was stunned by the completely false impression she had of herself.

Why did she think she was boring?

Contemplating the soft curve of her mouth and the shyness in her expression, Stefano strolled across his office towards her. He watched as her eyes widened slightly.

'Mr Lucarelli—Stefano…'

Without speaking, Stefano took her face in his hands, stared down into her startled green eyes for a few endless seconds and then brought his mouth down on hers. For a moment she didn't move a muscle, and then she made a soft sound and her lips parted under his.

He kissed her slowly and confidently, taking his time, holding her head exactly as he wanted it as he skilfully seduced her mouth. Only when her fingers curled into the front of his shirt and he felt her relax against him did he slide an arm around her waist and pull her into his body.

Boring?

She was exquisite.

Her hips were curved, her breasts full and the sudden explosion of raw lust that devoured him was so powerful that it took all his willpower to stop himself from slamming the door shut and just taking her on his desk.

Unsettled by the fierce intensity of his own response, Stefano dragged his mouth from hers and eased her away from him.

Liv swayed for a moment and then opened her eyes and looked at him. Her expression was so bemused that he suddenly wondered exactly how long it had been since anyone had kissed her properly.

'There's plenty that I don't know about you, Liv,' he said softly, dragging his thumb over the swollen softness of her mouth. 'But I intend to find out.'

CHAPTER SIX

'MUMMY, why are you staring out of the window and smiling?'

Liv turned at the sound of Max's voice. 'Oh…' she cleared her throat and picked up her coffee-mug. It was Saturday morning and she'd been up since dawn. 'I was just…thinking.' *About being kissed.* It wasn't the first time she'd been kissed, but it seemed that way. Unless her memory was defective, it had never felt like that.

Stefano Lucarelli kissed as well as he did everything else.

Max shook the contents of the cereal packet into his bowl and looked at her sympathetically. 'Are you worrying that Father Christmas might not come? I know how he gets round the whole world in one night.'

'You do?' *Why had he kissed her?* She didn't understand it, but it was impossible to erase the memory from her brain or her body. And he'd said that he wanted to know more about her. *What had he meant by that?*

'Mum? Are you listening?'

'I'm listening.'

'It's because he travels through different time zones,' Max said seriously. 'You know, he starts in Australia, then he moves on to…' swinging his legs, he carried on detailing

Father Christmas's route while Liv tried desperately to stop thinking about Stefano.

With a huge effort, she brought herself back to reality. 'OK. I'll stop worrying about Father Christmas's workload. So—plan for the day. Football in the park and then we'll buy the Christmas tree. How does that sound?'

'Brilliant.' Max crunched his way through the cereal and drank his milk. 'Pizza for tea?'

Liv laughed. *Why was she feeling so happy?* It was completely ridiculous, but she just couldn't help it. Determined to pull herself together, she rose to her feet. 'I'll make the dough now. You can help. Wash your hands.'

'Hayley's mum won't let her make pizza dough because she says it makes a mess.' Max reached for the weighing scales and lifted the flour out of the cupboard. 'I told her that you love mess.'

'Mess and I are certainly intimately acquainted,' Liv said dryly, glancing around her kitchen and wondering why it never stayed tidy.

Because she was happy to let her son make pizza dough.

Max emptied some flour onto the weighing scales. 'Oops.' He stood back as some of it sprinkled over his toes. 'You can do the water.'

The doorbell rang just as Max plunged his fingers into the gooey mixture.

'That will be the postman.' Liv wiped her hands and walked towards the door. She was still in her pyjamas, her hair was tumbling loose past her shoulders and her feet were bare, but as she had no intention of stepping outside, she decided that it didn't matter.

Keeping her body out of sight, she opened the door, a cheerful smile on her face as she popped her head round.

Stefano Lucarelli stood there, a large white box in his hands and a cool, confident look on his handsome face. He was wearing a long black coat over jeans and a chunky roll-neck jumper that brushed against the blue shadow of his jaw.

'*Buongiorno.*'

Memories of that amazing kiss came flooding back with disturbing clarity and for a moment she wondered whether he was real or whether her mind had conjured him up because she'd been thinking of him all morning. *Was he a product of wishful thinking?*

'What are you doing here?' Liv winced as she listened to herself. It was no wonder she was single. 'I'm sorry. That sounded rude. It's just that I—' *He looked far too good to be standing in her doorway.*

'Invite me in.' His silken command left her more flustered than ever.

'You must be joking.' She thought of the pyjamas she was wearing. 'Why would you want to come in?'

'Because I don't want to eat dessert on my own.'

Her gaze shifted from the gleam in his eyes to the box in his hands. 'You brought me dessert?'

'Belgian chocolate log, complete with whipped cream.'

Liv started to laugh. 'It's ten o'clock in the morning.'

Stefano gave a dismissive shrug. 'If you're going to commit a sin, you may as well get it over with early in the day.' His Italian accent somehow made the words seem more sinful than the subject and the way he was looking at her made her insides turn to liquid.

'You can't possibly come in,' she said in a strangled voice. 'If you leave your Ferrari there, it will be gone when you leave. And anyway, I'm still in my pyjamas.'

'Are you? You probably shouldn't have told me that.' His

gaze focused on her for a moment. 'You have amazing hair. I had no idea it was so long.'

His words were so unexpected that everything she'd been about to say fizzled and died in her head. *He liked her hair?*

No, of course he didn't. How could he possibly? 'Now, you're being ridiculous,' she said gruffly. 'I look as though I just crawled out of bed.'

'Precisely.' His low, sexy drawl somehow connected to every nerve ending in her body.

Scarlet with embarrassment, she kept her body behind the door. 'I can't let you in.'

He smiled. 'Yes, you can.' He stepped forward and nudged at the door with his powerful shoulders.

'What are you doing?'

'Blasting you out of your comfort zone.' He strolled into her flat, pushed the door shut and scanned her body with a single glance. 'Nice pyjamas.' Amusement shimmered in his dark eyes. 'Pink baby elephants are absolutely my favourite animal.'

Aware that only a thin layer of cotton lay between his disturbingly thorough gaze and her naked body, Liv tried to cover herself and then realised the futility of the gesture and gave up. Why was life so unfair? When he'd taken her to dinner she'd been wearing her most ancient skinny rib jumper and now he'd arrived at her flat and she was dressed in cosy pyjamas that clung to her bottom and did nothing to hide the generous proportion of her top half.

Why couldn't she have been wearing a skimpy lacy number?

Because skimpy lacy numbers were designed for sex and seduction, not sleep.

She was about to make an excuse and vanish into her bedroom when Max emerged from the kitchen, trailing dough behind him.

'Did the postman bring something, Mum?'

'No.' Suddenly confronted by an issue far more serious than her choice of nightwear, Liv cleared her throat and tried to work out how best to explain the presence of a strange man in their hallway without upsetting Max.

She never brought men home.

But she didn't have to explain because Stefano took over. 'I work with your mother.' He dropped to his haunches and smiled at the child. 'Is that pizza dough you're wearing?'

Max grinned. 'It sort of just sticks everywhere.'

Stefano nodded with understanding. 'You could try using a little less water.'

Max considered that advice for a moment and then looked at Liv. 'You're adding too much water, Mum.'

Liv smiled weakly. 'That's probably where I'm going wrong.' She watched nervously as her son gave Stefano the once over.

'Are you staying for breakfast?' He peered at the box, his face brightening. 'What is that? Is it a present?'

'Max!'

But Stefano simply smiled and rose to his feet. 'It is a present. An edible present.' He handed the box to Liv. 'I heard that your mother likes dessert.'

Max was jumping up and down, sending pizza dough flying everywhere. 'She loves dessert but we don't often have it because she says it makes her fat. Can I see? Is it chocolate?'

Liv held the box in front of her like armour. 'I really need to get dressed,' she began, but Max was tugging her towards the kitchen.

'You look great, Mum,' he said earnestly. 'Why would you want to get changed? They're my favourite pyjamas. They're just so happy.'

Intercepting Stefano's laughing gaze, Liv closed her eyes.

Great.

The sexiest man alive was standing in her tiny hallway and she was wearing 'happy' pyjamas.

Why was he doing this? Why was he here?

Didn't he have anywhere better to be on a cold, sunny Saturday in December?

Max was giggling. 'This is *awesome*. Mum won't usually let me eat dessert unless I've finished my vegetables and I've never had dessert for breakfast before.'

They moved through to the tiny kitchen and Stefano instantly made himself at home, pulling out a chair and helping himself to a glass of orange juice.

Liv watched him out of the corner of her eye, wondering what he'd make of her tiny kitchen. But he didn't appear interested in anything other than Max.

'You need to cut the ribbon.' Picking up a knife, he leaned forward and sliced through the ribbon. The box fell open to reveal a beautiful chocolate log, dusted with icing and decorated with a snowman.

Max sank onto his chair, speechless. 'Wow. Have you seen it, Mum?'

'I've seen it, sweetheart.' And she didn't even want to imagine how many calories would be in a single slice.

'It's *amazing*.'

'I hope so.' Stefano picked up the knife. 'Would you like the piece from the end? There's more chocolate on that piece.' He sliced through the cake in a typically decisive fashion and Liv turned to put on the kettle, her mind working overtime.

Was he charming Max to get to her?

No, of course not. He wasn't interested in her. Why would he be interested in her?

But he *was* in her flat on his day off.

Her head was full of questions, but she didn't dare ask any of them while Max was there so she made a fresh pot of coffee and placed it in front of Stefano with an awkward smile. 'It isn't Italian. Cuban, I think.'

He leaned back in his chair and lifted an eyebrow. 'What happened to the instant?'

'Fresh coffee is my Saturday morning treat.' Liv raked her fingers through her long hair and then wished she hadn't because the gesture drew his gaze and she froze, sensing a shift in the mood and the atmosphere.

'We're going to play football in the park.' Aware that the adults were distracted, Max slid his hand towards the cake and transferred another piece onto his plate. 'Are you going to come?'

'Max!' Embarrassed and horrified, Liv dragged her gaze away from Stefano's and poured coffee into two mugs. 'Mr Lucarelli can't—I mean, he's very busy and he has to go in a minute and—'

'No, I don't. I'd love to play football.' Stefano stretched his long legs out in front of him and winked at the boy. 'As long as you are gentle with me. It's a long time since I played.'

'Do you like football?'

'I'm Italian,' Stefano pointed out. 'All Italians are born loving pizza, football and fast cars.'

'Perhaps I'm Italian.' For a moment Max forgot about the chocolate cake. 'Do you have a fast car?'

'Very fast.' Stefano smiled and Liv sat down opposite him, nursing her mug in her hands, watching as Max chatted.

'Cool. I'd love to drive it but I'm not old enough yet. I'm trying to make it into the first team at school. Mum's coaching me.'

'I'm not sure I'd exactly describe it as coaching.' Liv removed the remains of the chocolate log before Max was tempted to take a third slice. 'That was delicious. Thank you, Stefano.'

'Awesome.' Max watched wistfully as she put the cake away. 'Can we eat the rest later? After we've played football, we're going to buy our Christmas tree.'

Liv watched her son, her heart in her mouth. He was so, so trusting and while that was lovely in a way, it also terrified her. Despite not having a father, his little life had been stable and secure. She'd made sure of it. He didn't even remember Jack and he had no idea how much pain and anguish lurked out there in the world.

He had no idea what it felt like to be hurt.

Suddenly she felt a rush of protectiveness and for the first time since Stefano had knocked on her door, her voice was steady. 'Max, go and get changed. And spend ten minutes tidying your room.'

'But—'

'Untidy room, no football.'

With an exaggerated groan, Max slid off the chair and huffed his way out of the kitchen.

Liv closed the door behind him and Stefano's eyes narrowed.

'I sense I'm in trouble,' he said softly. 'Was it the chocolate log?'

'I need to know what you're doing here.' She stood with her back to the door, wishing she'd changed out of her pyjamas before she'd started this conversation. 'And don't tell me you were just bringing me dessert.'

'You refused my dinner invitation.'

'And you always bring breakfast round to women who refuse you?' When he didn't answer immediately, she gave a hollow laugh. 'Oh, don't tell me—no one has ever said no to you before. Is that what is going on here? Is it a pursuit thing? Is this about your ego, Stefano?'

He stirred. 'I don't have a problem with my ego.' He placed his mug back on the table in a deliberate movement. 'But I do enjoy your company.'

She thought about that comment for a moment and then let out a little breath and lifted a hand to her hair. 'Stefano, we both know that there are a million women out there who would give their entire salary to have breakfast with you. Women who are thinner and much more interesting than I am. So what I want to know is—what are you doing in my kitchen?'

'I heard a rumour that you wore pink elephant pyjamas.'

'Why are you joking?'

'Why are you so lacking in confidence?' His voice was soft. 'Why is it so unlikely that I would seek out your company?'

Liv looked at him in exasperation, aware that Max could remerge at any moment. 'Do I really have to spell it out?'

'Yes, I think you probably do.' Eyes narrowed, he watched her. 'I'd like to know what I'm dealing with.'

'You're dealing with someone ordinary, that's what you're dealing with. I try to be a good mother and I hope I'm a good nurse, but I'm not interesting and I'm *certainly* not sexy. I've had a *child*.' Listening to herself, she gave a groan and rolled her eyes to the ceiling. 'I cannot *believe* I'm having this conversation with you.'

'How could you possibly believe that you're not sexy?'

'Because I have a perfectly good mirror in my bedroom.' Liv forced herself to look him in the eye. 'I honestly don't know what you want from me. If it's sex, and I can't imagine for a moment that it would be,' she added hastily, 'then it's only fair to warn you that it's been so long since I did it, I'm not sure I can even remember how. I can guarantee that it would be the most crashing disappointment of your life. Don't waste your time. I—I'm *ordinary*, Stefano.' The way he was looking at her made her hot and shivery at the same time.

'If you don't think you're sexy then there is clearly something wrong with your mirror.' His dark gaze lingered on her face. 'And I don't find you in the least bit "ordinary". You are warm, kind, independent and unselfishly devoted to your child. That makes you extraordinary, Liv, not ordinary.'

'Stefano—'

'I'm not here because you said no to me, I'm here because I enjoy your company and I want to spend the day with you. Do I want to have sex with you?' He gave a slow smile and a fatalistic lift of his broad shoulders. 'Yes, of course, I do. And if you have forgotten how then don't worry, I will remind you.'

'*Stefano!*'

'You're being honest, so I will be the same. I am Italian and you are *extremely* sexy. But I'm willing to delay that part until you feel a little more comfortable with me. Then we'll see. Perhaps you will decide you'd like hot sex for Christmas after all.'

The colour poured into her cheeks and she closed her eyes. 'So you *did* overhear our conversation.'

'Anna has a loud voice.'

'And she was voicing her own opinions, not mine,' Liv said in a strangled voice. 'I can't think of anything more horrifying than having hot sex with you—'

'*Grazie.*'

She covered her face with her hands. 'That didn't come out the way I meant it to come out. You must know how attractive you are—you don't need me to tell you that. It's just that—'

'You're a nervous wreck,' he said, watching her with a

faint hint of amusement in his lazy dark eyes. Unlike her, he was totally at ease with the conversation and with himself.

Her hands dropped to her sides and she gave a little shake of her head, knowing that whatever happened nothing would give her the courage to take her clothes off in front of this man.

'You don't want to go to a bed with a woman who eats chocolate log at ten in the morning.'

A slow, dangerous smile spread across his face. 'If you think that, *tesoro*...' he breathed gently '...then you truly know nothing about men. Being tempted by chocolate log in the morning, suggests a hedonistic, passionate nature and a real enjoyment of the good things in life. I look forward to uncovering more of this hidden side to you.'

The thought of him uncovering a single inch of her made her shrink with mortification, but at the same time her pulse was racing and her entire body was warm.

'Do you want to come and play football?' If there was one thing guaranteed to stop him looking at her in the way he was, it would be the sight of her shivering in goal with pink cheeks and blue lips.

He rose to his feet. 'Now that's an invitation I definitely can't refuse.'

It was the most entertaining day he'd had since his arrival in England.

The ground was hard and covered by frost, but Max sped down the field with the ball and kicked it into the goal. With whoops of joy he retrieved the ball and threw it to Stefano.

'Did you see me? Did you see me?' He was dancing on the spot with excitement and Stefano grinned.

'Great shot. But watch the position of your body,' he instructed, lining up the ball and demonstrating. 'Now you try.'

Max paused, distracted by two fire engines that raced along the nearby road, lights flashing, horns blaring. 'Wow,' he breathed, 'they're going so fast.'

Stefano glanced at them briefly and then took the opportunity to look at Liv.

She was standing in goal, occasionally shouting encouragement to her son. Her hands were in her pockets to keep them warm and she always seemed to move a few seconds after the ball had landed in the goal, but she was clearly doing her best.

And it was obvious that she hated football.

Stefano felt something shift inside him.

Offhand he couldn't think of a single other woman who would be prepared to spend an entire Saturday shivering, while a small boy kicked a ball into a net.

Yet she hadn't complained once, despite the fact that she was obviously freezing cold.

She'd changed out of her pyjamas into a thick wool sweater and a pair of jeans, but even with her wool coat and the addition of a thick scarf, he knew that she wasn't moving around enough to be able to stay warm. Her cheeks were pink, her lips were blue and suddenly he wanted to tackle her to the ground and warm her up in the most basic way known to man.

'Time for a break,' he called to both of them and together they strolled back towards the flat. Stefano was just wondering how to take the two of them out for lunch without triggering Liv's independent streak, when she gave a strangled cry.

'Oh no! Stefano, *no*! Those fire engines we saw—the fire is in our block of flats!'

Stefano turned his head and saw smoke and flames engulfing the building with horrifying speed. Two fire engines were parked outside and were tackling the blaze but even as they watched there was a small explosion and glass blew out of two upstairs windows.

With a horrified gasp, Liv started to run towards the flats and Stefano reached out and caught her arm in an iron grip. Her eyes still on her home, Liv tugged and tried to free herself but he closed his hands over her shoulders, holding her fast.

'No. You can't go in there. There's nothing you can do.' His tone was harsher than he'd intended but it seemed to have the desired effect because she stopped pulling and sagged against him.

'Our home. All our things...' Her voice was a helpless whisper and Max give a little sob and curled his fist into her coat for reassurance.

'Has our home gone, Mummy? Has it gone?'

'Oh, baby!' Forgetting her own anguish, she pulled away from Stefano and dropped to her knees, folding her son into her arms and squeezing him tightly. 'It's going to be fine, you'll see. It's just a little problem, but we can solve it together like we always do. Don't you worry.' Putting her own feelings to one side, she thought only of Max and Stefano watched in silence, at a loss to know what to say in the face of her personal disaster.

Remembering her reaction to the car, he knew how enormous this would be for her. But instead of falling apart and turning to him for support, she kept her emotions in check and concentrated on her child.

'Where will we live? Where will we sleep?' Max was crying now and he wrapped his arms round her neck and hung on tightly, clinging to his mother.

Stefano, who could never remember crying in his entire adult life, found that he had a lump in his throat.

'Hush. Hush now,' Liv said gently, 'that's enough. Stop

crying.' She eased him away from her and forced him to look at her. 'I'll fix it. You know I'll fix it.'

Even though everything she owned was in the building, currently being greedily devoured by flames, she held it together and the hand that stroked her son's head was remarkably steady.

Max's eyes swam. 'My toys are in there,' he choked, 'and my special moon and stars bed cover and my geography colouring.'

Stefano watched as Liv somehow conjured up a magical smile full of confidence and reassurance. 'Well, I'm willing to bet that Mr Thompson hasn't heard *that* excuse before for not handing in homework on time. I think he just might forgive you, this once.' Her tone was light and she leaned forward and kissed Max several times. 'It's people that matter, sweetheart, not things. Remember that. Things aren't important. They can always be replaced. We have each other, and that's all that really matters.' But although her words were brave and seemed to reassure Max, her face was as white as a winter frost and her eyes were blank with shock.

He needed to get both of them away from here.

Stefano was about to take charge when she straightened, still holding Max's hand.

'There's no point in standing here watching.' Her voice was steady and strong. 'It's upsetting for Max. There's a coffee-shop round the corner. I'll take him there while I ring the insurance company and work out what to do. They're going to have to arrange for us to stay somewhere tonight.'

A flicker of movement in the flats caught Stefano's eye. 'Liv—there's someone up there. One flat below yours.'

Still holding tightly to Max's hand, Liv followed the direction of his gaze. 'It's Emma,' she breathed in horror. 'She's eleven. Where's her mother? Why are they still in there?'

'She needs to get down on the floor,' Max muttered, pressing himself against Liv's leg. 'We were taught that in school. Smoke rises, so you need to get down on the floor.'

Stefano glanced at Liv. He didn't want to leave her, but she clearly read his mind because she gave him a push.

'We're fine. Go. Be careful.'

'Stay here,' Stefano ordered. 'Call an ambulance, Liv. At the very least she's going to suffer from smoke inhalation.'

By the time he'd identified himself to the crew, two firemen in breathing apparatus had appeared from the building carrying the child.

Swiftly Stefano carried out an initial assessment. 'Do we have any idea of the nature of the materials in her flat? Furniture, polyurethane foam?'

Liv appeared by his side, as cool and composed as she always was in a medical crisis. There was nothing to indicate that her own home had been one of those destroyed. 'Emma?' She stroked the child's hair gently. 'It's Liv, from upstairs— how are you feeling, sweetheart?'

'I didn't hear anything,' the little girl said hoarsely and then gave a choking cough. 'I was asleep.' She made a whistling sound as she inhaled and Stefano saw Liv glance at him.

'She has a degree of stridor. Do you want to intubate her?'

'I want to give her oxygen and get her to hospital. If I have to intubate her, I will, but this obviously isn't the best place.' Stefano cursed mentally, aware that Liv's home was burning behind him and he was going to have to make a difficult choice. The shriek of an ambulance siren announced the arrival of the paramedics.

'Max and I will follow in the car,' Liv said immediately. 'We might be able to help and at least we'll be able to give you a lift back here.'

Stefano thrust a hand in his pocket and withdrew his keys. 'Use my car.'

'You're joking.' Her expression was comical. 'I can't drive a Ferrari. I'll take the hire car and we can collect yours later.'

At that moment there was a piercing scream and a woman dropped her shopping and ran towards them. Food spilled over the pavement and a milk carton split and slowly leaked its contents into the gutter. 'Emma!' The woman stared at the stretcher and then put her hands to her mouth. 'Oh my God— is she? Is she—?'

About to transfer the child to the ambulance, Stefano cast a meaningful look in Liv's direction. She slid her arm round the woman, supporting and restraining her so that she didn't obstruct the transfer of her daughter into the ambulance.

'Emma's all right, Susan. But she's breathed in some of the smoke so we need to take her to the hospital. You can follow in the car with us.'

Susan looked over her shoulder at the smouldering building. 'Our home…'

'Let's worry about Emma first.' Liv didn't even glance towards her flat, but Susan started to sob.

'I've lost everything. Everything. All my Christmas presents were in there and I certainly can't afford to buy another lot.'

Stefano gritted his teeth. Her daughter was lying on a stretcher and she was worrying about her Christmas presents? Deciding that he would never cease to be disgusted by the shallowness of human nature, he climbed into the ambulance, wishing that he didn't have to leave Liv.

Just before the doors closed, he glanced back at her and saw her speaking reassuringly to Susan, while cuddling Max.

She supported everyone, he thought grimly. *But who supported her?*

CHAPTER SEVEN

THEY decided to admit Emma, and Liv was helping Susan make a call to the insurance company when Stefano strode into the room.

'Liv?'

Relieved to see him, she gently extracted herself from Susan's clutches. 'Go and see Emma.' Checking that Susan had everything she needed, Liv followed him out of the room. 'She's terribly upset.'

'I noticed. More upset about her things than her daughter,' he said in a cool tone.

'It's hard for her. Her husband left in the summer and she's been really struggling.' Liv ran her fingers over her forehead, trying to ease the throbbing ache. 'Anyway, Emma will be fine and that's the main thing. Are you going home now?' Just saying the word made her feel slightly strange because she realised that she didn't have a home to go back to. 'I need to talk to the fire service.'

'I've just done it. The blaze is out but it's too soon for them to assess the damage. They think it was caused by faulty Christmas-tree lights in a flat on the ground floor.' He frowned. 'You look awful. You need to rest. You and Max can stay with me for now.'

Liv was so stunned by his unexpected offer that for a moment she just gaped at him. Then she shook her head. 'No way. We couldn't possibly.'

'I'm not letting you refuse, so don't even waste time arguing.' His tone was forceful but she still hesitated.

'That's far too generous an offer. I just…couldn't.'

'Yes, you could. And you will.'

'Having me around will cramp your style.'

'What style is that?' His eyes gleamed with irony. 'Liv, you've seen my life. I work. When I get home, I sleep. You won't be cramping anything. I want you to move in.'

She couldn't believe he was making this offer. 'You've never let a woman move in with you.'

'That's because I don't like anyone tracking my movements. And I hate anyone asking what time I'm finishing work. You won't do that because the chances are that you'll be stuck at work, too. Now stop arguing and just say yes.'

It was such an overwhelming gesture that she felt her throat close. 'Max is a very lively little boy,' she said thickly. 'He'll break something. They say that trouble comes in threes. My car is dead, my flat is no more—perhaps the third thing will be Max breaking something valuable that I can't afford to replace.'

'He can break anything he likes. It's a home, not a museum.' Visibly exasperated, Stefano raked his fingers through his hair. 'Liv, for once just say yes.'

'Why?' She looked at him helplessly. 'Why are you doing this?'

'Because I like you.'

'You…do? You like me?' Her car was dying, her house had just burned down. But the way Stefano was looking at her made her feel as though something amazing had just happened.

'I like you.' A muscle flickered in his jaw. 'And I like Max.'

Overwhelmed, she took a step backwards. 'Don't do that,' she said hoarsely. 'Don't be nice to me, Stefano, or I'll bawl all over you again and you know how much you enjoyed it the last time.'

'I'm not giving you sympathy. I'm giving you a solution to your problems. Take it.' He paused as a nurse hurrying past shot them a curious look. 'Liv, Max is still waiting in my office. He's upset and worried. He needs to know where he is sleeping tonight and he doesn't need some anonymous hotel room. Go and talk to him. Explain that we're going to buy his Christmas tree. We can sort out where you're going to live permanently when Christmas is over.' Stefano pulled his phone out of his pocket. 'You fetch Max and meet me by the car. I'll do the rest.'

Stefano's apartment was in an exclusive red-brick building overlooking the wide expanse of Hyde Park.

Feeling as though she was living someone else's life, Liv held tightly to Max's hand as Stefano negotiated the tight security that formed an apparently impenetrable cordon at the base of the building.

Still shocked by everything that had happened, Max barely spoke until they were through the glass doors.

Then his youthful curiosity gradually reasserted itself. 'Wow, that scanner thing is amazing,' he breathed as Stefano gently urged them across the gleaming marble floor towards the lift. 'Like something out of a spy movie.'

'I smell of smoke.' Liv wrinkled her nose in distaste and Stefano flicked some debris from his long coat.

'It clings, doesn't it? As soon as we get upstairs, you can take a bath.'

And then what? She didn't have any clothes to change into but Liv didn't say anything. Presumably the insurance would eventually cover most of what they'd lost, but in the short term it was going to cost her a fortune.

A fortune that she didn't have.

Perhaps she would have to work Christmas Day after all, she thought miserably. *Just for the money.*

Suddenly it all seemed like too much.

She'd been holding it together for Max, but the sheer size of the problem she was facing made her want to curl into a ball and give up.

How was she going to cope?

The lift purred soundlessly upwards and when the doors finally opened Liv gave a gasp.

Max spoke first. 'Which bit is your house?' He spoke in a soft, awed voice and Stefano smiled and took his hand.

'All of it. It's not a house, it's an apartment. I own the whole of this floor. Come on, I'll show you your bedroom.'

'All of it? All of this is yours?' Max tilted his head back and stared up at the endless glass and spacious elegance. 'It's bigger than the hospital.'

Stefano picked him up and lifted him onto his shoulders. 'There—now it doesn't seem so big.'

'Wow, this is terrific!' Max whooped with excitement and dug his fingers into Stefano's hair. Liv winced but part of her was overwhelmed with gratitude because he'd made her little boy smile.

With her son on his shoulders, his bronzed hands holding the child steady, Stefano seemed nothing like the intimidating consultant she worked with in the emergency department.

'I'll show you the bedroom I think you'll like, but you can choose a different one if you prefer.' He strode across the pale wooden floor, opened a door and lifted the boy off his shoulders in an easy movement. 'What do you think?'

'It's like mine,' Max said in wonder. 'Only bigger. It's a space capsule, Mum.'

'Yes. Aren't you lucky?'

'I have twin nephews the same age as Max.' Stefano strolled across to the window. 'They chose the décor.'

'They like the same things as me.' Max clambered onto the cabin bed and vanished under a canopy of moons and stars. 'This is so cool. It's just like being at home only better.' His little head peeped round the side of the canopy. 'Is it OK to say that Mum? That doesn't make you sad, does it?'

'You never make me sad,' Liv said quickly. 'I'm pleased you like it. It's very kind of Stefano to have us.'

Stefano steered her out of the bedroom and back into the glorious living room that overlooked the park.

Beneath them she could see horses cantering sedately along a track, their breath forming clouds in the freezing air. Mothers wrapped up in scarves and long elegant coats pushed buggies and watched toddlers romping in the snow.

'It's a fabulous place.'

'You make it sound like a problem.'

She gave a wry smile, her eyes still on the view. 'I'm hoping that it won't be too much of a wrench for Max to go back to his real life after this.'

'Don't think about that and anyway, you're his real life. You're his security. As long as *you're* all right, so is he.' Stefano put his hands on her shoulders and turned her towards him, a frown in his eyes as he studied her face. 'You're exhausted. Can you stop thinking and worrying for just five minutes and let me sort things out? Max and I are going to buy a Christmas tree and you are going to lie in a hot bubble bath for an hour.'

'An hour?' She was horribly aware of him, her heart thudding in a crazy rhythm against her chest. 'I wouldn't know what to do in a bath for an hour.'

'That's the point.' Amusement gleamed in his eyes. 'You do nothing.' He gave a slow smile and then his gaze slid to her mouth and lingered.

'Mum?'

Liv jumped backwards. 'Yes?' Flustered, she licked her lips, as if Stefano's gaze had left a mark she had to remove. 'You're going to buy a Christmas tree. Don't buy a big one.' Reaching for her bag, she pulled out her purse. 'This is our budget. Don't argue.' She stuffed the money into Stefano's hand. 'Thank you.'

For a moment he didn't respond. He simply looked at the money in his hand and then glanced at her face. Then he smiled and slid the money into a soft billfold, as if he knew that to refuse would make her uncomfortable.

'*Grazie*. Now go and relax and leave everything to us boys.'

'Do you like that one?' Stefano watched as Max gazed at the huge, glittering Christmas tree in the window of the exclusive Knightsbridge store.

'It's amazing,' Max breathed, his head tilted backwards as he scanned it all the way to the top. 'Like something out of a Christmas movie.'

'Good.' Wishing all decisions were as easy, Stefano strode through the doors and into the store, Max by his side.

Within seconds he found an assistant, briefed her on what he wanted and then looked down at Max who was tugging at his sleeve. 'What's the matter? You've decided that you want a different one?'

'No, but—you can't buy the one in the window,' Max whispered. 'It isn't for sale.'

Stefano smiled. 'It is now.'

'Really?' Max glanced over his shoulder, as if checking that his imagination hadn't been playing tricks. 'What about the decorations?'

'Those too.'

'But what about the decorations you already have at home? Aren't you going to use those?'

'I don't have any decorations at home.'

Max looked startled. 'But what do you usually put on your tree?'

'Nothing.' Stefano handed his credit card to the assistant. 'I don't usually have a tree.'

'*You don't have a tree?*' Max looked shocked. 'Not even a small one?'

'No.'

'Why not?'

'I don't bother with a tree because I usually spend Christmas on my own.'

There was a long silence while Max digested that fact. 'That's terrible,' he said in a hushed voice. 'Mum told me that some people are on their own for Christmas and that's just the *worst* thing.' His expression sympathetic, he slid his arms round Stefano and gave him a hug. 'Well, this year you won't have to be lonely,' he said solemnly, 'because *we're* going to keep you company. We can stay as long as you need us.'

Oblivious to the team of sales assistants who were casting him covetous glances as they busily collated the decorations for the tree, Stefano stood still, too stunned by the child's warmth and generosity to answer immediately. Then he put his hand on the boy's shoulder and squeezed gently. '*Grazie*,' he said softly, '*thank you*.' The child was like his mother. *Always thinking about other people*.

'You're welcome. Mum always makes Christmas amazing.' Max's eyes widened as the assistant wrapped the boxes of decorations. 'I hope it isn't costing too much,' he whispered. 'It can't cost too much or Mum will just worry.'

'Does she worry a lot?'

'All the time. She thinks she's hiding it but I just *know*.' The child glanced up. 'Girls don't always say what they mean, do they?'

Stefano hid a smile. 'No,' he said wryly. 'They certainly don't.'

'It's weird really,' Max said frankly. 'I mean, if I'm worried about something I just say it straight out. Mum tries to hide it. Why does she do that?'

'I expect she doesn't want to worry you.'

'But I always know when she's worried because she has a different face. Her smile is bigger when she's really worried, like she's trying extra hard to hide the fact that she's worried. And when it's money that's worrying her she makes lots of lists and does a lot of adding up. Just to check she doesn't run out. But if something new comes along she has to cross something out.'

Stefano digested that information for a moment. 'So what do you think she'd like for Christmas?'

'Oh that's easy.' Max looked smug. 'A hug.'

'A *hug*?'

'Yes.' Max picked up a frosted bauble from the display and examined it closely. 'Whenever you ask Mum what she wants for Christmas, she always says "a really big hug". Which is

SARAH MORGAN 117

a bit weird, to be honest. I mean, I love anything with a remote control, but she's just happy with cuddles. Girls are pretty easy to please, aren't they?'

Never having encountered a girl who was easy to please, Stefano gave a sardonic smile. 'Your mother is easy to please.'

The assistant cleared her throat and returned his credit card. 'Could you give me a delivery address, sir?'

'We haven't finished shopping yet.' Making an instantaneous decision, Stefano took Max's hand. 'Come on. We need to replace some of the things you lost.'

Max hung back. 'Where's the money coming from? Did Mum sell her tickets to the ball or something?'

Tucking his credit card back into his wallet, Stefano looked at the child. 'She had tickets to a ball? The hospital ball?'

'Yes, she won them. But she doesn't want them so she's going to sell them to someone who can go. She can't go because she's not Cinderella.'

Stefano exhaled slowly and squatted down next to the little boy. 'Did she tell you that?'

'Yes. She said it the morning the tickets arrived in the post.' Max shrugged. 'She sort of looked at them in a funny way, said that she'd never won anything in her life before, and then put them back in the envelope. Then she said something like "I'm not Cinderella and I'm not going to a ball." But she hasn't given them away. They're in her handbag. I saw them when she gave me my pocket money.'

Stefano digested that information and then straightened, 'I don't know about you, Max,' he said idly, 'but it seems a terrible waste not to use those tickets.'

'She doesn't want to go because she thinks her bottom is too big and she doesn't have anything to wear. Girls really care about things like that,' Max said sagely and Stefano smiled.

'Then we'd better fix that, hadn't we? Are you any good at keeping secrets?'

Hearing laughter and Max's excited chatter, Liv emerged from the bathroom self-consciously, wrapped in a large soft robe that Stefano had given her.

'Mum, Mum come and see this tree!' Max was almost exploding with excitement and he darted across Stefano's apartment as if it had been his home all his life. 'We're going to decorate it together.'

'You bought decorations?' Eyeing the size of the tree and then the number of parcels and bags that now littered the floor of the room, Liv felt a flutter of panic.

Max immediately hurled himself across the room and hugged her. 'You're not to worry. Stefano needed a tree anyway and he needed decorations.' He lowered his voice. 'He didn't have any. Can you believe that?'

Liv glanced towards Stefano and he gave a wicked little smile.

'Nice bath?'

Suddenly conscious that she was naked under the robe, she blushed. 'Lovely. Thank you.'

'I bought you some clothes. Just some basic stuff to tide you over until you can go shopping yourself.' He handed her several bags, as if it were nothing. 'I hope they fit.'

Liv's stomach lurched as she stared at the label on the bags. 'You didn't—'

'You can't spend the next few weeks dressed in a bathrobe.' Stefano's eyes gleamed dangerously and then he turned back to Max and took the box of lights from him. 'Where do you want these?'

How could she argue when she needed something to wear? Resolving to find some way of paying him back, Liv picked up the bags. 'Thank you.'

She retreated to the beautiful bedroom and delved into the bags. Jeans? Her heart sank and she dropped them onto the bed. *Why did it have to be jeans?* This was going to be so *unbelievably* embarrassing. She could never find jeans to fit so there was no way he was going to have succeeded. The thought of confessing that she was actually three sizes larger than his estimate, made her shrink with embarrassment.

Postponing the moment when she had to try and pull them over her thighs, she delved into the bag again and hot colour flooded into her cheeks as she pulled out the pretty silk and lace bra. This was getting worse by the minute. How could she wear that? She needed something far more robust. Stefano had never seen her in anything that wasn't baggy, so obviously he wasn't going to have a clue what size—

Her thoughts tangled as she looked at the label. The bra was exactly the right size and she dropped it as if it were scalding hot.

How had he known what size to buy?

Horribly self-conscious, she turned and stared at the closed door, half expecting him to be watching her with that sexy smile on his face.

She couldn't even tell herself that it was because he was very, very experienced with women, because she didn't think for a moment that he would have had any experience with women of *her* size.

Pulling on the silk panties, she was momentarily sidetracked by the fact they felt so decadently luxurious against her skin. Then she tried the bra and was amazed to find that it not only felt secure, it looked fabulous.

He had excellent taste in underwear, she thought weakly, reaching for the jeans.

Braced for humiliation she pulled them up, but instead of becoming stuck on her thighs as she'd expected, they slid over her legs, moulded to her bottom and fastened easily.

Unable to believe he'd bought her a perfect pair of jeans when she'd never succeeded in doing that, Liv glanced at the label and then wished she hadn't because she knew instantly that they'd cost him a fortune.

She knew she ought to tell him to take them back. But then she glanced at herself in the mirror and they looked so impossibly good that she almost giggled with delight.

Her legs looked long and slender, her bottom curvy and—

Eyeing her cleavage, she sighed.

She needed a top.

Opening another bag, she found a luxuriously soft cashmere jumper in a shade of green that she loved, together with a scarf, a hat and an adorable pair of gloves.

Feeling like someone completely different, she strolled out into the living room.

'What is this? Make-over time?'

'No, those are the basics.' Stefano was reaching up to place a bauble at the top of the tree. 'A make-over is something entirely different. Do they fit? It was a bit of a rushed selection. Max and I didn't have much time.' He turned to look at her and his eyes swept over her in blatant masculine appraisal.

'These jeans are amazing.' Disconcerted by the look in his eyes, she looked down at herself. 'It's like having plastic surgery.'

'You don't need plastic surgery.' His tone exasperated, he

strolled towards her and took her face in his hands. 'You're gorgeous, Liv.'

Her eyes slid towards Max and Stefano exhaled slowly and let his hands drop to his sides. 'I'm glad everything fits.'

'I don't even want to know how you knew my size,' she muttered and he gave a knowing smile.

'Guesswork.' The way he was looking at her made her feel dizzy and breathless and the clothes made her feel—well, they made her feel *incredible*.

'Thank you.'

'It's a pleasure.' His gaze lingered on hers for a moment and then he turned his attention back to the tree.

But there was a tension in his broad shoulders that hadn't been there before and Liv felt a sudden rush of exhilaration because she knew that there was chemistry between them. She didn't understand it, but it was definitely there.

The question was, would she dare to do anything about it?

By the middle of December the whole hospital was buzzing with excitement at the prospect of the Snowflake Ball. Those without tickets were hoping desperately for a sudden flurry of returns and those with tickets spent the day of the ball discussing how to look glamorous and stay warm at the same time.

'Everyone has gone mad,' Liv grumbled as she handed Anna a pile of notes. 'It's just a dance. With all the same people they work with every day.'

'In case you hadn't noticed, a dinner jacket is so much more attractive than a scrub suit.'

'But once you've seen them in a scrub suit, there's no going back.' Liv said dryly. 'I'm glad I gave my tickets to you. What are you wearing?'

'Oh!' Anna avoided her gaze. 'I haven't decided yet.'

Liv looked at her in amazement. 'But it's tonight.'

'I know. But we finish at four. That gives me four hours to decide what to wear. That should just about be enough.'

'You should have let me have Sam for the night.'

'You don't think that two little boys in Stefano's flashy apartment would have been pushing things?' Anna smiled. 'Anyway, there's no need. Dave's mother has turned up for her annual Christmas take-over, so she might as well make herself useful. How's Max doing? Is he sleeping in his own bed yet?'

'Yes. He only slept with me for the first couple of nights. He seems to be fine, actually. And that's because of Stefano. Max is so cocooned in this wonderful masculine world of football and Ferraris that I think he's forgotten that his own home no longer exists.'

'Sam told me all about Stefano turning up at school in the Ferrari to collect Max.'

'Yes. That was probably the highlight of Max's life so far.'

Anna looked at her closely. 'And you're not happy about that?'

Liv bit her lip. 'I'm happy that he's happy, of course I am. But I'm also worried about what is going to happen in the new year. At the moment Max is living in style. He's made friends with the whole of the security team in Stefano's apartment block and they play spy games with him all the time. He goes for rides in Stefano's Ferrari. How is he going to adapt to returning to his own life?'

'He's just having fun. You're the reality of his life, Liv. You're the anchor. But that doesn't mean he can't have fun while it's on offer.' Anna touched her shoulder. 'And you should do the same. Just enjoy it while it's there. Life is a cold, hard thing as you well know. If there's any warmth available, then take it and make the most of it.'

'That's what I'm doing.' Liv thought of her new clothes and Stefano's incredible apartment. 'He has this balcony that wraps itself around the whole apartment. It's fabulous. And it's so, so peaceful.' She took a deep breath. 'And it feels safe. In the flat I always slept with one eye open in case someone tried to break in and there were often fights on the streets outside. Living in Knightsbridge is like moving to a different country.'

'All right, I've heard enough.' Laughing, Anna covered her ears with her hands. 'Any moment now I'm going to thump you. Just don't tell me that you've seen Stefano naked. That will *really* ruin my day.'

'One of the advantages of an extremely large apartment is that it's perfectly possible for two people not to see that much of each other.'

And that was a good thing, she told herself firmly. He'd been so generous that she was starting to imagine things she shouldn't imagine.

Yes, he'd said that he wanted to have sex with her, but he was a man, wasn't he? And she had no doubt at all that if Stefano ever caught a glimpse of her without the clothes he'd bought, he'd change his mind about finding her attractive.

Anna peered at her closely. 'Is something going on I should know about?'

Liv felt her heart bump. 'Nothing.' She wasn't going to mention that one incredible kiss in his office because since then he hadn't laid a finger on her so obviously he'd changed his mind about finding her attractive.

'Well you've been living with him for over a week so if there's nothing going on then you're a disgrace to the female race. You're living with the sexiest man alive. If you haven't used the opportunity to seduce him, you should be ashamed of yourself.'

Liv picked up another set of notes and went to call the patient. 'Seduction usually involves undressing. And I don't do undressing unless I'm by myself or I'm in the dark.'

Anna slid into Stefano's office. 'This is never going to work. You're never going to get her into a balldress and you're never going to persuade her to relax enough to dance with you.'

'That is my problem.' Stefano put his pen down. 'Is everything else arranged?'

'Yes, yes.' Anna paced nervously across the room. 'But she has *no* confidence, you know that, don't you?'

Yes, he knew that.

Accustomed to women who were tediously preoccupied with their own appearance, he was finding Liv a revelation. 'Stop worrying.'

Anna shot him a look. 'The suspense is killing me.' She folded her arms. 'I don't think I've actually ever kept a secret before. And how on earth has Max managed not to let it all spill out? Sam is the same age and he can't keep a secret if you pay him.'

'It helps to own a Ferrari,' Stefano said dryly and Anna laughed.

'You're bribing him with your car? You Italians have no sense of decency.'

'Max wants her to go to the ball. You're sure you haven't changed your mind?'

'About giving you the tickets? Of course not. But I'm not convinced this whole thing is going to work. Thanks to her delightful ex-husband, Liv doesn't think she's beautiful and no amount of Cinderella treatment is going to change that. Why are you smiling?'

'Because by the time I have finished,' Stefano murmured,

'Liv will *know* she's beautiful.' *It was going to give him enormous pleasure to take care of that. Personally.*

'Oh for heaven's sake.' Anna fanned herself and sank into the nearest chair. 'Just don't break her heart, Stefano, or I'll chop you into pieces. Do you need any advice? Her favourite colour? Best shoes to make a woman gasp? What to say to turn a woman to mush? No.' She chuckled and shook her head. 'You don't need any advice on women at all, do you, you sexy beast.'

'I think I can struggle through.' Amused, Stefano checked his watch. 'You won't forget to pick Max up from school?'

'Of course not.' Anna stood up again and paced the floor. 'Will you phone me with an interim report?'

'No. I intend to be fully occupied.'

Anna's own smile faded. 'Why are you doing this? Is it just about sex?'

'Would it matter if it was?' Stefano watched her closely. She was Liv's best friend. She knew her better than anyone. 'Incredibly good sex can make a woman feel beautiful, too.'

'Just as long as she isn't dumped immediately afterwards,' Anna muttered. 'I suppose I just feel responsible. I agreed to go along with all this because it sounds pretty romantic to me, but if it's all going to end in—'

'Anna,' Stefano interrupted her gently. 'It's half past three.'

'Yes, yes. I'm going to pick the kids up now. Just make sure you live up to your reputation, Mr Lucarelli.'

'You believe what you read in newspapers?'

'In this case, I want to.' Anna glared at him. 'I want you to be as good as that disgustingly skinny ex-girlfriend of yours says you are, or Father Christmas just might do something unspeakable to your Ferrari.'

CHAPTER EIGHT

LIV changed slowly, lifted her bag from the locker and smiled at a couple of her colleagues who were buzzing with excitement and on their way to the hairdresser's in preparation for the ball.

She was going to have a lovely evening with Max.

They'd make pizza. Maybe they could curl up and watch a film in Stefano's den. It had deep squashy sofas and a huge cinema screen and it was definitely Max's favourite room.

She wasn't going to think about the fact that Stefano hadn't made a single move towards her since she'd moved into his apartment. Of course he hadn't. That kiss had just been a— Well she didn't exactly know what it was, but it certainly hadn't meant anything.

She left the hospital and walked across the car park. And then stopped as she saw Stefano. He was leaning against the Ferrari, his arms folded, obviously waiting for her.

He looked so spectacularly handsome that for a moment her mind just emptied and then she remembered that he wasn't supposed to be here.

Anxiety rushed over her. 'I thought you were picking Max up.'

'Slight change in the arrangements.' He opened the car door. 'Get in.'

'But—'

'Max is safe.' He slid into the driver's seat next to her. 'He's gone to Anna's for the night. And for the next twelve hours at least I don't want you to argue with me or question me. I just want you to say "*Sì*, Stefano."'

Bemused, Liv just looked at him, a hundred questions bubbling round in her head. 'That isn't fair. I need to know—'

'Do you trust me?' His voice was deep and velvety smooth and she felt her mouth dry.

'Yes. No.' Her eyes met his. 'I trust you with my son. I think.'

He smiled. 'That's good enough.' The Ferrari gave a throaty growl and several heads turned towards them as he drove out of the car park.

'Am I allowed to ask where we're going?'

'No.'

'Am I allowed to talk to Max?'

He glanced towards her. 'Would it make you feel better if you did?'

'I just need to know he's happy.'

'Then call.'

'He's at Anna's?'

'They might have gone for a treat. Call Anna's mobile.'

'But she'll be getting ready for the ball.' Wishing she knew what was going on, Liv dialled and spoke to Anna who immediately passed the phone to Max.

Liv hung up feeling better, but none the wiser. 'Why did he say "have a nice evening"?'

'Probably because he wants you to have a nice evening.' Stefano pulled up outside a top London hotel.

A uniformed man immediately stepped forward and opened the door. 'Miss Winchester? We've been expecting you.'

They had? Liv glanced at Stefano but he simply smiled.

'I'll pick you up in three hours. Enjoy.'

Enjoy what? What was she going to do for three hours?

'What's this all about? Please tell me.'

Stefano took her face in his hands and lowered his head so that his mouth was almost touching hers. Almost, but not quite. 'The next three hours are about *you*, Liv,' he said softly. 'And after that, it's about *us*. Lie there and think about that while you're being pampered.'

Pampered?

The questions flew from her brain as his mouth brushed hers in a seductive, deliberate kiss designed to tantalise rather than provide satisfaction.

Liv's head swam dizzily as he slowly lifted his mouth from hers and smiled.

'Enjoy yourself. Think about nothing but yourself. Promise?'

How could one kiss cause so much havoc?

Trying to control the fireworks in her insides, Liv allowed herself to be led through the elegant hotel lobby. Feeling like the only person in the world who wasn't in on a secret, she followed the man into a lift, which slid soundlessly upwards to the top floor of the hotel. The doors opened onto a tranquil, luxurious spa overlooking the rooftops of London.

Stunned, Liv glanced around her at the acres of cool marble, glass and mirrors. 'What is this place?'

'I believe that most women believe it to be the place closest to heaven, madam,' the man said dryly, guiding her towards an immaculately groomed woman in a white uniform. 'This is Irina. She will take very good care of you.'

The next three hours passed in a blur of scented oils and relaxation. Liv was taken into a softly lit room filled with the exotic flowers and the relaxing sounds of tiny, bubbling fountains. Having changed into a soft white robe, she was given a massage that almost sent her to sleep.

'I've never had one of these before,' she murmured, 'but it's heaven. I don't want it to end.'

Irina covered her with a warm towel. 'Unfortunately it has to be a little shorter than usual because we still need to do your nails, hair and make-up. We don't have much time.'

Liv lifted her head. 'Before what?'

The girl smiled. 'Before Stefano Lucarelli picks you up. The car will be here just before eight. And we want you to look your best.'

'I have no idea what is going on, and I don't even care any more,' Liv murmured, closing her eyes again. 'The only downside is realising what I've been missing all these years. I'm not sure I'm going to be able to get through the rest of my life without a massage a day.'

Glancing at his watch, Stefano strode through the doors of the hotel and into the foyer.

They were cutting it fine, but hopefully the traffic would be in their favour.

Unless she was late.

Simmering with impatience because he'd given the staff of the spa a *very* precise brief, Stefano lifted his phone out of his pocket and was just about to blast someone into outer space when he saw her.

Her silver gown shimmered and sparkled under the lights. It fell from her neck to the floor, skimming her incredible curves and displaying just enough cleavage to ensure that none of the men in the hotel were able to continue a conversation. Her hair had been swept up in a style that was both elegant and contemporary and was held in place by a single white gold and diamond snowflake.

Stefano gave a satisfied smile. The white gold and diamond snowflake that *he'd* chosen. Matching diamond snowflakes dangled from her ears, sparkling against the slender column of her throat.

The only colour was the vivid red of her scarlet mouth and the green of her eyes, which were looking at him with a mixture of excitement and nerves.

Mentally congratulating himself, Stefano strode across to her and lifted her hand to his lips. 'You look stunning.'

Her eyes were on his, anxious, seeking reassurance. 'Really?'

'Do you need proof?' He slid his other arm round her waist and pulled her against him. 'I'm beginning to wish we weren't going out.' His eyes drifted to the tempting shadow of her cleavage. The way he was feeling, he just wanted to check into the nearest room and rip the silver dress from her delicious body.

'I'm presuming we're going to the ball?'

Her excitement was infectious and he smiled. 'What makes you think that?'

'I don't suppose you went to all this trouble to take me for a bowl of spaghetti at Luigi's,' she joked, 'and given that Anna currently has my child, and I'm wearing an amazing dress— Did you choose the dress?'

'I gave them the jewellery and a brief.' A brief to make sure that she looked sexy, glamorous and incredibly feminine.

They'd excelled themselves, he decided, dragging his gaze from her lips and scanning her body.

'This dress is amazing and the diamonds…' She lifted her fingers to the snowflakes dangling from her ears. 'I'm scared to wear them. What if I lose them?'

'They're yours to lose or to keep.' Stefano shrugged. 'Enjoy them.' Knowing how fiercely independent she was, he braced himself for an argument, but she gave him a delicious smile that increased the heat in his groin by a thousand degrees.

'I *know* I ought to argue with you and insist on giving them back,' she confided, 'but I can't. I love them too much. Does that make me greedy?'

'No, it makes you a woman.' A gorgeous, captivating sexy woman. 'It also makes me pleased. It's always nice to know that a gift is well received.' Engulfed by an explosion of raw, savage lust, Stefano was starting to wish he'd arranged for a private dinner instead of a very public, glittering Christmas ball.

'I *feel* like a woman. I feel...*fabulous*. The dress is just amazing and I'm never going to take it off.'

She glowed like a candle and he couldn't take his eyes from her face.

'I will be the one taking it off, *tesoro*,' Stefano murmured huskily and watched with satisfaction as her pupils dilated and her lips parted. Soft colour touched her cheeks and the fact that she couldn't hide the way she felt about him simply intensified the almost agonising ache in his groin.

'Stefano.' she sounded breathless. 'I honestly— It's been such a long time—'

He covered her mouth with the tips of his fingers. 'Anything you have forgotten, I will remind you.' Seriously aroused, Stefano dragged his eyes from her lush, quivering body and glanced towards Reception. Check in, find the room—*he could be working on her self-confidence in less than four minutes.*

'What's the matter? Shouldn't we be going?' She tugged

at his sleeve. 'We don't want to be late. I don't want to miss a single minute of the dancing.'

Torn, Stefano glanced into her sparkling, excited eyes. 'You want to dance?'

'Of course I do. Have you any idea how long it is since I danced?'

'The same length of time since you last had sex?'

'Longer. You're going to have to tear me off the dance floor. I just love the way this dress feels against my skin.' Clearly enjoying her transformation, Liv circled her hips seductively and Stefano inhaled sharply, wondering how he was going to make it through the evening without exploding.

A man seated nearby dropped his glass and it shattered on the marble floor much to the irritation of his large, rather plain wife.

Deciding that he'd better remove Liv from the hotel before she was responsible for more marital disharmony, Stefano drew her arm through his. 'Did they give you a coat of some sort?' He glanced towards the door. 'It's snowing outside. You'll be freezing.'

She turned and picked up a wrap of soft, white fur from the sofa next to them. 'It isn't real fur of course, but it looks amazing, don't you think? It's like being wrapped in a cloud.'

Pleased by the change in her, Stefano smiled. 'What's happened to the woman who loved her elephant pyjamas?'

Liv's eyes sparkled as brightly as the diamonds she was wearing. 'You've corrupted me. I've discovered that being rich and pampered is a life I could enjoy. Does that worry you? Because it probably should. I think I might be about to transform into a greedy, grabbing gold-digger.'

'You have a great deal to learn before you reach the status of gold-digger.' He glanced at his watch. 'We need to leave. The ball started five minutes ago.'

'We're late?'

'Just late enough to make a grand entrance.'

Liv stood at the top of the sweeping staircase that led down to the ballroom. 'Oh my goodness, it's so pretty. I feel really Christmassy all of a sudden.'

Beneath her the room sparkled with festive lights and every table was sprinkled with tiny silver stars and decorated with generous bunches of holly and mistletoe. In the centre of the room a Christmas tree rose up towards the ceiling and a huge star rotated slowly, sending shards of light across the dance floor.

A jazz band was playing Christmas songs to welcome the guests and Liv smiled, so caught up in the excitement of the atmosphere and the sheer indulgence of the moment that it took her a moment to realise that the hum of conversation had dipped and that everyone was staring at her.

'Oh…' Her courage faltered slightly and then she felt Stefano's hand cover hers.

'You're stunning. That's why they're staring.' His tone was amused as he smiled down at her and his smile was so intimate and sexy that she couldn't look away.

'They're probably wondering how long it's going to take me to fall out of this dress,' she muttered. 'I don't want to create a spectacle.'

With a slow, deliberate movement, he pulled her against him and brought his mouth down on hers, kissing her in full view of the entire hospital staff. His kiss was as skilled as it had been that first time and Liv melted like wax under a flame, oblivious to the stir they were causing. It was only when Stefano reluctantly lifted his head that she realised that a dreamy silence had descended on the ballroom. And everyone was still staring.

'I was trying to stay *out* of the limelight,' she said in a strangled voice. 'What do you think you're doing?'

'Staking my claim,' Stefano said calmly, leading her down the stairs. He stopped a waiter, helped himself to two glasses of champagne and handed her one. 'Every man in the room was looking at you. I just wanted to make it clear that you're mine.' His possessive declaration made her stomach flip.

'I'm not yours!'

'Not yet…' The devil danced in his eyes as he lifted his glass in a silent toast. 'But you will be, *tesoro*.'

His words robbed her of thought and breath and Liv forgot about the people watching them. Standing in the full glare of his appreciative masculine gaze, she felt truly beautiful. *And desperately nervous*. He really did seem to be suggesting that— He was implying—

'I've been living under your roof for two weeks and you…' she licked her lips '…you haven't—'

'No, I haven't.' His eyes held hers and a faint smile touched his mouth. 'Max was understandably unsettled by all the changes and I didn't want to make things worse by introducing yet another new factor into his life. I'm assuming from Anna's comments about your sex life that he isn't used to seeing you with a man.'

'So is this what tonight is all about? Are you delivering Anna's Christmas present?'

'This has nothing to do with Anna.' Stefano lifted a lean brown hand and gently brushed his fingers over her cheek. 'This is about us. I'm doing what I've wanted to do since the first moment I laid eyes on you. The past fortnight has been a real test of willpower, believe me.'

Liv had to force herself to breathe. *Stefano Lucarelli wanted her*. This staggeringly handsome, rich, sophisticated man wanted *her.* And this time she didn't doubt his sincerity because it shimmered in his eyes in a blaze of raw sexuality.

She felt light-headed, dizzy and ecstatic, as if she'd just swallowed the entire glass of champagne in one gulp. Having lived like a nun for four long years, believing that no man would ever find her attractive again, it was a heady experience to suddenly have an incredibly sexy man looking at her in the way Stefano was looking at her. The fact that he wanted her filled her with elation and trepidation.

He didn't love her, she knew that.

She wasn't going to fool herself that for him it was anything more than sexual attraction.

But what was it for her?

She didn't know. She certainly hadn't contemplated another relationship.

And while he was looking at her the way he was looking at her, she couldn't think rationally.

Maybe it didn't matter, she thought helplessly.

Even if she only had this one night, maybe that was just what she needed. Proof that she was an attractive woman. *A boost to her confidence.*

He was still holding her, his strong hand in the centre of her back, his thumb stroking her bare flesh as the chemistry devoured them both. His head was bent towards hers, and she found herself mesmerised by the sheer masculinity of his features. His face was lean and handsome and his jaw was already showing the beginnings of dark shadow, but what really held her attention was the heat in his eyes.

The atmosphere between them was so charged that Liv couldn't think straight. Trying to catch her breath, she placed her hand in the centre of his chest and felt the steady thud of his heart under her fingers. For a moment she was totally lost in him, transfixed by the look in his eyes, seduced by the feel of hard male muscle and warm skin.

Neither of them said a word and yet with look and touch they shared something impossibly intimate and she knew that had they not been in public, it would have been now. Right now. *Right here.*

Stefano said something in Italian and released her with obvious reluctance, and she sensed the sudden dramatic increase in his tension levels.

Breathless, excited and dizzy with longing, Liv was wondering why he'd let her go when she realised that everyone was sitting down to dinner.

As he steered her towards their table, she was hyper-aware of him, her heart rate doubling with every glance he sent her, her skin tingling with anticipation as his arm brushed against hers.

Part of her wanted to be outrageous and suggest in his ear that they just go home, but another part of her was enjoying the glamour, the glitz and the sparkle of the Christmas ball. *And the intoxicating, dizzying knowledge that Stefano Lucarelli wanted her.*

She felt irresistible, and she wanted the feeling to last for ever.

It was hard to give any attention to the man seated on her other side because for her no one existed except for Stefano and just the thought of what was to come made her stomach perform acrobatics.

The waiters removed her first course untouched and then served her main course.

'I thought working mothers need carbohydrates.' Lifting his glass to his lips, Stefano glanced at her untouched plate. 'What has happened to your appetite? You're not hungry, *tesoro*?'

'No.' Her stomach performed another flip. 'Not really.'

He rose to his feet and held out his hand. 'Then let's dance.'

Liv wasn't sure that her legs would hold her but she let him lead her onto the dance floor.

He curved her against him in a decisive, possessive gesture that made her heart skip. Brought into close contact with his lean, hard body, she felt an unfamiliar flash of heat explode inside her. Her hands slid upwards to his powerful shoulders and then locked around his neck.

The music had tempted quite a few couples onto the dance floor, but Liv was oblivious to everyone except Stefano and she had a feeling that that was exactly the way he wanted it.

The anticipation of what was to come was almost suffocating. Warmth spread through her pelvis, turning her limbs to liquid and Liv gave a little shiver and slid her hands through the hair at the back of his neck.

The tension levels between them had reached the point of explosion and when a shower of tiny silver stars drifted onto the dance floor drawing gasps of delight from all around them, Stefano finally eased her away from him and stared down at her.

'Time to go home, I think,' he breathed softly and guided her back to the table. They collected her bag and her wrap and left the ballroom to find the limousine waiting.

Liv slid into the warmth of the luxurious interior, but it was impossible to relax. Instead of savouring every second of the experience, she found herself desperate to arrive at his apartment and she suspected he was experiencing a similar degree of urgency because he suddenly lifted a hand, undid his tie and loosened his top button.

His eyes met hers for a brief, electrifying moment and she felt that look right through her body.

Why was she feeling this way?

Was it just because she hadn't had sex for such a very long time?

Or was it something more?

She didn't know. All she knew was that being with him felt right. Slightly scary, but right.

Outside, the streets of London were eerily empty, the snowfall muffling sounds and giving the city an ethereal quality that seemed to add to the tension of the moment. Shop windows shone and sparkled with festive decorations as the car purred silently through the wintry atmosphere and emerged in Knightsbridge.

Her high heels echoed on the marble floor of his apartment building, the sound reminding her of a dramatic drum roll announcing the grand finale of the evening. It was only as they walked into the lift and Stefano pressed the button for the top floor that reality hit her.

Suddenly consumed by a violent attack of nerves, Liv tried to extract her hand from Stefano's, but his fingers held her firmly.

'You are glamorous and beautiful and stop thinking otherwise.'

Wondering how he could read her so easily, she shot him an embarrassed glance. 'Am I that transparent?'

'Yes,' he murmured, his eyes surprisingly gentle. 'Unlike most women, you are refreshingly easy to understand.'

'It's the dress that's glamorous and beautiful,' she said in a strangled voice. 'Underneath, I'm still me.'

'I really hope so. I'm relying on that fact.' Turning her to face him, Stefano slid his hands over the curve of her bottom and drew her against him. And then he brought his mouth down on hers.

He'd kissed her before, but this time felt different. The desire had been building between them all evening and this time there was no gentle promise or slow, sensual hint of more to come. This time his kiss was a declaration of intent, a skilled deliberate assault on her senses designed to trigger a similarly explosive response from her. There was a whisper of silk as he slid the silver dress up her thigh with a purposeful movement of his hand and then his mouth moved to her neck and lower still.

The lift doors opened and Liv gave a gasp of surprise as he scooped her easily into his arms and carried her into his apartment.

'Stefano, you can't—' Her faint protest was smothered by the possessive demands of his mouth and her wrap slid to the floor, closely followed by the silver bag.

Without lifting his head from hers, he carried her through to his bedroom and then lowered her gently to the floor.

Beyond the huge glass windows stretched the winter wonderland that was Hyde Park, but Liv was so dazed from his kiss and from the look in his glittering dark eyes that she couldn't focus on anything except him. For her, Christmas was in this apartment, with this man.

Cupping her face in his hands, Stefano brought his mouth down on hers again and this time she just melted against him, so excited that she could hardly breathe. He kissed her slowly and thoroughly and with such skill and expertise that her body threatened to explode. Lost in his kiss, she barely felt the sensual slide of his strong hands over her body and when her dress pooled on the floor she gave a murmur of shock and pulled away slightly.

'Stefano—'

'You have the most amazing body,' he said hoarsely and the raw appreciation in his eyes doused the sudden flicker of insecurity that had threatened to disturb the moment.

He tipped her back onto the bed and came down on top of her, his expert hands tracing every contour of her shivering, excited body. His mouth lingered on the sliver of lace that framed the tantalising dip between her breasts and then suddenly she was naked from the waist up, totally exposed to his disturbing masculine gaze.

Blindly wondering how he managed to undress her without her even noticing, Liv was just about to protest when he drew his tongue over one pink-tipped nipple and she felt a spasm of sexual heat connecting with the most intimate part of her. With a moan of disbelief, she arched against his clever mouth and with the skilled flick of his tongue and fingers he drove all traces of shyness from her brain.

Liv was no longer thinking about the fact that she was virtually naked. Neither did she care that the moon was providing sufficient light for him to enjoy a leisurely visual survey of her body.

Her body ached and throbbed and she writhed her hips against the silk sheets, needing him to touch her but far too shy to ask. The air vibrated with sexual tension but Stefano took his time, driving her to screaming pitch with the deliberate touch of his mouth and his fingers. When he slowly drew away from her and stood up, she almost sobbed out a protest and then realised that he was removing his own clothes. His eyes didn't once leave hers as he swiftly dispensed with his shirt and dropped those lean, clever fingers to the button of his trousers.

His chest was broad and muscular, the bronzed skin darkened with crisp curls of male hair that drew the eye inexorably downwards over his board-flat abdomen to the bold thrust of his erection.

He discarded his clothes in a careless heap and his firm mouth curved into a sexy smile full of masculine promise.

The mattress dipped as he came down beside her and Liv felt her stomach knot in wicked anticipation as he slid a hard, muscular thigh over her legs, trapping her.

'Do you know how long I have waited for this?' With an appreciative murmur, he slid a leisurely hand down her body and Liv shivered with helpless longing.

She would have expected to feel self-conscious, but he was looking at her with such a blaze of sexual hunger that it was impossible to feel anything other than beautiful and seductive.

When his clever mouth closed over one pink nipple she gasped, and as his warm, strong hand slid confidently over her thigh she shifted her hips to try and relieve the nagging ache that was building inside her.

She didn't feel like herself. *Everything* about her world suddenly seemed different. She was hot, burning and just dizzy with longing as he introduced her to an eroticism that she'd never before known.

Her fingers slid over the hard muscle of his shoulders and he lifted his head and looked at her, his glittering eyes half-shielded by thick, black lashes.

'You are spectacular.' He shifted slightly and brought his mouth down on hers and every single part of her shivered and quivered with agonising sexual tension. Their eyes held as his tongue danced with hers and Liv squirmed underneath him, her thigh sliding against the rough hardness of his.

His hand slid between her legs and she cried out as she felt the expert stroke of his fingers touching her moist femininity. The pleasure was so wickedly intense that the world around her suddenly ceased to exist and there was nothing but him.

'Stefano…' She gasped his name against his mouth in a desperate plea and he shifted her underneath him in a swift, decisive move.

'I need you now,' he groaned thickly, 'I can't wait.'

Liv felt the hard probe of his erection against her and dug her nails into his shoulder. As she arched her hips towards him, he slid his hand into her hair and for a moment he stared down into her eyes, his gaze fierce and hot. Then he shifted his weight and sank into her with a purposeful thrust that drew a harsh groan from the back of his throat and a startled gasp from her.

He was powerfully male and for a moment the feel of him inside her was so overwhelming that she couldn't move or breathe. His eyes were dark and demanding, the atmosphere was steamy and hot and each thrust of his body drove her deeper and deeper into an ecstasy that she'd never known before.

The excitement bordered on terrifying and as he drove her higher and higher she clung to the hard muscle of his shoulders. Consumed by unbearable pleasure, her world exploded in a shower of exquisite sensation and her body tightened around his as she fell, spiralling down and down in a dizzying, endless tumble of ecstasy.

Stefano groaned in agonising pleasure and reached his own peak, his passion so intense and demanding that it prolonged her own pulsing excitement. Liv wrapped her arms around him, holding him as tightly as he was holding her, shocked and dazed by sensation and wishing that they could stay like this for ever.

She woke to bright sunshine and the knowledge that she was naked in Stefano's arms.

Memories of the night before filled her head but her initial rush of elation was swiftly swamped by her old feelings of insecurity. Conscious that moonlight created a very different atmosphere from the harsh honesty of daylight, Liv felt a sudden desperate urge to put some clothes on and wondered how she was going to extract herself without waking him up.

The fabulous silver dress still lay in a pool on the floor, a reminder that the magical night was well and truly over.

Willing him not to open his eyes, she turned her head to look at him. He was intensely masculine and for a moment her gaze lingered on the hard lines of his face and his firm, sensual mouth. His lashes were thick and dark and his jaw was blue with stubble. Even in sleep he was breathtakingly, impossibly handsome and her insides squirmed as she remembered the intimacies they'd shared the night before.

How could she have ever thought that one night with this man would be enough?

The trouble with discovering the existence of really, really good sex, she thought to herself, *was that one didn't want to give it up*.

No wonder women were disgruntled when he ended a relationship. They knew that they'd just lost perfection.

And now she had to find a way of leaving the bed without disturbing him.

Gently and slowly she tried to ease away from him but he tightened his grip and pulled her back against him. 'Where do you think you're going?'

Agonisingly aware of the brush of his thigh against hers, she stilled. 'I was going to get dressed.'

'Don't bother,' he murmured softly, rolling her underneath him and combing her hair away from her face with a gentle hand. 'We don't have to collect Max until four o'clock. That gives us all day.'

Her heart thudding, she stared up at him. 'I'm naked.'

'I know, *tesoro*. And you are beautiful. *Molto bella*.' With a sexy smile, he shifted his body subtly and she gasped as she felt the hard thrust of his arousal.

'Stefano—'

He lowered his head and kissed her mouth, cutting her off before she could say what she wanted to say. 'You have a glorious, fabulous body and to let you wear clothes would be criminally irresponsible.'

'I was going to have a shower,' she murmured, distracted by the touch of his mouth on her neck. How did he know exactly where to touch her?

'Good idea. We'll take one together.' Delivering a last, lingering kiss on her mouth, Stefano sprang out of bed, gloriously naked and as confident and unselfconscious as ever.

Maybe if she looked as good as him, she'd be confident too, Liv thought and then gave a gasp of shock as he swung her into his arms.

Ignoring her muttered confession that she'd never showered with anyone before, he carried her into his enormous bathroom and lowered her gently to the floor. Then he hit a button on the wall and jets of deliciously warm water cascaded over both of them.

'The great thing about showering *with* someone,' he said, his Italian accent suddenly very pronounced, 'is that they do all the work.' Reaching for the soap, he gave a her a wicked smile and slid his hands slowly and deliberately over her body. 'Tell me—what is it that you don't like about your body?'

'I don't know, I can't think when you're doing that to me!' She tilted her head back and then gasped as the water hit her full in the face. 'I'm drowning...'

Laughing, he nudged her gently back against the wall of the shower, away from the direct flow of the jets of water. 'Better?'

She opened her mouth to answer but then his hand slid

between her thighs and the only sound she was capable of making was a low moan of pleasure and desperation. The water flowed over her but she was only aware of the expert slide of his fingers against her flesh. His touch was wickedly skilled and when he dropped to his knees in front of her, she gave a whimper of disbelief.

She had to stop him. She knew she had to stop him but then he parted her gently and the only sound that emerged was a low moan of pleasure.

The heated, moist sensation of his mouth drove the breath from her body and every rational thought from her head as he licked her with slow strokes of his tongue and then teasing flickers that drove her wild with desire.

Her pelvis ached and throbbed and she moved restlessly, overtaken by the heat that he was creating. The tremors started to engulf her and then he slid his fingers deep and she exploded into an orgasm so intense that for a moment the world went black and she forgot where she was and who she was with. She lost control totally and it felt like endless minutes before she was finally able to open her eyes and look at him.

Stefano rose to his feet, paused long enough to protect her and then he put his hands under her hips and lifted her, his eyes impossibly dark and slumberous as he held her gaze. 'I think you are fabulous and beautiful, Liv—' His voice was husky. 'Are you getting the message yet?' His arms and shoulders were thickened with muscle and he held her easily, his erection hot and heavy against her as he positioned her to his satisfaction. His strong fingers bit hard into her thighs and she cried out in ecstasy as he surged into her body with a single, decisive thrust. She felt the warmth and fullness of him deep, deep inside her and he paused for a moment as sexual chemistry threatened to devour them both. Stefano groaned something in Italian and withdrew slightly, only to thrust again, this time deeper than the last time. Holding her securely, he began a sensual, erotic rhythm that felt so agonisingly, impossibly good that Liv felt the immediate response of her body. She wanted to move her hips but he was the one in control, his body pressed hard against hers, his shoulders and arms taking her weight as he drove into her again and again. Ripples of exquisite excitement turned to an explosion of ecstasy and she felt him shudder against her as her own body was suddenly showered with sensation.

She clung to him, ignoring the drenching flow of the shower and the relentless patter of her heartbeat. It was only when he finally lowered her gently to the floor and smiled at her that she realised just how much trouble she was in.

Nothing was ever going to be the same again. How could it be after a night with this man? Before the previous night she'd managed to convince herself that she was happy being single, that her life with her little boy was enough. All her fulfilment and satisfaction had come from her role as a mother and she hadn't dared explore the world beyond. She'd been too afraid. Jack's cruel rejection had acted like chains, preventing her from exploring her needs as a woman.

But one night with Stefano had set her free from those restraints.

With soft words and skilled touch, he'd made her feel like a beautiful, confident woman and she knew that she'd never again be able to shut that part of herself down. She wanted to share her life with a man, but not just any man.

Stefano.

Which meant that she was heading for disaster, because this was a man who had confessed himself unable to find that one special woman.

CHAPTER NINE

'I NEED you to look straight ahead,' Liv said gently, her hands holding the child's as she coaxed the little boy to do as she wanted. 'Mr Lucarelli is going to look in your eyes. Good boy.'

'That light thing feels funny.'

'Don't think about the light thing. Think about me, instead. Tell me what you're hoping to have for Christmas.' She kept the conversation going, hoping that she looked and sounded normal. She certainly didn't feel normal. *Everything* about her had changed. Her view of life, her view of herself, her view of her body...

'A skateboard.'

'Wow!' Liv let go of one of his hands so that she could hand Stefano the equipment he needed. She was careful not to look at him. If she looked at him then she thought of sex and if she started thinking about sex, then she wouldn't be able to concentrate. She was desperate to ask him what was going to happen now, but at the same time she didn't dare because she was so afraid of the answer. For him it had been a fling, she was sure of that. And there hadn't even been an opportunity to continue the relationship because Max was now back in the apartment. 'A skateboard? That is fantastic. Have you ever been on one before?'

'Once. At my cousin's house. I fell off and hurt my arm.'

'Better make sure you ask Father Christmas for some protective pads then, and a good helmet. Tilt your head for us slightly, good boy.' Liv moved slightly so that Stefano could get a better view. Was he finding it as difficult as she was? No, apparently not. In public he was his usual cool, composed self, but in private…

She gave a tiny smile, thinking of the long conversations they'd shared after Max had fallen asleep, curled up together on his deep, comfortable sofa. Conversations designed to take their minds off the powerful attraction that drew them together. Liv didn't feel comfortable making love while Max was in the apartment and she suspected that Stefano felt the same way because he hadn't pushed the point. And he still wanted her, she knew he did. Maybe they could find an opportunity. Maybe she could talk to Anna—

'Drops, Liv.' Stefano's tone was impatient and she gave a start and handed him the drops, allowing herself a slight smile. Even their special relationship didn't allow her any concessions when it came to efficiency.

'Do you want him to have an eye patch?' She forced her mind back to the job and smiled at the little boy. 'I hope Father Christmas brings you everything you want.'

'That's fine. I'm done. No eye patch, but I want him to have chloramphenicol.' Stefano stepped away from the little boy and ripped off his gloves. 'Well done, Nick. You were very brave. There's a little scratch in your eye but we'll give you some ointment to help.'

His mother stood up. 'He needs a prescription?'

Stefano talked to her about the care Nick was going to need and then strolled out of the cubicle.

Counting the hours until they could go home, Liv sorted

out the eye ointment, gave them an advice sheet to take home and then went back to tidy the cubicle.

Moments later, Anna slid into the room. 'All right, I've had enough of this. I want to know everything.'

'Everything about what?'

'Liv, I've waited *four days* for you to tell me what happened on the night of the ball, but you've been avoiding me. I gave up my ticket so that you could go. The least you can do is tell me whether my sacrifice was worth it. Judging from the smile on your face, I'm guessing that it was.'

'I had a nice time, yes. I've already told you that. The food was great…' *even though she hadn't eaten any* '…and the band was fantastic.'

'I'm not remotely interested in the band or the food. *I want to know about Stefano.*'

Just the sound of his name sent a tiny thrill through her body. 'I had a lovely time.'

'Lovely time?' Anna gritted her teeth. 'You spent the night with the sexiest man on the planet and all you can say is that you had a lovely time? How much of a lovely time?'

'It was nice.'

'Nice? What sort of feedback is that? I want details! Did you—you know…?' Anna waggled her eyebrows suggestively. 'Please tell me you did. I'm guessing that you did, because you're suddenly smiling all the time.'

'Anna!' Liv blushed. 'I am *not* answering that!'

'So obviously you did.' Anna rested her bottom on the table, a satisfied smile on her face. 'Well? Were you a buttoned-up prude or a brazen hussy?'

'Oh, definitely a brazen hussy,' Liv said lightly, remembering the raw explosive passion they'd shared.

Anna sighed. 'Thank goodness for that. Tell me about it.'

'He's wonderful,' Liv said simply. 'I know he can be controlling sometimes, but to be honest I quite like that because I'm totally exhausted with having to make every decision by myself. I've discovered that sometimes it's just wonderful to let someone take over. And he *really* cares about Max. He has nephews Max's age and he really understands how they—'

'Yes, yes, I know he's good with kids, I've seen him in Resus,' Anna said impatiently. '*But what about the sex?* Was he amazing?'

Amazing? No, he'd been more than just amazing. Liv's legs trembled. 'It would be totally wrong of me to talk about that.'

'That good, hmm?' Anna grinned. 'And did he have stamina?'

Liv's face turned scarlet. 'Anna, for goodness' sake…'

'All right, now I'm starting to hate you.' Anna's laughter faded and she studied her friend. 'And there was me, worrying that when it came to the crucial moment, you'd refuse to take your clothes off.'

'I didn't even think about it,' Liv said honestly. 'He made me feel—beautiful.'

'That's because you are beautiful. Believe me, the guy isn't doing you a favour. He's struck gold and he knows it. And I have to say, I'm loving the new you.'

'I'm loving the new me, too.' Liv glanced sideways to check that no one was listening and gave a secretive smile. 'I feel alive. I adored the life I had with Max, but it was hard and I can't pretend otherwise. I used to lie awake at night worrying about the boiler going and not being able to afford the repair, and now I'm awake at night because I'm thinking about—' She broke off and Anna groaned.

'All right, enough or I'll have to punch you. So what happens now? You carry on having hot sex over Christmas?'

Liv turned and dropped the remains of the dressing pack into the bin. 'No. Obviously we have Max to think of.'

Anna gaped at her. 'So you haven't done it since…' She waved a hand. 'You're kidding.'

'No.' Liv rubbed her fingers over her forehead. 'It's not just about the two of us, Anna. Max has just had a huge amount of change in his life. I'm worried it will upset him.'

'He loves Stefano. He talks about him all the time.'

'I know he loves him, but that still doesn't mean I want him to see Stefano and I in bed together. It just doesn't feel right.'

'So now I know why Stefano's fuse is even shorter than usual,' Anna said dryly. 'What does he say about the situation?'

'We haven't talked about the future, if that's what you mean.' Liv walked across to the sink and washed her hands. 'I don't know what's going to happen. But the flat won't be habitable for a couple of months at least because there was some structural damage.'

'Well the two of you aren't going to be able to keep your hands off each other for that long. You're crazy about him, aren't you?'

Liv didn't even bother denying it. 'I don't think I'm one of those women who can just have a night of hot sex and move on. For me it's—' She swallowed. 'It's emotional.'

'So basically you love him.'

Liv looked away, shocked by how those words sounded and felt. 'Don't be ridiculous,' she said hoarsely. 'I've only known him for a few weeks.'

'Time is irrelevant as we both know. Does he feel the same way?'

Liv stared at the poster on the wall without seeing it. 'I think he cares about me.'

The sound of an ambulance siren disturbed their conversation and Liv glanced behind her. 'Are we expecting someone?'

'Child with a temperature. Greg is going to see him to begin with but I've asked Stefano to check on things when he's free. He's been keeping a close eye on Greg, as you know. In the meantime you'd better get in there and do your stuff. A few weeks under the boss's eye has improved Greg's performance, but he's still far too reluctant to ask for help.'

'I'll go. I need distraction.' Liv washed her hands and glanced at her friend with a soft smile. 'All I seem to think about now is sex and it's all your fault.'

'I know. I'm so pleased with myself. I'm going to give up my job and run a dating agency.'

Laughing, Liv walked out of the room and hurried towards Resus. She was still smiling when she opened the swing doors but the smile faded the instant she saw the little boy seated on his mother's lap. He was ominously quiet and was leaning with his chin slightly forward, as if he was sniffing something.

Liv's instincts screamed a warning and she turned to Greg, ready to voice her concerns.

'Dr Hampton, I think we should—'

'Great, now you're here, I can examine him.' Although Greg's tone was civil enough, she could see the flash of irritation in his eyes. 'I've taken a history but I want to lay him down on the trolley so that I can take a proper look.'

'No, don't move him!' Realising from the sudden tightening of his mouth that she'd overstepped the mark, Liv tried again. 'He's probably best on his mother's lap for now,' she said tactfully, knowing that the child had chosen the position that was most comfortable for him. 'I expect you want me to give him some humidified oxygen.' As she dealt with that, she glanced swiftly at the notes, checking mother's and child's names. 'Hello, Tom. You're obviously feeling very poorly, sweetheart.'

The child made no attempt to respond and Liv adjusted the flow of oxygen and then turned to the mother. 'Has he been like this for long, Kelly?'

'He was fine yesterday. I think he's just fussing.' The mother sounded tired and irritable. 'He just wants a bit of sympathy.' She was little more than a child herself and Liv could see that she had no idea how sick her little boy was. Unfortunately, Greg didn't appear aware of it, either.

'Has your GP seen him?'

'Are you kidding?' The girl rolled her eyes. 'Couldn't get an appointment. To start with I thought Tom was just playing up because he didn't want to go to school, then he felt hot so I thought I'd bring him down and get him checked. He had me up all night and I'm not going through that again tonight. He's really clingy. I just want you to give him something to sort him out.'

'Let's get him on the trolley,' Greg said briskly but Liv gave a brief shake of her head and took him to one side, knowing that they were dealing with a potentially life-threatening situation.

'Greg.' She kept her voice soft so that neither child nor mother could overhear her words. 'This child has serious breathing problems. We shouldn't move him. He's naturally adopted the position that's most comfortable for him, which is upright. I expect you'd like me to call an anaesthetist and an ENT surgeon right now.' She'd phrased it in such a way that he could simply agree without losing face, but his eyes narrowed defensively.

'I'll make that judgement if and when it needs to be made. You're overreacting. There is no stridor and no cough.'

'I'm aware of that, but…' Liv bit her lip and swiftly questioned her own judgement. *Was she overreacting?* 'It's the way he's holding his head. I think he could have epiglottitis. I've seen it once before.'

'I've already taken a history and he's been fully immunised.'

'It could be a vaccine failure.'

'The haemophilus influenza vaccine is ninety-eight per cent effective,' Greg said impatiently and Liv nodded.

'I know that. I know it's unlikely. But I also know what I'm seeing and to be honest the question "why" is irrelevant at the moment. This child is showing signs of progressive airway obstruction and we need to deal with that. Fast.'

Greg leaned towards her, his eyes hard. 'Sorry, but am I the doctor here, or are you?'

'You, but I've worked in the emergency department for five years and—'

'And perhaps you've become addicted to drama. Five years here still doesn't make you a doctor.' He smiled pleasantly. 'I'll examine him. Then I'll decide who to refer him to. And I'll let you know so that you can make the call.'

Her heart pounded because she absolutely *hated* conflict and normally would have done everything possible to avoid it. *But this was different.* She knew that any delay could be serious.

Where was Stefano?

Hadn't Anna said that she'd asked him to check the child?

She glanced towards the little boy, knowing that if anything happened to him because she hadn't acted, she wouldn't be able to live with herself.

Feeling physically sick at the thought of what she was about to do, Liv moved towards the phone, ignoring Greg's fierce warning glare. As she called Switchboard and asked for them to emergency bleep the on-call anaesthetist and the ENT surgeon, her hands were shaking and she wondered how she was ever going to be able to salvage her working relationship with the junior doctor. *He was due to leave in January*, she reminded herself. She just had to get through another few weeks. And even if he never spoke to her again, it didn't matter.

Pushing aside that worry for later, she checked the child's weight from the notes and reached for an ampoule of adrenaline just as Stefano strode into the room.

'Anna asked me to see a patient?' He looked as cool and confident as ever, the blue scrub suit emphasising the width and power of his shoulders and Liv had never been so pleased to see anyone in her life. She felt her limbs weaken, but this time it was not because he was exceptionally good-looking but simply because she needed senior back-up and one glance at Stefano inspired confidence.

Kelly's eyes widened and she transformed from being tired and irritable to alert and interested. Instinctively she lifted a hand and smoothed her hair but Stefano wasn't looking at her. He was looking at the child. And that one look was clearly enough for him, as it had been for Liv.

He focused his gaze on Greg. 'Have you bleeped the on-call anaesthetist and the ENT surgeon?'

The colour drained from Greg's cheeks and he stood a little straighter. 'Yes,' he muttered and Stefano relaxed slightly and nodded his approval.

'Good.' He turned to Liv. 'Let's give him nebulised adrenaline.'

'I have it here.' She handed him the tray and showed him the ampoule. 'I've checked his weight and given him point-five millilitres per kilogram. Are you happy with that?'

'Give it.' Having delegated that task, Stefano crouched down next to the child, his eyes gentle. 'You are having problems with your breathing, but we are going to help you with that.'

Greg cleared his throat. 'Do you want to do a lateral chest X-ray?'

'In this case it's not necessary and potentially hazardous.' Stefano straightened and looked at Liv. 'I want a 16-gauge cannula ready.'

'I already have it.' As always, her mind had been working along the same lines as his. She knew that he was afraid that the child's airway might become completely obstructed and he wanted to ensure that everything was within reach so that he could create an airway with the needle if he had to.

'Cefotaxime?'

'I have that ready, too, but I thought you might like to wait until the anaesthetist has assessed him.'

Stefano gave a faint smile and was about to comment when the anaesthetist walked into the room along with the ENT consultant.

It was another hour before the child was stabilised and transferred out of the emergency department.

'Greg.' Stefano's tone was cool and businesslike. 'You need to talk to the mother about contacts and arrange treatment. You did well. A case of epiglottitis is extremely rare, but still you considered it and managed the case accordingly. You didn't sit the child up, you didn't examine the throat and you called for help early. I'm impressed.'

Greg's gaze flickered to Liv and she looked at him, waiting for him to tell the truth. But the doctor simply smiled.

'Thanks. Good teamwork, Liv. I'll go and talk to the mother about antibiotic cover.'

He left the room and Liv turned away, struggling with an unpleasant ethical dilemma. If she hadn't acted, Greg's

actions could have put the patient in danger. She had to say
something but it felt like a very uncomfortable thing to do.

'So...' Stefano's accented drawl came from directly behind
her. 'Having just established that Greg Hampton is a coward
who is afraid to take responsibility for his own actions, I'm
relying on you to have the courage to tell me the truth about
what just happened in here.'

Liv turned slowly. 'You knew?'

'Did you really think that I wouldn't sense that something was going on? You were panicking when I walked into
the room,' he said softly, his dark eyes fixed on her face,
'and I've never seen you panic before. And Greg kept
looking at you as if he was afraid you might say something
you shouldn't. So, I'll ask you the question once again.
What happened here?'

Liv took a deep breath. 'Dr Hampton and I had a slight difference of opinion over the correct management of the patient.'

'Who rang the anaesthetist?' Stefano studied her face for
a moment and then his mouth tightened. 'You, obviously.'

Feeling slightly shaky, Liv took a deep breath. 'I went over
his head. I shouldn't have done it, I know, but—'

'You were absolutely right to do it.' Stefano's tone was cool
and unemotional. 'In this department we put patient welfare
before staff egos. That child could have died.'

'You think I did the right thing?'

'You know you did.'

'I suppose I do, but that doesn't stop me feeling very bad
about it,' she confessed. 'I've never had an incident like that in
five years of working here. Normally doctors are happy to work
as a team and exchange ideas, but Dr Hampton never—'

'He never listens. And he thinks he's always right. I'll deal
with it. It's no longer your problem.' He looked at her thought-

fully and then frowned slightly. 'You're shaking. Is that because of the medical emergency?'

'No.' Exasperated with herself, she gave a shrug. 'It's because I hate confrontation. Pathetic, isn't it?'

'It isn't pathetic. It's what makes you who you are.' His sexy mouth curved slightly. 'You're gentle and caring and I really love that. Forget Dr Hampton. I will deal with him.'

Now that the crisis was over she was suddenly very aware of him and it was a struggle to keep her eyes averted from the hint of bronzed male skin visible at the neck of the scrub suit.

Having not thought about sex for years, suddenly she was thinking about nothing else.

Stefano's gaze lingered on her flushed cheeks and then his hand closed around her wrist and he hauled her against him.

'If I don't kiss you, I'm going to explode,' he breathed and brought his mouth down on hers in a hard, possessive kiss that sent hungry tremors through her body.

'Stefano…' She wrapped her arms round his neck and kissed him back, oblivious to everything except the shocking expertise of his kiss. It was hot, explosive and out of control and it was only the sound of voices outside the door that made them both break apart.

'*Accidenti.*' Stefano released her suddenly and raked his hands through his hair. 'I have never before kissed a woman at work. That's how desperate I am,' he muttered and she found herself unable to breathe.

'You're desperate?'

'Do you doubt it? Soon I will be ready to give Max the keys to my Ferrari in exchange for an hour alone with you. It's Christmas in three days' time and neither of us is working.' His eyes dropped to her mouth. 'I'm taking you to Italy. We'll spend the holiday at the chalet. I want to take you to meet my family.'

He wanted her to meet his family?

Joy, hope and excitement mingled together in a dizzying cocktail that made her head spin.

Would he take her to meet his family if their relationship meant nothing more to him than sex? Suddenly her mind was full of questions, but she had no opportunity to ask any of them because Stefano cast an impatient glance at his watch.

'I have a meeting with the chief executive in ten minutes and I need to talk to Greg.' He looked back at her. 'Go shopping. Use the card I gave you and buy plenty of warm clothes. Max is going to have snow for Christmas.'

CHAPTER TEN

'YOU'RE going to Italy to stay with his family?' Anna handed a set of notes to a nurse who was passing. 'Well that sounds like happily ever after if ever I heard it.'

'Not really.' Liv was trying to keep a lid on her excitement. 'I mean, he can hardly leave us alone in his flashy apartment, can he? We'd set off all the alarms.'

'And you think that's the reason he's taking you home to meet his dad and sister at Christmas? I don't think so. Don't you remember that interview with the actress? She said that he'd never taken a woman to meet his family.'

'Stop it, Anna.' Liv covered her ears with her hands. 'Stop making me hope.'

'What's wrong with hope? Hope is what stops us all from jumping on the tracks. Trust me.' Anna lowered her voice. 'When a rich, good-looking guy takes you to meet his family, you're home and dry. I smell diamonds for Christmas. Except he's already given you diamonds. More diamonds, then. Have I told you lately how much I hate you?'

Liv was laughing. 'Enough!' She walked away from her friend, but her imagination was already working overtime, as it had been since he'd issued the invitation.

Actually it had been more of a command than an invitation, she thought wryly, which was typical of Stefano. But command or invitation, it held meaning.

It wasn't even as if he was taking her to some anonymous hotel somewhere. He was taking her to meet his family and obviously that wasn't something he did with every woman he met.

They hadn't actually spoken about their feelings, that was true, but wasn't it true that actions spoke louder than words? Surely the fact that he was taking her home to meet his family must mean something?

Excitement bubbled up inside her and she tried desperately to squash it down.

'How does it stay in the sky? Where are all the other passengers?' Max bounced in his seat, so excited that he was finding it impossible to sit still. 'Are we in Italy yet?'

Stefano watched him with amusement. 'There are no other passengers because this plane is owned by my family, we're not in Italy yet and we stay in the sky because—' He broke off and exhaled slowly. 'I don't know what level of explanation is suitable for a seven-year-old.'

'Just tell me,' Max said earnestly. 'If it's too complicated, I'll say so.'

Listening to Stefano talk about thrust and lift, Liv smiled to herself. It was utter bliss to allow someone else the privilege of delivering simple answers to complicated questions.

Max was transfixed. 'And what happens if—?'

'That's enough, Max.' Liv intervened finally. 'You've been firing questions at Stefano since we took off from the airport. Aren't you tired? Wouldn't you like a nap?'

'Babies nap. I'm seven, Mum.' Max gave her a pitying look and then slipped his hand into Stefano's. 'What are we going to do when we land? Are we going to the mountains straight away? Will there be enough snow to build a snowman? Can I go sledging?'

'You can do all those things.' Stefano glanced at his watch. 'Providing that we are not delayed.' He stretched his legs out in front of him and Liv quickly looked away, wishing that every movement he made didn't remind her of the night of the ball.

She really needed to get herself under control before she met his family, otherwise she was going to embarrass both of them.

As Stefano drove the last few kilometres towards the chalet, Max was bouncing in his seat.

'I didn't know this much snow existed anywhere. In London we just have a tiny bit, never enough for a snowman. It's all over the roads and the roofs and it's higher than me.' His tone was awed as he gazed around him. 'Now I see why you had to use a four-wheel drive.'

'The Ferrari is not designed for winter in the mountains.' Stefano took another hairpin bend and slowed down. 'We're here.'

In her mind, Liv had imagined a tiny log cabin but the home in front of her was something entirely different. A traditional wooden chalet with a sloping roof buried under at least a foot of snow, it was sheltered to one side by tall fir trees and surrounded by a beautifully carved wooden balcony. Beneath them in the valley she could see the sparkling lights of the village and a church.

'It's stunning.'

'The village is pretty crowded at this time of year, so being up here away from the hordes is a good thing. But we'll go down tomorrow and I'll show you around.' He parked the car and switched off the engine. 'Max will like it. Horse-drawn sleighs, ice skating—pretty much a child's heaven.'

And an adult's heaven too, Liv thought wistfully as she jumped down from the car. It was easily the most beautiful, peaceful place she'd ever seen. There was no sound apart from the soft crunch as their feet broke through the fragile crust of snow and the occasional muffled thud as lumps of snow fell from the heavily laden trees onto the ground below.

She breathed in, loving the smell of woodsmoke and pine trees. The cold air stung her cheeks and Liv gave a little shiver as she reached out her arms to lift Max down from the car.

'Mum, have you seen the snow?' Max was almost incoherent with excitement and Liv smiled.

'I've seen it. In fact I'm standing in it and my feet are cold. Hurry up.'

Stefano swung two of the cases out of the boot. 'Most of these snowdrifts are probably deeper than you are tall so don't wander off.'

For a man who didn't have children he was remarkably in tune with the way children thought. And then she remembered that he worked in the emergency department and was constantly exposed to the consequences of a child's need to explore and push the boundaries.

'Can we build a snowman now?' Max bent down and started to scoop snow into his palms. 'This is awesome.' He straightened and Liv caught the mischievous look in his eye too late to avoid the inevitable snowball.

She gasped and closed her eyes as a freezing shower of snow smacked into her hair and trickled down her neck. 'Oh my goodness, that's *freezing*! Max you are in serious trouble now!' Her eyes glinted and she stooped and gathered her own ball of snow while Max squealed in delighted terror.

Giggling like a child, Liv carefully lobbed the snowball into the middle of his back, where she knew it would cause the least damage in terms of wet and cold. Then she caught Stefano's gaze and smiled. 'Sorry. I'm as bad as he is, I know. It's just that neither of us have seen snow like this before. It's like waking up in the middle of a fairy-tale.'

But the best part of the fairy-tale was being here with him.

The door of the chalet suddenly opened sending shafts of bright light across the snow. There was a chorus of welcome and then suddenly there were people everywhere and they were engulfed by hugging, kissing, laughter and lots of unintelligible Italian.

Overwhelmed, Max dropped the snow he'd been holding and shrank against Liv. She slid an arm round him, feeling equally daunted by the noisy exuberance of Stefano's *extremely* large family. Two big dogs bounded towards them and Stefano spoke a sharp command in Italian. Both of them skidded to a halt, sending soft snow showering everywhere. Then they whimpered and sat, watching him expectantly.

'Are they friendly?' Still holding onto Liv, Max gazed at the dogs in fascination and Stefano dropped to his haunches next to him.

'*Sì*, they are friendly. Put your hand out and let them smell you.'

Max stuck his hand out and both dogs sidled towards him and licked him frantically, their tails sending more snow flying in all directions. 'Ew!' Giggling and cringing at the same time, Max jerked his hand away. 'That's so wet. It's gross.' But he was enchanted by the dogs, and the animals were enough to break the ice.

'This is all a bit much for you, I'm so sorry.' A dark-haired woman with a warm smile pulled Liv towards her and kissed her on both cheeks. 'It's just that we don't see enough of Stefano. You're *very* welcome. I'm his sister, Isabella.' She smiled at Max. 'The dogs are Leo and Angelo. Everyone else can be introduced at some other point. It's freezing out here. Let's go inside.'

Dinner was a noisy, lengthy affair with simultaneous conversations and much friendly argument and disagreement.

Stefano's father, Bernardo, sat at the head of the table watching over the proceedings like a benign monarch. Occasionally Liv caught his warm, approving gaze and she wondered exactly what Stefano had said about their relationship.

'In Italy we have a saying,' Stefano told her dryly as he handed her a plate of food, '*Natale con i tuoi, Pasqua con i vuoi*—which roughly translated means, Christmas with the family, Easter with who you like. Food is an important part of the Lucarelli family Christmas. I hope your appetite is healthy.'

But she wasn't part of his family, was she?

Feeling slightly awkward, Liv smiled at his father. 'I hope we're not intruding too much on your celebrations.'

'The biggest celebration is that my son has brought a lovely woman home for Christmas.' He lifted his glass and Stefano said something soft in Italian but the older man simply smiled and drank deeply.

Captivated by his warm, demonstrative family, Liv ate and watched the family dynamics.

Stefano's grandmother was in charge of the kitchen with Isabella and two of the female cousins were also roped in to help.

Liv noticed that one of them—was her name Donatella?—kept casting shy, dreamy looks in Stefano's direction but he didn't seem to notice because he was occupied in an argument with his father which seemed to be about whether or not they should buy an ailing local company.

'No business at the table,' Isabella said sharply, putting plates laden with food in front of them, 'this is Christmas. We don't talk business at Christmas.'

The meal was spectacular and Liv was fascinated by the interaction between everyone at the table. It felt good to be part of a large noisy group. And it was good for Max.

He was seated between Stefano's twin nephews and was happily occupied improving their English.

'We have Father Christmas,' he said solemnly. 'What do you have?'

'*Babo Natale*,' one of the boys said. 'And *La Befana*, she brings us presents in January.'

Suddenly horrified, Max looked at Liv. 'How will Father Christmas know I'm here? What if he takes my presents to our old flat?'

Visibly moved, Isabella put her hand on her heart, murmured something in Italian and then shot out of her seat and hugged Max tightly. 'He will know you are here,' she said firmly. 'We will hang up a sock, yes? And write him a note—in English and Italian just to be sure. Why don't you go and play now? My boys will show you their toys.' Isabella stood up, waved the children away from the table and then glanced at the fire. 'We need another log and that's man's work.' She looked pointedly at her brother and he gave a faint smile and rose to his feet.

'I'll go then, shall I?.' He held out a hand to Liv. 'Come with me. I'll show you the rest of the chalet.'

Liv followed him down two flights of stairs to a basement and then out into the crisp night air. 'I love the smell of wood-smoke. And I love your family. You're very lucky.'

'I thought you might be feeling completely overwhelmed.' He hauled her into his arms and curved his hands over her bottom. 'They are noisy and interfering.'

'I think they're lovely. And they love you.' It was exciting, being on her own with him, even if only for a moment. The air was electric and she knew from the glitter in his eyes that he was as aroused as she was. Trying to keep herself in check, she chose a neutral subject. 'Donatella is sweet. She adores you, that's obvious.'

He stilled. 'She's very young,' he said carefully. 'And I'm hoping that she will soon get the message.'

What message? Liv was about to question him further when he brought his mouth down on hers and kissed her hard.

Forgetting everything except the way he made her feel, she kissed him back, oblivious to the cold and the peal of church bells from the village below.

He cared, she thought to herself, her head swimming dizzily. Surely he cared?

Liv woke on Christmas Eve to bright blue skies. Fresh snow had fallen overnight and there was no longer any sign of their footprints of the night before. Branches sagged under the weight of the snow and the valley below them looked as though it had been covered by a thick layer of icing.

Hearing squeals from outside, Liv dressed quickly, relieved that she'd followed Stefano's instructions and purchased some suitable clothes. At some point she was going to have to think about paying him back, but for now she was determined to enjoy the moment.

Pulling on her boots, she stepped outside and saw Max stretching up to put a hat on a large, fat snowman. Isabella and the twins were helping and snow flew through the air with predictable regularity, covering all three boys in soft white clumps.

'Mum, come and see!' Max stamped his boots in the snow and pressed two dark glossy pebbles into the snowman's 'face'. 'Isn't he amazing?'

'We think he looks like Stefano,' Isabella said cheerfully, winking at Liv. 'He always looks grumpy in the mornings.' Leaving the children to finish off the snowman, she wrapped her scarf more firmly round her throat and walked over to Liv. 'Did you sleep?'

'Oh yes.' Liv pushed her hands into her pockets. 'Better than ever before.'

'I always sleep well in the mountains.' Isabella breathed in the cold air and smiled. 'Can I interest you in some serious shopping? Cortina is a shopaholic's paradise, I can assure you.'

Liv shook her head. 'I'd love to see the village but my budget won't stretch to shopping.'

'Stefano will pay,' Isabella said dismissively, knocking snow from the toe of her soft leather boot. 'It's the least he can do given that you've come all this way just to solve his problems.'

Liv looked at her. 'His problems?'

'You must have noticed Donatella.' Isabella rolled her eyes. 'I mean, she can't take her eyes off him. I warned Stefano three weeks ago that she is as much in love with him as ever. To be honest, I even wondered whether he might not come this year, because he hates being cornered by women, but Stefano always finds a solution to everything. Clearly, he decided that bringing you would solve everyone's problems.'

'Really?' Liv's mouth was dry.

'Yes, well...' Isabella looked awkward. 'He did tell me that you'd lost your home. I hope you don't mind. We weren't gossiping or anything—Stefano never gossips. Clearly you've done each other a favour.'

'Yes.' Somehow Liv managed to form the words. 'We have.'

'You're shivering.' Isabella frowned. 'Should we go inside?'

'No. In fact I might go for a walk,' Liv said quickly, buttoning up her coat. 'It's so pretty and I haven't had a chance to take a proper look yet.'

Was it true?

Had he really invited her to spend Christmas with his family just to keep Donatella at a distance?

Isabella seemed about to say something else but there was another snowball fight starting between the children and she hurried across to sort them out.

Taking advantage of the opportunity to escape, Liv walked as quickly as she could up the snow-covered road, suddenly feeling terribly, terribly cold. Although the air was freezing she knew that the chill inside her had more to do with Stefano than the weather.

Why hadn't he told her the truth?

Why had he let her believe that he'd actually wanted her to join him for Christmas?

Why had he let her hope and dream?

She remembered the way Donatella had looked at him and the way that he'd suddenly stilled when she'd mentioned the fact that Donatella clearly liked him.

Oh dear God—she'd been a fool. She'd done it again, taken her dreams and somehow managed to entangle them with reality. She'd turned the world into what she wanted it to be, rather than what it really was.

She'd seen what she'd wanted to see.

Stefano was a man, wasn't he? They'd shared amazing sex

and for him their relationship was nothing more than that. And it wasn't really his fault. *She* was the one who had turned amazing sex into something warmer and deeper. She'd been stupid and careless and—

Blinded by tears, she stumbled into the deep snow at the side of the road and suddenly she just wanted to sink into the cold, white powder and sob. She felt as though she was dying inside and realised that the loss of her dream was much, much more devastating than anything else that had ever happened to her.

'Liv!' Stefano's strong voice carried through the frozen air and Liv stood still, wanting to run but knowing that there was nowhere to run to.

He was wearing sturdy boots, his strong legs were encased in soft fleece trousers and a thick jumper brushed against his darkened jaw. Liv's heart bumped frantically as she watched him approach because he was impossibly, shockingly good-looking and one glance at his face turned her limbs to liquid.

But she shouldn't feel that way, should she?

Not any more.

She felt a flash of desperation. If he came any closer he might see how she felt because she was hopeless at hiding her feelings. She couldn't face him.

But where was she going to go?

With no choice but to wait for him to catch up with her, she took a few deep breaths and told herself that she'd coped with rejection before and she would do it again.

'What are you doing?' His tone was forceful. 'Where are you going?'

Liv concentrated on the snow at her feet. 'For a walk. I needed to be on my own for a while.'

'Why?' His hand closed over hers like a vice. '*Accidenti*, you are as white as a sheet. *What* has happened?'

'Nothing.'

'Nothing doesn't send you stumbling into a snowdrift,' he said grimly, pulling her towards him with firm hands. 'You're upset and I want to know why.'

She felt like too much of a fool to admit the truth. He'd laugh, wouldn't he? He'd laugh if she admitted that she'd thought they shared something more than hot sex. He'd tell her that she was foolish and old-fashioned and that the world just wasn't like that any more.

'I'm just— Nothing.'

Stefano muttered something under his breath in Italian and then took her face in his hands. 'One of the things I love about you is that you are so straightforward and honest. You say what you think and I like that. *Don't* change now. Tell me what's wrong.'

Perhaps if he hadn't used the word 'love' she might have managed to hold it all in, but something pinged inside her and she pulled away, engulfed by an emotion that she couldn't control.

'All right, I'll tell you.' Her breath was coming in rapid pants, as if she'd been running instead of standing still. 'I just—I can't do this. I can't do this any more. The sex was amazing, yes. But I just can't have sex without wanting…more. And I *know* that's my fault, not yours, but I still think you could have been a little bit more honest with me about the reason you invited me here.'

His eyes narrowed. 'Why do you think I invited you here?'

Liv blinked rapidly to clear her vision. 'I *thought* you wanted me to meet your family and then I discover that *actually* you invited me here because you need to keep Donatella at a distance.'

Stefano stilled and his hands dropped to his sides. 'Who told you that?'

'It doesn't matter.' Liv felt a stab of pain that he hadn't denied it. 'And do you know what? The reason we're here shouldn't matter either. It's a beautiful, magical place and Max is having a wonderful time and he's so, so happy playing with your nephews in the snow. I should be relieved and delighted and I *am*, but…' Her words tangled and her emotions raw, she took a breath. 'None of this is your fault. It's me. It's all me. I mean, it should have been obvious to me from the start that our relationship was just about sex, I mean you have…' she waved her hand despairingly '…*all this money*, and what do I have? I live in a tiny flat in a grotty part of London with my son and you live in this flashy apartment with more security than a palace and a lifestyle that makes me drool with envy.'

'Liv—'

'Don't say a word!' Sniffing hard, she lifted a hand to stop him speaking. 'It really isn't your fault that I have fantasies and that I'm basically extremely stupid. You didn't lead me on. You didn't promise me anything. I imagined it all by myself with no help from you. I don't know whether it's the way I'm wired or whether it's because I'm so sensitive about Max, but I just can't seem to do casual relationships. You've been great to Max and without you he would have had a horrible, horrible Christmas and I'll always be grateful to you for that. And now I need to…' She backed away a few steps. 'I need to walk by myself for a bit. Please, please don't follow me.' And without looking at him, she turned and walked up the snowy path as fast as she could without slipping and breaking her neck.

'Mum, he's been! The letter must have worked. He knew I was in Italy and he's brought all my presents here.' Dragging a long, colourful sock behind him Max came charging into her bedroom and Liv sat up and smiled. It was Christmas morning and she was gritty-eyed from lack of sleep and her head felt as though someone was attacking it from the inside with a pick axe.

'That's great, Max.' She glanced towards the window. 'What time is it? Max, it's dark out there!'

'No, it's not. It's snowed again but Stefano says it's going to be a beautiful day and when we've opened our presents he's taking us on a special sleigh ride. It has bells and everything. Are you coming, Mum? The twins and I are going to open our stockings in front of the fire. You don't want to miss it.' Jumping with excitement, he trailed the bulging stocking out of her bedroom and Liv slid out of bed and dressed slowly, knowing that she couldn't avoid seeing Stefano.

When she'd eventually returned to the chalet from her walk on the previous day, there had been no sign of him and Isabella had told her that he'd gone skiing with his father for the day.

So Liv and Max had spent the day with Isabella and her two sons, and her husband had arrived from work in Milan and it had been fun. Together they'd prepared the elaborate Christmas Eve dinner and somehow she'd been so busy that she'd managed to bury her disappointment and her silly fantasies and enjoy herself. His family was warm and demonstrative and at least she hadn't had to look Stefano in the face.

When he and his father had finally returned there had been so much activity and bustle in the chalet that there had been no awkward moments, no intimate opportunities for the two of them to be alone or for him to respond to what she'd said to him in that frozen, solitary moment when she'd bared her soul.

It would be the same today, she told herself as she pulled on the soft cashmere jumper he'd bought her only a few weeks earlier. It would be a busy family day with no opportunity for private moments and then tomorrow they'd be going home to England.

And then she'd rent a flat of her own, forget about Italian millionaires and try and get on with her life.

The next couple of hours passed in a blur of excited squeals, wrapping paper and laughter as everyone passed around presents and Isabella and Stefano's grandmother served breakfast.

Stefano had given Max tickets to see a football match at the famous San Siro stadium in Milan and the little boy was speechless with excitement. 'So we're coming back to Italy? Wow, that is so cool.'

'It's certainly cool,' Isabella agreed cheerfully. 'Minus five today. Make sure you wrap up when you go out.'

Liv glanced at Stefano, grateful that he was obviously intending to carry on spending time with her son and seriously worried as to how she'd be able to maintain a simple friendship with him without making a fool of herself.

Liv handed Max her present to him and found herself with a lump in her throat as he ripped open the paper and found the football boots. 'Oh, Mum…' For a moment he couldn't speak and then he looked at her, eyes shining. 'You're just the best and I love you.' He flung his arms around her and Liv hugged him tightly, reminding herself of what was important in life. She had her lovely, wonderful son and Stefano clearly didn't mean to stop seeing the boy just because they weren't together any more and she was grateful for that. She was lucky. Really lucky.

Max sprinted back to the Christmas tree. 'I've got presents for you and Stefano.' He lifted up two haphazardly wrapped parcels and handed one to Stefano and one to Liv. 'I made them.'

Liv glanced at Stefano, hoping that he wouldn't wince when he saw his present.

He opened it carefully and pulled out a childish drawing of a car.

'It's your Ferrari. I went down to the garage and copied it. That nice security man helped me.' Max watched him anxiously, gauging his reaction. 'I'm not sure I got the nose right.'

Stefano was silent for a moment and then he cleared his throat. 'The nose is perfect,' he said huskily. 'Thank you.'

The fact that he was so careful with Max's feelings somehow made everything seem even worse and Liv dipped her head and concentrated on opening her own present. 'Oh Max…' She lifted the painted pasta necklace from the wrapping. 'It's beautiful.' Slipping it over her head, she smiled at him and his eyes shone with pride.

'Well, you're a girl and Stefano says girls like jewellery and things. He gave you earrings and that thing for your hair, but he didn't give you a necklace.' Max slid his arms round her and Liv hugged him tightly.

'I love it. It's really beautiful.' She watched with a lump in her throat while the twins ripped the paper off their presents and then Isabella tilted her head.

'I hear bells outside—did anyone order a sleigh?'

Stefano rose to his feet. 'We'll see you later. Don't eat lunch without us.'

'Isn't everyone coming?' As Liv slipped her arms into her coat, she glanced around her but the group was already breaking up and doing different things. Donatella was going skiing with the other cousins, Isabella was joining her grandmother in the kitchen to prepare the meal.

Max was speechless with delight when he saw the horse-drawn sleigh waiting on the snowy path outside the chalet. 'We're going to ride in that?'

'You certainly are.' Stefano scooped him up and deposited

him in the back of the sleigh on a deep pile of sheepskin rugs and soft cushions. Following more slowly, Liv climbed up beside him, horribly conscious that it was just the three of them.

She really didn't want to be alone with Stefano. But what choice did she have? If she made an excuse, she'd spoil Max's fun and she didn't want to do that. So she said nothing and tried to look as though this was her idea of a perfect trip.

And in different circumstances it probably would have been.

The driver urged the horses forward and the sleigh moved smoothly along the snowy track that snaked up the mountain through tall pine trees. The only sounds were the muffled thud of horses' hooves, the creak of the oiled leather harness and the tinkle of sleigh bells.

Just enjoy the moment, Liv told herself desperately, and then she glanced at Max's face and felt herself soften with love. She would have been willing to face a thousand demons if it meant seeing her little boy smile the way he was smiling right now.

'It's magical,' she murmured and Stefano spread a blanket over her knees.

'Magical and freezing. Are you cold?'

'No.' *How could she be cold when he was so close?* Reminding herself not to get any ideas, Liv shrank back against the soft cushions and concentrated on the view.

The pain of not being with him would fade in time, wouldn't it?

And if it didn't, she'd somehow learn to live with it.

Max peered ahead of them, oblivious to the tension between the adults and fascinated by the horses. 'Can they go faster? Can we gallop? Can I help to drive them?'

'No, to all those questions,' Stefano said dryly, his eyes amused as he watched the child. 'We don't want to end up at the bottom of the valley. I think, for now, we'll leave the driving to the expert.'

'It was kind of you to do this for him.' Liv risked a glance and then looked away quickly, appalled by the sudden stab of need that swamped her.

'I didn't do it for him.' Stefano's voice was soft. 'I did it for myself. Because it's the only way to escape from my enormous family. Families can give you many things, but not privacy and peace and quiet. I can't quite believe that I've resorted to hiring a horse and sleigh, but that should give you some indication of how desperate I am.'

Desperate?

'Don't lean that far out, Max.' Anxious about safety, Liv reached out a hand and pulled the child back and then glanced at Stefano. 'Why do you need privacy?'

'Because I refuse to propose to you with my entire family watching.'

There was a long silence and Liv sat absolutely still, unable to speak or move, sure that she'd misheard him. He couldn't possibly have said what she thought he'd just said. She recited his words back to herself in her head. Then she turned her head slowly and their eyes met and held. 'What did you say?'

'What you thought I said. Marry me, Liv.' The look in his eyes made her body tingle and warm.

'Stefano—'

'*Te amo*. I love you. I should have told you that days ago and I'm sorry I didn't, but until yesterday I wasn't sure you'd say yes.'

'You should have asked me,' Max chipped in breathlessly. 'I could have told you she'd say yes. She's always staring at you and looking goopy and she smiles *all* the time, especially when you've just said something to her.'

Liv blushed, amazed that Max had noticed so much.

Stefano laughed, but his eyes didn't leave Liv's face for a moment. '*What* is "goopy"? This is not a word I know.'

'It's sort of…' Max pulled a face and shuddered as he tried to explain. 'Girly. I had to marry one of the girls in my class in a play this term and it was the grossest thing that has ever happened to me. She looked as though she was going to *eat* me or something. And she said lots of mushy stuff. If Mum marries you do we get to live in your cool apartment and play with all the gadgets?'

A wry smile on his face, Stefano spoke to the driver in Italian and the sleigh immediately glided to a halt.

The horses snorted and tossed their heads, their breath clouding the freezing air, their hooves making a muffled sound as they stamped the snowy ground.

'How would you like to exchange a few words with the horses, Max?' Stefano lifted the little boy down from the sleigh and Max eagerly sprinted forward to stroke the horses.

Beneath them lay the valley. Smoke curled upwards from chimneys, snow sparkled in the bright sunshine and the mountains rose up with pride, dominating the breathtaking landscape with their stark, wild beauty. Breathing in the crisp cold air and the scent of pine trees, Liv knew that she'd never forget this moment as long as she lived. 'You love me?'

'I love you. Do you want me to say it again?' Stefano took her face in his hands and looked at her, his dark eyes serious. 'I love you, *tesoro*.'

Her heart was thumping and her mouth was dry. 'But…' She swallowed hard. 'I'm no one.'

Stefano gave a slow smile that turned him from handsome to devastating. 'You're the woman I'm going to marry.'

She felt dizzy and shaky. *Marry?* 'I thought—I thought that for you it was just sex,' Liv whispered. 'I wanted it to be more. I really, really wanted it to be more, but that was all in my own head.'

'It wasn't in your head.' His eyes were gentle on hers. 'It was real. And it wasn't just sex.'

'But…you didn't say anything.'

'Liv, you haven't been with a man for four years.' He spoke the words quietly, just for her. 'I know what a big thing this is for you, even more so because you have always put your son's needs before your own. To begin with you rejected everything I gave you. You were *so* independent. I was giving you time to get used to the idea of being with me. That's why I wanted you to come home with me for Christmas.'

'When you first invited me I was so excited. I thought it meant that you cared, but then Isabella told me that you wanted to keep Donatella at a distance—'

'So it was Isabella.' His eyes narrowed wrathfully. 'Remind me to drop my sister in a snowdrift later. Liv, you're an intelligent woman. Do I look as though I need help keeping women at a distance?'

Liv bit her lip, her eyes scanning every detail of his handsome face. 'I suppose by now you must be pretty experienced at managing the expectations of the opposite sex.'

A smile touched the corners of his mouth. 'I have had some practice, I admit. But this isn't about me, is it, *tesoro*? It's about you.' His eyes held hers, demanding her full attention. 'You still don't believe that you are lovable and sexy. You are so lacking in confidence that when someone suggests I might have had an ulterior motive for bringing you here, you don't even question it.'

Dragging her gaze from his, Liv realised that her heart was pounding. 'Stefano—'

Strong fingers caught her chin and he forced her to look at him again. 'I'm going to make you see yourself as others see you, Liv. Warm, beautiful, talented, clever and a wonderful mother. And sexy.' He drew her head towards his and his eyes glittered dark with sexual promise. 'Very, very sexy. I have never brought a woman here before. What does that say to you?'

Hypnotised, Liv stared up at him and he slowly brought his mouth down to hers.

'It says that I'm crazy about you,' he murmured against her lips. 'It says that I cannot bear to be without you, even for a few days. That is why I brought you here, *tesoro*. And I wanted to see how you coped with my family.' He pulled back slightly, a sardonic gleam in his eyes. 'As you've already gathered, being with me comes with a great deal of family interference. Do you think you can stand it?'

Still in a state of suspended disbelief, Liv couldn't think properly. 'I— Does your father know that—? What if he doesn't approve? I have a child, Stefano. Donatella would probably be a far more suitable Italian wife.'

'Donatella and I would drive each other mad in less than a day. She isn't the right woman for me.' He sat back in his seat, his arm draped along the back of the carriage, very much his own man. 'You, on the other hand, enchant me and fascinate me and have done since the first moment I saw you hugging Anna.'

'That was so embarrassing—'

'I heard her say that she wanted to buy you hot sex for Christmas and you looked so appalled that I was instantly intrigued. A woman like you should be having hot sex every night of her life.'

Liv blushed. 'You were *so* kind to me. That night the car broke down and then with my flat—'

'It wasn't kindness, Liv.' Stefano slid his arm round her and curved her against him. 'I've never felt so protective towards a woman. I don't know what happens to me when I'm with you but I just want to wrap you up and keep you safe.'

His words brought a lump to her throat. 'Stefano—'

'I make you this promise, *tesoro*,' he said huskily, 'I won't let you be hurt ever again if it is in my power to prevent it. I won't let you struggle and I won't let you make any more sacrifices.'

His words drove the last of the breath from her quivering body. The emotions inside her swelled to a point that she could barely contain them. When had anyone ever taken care of her before? She'd always had to do it herself. On her own. She'd fought, struggled and worried her way through parent-hood, with no one to share the burden. And now this man was telling her that she no longer had anything to worry about. She was afraid to move in case the dream shattered into a million tiny fragments.

'I thought it was because you felt sorry for me.'

'It was because I was falling in love with you. Almost from that first moment. You're very easy to love.'

Tears pricked her eyes and her throat felt full. 'This sort of thing doesn't happen to me.'

'Yes, it does. It's happening now.' He was smiling and Liv shook her head, the tears blurring her vision.

'No. It doesn't—and I can't…' She brushed her hand across her face. 'Any moment now you're going to tell me this is a joke.'

'Then perhaps this will convince you.' Stefano reached into his pocket and pulled out a tiny silver box. 'I went out yesterday and bought this for you.'

'Yesterday? But you were skiing…' Her voice cracked and she stared at the box, wondering whether it was real or whether her mind had conjured up this whole situation.

'I was choosing a ring suitable for my future wife. I knew it had to be something extremely special because *she* is extremely special.' Stefano flicked open the box and a huge diamond solitaire winked and flashed in the winter sunlight.

Liv gave a gasp of shock and then lifted her eyes to his. 'It's…a ring. You bought me a ring.'

'You're right.' His eyes laughed into hers. 'It's a ring. It's tradition for the man to give his woman a ring when he's proposing.'

She could hardly breathe. 'You want to marry me.'

'That's what I've been saying for the past five minutes.' Stefano's gaze flickered briefly to the front of the sleigh. 'I hate to hurry this romantic moment, but Max is going to get bored with those horses shortly and then the goopy, mushy stuff is going to have to finish.'

'Your father—'

'My father loves you, but even if he didn't it wouldn't make a difference. He's not the one marrying you. I am.'

'You are?' She looked at him, unable to believe that life could transform from misery to perfect pleasure in such a short time. 'But yesterday, when I told you how I felt—'

'I was so stunned by what you said that I didn't even stop you walking away. But you did me a favour. I realised that there was no point in holding back and giving you time to adjust to the fact that we were together. I could see that words alone wouldn't be enough to convince you that I love you.'

Hardly daring to breathe, Liv gazed at the glittering diamond and then at him. 'Stefano, you couldn't have found a woman with less to offer you. I don't have any money at all and—'

'Fortunately I have more than enough for both of us.' His possessive gaze was fixed on her in blatant appreciation and she felt herself blushing.

'Don't look at me like that.'

'I'm going to be looking at you like that for the next fifty years at least, *tesoro*,' he drawled softly, 'so you'd better get used to it.'

Liv lifted a hand to her throat. 'I want to be with you more than anything, you know that. But I can't marry you.'

His dark eyes narrowed ominously. *'Liv—'*

'How can I marry you? I don't have a single penny in my bank account and you're a multi-millionaire. You've bought me a ring that must have cost more than I earn in a year! It's very easy for you to dismiss that, but it matters! If I marry you, you'll think I'm a gold-digger,' she said passionately and when he started to roar with laughter she glared at him in exasperation. 'Why is that funny?'

'Because for a moment I really thought you were refusing me,' he gasped through his laughter, 'and having never proposed to a woman before, you might have done irreparable harm to my arrogance and my ego.'

'I'm being serious, Stefano.'

'So am I. Fortunately for both of us, I have considerable experience with gold-diggers, *tesoro*. Believe me, you don't have any of the necessary qualifications.'

'You don't understand. I like the fact that you have money,' Liv said honestly, watching for his reaction with something close to dread, afraid that she might drive him away. *'I like the money, Stefano!* I like the fact that you don't have to worry about paying bills. I like the fact you can just wave your credit card, snap your fingers and solve a million problems. I even like being given diamond earrings and beautiful clothes! There. Does that shock you?'

'Liv, you've been counting every penny for the past four years. It's entirely natural that having access to money should come as a relief. To not like the money would make you stupid, no? And you *certainly* are not stupid.' He was watching her with a considerable degree of amusement in his eyes. 'Just enjoy it. Why are you worrying?'

'Because I'm afraid you'll think my feelings for you are tied up with the money.'

Stefano smiled and took her face in his hands. 'Liv, I've always known what your feelings for me are, *tesoro*. Fortunately for me, you aren't experienced enough to hide them. I can even describe the moment when you first realised that you loved me.'

Her eyes widened. 'You can?'

'Of course. It was when you woke up in my bed the morning after the ball.'

'Oh.' Liv gave a shocked laugh. 'How can you be so confident about everything?'

'Because, unlike you, no one has ever dented my self-esteem.' Bending his head, he kissed her gently, his mouth lingering against hers. 'I love the fact that you can't hide your feelings. I also love your kindness, your honesty, your total selflessness, your amazing confidence and skill at work, your sense of humour, your incredibly sexy body—'

'Stop!' Laughing, Liv shook her head and pulled away slightly. 'That's not me you're describing. I'm not used to so many compliments.'

'Then get used to it because there is no end of compliments coming your way, *tesoro*.' Gently, Stefano stroked her flushed cheek with the backs of his fingers then he lifted the ring out of the velvet case. 'Stop worrying about the money and enjoy it. Given that my life is about to become your life, it would be a little complicated if you didn't like the money.'

He really wanted to marry her?

It was too much to absorb. 'I can't believe this is happening.' Liv stared at the beautiful ring in his hand. Her heart was pounding, her legs were shaking and she didn't know whether to laugh or cry. 'I've shut myself away for so long. That first night when you took me to that Italian restaurant, I just wanted to shrink into the woodwork.'

'I had a good time, but you had absolutely *no* confidence.'

'It had been ages since I'd been out with a man and I had no idea what to say. I was worried that you were terribly bored.'

'You have never bored me,' Stefano breathed, 'and I couldn't believe that you hadn't been with a man for so long.'

'I just wasn't interested,' she admitted, checking that Max was still patting the horses. 'I suppose I was terrified of rejection. Anna despaired of me, but I honestly couldn't imagine wanting to have sex ever again. Then I met you and sex with you was so amazing that suddenly I couldn't imagine living without it. You've turned me into a sex maniac.'

With a husky laugh, Stefano took her hand in his and slid the ring onto her finger. 'Then the sooner we are married, the better. I am willing to sacrifice myself by marrying a sex maniac,' he said dryly, 'just as long as there is no confusion as to whose woman you are.'

Liv stared down at the diamond that sparkled on her finger. 'It's stunning.'

'It tells the world that you are mine.' Stefano gave a satisfied smile and Liv tore her eyes away from the ring, a lump building in her throat as she looked up at him.

'What can I ever give you in return?'

'Love, *tesoro*.' His hands strong and confident, he drew her against him. 'You're giving me love, and that's a gift beyond price.'

'Yuck!' Max scrambled up beside them. 'Did she say no or something?'

Still sniffing, Liv pulled out of Stefano's arms. 'I said yes, Max.'

'So why are you crying?'

'Because I'm happy.'

Max stared at her bemused and then exchanged a look with Stefano, man to man. 'She cries when she's sad and she cries when she's happy. Girls are so confusing, aren't they?'

'Very confusing.' With a smile, Stefano released Liv and lifted the child onto his lap. 'How would you fancy coming to live with me, Max?'

'For ever?'

'Yes, for ever.'

Liv couldn't help it. The tears were pouring down her face and she turned her head and buried her face in Stefano's sleeve, feeling like a complete idiot and so deliriously happy that she wanted to dance with joy.

Max was concentrating on the important issues. 'Will we live in your apartment?'

'To start with. But then I thought we might look around for a nice big house. We need a garden so that we can have a goal.'

'My own goal?' Max bounced on his lap and Stefano winced.

'I hope you didn't want more children,' he muttered under his breath, and Liv started to laugh because her life suddenly seemed so amazing and everything around her was just perfect.

'Can we go and get married straight away in case you change your mind?'

'He won't change his mind.' Max settled himself between them. 'Stefano was lonely until we came along. He had no Christmas decorations of his own, can you believe that? Now he has us, we'll be able to help him with his Christmas tree every year. And you'll be able to sleep in his bed, like married people are supposed to.'

The sleigh bells jangled as the horses moved back up the road towards the chalet and Liv and Stefano exchanged a look over the top of his head.

'I love you, Stefano.' Saying the words suddenly made it all seem real and she suddenly discovered that it was perfectly possible to smile and cry at the same time. 'I love you *so much* and this is the best Christmas I could possibly have imagined.'

His dark eyes flared with emotion. 'And I love you, *tesoro*. You're mine. Always.'

'Oh please!' Giggling and squirming between them, Max covered his ears and shuddered. 'Someone let me out of here before I'm sick. I'm sure Father Christmas doesn't have to listen to this in *his* sleigh.'

CHRISTMAS ANGEL
FOR THE
BILLIONAIRE
LIZ FIELDING

Liz Fielding was born with itchy feet. She made it to Zambia before her twenty-first birthday and, gathering her own special hero and a couple of children on the way, lived in Botswana, Kenya and Bahrain—with pauses for sightseeing pretty much everywhere in between. She finally came to a full stop in a tiny Welsh village cradled by misty hills, and these days mostly leaves her pen to do the travelling. When she's not sorting out the lives and loves of her characters, she potters in the garden, reads her favourite authors and spends a lot of time wondering 'What if...?' For news of upcoming books—and to sign up for her occasional newsletter—visit Liz's website at www.lizfielding.com.

PROLOGUE

Daily Chronicle, 19th December, 1988

MARQUESS AND WIFE SLAIN ON CHARITY MISSION
The Marquess and Marchioness of St Ives, whose fairy-tale romance captured the hearts of the nation, were slain yesterday by rebels who opened fire on their vehicle as they approached a refugee camp in the war-torn region of Mishona. Their driver and a local woman who worked for the medical charity Susie's Friends *also died in the attack.*

HM the Queen sent a message of sympathy to the Duke of Oldfield, the widowed father of the Marquess, and to the slaughtered couple's six-year-old daughter, Lady Roseanne Napier.

The Marchioness of St Ives, Lady Susanne Napier, who overcame early hardships to train as a doctor, founded the international emergency charity with her husband shortly after their marriage.

Daily Chronicle, 24th December, 1988

WE MUST ALL BE HER FAMILY NOW...
Six-year-old Lady Roseanne Napier held her grandfather's hand as the remains of her slain mother and father were laid to rest in the family vault yesterday afternoon. In his oration,

praising their high ideals, the grieving Duke said, 'We must all be her family now…'

Daily Chronicle, 18th December, 1998

A PERFECT ANGEL…
Today, on the tenth anniversary of the slaying of her parents while helping to co-ordinate relief in war-ravished Mishona, Lady Rose Napier opened Susanne House, a children's hospice named to honour her mother. After unveiling a plaque, Lady Rose met the brave children who are being cared for at Susanne House and talked to their parents. 'She was so caring, so thoughtful for someone so young,' one of the nurses said. 'A perfect angel. Her mother would have been so proud of her.'

Her mother isn't here to tell her that, so we are saying it for her.

We are all proud of you, Lady Rose.

CHAPTER ONE

ANNIE smothered a yawn. The room was hot, the lingering scent of food nauseating and all she wanted to do was lay her head on the table in front of her, close her eyes and switch off.

If only.

There was a visit to a hospital, then three hours of Wagner at a charity gala to endure before she could even think about sleep. And even then, no matter how tired she was, thinking about it was as close as she would get.

She'd tried it all. Soothing baths, a lavender pillow, every kind of relaxation technique without success. But calming her mind wasn't the problem.

It wasn't the fact that it was swirling with all the things she needed to remember that was keeping her awake. She had an efficient personal assistant to take care of every single detail of her life and ensure that she was in the right place at the right time. A speech writer to put carefully chosen words into her mouth when she got there. A style consultant whose job it was to ensure that whenever she appeared in public she made the front page.

That *was* the problem.

There was absolutely nothing in her mind to swirl around. It was empty. Like her life.

In just under a minute she was going to have to stand up

and talk to these amazing people who had put themselves on the line to alleviate suffering in the world.

They had come to see her, listen to her inspire them to even greater efforts. And her presence ensured that the press was here too, which meant that the work they did would be noticed, reported.

Maybe.

Her hat, a rich green velvet and feather folly perched at a saucy angle over her right eye would probably garner more column inches than the charity she was here to support.

She was doing more for magazine and newspaper circulation than she was for the medical teams, the search units, pilots, drivers, communications people who dropped everything at a moment's notice, risking their lives to help victims of war, famine, disaster—a point she'd made to her grandfather more than once.

A pragmatist, he had dismissed her concerns, reminding her that it was a symbiotic relationship and everyone would benefit from her appearance, including the British fashion industry.

It didn't help that he was right.

She wanted to do more, *be* more than a cover girl, a fashion icon. Her parents had been out there, on the front line, picking up the pieces of ruined lives and she had planned to follow in their footsteps.

She stopped the thought. Publicity was the only gift she had and she had better do it right but, as she took her place at the lectern and a wave of applause hit her, a long silent scream invaded the emptiness inside her head.

Noooooo…

'Friends…' she began when the noise subsided. She paused, looked around her, found faces in the audience she recognised, people her parents had known. Took a breath, dug deep, smiled. 'I hope I've earned the right to call you that…'

She had been just eighteen years old when, at her grandfather's urging, she'd accepted an invitation to become patron of Susie's Friends. A small consolation for the loss of her dream of following her mother into medicine.

All that had ended when, at the age of sixteen, a photograph of her holding the hand of a dying child had turned her, overnight, from a sheltered, protected teen into an iconic image and her grandfather had laid out the bald facts for her.

How impossible it was. How her fellow students, patients even, would be harassed, bribed by the press for gossip about her because she was now public property. Then he'd consoled her with the fact that this way she could do so much more for the causes her mother had espoused.

Ten years on, more than fifty charities had claimed her as a patron. How many smiles, handshakes? Charity galas, first nights?

How many children's hands had she held, how many babies had she cradled?

None of them her own.

She had seen herself described as the 'most loved woman in Britain', but living in an isolation bubble, sheltered, protected from suffering the same fate as her parents, it was a love that never came close enough to touch.

But the media was a hungry beast that had to be fed and it was, apparently, time to move the story on. Time for a husband and children to round out the image. And, being her grandfather, he wasn't prepared to leave anything that important to chance.

Or to her.

Heaven forbid there should be anything as messy as her own father's passionate romance with a totally unsuitable woman, one whose ideals had ended up getting them both killed.

Instead, he'd found the perfect candidate in Rupert Devenish, Viscount Earley, easing him into her life so subtly that she'd barely noticed. Titled, rich and almost too good-looking to be true, he was so eligible that if she'd gone to the 'ideal husband' store and picked him off the shelf he couldn't be more perfect.

So perfect, in fact, that unless she was extremely careful, six months from now she'd find herself with a ring on her finger and in a year she'd be on every front page, every magazine cover, wearing the 'fairy-tale' dress. The very thought of it weighed like a lump of lead somewhere in the region of her heart. Trapped, with nowhere to turn, she felt as if the glittering chandeliers were slowly descending to crush her.

She dug her nails into her palm to concentrate her mind, took a sip of water, looked around at all the familiar faces and, ignoring the carefully worded speech that had been written for her, she talked to them about her parents, about ideals, about sacrifice, her words coming straight from the heart.

An hour later it was over and she turned to the hotel manager as he escorted her to the door. 'Another wonderful lunch, Mr Gordon. How is your little girl?'

'Much improved, thank you, Lady Rose. She was so thrilled with the books you sent her.'

'She wrote me the sweetest note.' She glanced at the single blush-pink rose she was holding.

She yearned to be offered, just once, something outrageous in purple or orange, but this variety of rose had been named for her and part of the proceeds of every sale went to Susanne House. To have offered her anything else would have been unthinkable.

'Will you give her this from me?' she said, offering him the rose.

'Madam,' he said, pink with pleasure as he took it and Annie felt a sudden urge to hug the man. Instead, she let her hand rest briefly on his arm before she turned to join Rupert, who was already at the door, impatient to be away.

Turned and came face to face with herself.

Or at least a very close facsimile.

A look in one of the mirrors that lined the walls would have shown two tall, slender young women, each with pale gold hair worn up in the same elegant twist, each with harebell-blue eyes.

Annie had been aware of her double's existence for years. Had seen photographs in magazines and newspapers, courtesy of the cuttings agency that supplied clippings of any print article that contained her name. She'd assumed that the amazing likeness had been aided by photographic manipulation but it wasn't so. It was almost like looking in the mirror.

For a moment they both froze. Annie, more experienced in dealing with the awkward moment, putting people at their ease, was the first to move.

'I know the face,' she said, feeling for the woman—it wasn't often a professional 'lookalike' came face to face with the real thing. With a smile, she added, 'But I'm afraid the name escapes me.'

Her double, doing a remarkable job of holding her poise under the circumstances, said, 'Lydia, madam. Lydia Young.' But, as she took her hand, Annie felt it shaking. 'I'm s-so sorry. I promise this wasn't planned. I had no idea you'd be here.'

'Please, it's not a problem.' Then, intrigued, 'Do you—or do I mean I?—have an engagement here?'

'Had. A product launch.' Lydia gave an awkward little shrug as she coloured up. 'A new variety of tea.'

'I do hope it's good,' Annie replied, 'if I'm endorsing it.'

'Well, it's expensive,' Lydia said, relaxing sufficiently to smile back. Then, 'I'll just go and sit down behind that pillar for ten minutes, shall I? While I'm sure the photographers out there would enjoy it if we left together, my clients didn't pay me anywhere near enough to give them that kind of publicity.'

'It would rather spoil the illusion if we were seen together,' Annie agreed. About to walk on, something stopped her. 'As a matter of interest, Lydia, how much do you charge for being me?' she asked. 'Just in case I ever decide to take a day off.'

'No charge for you, Lady Rose,' she replied, handing her the rose that she was, inevitably, carrying as she sank into a very brief curtsey. 'Just give me a call. Any time.'

For a moment they looked at one another, then Annie sniffed the rose and said, 'They don't have much character, do they? No scent, no thorns...'

'Well, it's November. I imagine they've been forced under glass.'

Something they had in common, Annie thought.

She didn't have much character either, just a carefully manufactured image as the nation's 'angel', 'sweetheart'.

Rupert, already through the door, looked back to see what was keeping her and, apparently confident enough to display a little impatience, said, 'Rose, we're running late...'

They both glanced in his direction, then Lydia looked at her and lifted a brow in a 'dump the jerk' look that exactly mirrored her own thoughts.

'I don't suppose you fancy three hours of Wagner this evening?' she asked but, even before Lydia could reply, she shook her head. 'Just kidding. I wouldn't wish that on you.'

'I meant what I said.' And Lydia, taking a card from the small clutch bag she was carrying, offered it to her. 'Call me. Any time.'

Three weeks later, as speculation in the press that she was about to announce her engagement reached fever-pitch, Annie took out Lydia's card and dialled the number.

'Lydia Young...'

'Did you mean it?' she asked.

George Saxon, bare feet propped on the deck rail of his California beach house, laptop on his knees, gave up on the problem that had been eluding him for weeks and surfed idly through the headlines of the London newspapers.

His eye was caught by the picture of a couple leaving some gala. She was one of those tall patrician women, pale blonde hair swept up off her neck, her fabulously expensive gown cut low to reveal hollows in her shoulders even deeper than those in her cheeks.

But it wasn't her dress or the fact that she'd so obviously starved herself to get into it that had caught and held his attention. It was her eyes.

Her mouth was smiling for the camera, but her eyes, large, blue, seemed to be looking straight at him, sending him a silent appeal for help.

He clicked swiftly back to the program he'd been working on. Sometimes switching in and out of a problem cleared the blockage but this one was stubborn, which was why he'd left his Chicago office, lakeside apartment. Escaping the frantic pre-Christmas party atmosphere for the peace—and warmth—of the beach.

Behind him, inside the house, the phone began to ring. It would be his accountant, or his lawyer, or his office but success had insulated him from the need to jump when the phone rang and he left it for the machine to pick up. There was nothing, no one—

'George? It's your dad…'

But, then again, there were exceptions to every rule.

Tossing a holdall onto the back seat of the little red car that was Lydia's proudest possession, Annie settled herself behind the wheel and ran her hands over the steering wheel as if to reassure herself that it was real.

That she'd escaped…

Three hours ago, Lady Rose Napier had walked into a London hotel without her unshakeable escort—the annual Pink Ribbon Lunch was a ladies-only occasion. Two hours later, Lydia had walked out in her place. And ten minutes ago she'd left the same hotel completely unnoticed.

By now Lydia would be on board a private jet, heading for a week of total luxury at Bab el Sama, the holiday home of her friend Lucy al-Khatib.

Once there, all she had to do was put in an occasional appearance on the terrace or the beach for the paparazzi who, after the sudden rash of 'Wedding Bells?' headlines, would no doubt be sitting offshore in small boats, long-range cameras at the ready, hoping to catch her in flagrante in this private 'love-nest' with Rupert.

She hoped they'd packed seasick pills along with their sunscreen since they were going to have a very long wait.

And she grinned. She'd told her grandfather that she needed time on her own to consider her future. Not true. She wasn't going to waste one precious second of the time that Lydia— bless her heart—had given her thinking about Rupert Devenish.

She had just a week in which to be anonymous, to step outside the hothouse environment in which she'd lived since her parents had been killed. To touch reality as they had done. Be herself. Nothing planned, nothing organised. Just take life as it came.

She adjusted the rear-view mirror to check her appearance. She'd debated whether to go with a wig or colour her hair but, having tried a wig—it was amazing what you could buy on the Internet—and realising that living in it 24/7 was not for her, she'd decided to go for a temporary change of hair colour, darkening it a little with the temporary rinse Lydia had provided.

But that would have taken time and, instead, in an act of pure rebellion, of liberation, she'd hacked it short with a pair of nail scissors. When she'd stopped, the short, spiky result was so shocking that she'd been grateful for the woolly hat Lydia had provided to cover it.

She pulled it down over her ears, hoping that Lydia, forced to follow her style, would forgive her. Pushed the heavy-framed 'prop' spectacles up her nose. And grinned. The sense of freedom was giddying and, if she was honest, a little frightening. She'd never been completely on her own before and, shivering a little, she turned on the heater.

'Not frightening,' she said out loud as she eased out of the parking bay and headed for the exit. 'Challenging.' And, reaching the barrier, she encountered her first challenge.

Lydia had left the ticket on the dashboard for her and she stuck it in the machine, expecting the barrier to lift. The machine spat it back out.

As she tried it the other way, with the same result, there was a series of impatient toots from the tailback building up behind her.

So much for invisibility.

She'd been on her own for not much more than an hour and already she was the centre of attention…

'What's your problem, lady?'

Annie froze but the 'Rose' never came and she finally looked up to find a car park attendant, a Santa Claus hat tugged down to his ears against the cold, glaring at her.

Apparently he'd used the word 'lady' not as a title, but as something barely short of an insult and, like his sour expression, it didn't quite match the 'ho, ho, ho' of the hat.

'Well?' he demanded.

'Oh. Um…' *Concentrate!* 'I put the ticket in, but nothing happened.'

'Have you paid?'

'Paid?' she asked. 'Where?'

He sighed. 'Can't you read? There's a notice ten feet high at the entrance.' Then, since she was still frowning, he said, very slowly, 'You have to pay before you leave. Over there.' She looked around, saw a machine, then, as the hooting became more insistent, 'In your own time,' he added sarcastically.

And *Bah! Humbug…* to you, she thought as she grabbed

her bag from the car and sprinted to the nearest machine, read the instructions, fed in the ticket and then the amount indicated with shaking fingers.

She returned to the car, calling, 'Sorry, sorry…' to the people she'd held up before flinging herself back into the car and finally escaping.

Moments later, she was just one of thousands of drivers battling through traffic swollen by Christmas shoppers and visitors who'd come up to town to see the lights.

Anonymous, invisible, she removed the unnecessary spectacles, dropping them on the passenger seat, then headed west out of London.

She made good time but the pale blue winter sky was tinged with pink, the trees black against the horizon as she reached the junction for Maybridge. A pretty town with excellent shops, a popular riverside area, it was not too big, not too small. As good a place as any to begin her adventure and she headed for the ring road and the anonymous motel she'd found on the Internet.

Somewhere to spend the night and decide what she was going to do with her brief moment of freedom.

George Saxon's jaw was rigid as he kept his silence.

'No one else can do it,' his father insisted.

A nurse appeared, checked the drip. 'I need to make Mr Saxon comfortable,' she said. Then, with a pointed look at him, 'Why don't you take your mother home? She's been here all day.'

'No, I'll stay.' She took his father's hand, squeezed it. 'I'll be back in a little while.'

His father ignored her, instead grabbing his wrist as he made a move.

'Tell me you'll do it!'

'Don't fret,' his mother said soothingly. 'You can leave George to sort things out at the garage. He won't let you down.'

She looked pleadingly across the bed at him, silently imploring him to back her up.

'Of course he'll let me down,' his father said before he could speak. 'He never could stand getting his hands dirty.'

'Enough!' the nurse said and, not waiting for his mother, George walked from the room.

She caught up with him in the family room. 'I'm sorry—'

'Don't! Don't apologise for him.' Then, pouring her a cup of tea from one of the flasks on the trolley, 'You do realise that he's not going to be able to carry on like this?'

'Please, George…' she said.

Please, George…

Those two words had been the soundtrack to his childhood, his adolescence.

'I'll sort out what needs to be done,' he said. 'But maybe it's time for that little place by the sea?' he suggested, hoping to get her to see that there was an upside to this.

She shook her head. 'He'd be dead within a year.'

'He'll be dead anyway if he carries on.' Then, because he knew he was only distressing his mother, he said, 'Will you be okay here on your own? Have you had anything to eat?'

'I'll get myself something if I'm hungry,' she said, refusing to be fussed over. Then, her hand on his arm, 'I'm so grateful to you for coming home. Your dad won't tell you himself…' She gave an awkward little shrug. 'I don't have to tell you how stubborn he can be. But he's glad to see you.'

The traffic was building up to rush-hour level by the time Annie reached the far side of Maybridge. Unused to driving in heavy traffic, confused by the signs, she missed the exit for the motel, a fact she only realised when she passed it, seeing its lights blazing.

Letting slip a word she'd never used before, she took the next exit and then, rather than retracing her route using the ring road, she turned left, certain that it would lead her back to the motel. Fifteen minutes later, in an unlit country lane that had meandered off in totally the wrong direction, she admitted defeat and, as her headlights picked up the gateway to a field, she pulled over.

She found Reverse, swung the wheel and backed in. There was an unexpectedly sharp dip and the rear wheels left the tarmac with a hard bump, jolting the underside of the car.

Annie took a deep breath, told herself that it was nothing, then, having gathered herself, she turned the steering wheel in the right direction and applied a little pressure to the accelerator.

The only response was a horrible noise.

George sat for a moment looking up at the sign, George Saxon and Son, above the garage workshop. It was only when he climbed from the car that he noticed the light still burning, no doubt forgotten in the panic when his father had collapsed.

Using the keys his mother had given him, he unlocked the side door. Only two of the bays were occupied.

The nearest held the vintage Bentley that his father was in such a state about. Beautiful, arcane, it was in constant use as a wedding car and the brake linings needed replacing.

As he reached for the light switch he heard the familiar clang of a spanner hitting concrete, a muffled curse.

'Hello?'

There was no response and, walking around the Bentley, he discovered a pair of feet encased in expensive sports shoes, jiggling as if in time to music, sticking out from beneath the bonnet.

He didn't waste his breath trying to compete with whatever the owner of the feet was listening to, but instead he tapped one of them lightly with the toe of his shoe.

The movement stopped.

Then a pair of apparently endless, overall-clad legs slid

from beneath the car, followed by a slender body. Finally a girl's face appeared.

'*Alexandra?*'

'*George?*' she replied, mocking his disbelief with pure sarcasm. 'Gran told me you were coming but I didn't actually believe her.'

He was tempted to ask her why not, but instead went for the big one.

'What are you doing here?' And, more to the point, why hadn't his mother warned him that his daughter was there when she'd given him her keys?

'Mum's away on honeymoon with husband number three,' she replied, as if that explained everything. 'Where else would I go?' Then, apparently realising that lying on her back she was at something of a disadvantage, she put her feet flat on the concrete and rose in one fluid, effortless movement that made him feel old.

'And these days everyone calls me Xandra.'

'Xandra,' he repeated without comment. She'd been named, without reference to him, after her maternal grandmother, a woman who'd wanted him put up against a wall and shot for despoiling her little princess. It was probably just as well that at the time he'd been too numb with shock to laugh.

Indicating his approval, however, would almost certainly cause her to change back. Nothing he did was ever right. He'd tried so hard, loved her so much, but it had always been a battle between them. And, much as he'd have liked to blame her mother for that, he knew it wasn't her fault. He simply had no idea how to be a dad. The kind that a little girl would smile at, run to.

'I have no interest in your mother's whereabouts,' he said. 'I want to know why you're here instead of at school?'

She lifted her shoulders in an insolent shrug. 'I've been suspended.'

'Suspended?'

'Indefinitely.' Then with a second, epic, I-really-couldn't-care-less shrug, 'Until after Christmas, anyway. Not that it matters. I wouldn't go back if they paid me.'

'Unlikely, I'd have said.'

'If you offered to build them a new science lab I bet they'd be keen enough.'

'In that case *I'd* be the one paying them to take you back,' he pointed out. 'What has your mother done about it?'

'Nothing. I told you. She's lying on a beach somewhere. With her phone switched off.'

'You could have called me.'

'And what? You'd have dropped everything and rushed across the Atlantic to play daddy? Who knew you cared?'

He clenched his teeth. He was his father all over again. Incapable of forming a bond, making contact with this child who'd nearly destroyed his life. Who, from the moment she'd been grudgingly placed in his arms, had claimed his heart.

He would have done anything for her, died for her if need be. Anything but give up the dream he'd fought tooth and nail to achieve.

All the money in the world, the house his ex-wife had chosen, the expensive education—nothing he'd done had countered that perceived desertion.

'Let's pretend for a moment that I do,' he said, matter-of-factly. 'What did you do?'

'Nothing.' She coloured slightly. 'Nothing much.' He waited. 'I hot-wired the head's car and took it for a spin, that's all.'

Hot-wired...

Apparently taking his shocked silence as encouragement to continue, she said, 'Honestly. Who'd have thought the Warthog would have made such a fuss?'

'You're not old enough to drive!' Then, because she'd grown so fast, was almost a woman, 'Are you?'

She just raised her eyebrows, leaving him to work it out for himself. He was right. He'd been nineteen when she was born, which meant that his daughter wouldn't be seventeen until next May. It would be six months before she could even apply for a licence.

'You stole a car, drove it without a licence, without insurance?' He somehow managed to keep his voice neutral. 'That's your idea of "nothing much"?'

He didn't bother asking who'd taught her to drive. That would be the same person who'd given him an old banger and let him loose in the field out back as soon as his feet touched the pedals. Driving was in the Saxon blood, according to his father, and engine oil ran through their veins.

But, since she'd hot-wired Mrs Warburton's car, clearly driving wasn't all her grandfather had taught her.

'What were you doing under the Bentley?' he demanded as a chill that had nothing to do with the temperature ran through him.

'Just checking it out. It needs new brake linings…' The phone began to ring. With the slightest of shrugs, she leaned around him, unhooked it from the wall and said, 'George Saxon and Granddaughter…'

What?

'Where are you?' she asked, reaching for a pen. 'Are you on your own…? Okay, stay with the car—'

George Saxon and Granddaughter…

Shock slowed him down and as he moved to wrest the phone from her she leaned back out of his reach.

'—we'll be with you in ten minutes.' She replaced the receiver. 'A lone woman broken down on the Longbourne Road,' she said. 'I told her we'll pick her up.'

'I heard what you said. Just how do you propose to do that?' he demanded furiously.

'Get in the tow-truck,' she suggested, 'drive down the road…'

'There's no one here to deal with a breakdown.'

'You're here. *I'm* here. Granddad says I'm as good as you were with an engine.'

If she thought that would make him feel better, she would have to think again.

'Call her back,' he said, pulling down the local directory. 'Tell her we'll find someone else to help her.'

'I didn't take her number.'

'It doesn't matter. She won't care who turns up so long as someone does,' he said, punching in the number of another garage. It had rung just twice when he heard the clunk as a truck door was slammed shut. On the third ring he heard it start.

He turned around as a voice in his ear said, 'Longbourne Motors. How can I…'

The personnel door was wide open and, as he watched, the headlights of the pick-up truck pierced the dark.

'Sorry,' he said, dropping the phone and racing after his daughter, wrenching open the cab door as it began to move. 'Turn it off!'

She began to move as he reached for the keys.

'Alexandra! Don't you dare!' He hung onto the door, walking quickly alongside the truck as she moved across the forecourt.

'It's Granddad's business,' she said, speeding up a little, forcing him to run or let go. He ran. 'I'm not going to let you shut it down.' Then, having made her point, she eased off the accelerator until the truck rolled to a halt before turning to challenge him. 'I love cars, engines. I'm going to run this place, be a rally driver—'

'What?'

'Granddad's going to sponsor me.'

'You're sixteen,' he said, not sure whether he was more horrified that she wanted to race cars or fix them. 'You don't know what you want.'

Even as he said the words, he heard his father's voice. *'You're thirteen, boy. Your head is full of nonsense. You don't know what you want…'*

He'd gone on saying it to him even when he was filling in forms, applying for university places, knowing that he'd get no financial backing, that he'd have to support himself every step of the way.

Even when his 'nonsense' was being installed in every new engine manufactured throughout the world, his father had still been telling him he was wrong…

'Move over,' he said.

Xandra clung stubbornly to the steering wheel. 'What are you going to do?'

'Since you've already kept a lone woman waiting in a dark country lane for five minutes longer than necessary, I haven't got much choice. I'm going to let you pick her up.'

'Me?'

'You. But you've already committed enough motoring offences for one week, so I'll drive the truck.'

CHAPTER TWO

ANNIE saw the tow-truck, yellow light flashing on the roof of the cab, looming out of the dark, and sighed with relief as it pulled up just ahead of her broken-down car.

After a lorry, driving much too fast along the narrow country lane, had missed the front of the car by inches, she'd scrambled out and was standing with her back pressed against the gate, shivering with the cold.

The driver jumped down and swung a powerful torch over and around the car, and she threw up an arm to shield her eyes from the light as he found her.

'George Saxon,' her knight errant said, lowering the torch a little. 'Are you okay?' he asked.

'Y-y-yes,' she managed through chattering teeth. She couldn't see his face behind the light but his voice had a touch of impatience that wasn't exactly what she'd hoped for. 'No thanks to a lorry driver who nearly took the front off the car.'

'You should have switched on the hazard warning lights,' he said unsympathetically. 'Those sidelights are useless.'

'If he'd been driving within the speed limit, he'd have seen me,' she replied, less than pleased at the suggestion that it was her own fault that she'd nearly been killed.

'There is no speed limit on this road other than the national limit. That's seventy miles an hour,' he added, in case she didn't know.

'I saw the signs. Foolishly, perhaps, I assumed that it was the upper limit, not an instruction,' she snapped right back.

'True,' he agreed, 'but just because other people behave stupidly it doesn't mean you have to join in.'

First the car park attendant and now the garage mechanic. Irritable men talking to her as if she had dimwit tattooed across her forehead was getting tiresome.

Although, considering she could be relaxing in the warmth and comfort of Bab el Sama instead of freezing her socks off in an English country lane in December, they might just have a point.

'So,' he asked, gesturing at the car with the torch, 'what's the problem?'

'I thought it was your job to tell me that,' she replied, deciding she'd taken enough male insolence for one day.

'Okaaay…'

Back-lit by the bright yellow hazard light swinging around on top of the tow-truck, she couldn't make out more than the bulk of him but she had a strong sense of a man hanging onto his temper by a thread.

'Let's start with the basics,' he said, making an effort. 'Have you run out of petrol?'

'What kind of fool do you take me for?'

'That's what I'm trying to establish,' he replied with all the long-suffering patience of a man faced with every conceivable kind of a fool. Then, with a touch more grace, 'Maybe you should just tell me what happened and we'll take it from there.'

That was close enough to a truce to bring her from the safety of the gate and through teeth that were chattering with the cold—or maybe delayed shock, that lorry had been very close—she said, 'I t-took the wrong road and t-tried to—'

'To' turned into a yelp as she caught her foot in a rut and was flung forward, hands outstretched, as she grabbed for anything to save herself. What she got was soft brushed leather and George Saxon, who didn't budge as she cannoned into him but, steady as a rock, caught her, then held her as she struggled to catch her breath.

'Are you okay?' he asked after a moment.

With her cheek, her nose and her hands pressed against his chest, she was in no position to answer.

But with his breath warm against her skin, his hands holding her safe, there wasn't a great deal wrong that she could think of.

Except, of course, all of the above.

She couldn't remember ever being quite this close to a man she didn't know, so what she was feeling—and whether 'okay' covered it—she couldn't begin to say. She was still trying to formulate some kind of response when he moved back slightly, presumably so that he could check for himself.

'I think so,' she said quickly, getting a grip on her wits. She even managed to ease back a little herself, although she didn't actually let go until she'd put a little weight on her ankle to test it.

There didn't appear to be any damage but she decided not to rush it.

'I'm in better shape than the car, anyway.'

He continued to look at her, not with the deferential respect she was used to, but in a way that made her feel exposed, vulnerable and, belatedly, she let go of his jacket, straightened the spectacles that had slipped sideways.

'It was d-dark,' she stuttered—*stuttered?* 'And when I backed into the gate there was a bit more of a d-drop than I expected.' Then, realising how feeble that sounded, 'Quite a lot more of a drop, actually. This field entrance is very badly maintained,' she added, doing her best to distance herself from the scent of leather warmed by a man's body. From the feel of his chest beneath it, his solid shoulders. The touch of strong hands.

And in the process managed to sound like a rather pompous and disapproving dowager duchess.

'Good enough for a tractor,' he replied, dropping those capable hands and taking a step back. Leaving a cold space between them. 'The farmer isn't in the business of providing turning places for women who can't read a map.'

'I…' On the point of saying that she hadn't looked at a map, she thought better of it. He already thought she was a fool and there was nothing to be gained from confirming his first impression. 'No. Well…' She'd have taken a step back herself if she hadn't been afraid her foot would find another rut and this time do some real damage. 'I banged the underside of the car on something as I went down. When I tried to drive away it made a terrible noise and…' She shrugged.

'And what?' he persisted.

'And nothing,' she snapped. Good grief, did he want it spelling out in words of one syllable? 'It wasn't going anywhere.' Then, rubbing her hands over her sleeves, 'Can you fix it?'

'Not here.'

'Oh.'

'Come on,' he said and, apparently taking heed of her comments about the state of the ground, he took her arm and supported her back onto the safety of the tarmac before opening the rear door of the truck's cab. 'You'd better get out of harm's way while we load her up.'

As the courtesy light came on, bathing them both in light, Annie saw more of him. The brushed leather bomber jacket topping long legs clad not, as she'd expected, in overalls, but a pair of well-cut light-coloured trousers. And, instead of work boots, he was wearing expensive-looking loafers. Clearly, George Saxon hadn't had the slightest intention of doing anything at the side of the road.

Her face must have betrayed exactly what she was thinking because he waved his torch over a tall but slight figure in dark overalls who was already attaching a line to her car.

'She's the mechanic,' he said with a sardonic edge to his voice. His face, all dark shadows as the powerful overhead light swung in the darkness, matched his tone perfectly. 'I'm just along for the ride.'

She? Annie thought as, looking behind her, he called out, 'How are you doing back there?'

'Two minutes…'

The voice was indeed that of a girl. Young and more than a little breathless and Annie, glancing back as she reached for the grab rail to haul herself up into the cab, could see that she was struggling.

'I think she could do with some help,' she said.

George regarded this tiresome female who'd been wished on him by his daughter with irritation.

'I'm just the driver,' he said. Then, offering her the torch, 'But don't let me stop you from pitching in and giving her a hand.'

'It's okay,' Xandra called before she could take it from him. 'I've got it.'

He shrugged. 'It seems you were worrying about nothing.'

'Are you sure?' she asked, calling back to Xandra while never taking her eyes off him. It was a look that reminded him of Miss Henderson, a teacher who had been able to quell a class of unruly kids with a glance. Maybe it was the woolly hat and horn-rimmed glasses.

Although he had to admit that Miss Henderson had lacked the fine bone structure and, all chalk and old books, had never smelt anywhere near as good.

'I'm done,' Xandra called.

'Happy?' he enquired.

The woman held the look for one long moment before she gave him a cool nod and climbed up into the cab, leaving him to close the door behind her as if she were royalty.

'Your servant, ma'am,' he muttered as he went back to see how Xandra was doing.

'Why on earth did you say that to her?' she hissed as he checked the coupling.

He wasn't entirely sure. Other than the fact that Miss Henderson was the only woman he'd ever known who could cut his cocky ten-year-old self down to size with a glance.

'Let's go,' he said, pretending he hadn't heard.

Back in the cab, he started the engine and began to winch the car up onto the trailer but, when he glanced up to check the road, his passenger's eyes, huge behind the lenses, seemed to fill the rear-view mirror.

'Can we drop you somewhere?' he asked as Xandra climbed in beside him. Eager to be rid of her so that he could drop the car off at Longbourne Motors.

That took the starch right out of her look.

'What? No... I can't go on without my car...'

'It's not going anywhere tonight. You don't live locally?' he asked.

'No. I'm... I'm on holiday. Touring.'

'On your own? In December?'

'Is there something wrong with that?'

A whole lot, in his opinion, but it was none of his business. 'Whatever turns you on,' he said, 'although Maybridge in winter wouldn't be my idea of a good time.'

'Lots of people come for the Christmas market,' Xandra said. 'It's this weekend. I'm going.'

All this and Christmas too. How much worse could it get? he thought before turning to Xandra and saying, 'You aren't going anywhere. You're grounded.' Then, without looking in the mirror, he said, 'Where are you staying tonight?'

'I'm not booked in anywhere. I was heading for the motel on the ring road.'

'We'd have to go all the way to the motorway roundabout to get there from here,' Xandra said before he could say a word, no doubt guessing his intention of dropping the car off at Longbourne Motors. 'Much easier to run the lady back to the motel through the village once we have a better idea of how long it will take to fix her car.'

She didn't wait for an answer, instead turning to introduce herself to their passenger. 'I'm sorry, I'm Xandra Saxon,' she said, but she was safe enough. This wasn't an argument he planned on having in front of a stranger.

Annie relaxed a little as George Saxon took his eyes off her and smiled at the girl beside him, who was turning into something of an ally.

'Hello, Xandra. I'm R-Ro...'

The word began to roll off her tongue before she remembered that she wasn't Rose Napier.

'Ro-o-owland,' she stuttered out, grabbing for the first name that came into her head. Nanny Rowland... 'Annie Rowland,' she said, more confidently.

Lydia had suggested she borrow her name but she'd decided that it would be safer to stick with something familiar. Annie had been her mother's pet name for her but, since her grandfather disapproved of it, no one other than members of the household staff who'd known her since her mother was alive had ever used it. In the stress of the moment, though, the practised response had gone clean out of her head and she'd slipped into her standard introduction.

'Ro-o-owland?' George Saxon, repeating the name with every nuance of hesitation, looked up at the rear-view mirror and held her gaze.

'Annie will do just fine,' she said, then, realising that man and girl had the same name, she turned to Xandra. 'You're related?'

'Not so's you'd notice,' she replied in that throwaway, couldn't-care-less manner that the young used when something was truly, desperately important. 'My mother has made a career of getting married. George was the first in line, with a shotgun to his back if the date on my birth certificate is anything—'

'Buckle up, Xandra,' he said, cutting her off.

He was her father? But she wasn't, it would appear, daddy's little girl if the tension between them was anything to judge by.

But what did she know about the relationship between father and daughter? All she remembered was the joy of her father's presence, feeling safe in his arms. If he'd lived would she have been a difficult teen?

The one thing she wouldn't have been was isolated, wrapped in cotton wool by a grandfather afraid for her safety. She'd have gone to school, mixed with girls—and boys—her own age. Would have fallen in and out of love without the eyes of the entire country on her. Would never have stepped into the spotlight only to discover, too late, that she was unable to escape its glare.

'Are you warm enough back there?' George Saxon asked.

'Yes. Thank you.'

The heater was efficient and despite his lack of charm, he hadn't fumbled when she'd fallen into his arms. On the contrary. He'd been a rock and she felt safe enough in the back of his truck. A lot safer than she'd felt in his arms. But of course this was her natural place in the world. Sitting in the back with some man up front in the driving seat. In control.

Everything she'd hoped to escape from, she reminded herself, her gaze fixed on the man who was in control at the moment. Or at least the back of his head.

Over the years she had become something of a connoisseur of the back of the male head. The masculine neck. All those chauffeurs, bodyguards...

George Saxon's neck would stand comparison with the best, she decided. Strong, straight with thick dark hair expertly cut to exactly the right length. His shoulders, encased in the soft tan leather of his jacket, would take some beating too. It was a pity his manners didn't match them.

Or was she missing the point?

Rupert's perfect manners made her teeth ache to say or do something utterly outrageous just to get a reaction, but George Saxon's hands, like his eyes, had been anything but polite.

They'd been assured, confident, brazen even. She could still feel the imprint of his thumbs against her breasts where his hands had gripped her as she'd fallen; none of that Dresden shepherdess nonsense for him. And his insolence as he'd offered her the torch had sent an elemental shiver of awareness running up her spine that had precious little to do with the cold that had seeped deep into her bones.

He might not be a gentleman, but he was real—dangerously so—and, whatever else he made her feel, it certainly wasn't desperation.

Annie didn't have time to dwell on what exactly he did make her feel before he swung the truck off the road and turned onto the forecourt of a large garage with a sign across the workshop that read, George Saxon and Son.

Faded and peeling, neglected, it didn't match the man, she thought as he backed up to one of the bays. He might be a little short on charm but he had an animal vitality that sent a charge of awareness running through her.

Xandra jumped down and opened the doors and then, once he'd backed her car in, she uncoupled it, he said, 'There's a customer waiting room at the far end. You'll find a machine for drinks.' Dismissed, she climbed down from the truck and walked away. 'Annie!'

She stopped. It was, she discovered, easy to be charming when everyone treated you with respect but she had to take a deep breath before she turned, very carefully, to face him.

'Mr Saxon?' she responded politely.

'Shut the damn door!'

She blinked.

No one had ever raised their voice to her. Spoken to her in that way.

'In your own time,' he said when she didn't move.

Used to having doors opened for her, stepping out of a car without so much as a backward glance, she hadn't even thought about it.

She wanted to be ordinary, she reminded herself. To be treated like an ordinary woman. Clearly, it was going to be an education.

She walked back, closed the door, but if she'd expected the courtesy of a thank you she would have been disappointed.

Always a fast learner, she hadn't held her breath.

'Take no notice of George,' Xandra said as he drove away to park the truck. 'He doesn't want to be here so he's taking it out on you.'

'Doesn't…? Why not? Isn't he the "and Son"?'

She laughed, but not with any real mirth. 'Wrong generation. The "and Son" above the garage is my granddad but he's in hospital. A heart attack.'

'I'm sorry to hear that. How is he?'

'Not well enough to run the garage until I can take over,' she said. Then, blinking back something that looked very much like a tear, she shrugged, lifted her head. 'Sorry. Family business.' She flicked a switch that activated the hoist. 'I'll take a look at your car.'

Annie, confused by the tensions, wishing she could do something too, but realising that she'd been dismissed—and that was new, as well—said, 'Your father mentioned a waiting room?'

'Oh, for goodness' sake. It'll be freezing in there and the drinks machine hasn't worked in ages.' Xandra fished a key out of her pocket. 'Go inside where it's warm,' she said, handing it to her. 'Make yourself at home. There's tea and coffee by the kettle, milk in the fridge.' Xandra watched the car as it rose slowly above them, then, realising that she hadn't moved, said, 'Don't worry. It won't take long to find the problem.'

'Are you quite sure?' she asked.

'I may be young but I know what I'm doing.'

'Yes...' Well, maybe. 'I meant about letting myself in.'

'Gran would invite you in herself if she were here,' she said as her father rejoined them.

In the bright strip light his face had lost the dangerous shadows, but it still had a raw quality. There was no softness to mitigate hard bone other than a full lower lip that oozed sensuality and only served to increase her sense of danger.

'You shouldn't be in here,' he said.

'I'm going...' She cleared her throat. 'Can I make something for either of you?' she offered.

He frowned.

She lifted her hand and dangled the door key. 'Tea? Coffee?'

For a moment she thought he was going to tell her to stay on her own side of the counter—maybe she was giving him the opportunity—but after a moment he shrugged and said, 'Coffee. If there is any.'

'Xandra?'

'Whatever,' she said, as she ducked beneath the hoist, clearly more interested in the car than in anything she had to say and Annie walked quickly across the yard, through a gate and up a well-lit path to the rear of a long, low stone-built house and let herself in through the back door.

The mud room was little more than a repository for boots and working clothes, a place to wash off the workplace dirt, but as she walked into the kitchen she was wrapped in the heat being belted out by an ancient solid fuel stove.

Now this was familiar, she thought, relaxing as she crossed to the sink, filled the kettle and set it on the hob to boil.

This room, so much more than a kitchen, was typical of the farmhouses at King's Lacey, her grandfather's Warwickshire estate.

Her last memory of her father was being taken to visit

the tenants before he'd gone away for the last time. She'd been given brightly coloured fizzy pop and mince pies while he'd talked to people he'd known since his boyhood, asking about their children and grandchildren, discussing the price of feedstuff, grain. She'd played with kittens, fed the chickens, been given fresh eggs to take home for her tea. Been a child.

She ran her hand over the large, scrubbed-top table, looked at the wide dresser, laden with crockery and piled up with paperwork. Blinked back the tear that caught her by surprise before turning to a couple of Morris armchairs, the leather seats scuffed and worn, the wooden arms rubbed with wear, one of them occupied by a large ginger cat.

A rack filled with copies of motoring magazines stood beside one, a bag stuffed with knitting beside the other. There was a dog basket by the Aga, but no sign of its owner.

She let the cat sniff her fingers before rubbing it behind the ear, starting up a deep purr. Comfortable, it was the complete opposite of the state-of-the-art kitchen in her London home. Caught in a nineteen-fifties time warp, the only concession to modernity here was a large refrigerator, its cream enamel surface chipped with age, and a small television set tucked away on a shelf unit built beside the chimney breast.

The old butler's sink, filled with dishes that were no doubt waiting for Xandra's attention—George Saxon didn't look the kind of man who was familiar with a dish mop—suggested that the age of the dishwasher had not yet reached the Saxon household.

She didn't have a lot of time to spare for basic household chores these days, but there had been a time, long ago, when she had been allowed to stand on a chair and wash dishes, help cook when she was making cakes and, even now, once in a while, when they were in the country, she escaped to the comfort of her childhood kitchen, although only at night, when the staff were gone.

She wasn't a child any more and her presence was an intrusion on their space.

Here, though, she was no one and she peeled off the woolly hat and fluffed up her short hair, enjoying the lightness of it. Then she hung her padded jacket on one of the pegs in the mud room before hunting out a pair of rubber gloves and pitching in.

Washing up was as ordinary as it got and she was grinning by the time she'd cleared the decks. It wasn't what she'd imagined she'd be doing this evening, but it certainly fulfilled the parameters of the adventure.

By the time she heard the back door open, the dishes were draining on the rack above the sink and she'd made a large pot of tea for herself and Xandra, and a cup of instant coffee for George.

'Oh…' Xandra came to an abrupt halt at the kitchen door as she saw the table on which she was laying out cups and saucers. 'I usually just bung a teabag in a mug,' she said. Then, glancing guiltily at the sink, her eyes widened further. 'You've done the washing-up…'

'Well, you did tell me to make myself at home,' Annie said, deadpan.

It took Xandra a moment but then she grinned. 'You're a brick. I *was* going to do it before Gran got home.'

A brick? No one had ever called her that before.

'Don't worry about it,' she replied, pouring tea while Xandra washed her hands at the sink. 'Your gran is at the hospital with your grandfather, I imagine?'

Before Xandra could answer, George Saxon followed her into the kitchen, bringing with him a metallic blast of cold air.

He came to an abrupt halt, staring at her for a moment. Or, rather, she thought, her hair, and she belatedly wished she'd kept her hat on, but it was too late for that.

'Has she told you?' he demanded, finally tearing his gaze away from what she knew must look an absolute fright.

'Told me what?' she asked him.

'That you've broken your crankshaft.'

'No,' she said, swiftly tiring of the novelty of his rudeness. A gentleman would have ignored the fact that she was having a seriously bad hair day rather than staring at the disaster in undisguised horror. 'I gave my ankle a bit of a jolt in that pothole but, unless things have changed since I studied anatomy, I don't believe that I have a crankshaft.'

Xandra snorted tea down her nose as she laughed, earning herself a quelling look from her father.

'You've broken the crankshaft that drives the wheels of your car,' he said heavily, quashing any thought she might have of joining in. 'It'll have to be replaced.'

'If I knew what a crankshaft was,' she replied, 'I suspect that I'd be worried. How long will it take?'

He shrugged. 'I'll have to ring around in the morning and see if there's anyone who can deal with it as an emergency.'

Annie heard what he said but even when she ran through it again it still made no sense.

'Why?' she asked finally.

He had the nerve to turn a pair of slate-grey eyes on her and regard her as if her wits had gone begging.

'I assume you want it repaired?'

'Of course I want it repaired. That's why I called you. You're a garage. You fix cars. So fix it.'

'I'm sorry but that's impossible.'

'You don't sound sorry.'

'He isn't. While Granddad's lying helpless in hospital he's going to shut down a garage that's been in the family for nearly a hundred years.'

'Are you?' she asked, keeping her gaze fixed firmly on him. 'That doesn't sound very sporting.'

He looked right back and she could see a pale fan of lines around his eyes that in anyone else she'd have thought were laughter lines.

'He flew all the way from California for that very purpose,' his daughter said when he didn't bother to answer.

'California?' Well, that certainly explained the lines around his eyes. Screwing them up against the sun rather than an excess of good humour. 'How interesting. What do you do in California, Mr Saxon?'

Her life consisted of asking polite questions, drawing people out of their shell, showing an interest. She had responded with her 'Lady Rose' voice and she'd have liked to pretend that this was merely habit rather than genuine interest, but that would be a big fat fib. There was something about George Saxon that aroused a lot more than polite interest in her maidenly breast.

His raised eyebrow suggested that what he did in the US was none of her business and he was undoubtedly right, but his daughter was happy to fill the gap.

'According to my mother,' she said, 'George is a beach bum.'

At this point 'Lady Rose' would have smiled politely and moved on. Annie didn't have to do that.

'Is your mother right?' she asked.

'He doesn't go to work unless he feels like it. Lives on the beach. If it looks like a duck and walks like a duck…'

She was looking at George, talking to him, but the replies kept coming from his daughter, stage left, and Annie shook her head just once, lifted a hand to silence the girl, waiting for him to answer her question.

CHAPTER THREE

'I'M AFRAID it's your bad luck that my daughter answered your call,' George replied, not bothering to either confirm or deny it. 'If I'd got to the phone first I'd have told you to ring someone else.'

'I see. So why didn't you simply call another garage and arrange for them to pick me up?' Annie asked, genuinely puzzled.

'It would have taken too long and, since you were on your own...' He let it go.

She didn't.

'Oh, I *see*. You're a gentleman beach bum?'

'Don't count on it,' he replied.

No. She wouldn't do that, but he appeared to have a conscience and she could work with that.

She'd had years of experience in parting millionaires from their money in a good cause and this seemed like a very good moment to put what she'd learned to use on her own behalf.

'It's a pity your concern doesn't stretch as far as fixing my car.' Since his only response was to remove his jacket and hang it over the back of a chair, the clearest statement that he was going nowhere, she continued. 'So, George...' use his name, imply that they were friends '...having brought me here under false pretences, what do you suggest I do now?'

'I suggest you finish your tea, Annie…' and the way he emphasized her name suggested he knew exactly what game she was playing '…then I suggest you call a taxi.'

Well, that didn't go as well as she'd hoped.

'I thought the deal was that you were going to run me there,' she reminded him.

'It's been a long day. You'll find a directory by the phone. It's through there. In the hall,' he added, just in case she was labouring under the misapprehension that he would do it for her. Then, having glanced at the cup of instant coffee and the delicate china cups she'd laid out, he took a large mug—one that *she'd* just washed—from the rack over the sink and filled it with tea.

Annie had been raised to be a lady and her first reaction, even under these trying circumstances, was to apologise for being a nuisance.

There had been a moment, right after that lorry had borne down on her out of the dark and she'd thought her last moment had come, when the temptation to accept defeat had very nearly got the better of her.

Shivering with shock at her close brush with eternity as much as the cold, it would have been so easy to put in the call that would bring a chauffeur-driven limousine to pick her up, return her home with nothing but a very bad haircut and a lecture on irresponsibility from her grandfather to show for her adventure.

But she'd wanted reality and that meant dealing with the rough as well as the smooth. Breaking down on a dark country road was no fun, but Lydia wouldn't have been able to walk away, leave someone else to pick up the pieces. She'd have to deal with the mechanic who'd responded to her call, no matter how unwillingly. How lacking in the ethos of customer service.

Lydia, she was absolutely certain, wouldn't apologise to him for expecting him to do his job, but demand he got on with it.

She could do no less.

'I'm sorry,' she began, but she wasn't apologising for being a nuisance. Far from it. Instead, she picked up her tea and polite as you please, went on. 'I'm afraid that is quite unacceptable. When you responded to my call you entered into a contract and I insist that you honour it.'

George Saxon paused in the act of spooning sugar into his tea and glanced up at her from beneath a lick of dark hair that had slid across his forehead.

'Is that right?' he asked.

He didn't sound particularly impressed.

'Under the terms of the Goods and Services Act,' she added, with the poise of a woman for whom addressing a room full of strangers was an everyday occurrence, 'nineteen eighty-three.' The Act was real enough, even if she'd made up the date. The trick was to look as if you knew what you were talking about and a date—even if it was the first one that came into her head—added veracity to even the most outrageous statement.

This time he did smile and deep creases bracketed his face, his mouth, fanned out around those slate eyes. Maybe not just the sun, then...

'You just made that up, Annie Rowland,' he said, calling her bluff.

She pushed up the spectacles that kept sliding down her nose and smiled right back.

'I'll just wait here while you go to the local library and check,' she said, lowering herself into the unoccupied Morris chair. 'Unless you have a copy?' Balancing the saucer in one hand, she used the other to pick up her tea and sip it. 'Although, since you're clearly unfamiliar with the legislation, I'm assuming that you don't.'

'The library is closed until tomorrow morning,' he pointed out.

'They don't have late-night opening? How inconvenient

for you. Never mind, I can wait.' Then added, 'Or you could just save time and fix my car.'

George had known the minute Annie Ro-o-owland had blundered into him, falling into his arms as if she was made to fit, that he was in trouble. Then she'd looked at him through the rear-view mirror of the truck with those big blue eyes and he'd been certain of it. And here, in the light of his mother's kitchen, they had double the impact.

They were not just large, but were the mesmerizing colour of a bluebell wood in April, framed by long dark lashes and perfectly groomed brows that were totally at odds with that appalling haircut. At odds with those horrible spectacles which continually slipped down her nose as if they were too big for her face...

As he stared at her, the certainty that he'd seen her somewhere before tugging at his memory, she used one finger to push them back up and he knew without doubt that they were nothing more than a screen for her to hide behind.

Everything about her was wrong.

Her car, bottom of range even when new, was well past its best, her hair was a nightmare and her clothes were chain-store basics but her scent, so faint that he knew she'd sprayed it on warm skin hours ago, probably after her morning shower, was the real one-thousand-dollar-an-ounce deal.

And then there was her voice.

No one spoke like that unless they were born to it. Not even twenty-five thousand pounds a year at Dower House could buy that true-blue aristocratic accent, a fact he knew to his cost.

He stirred his tea, took a sip, making her wait while he thought about his next move.

'I'll organise a rental for you while it's being fixed,' he offered finally. Experience had taught him that, where women were concerned, money was the easiest way to make a problem go away. But first he'd see how far being helpful would get him. 'If that would make things easier for you?'

She carefully replaced the delicate bone china cup on its saucer. 'I'm sorry, George. I'm afraid that's out of the question.'

It was like a chess game, he thought. Move and countermove. And everything about her—the voice, the poise—suggested that she was used to playing the Queen.

Tough. He wasn't about to be her pawn. He might be lumbered with Mike Jackson's Bentley—he couldn't offload a specialist job like that at short notice as his father well knew—but he wasn't about to take on something that any reasonably competent mechanic could handle.

Maybe if she took off her glasses…

'As a gesture of goodwill, recognising that you have been put to unnecessary inconvenience,' he said, catching himself—this was not the moment to allow himself to be distracted by a pair of blue eyes, pale flawless skin, scent that aroused an instant go-to-hell response. He didn't do 'instant'. It would have to be money. 'I would be prepared to pay any reasonable out-of-pocket expenses.'

Check.

He didn't care how much it cost to get her and her eyes out of the garage, out of his mother's kitchen, out of his hair. Just as long as she went.

'That's a most generous offer,' she replied. 'Unfortunately, I can't accept. The problem isn't money, you see, but my driving licence.'

'Oh?' Then, 'You do *have* a valid licence?'

If she was driving without one all bets were off. He could ground his daughter for her reckless behaviour—maybe—but Annie Rowland would be out of here faster than he could call the police.

But she wasn't in the least bit put out by his suggestion that she was breaking the law.

'I do have a driving licence,' she replied, cool as you like. 'And, in case you're wondering, it's as clean as the day it was issued. But I'm afraid I left it at home. In my other bag.' She shrugged. 'You know how it is.' Then, looking at him as if she'd only just noticed that he was a man, she smiled and said, 'Oh, no. I don't suppose you do. All a man has to do is pick up his wallet and he has everything he needs right there in his jacket pocket.'

He refused to indulge the little niggle that wanted to know whose wallet, what man…

'And where, exactly, is home?' he asked, trying not to look at her hand and failing. She wasn't wearing a ring but that meant nothing.

'London.'

'London is a big place.'

'Yes,' she agreed. 'It is.' Then, without indulging his curiosity about which part of London, 'You must know that no one will rent me a car without it. My licence.'

Unfortunately, he did.

Checkmate.

'Oh, for goodness' sake!' Xandra, who'd been watching this exchange with growing impatience, said, 'If you won't fix Annie's car, I'll do it myself.' She put down her cup and headed for the door. 'I'll make a start right now.'

'Shouldn't you be thinking about your grandmother?' he snapped before she reached it. 'I'm sure she'd appreciate a hot meal when she gets back from the hospital. Or are you so lost to selfishness that you expect her to cook for you?'

'She doesn't…' Then, unexpectedly curbing her tongue, she said, 'I'm not the selfish one around here.'

Annie, aware that in this battle of wits Xandra was her ally, cleared her throat. 'Why don't I get supper?' she offered.

They both turned to stare at her.

'Why would you do that?' George Saxon demanded.

'Because I want my car fixed?'

'You won't get a better offer,' Xandra declared, leaping in before her father could turn down her somewhat rash offer.

'My limit is baked beans on toast. I'm sure Annie can do better than that,' she said, throwing a pleading glance in her direction.

'Can you?' he demanded.

'Do better than baked beans on toast?' she repeated. 'Actually, that won't be…' She broke off, distracted by the wild signals Xandra was making behind her father's back. As he turned to see what had caught her attention she went on. 'Difficult. Not at all.'

He gave her a long look through narrowed eyes, clearly aware that he'd missed something. Then continued to look at her as if there was something about her that bothered him.

She knew just how he felt.

The way he looked at her bothered her to bits, she thought, using her forefinger to push the 'prop' spectacles up her nose. They would keep sliding down, making it easier to look over them than through them, which made wearing them utterly pointless.

'How long do you think it'll take?' she asked, not sure who she was attempting to distract. George or herself.

He continued to stare for perhaps another ten seconds—clearly not a man to be easily distracted—before he shrugged and said, 'It depends what else we find. Your car is not exactly in the first flush. Once something major happens it tends to have a knock-on effect. You're touring, you say?'

She nodded. 'That was the plan. Shropshire, Cheshire, maybe. A little sightseeing. A little shopping.'

'There aren't enough sights, enough shops in London?' he enquired, an edge to his voice that suggested he wasn't entirely convinced.

'Oh, well…' She matched his shrug and raised him a smile. 'You know what they say about a change.'

'Being as good as a rest?' He sounded doubtful. 'This isn't a great time of year to break down, especially if you're stranded miles from anywhere,' he pointed out.

He didn't bother to match her smile.

'It's never a good time for that, George.'

'It's a lot less dangerous when the days are long and the nights warm,' he said, leaving her to imagine what it would be like if she broke down way out in the country, in the dark, with the temperature below freezing. Then, having got that off his chest, 'Are you in a hurry to be anywhere in particular?'

He sounded hopeful.

'Well, no. That's the joy of touring, isn't it? There's no fixed agenda. And now Xandra has told me about the Christmas market in Maybridge this weekend…' she gave another little shrug, mainly because she was certain it would annoy him '…well, I wouldn't want to miss that.' It was a new experience. Annoying a man. One she could grow to enjoy and, taking full advantage of this opportunity, she mentally crossed her fingers and added, 'Ho, ho, ho…'

That earned her another snort—muffled this time—from Xandra, who got a look to singe her ears from her father before he turned back to her and, ignoring her attempt at levity, asked, 'Have you spoken to your insurance company?'

'Why would I do that?'

'Because you've had an accident?'

'Oh. Yes.' The prospect of contacting her insurance company and what that would mean took all the fun out of winding up George Saxon. 'I suppose I have. It never occurred to me…'

'No?' He gave her another of those thoughtful looks. 'Maybe you should do it now although, bearing in mind the age of the car and the likely cost of repairs, their loss adjuster will probably decide to simply write it off.'

'What? They can't do that!'

'I think you'll find they can.'

'Only if I make a claim.'

He didn't answer. And this time Xandra didn't leap in to defend her.

'I *am* insured,' she said hurriedly, before George asked the question that was clearly foremost in his mind.

She didn't blame him. First she wasn't able to produce her licence and now she didn't want her insurance company involved. Anyone with two brain cells to rub together would believe she had something to hide.

Obviously not whatever scenario was going through his mind right now, but something. And they'd be right to be suspicious.

But she was insured.

She'd checked that Lydia's car was covered by her own insurance policy but now, faced with the reality of accidental damage, she realised that it wasn't that simple. If, on the day she made a claim for an accident in Maybridge, the entire world knew she was flying to Bab el Sama—and they would, because she'd made absolutely sure that the press knew where she was going; she wanted them there, establishing her alibi by snatching shots of 'her' walking on the beach—well, that really would put the cat among the pigeons.

She couldn't tell him that, of course, but she was going to have to tell him something and the longer she delayed, the less likely it was that he would believe her. From being in a position of power, Annie now felt at a distinct disadvantage in the low chair and, putting down her cup, she stood up so that she could look him in the eye.

'You needn't worry that I won't pay you. I have money.' And, determined to establish her financial probity at least, she tugged at the neck of the V-neck sweater she was wearing, reached down inside her shirt and fished a wad of fifty-pound notes from one cup of her bra and placed it on the table.

'Whoa!' Xandra said.

'Will a thousand pounds cover it?' she asked, repeating the performance on the other side before looking up to discover that George was staring at her.

'Go and check the stores to see what spares we have in stock, Xandra,' he said, not taking his eyes off her.

His daughter opened her mouth to protest, then, clearly thinking better of it, stomped out, banging the back door as she went.

For a moment the silence rang in her ears. Then, with a gesture at the pile of banknotes, George said, 'Where did that come from?'

Realising she'd just made things ten times worse, that she was going to have to tell him at least some version of the truth, Annie said, 'It's mine.' He didn't move a muscle. 'Truly. I don't want to use credit cards for the same reason I can't call my insurance company.'

'And why is that?' he asked, stony-faced as a statue.

'It's difficult…'

'No licence, no insurance and a pile of hard cash? I'll say it's difficult. What exactly is your problem, Annie?' he asked. 'Who are you running away from? The police?'

'No! It's nothing like that. It's…' Oh, help… 'It's personal.'

He frowned. 'Are you telling me that it's a domestic?'

Was he asking her if she was running from an abusive husband?

'You're not wearing a ring,' he pointed out, forestalling the temptation to grab such a perfect cover story.

'No. I'm not married.'

'A partner, then. So why all the subterfuge?' he said, picking up one of the wads of banknotes, flicking the edge with his thumb. 'And where did this come from?'

'My parents left me some money. I daren't use credit cards—'

'Or claim on your motor insurance.'

She nodded.

'Is he violent?'

'No!'

'But unwilling to let you go.'

She swallowed and he accepted that as an affirmative. This was going better than she'd hoped.

'How will he trace you? You understand that I have to think about Xandra. And my mother.'

'There's a security firm he uses, but they think I've left the country. As long as I don't do anything to attract attention, they won't find me.'

'I hope you didn't leave your passport behind.'

'No. The clothes I'm wearing, the car, belong to the friend who helped me get away,' she said before he asked her why her 'partner' was in the habit of hiring a security firm to keep tabs on her. 'You can understand why I feel so bad about what's happened to the car. Will you be able to fix it?'

He looked at her for a long time before shaking his head. 'I knew you were trouble from the first moment I set eyes on you,' he said, 'and I know I'm going to regret this, but I'll see if your car is salvageable so I can get you on your way. I just hope I don't live to see the name Annie Rowland linked with mine in the headlines.'

'That won't happen,' she promised.

'Of course it won't. The only thing I am sure of where you're concerned is that your name isn't Rowland.'

'It *is* Annie,' she said, glad for some reason that she couldn't begin to fathom that she had chosen to use her own best name.

'Then let's leave it at that,' he said, putting down the mug as he pushed himself away from the table. 'But whatever you plan on cooking for dinner, Annie, had better be worth all the trouble you're causing.'

'I can guarantee that it'll be better than beans on toast,' she promised. 'Thank you for trusting me, George.'

'Who said I trusted you?' He looked at her as if he was going to say more, but let it go. 'Save your thanks and put that out of sight,' he said, pointing at the pile of notes lying on the kitchen table. Then, as she made a move to stuff it back in her bra, 'No! I didn't mean…' He took a deep breath. 'Just wait until I've gone.'

She blushed furiously. 'Sorry.'

'So am I,' he muttered as he left the kitchen. 'So am I.'

CHAPTER FOUR

ANNIE hadn't been aware of holding her breath, but the minute the back door closed she covered her hot cheeks with her hands and let out something very close to a, 'Whew.'

That had been intense.

She appeared to have got away with it, though. For now, at any rate. And she hadn't told any outright lies, just left George to answer his own questions. A bit of a grey area, no doubt, but she was sure he'd rather not know the truth and twenty-four hours from now she'd be miles away from Maybridge with no harm done.

The cat leapt from the chair as she crossed to the fridge, chirruping hopefully as it nuzzled its head against her ankle.

'Hello, puss. Are you hungry too?'

She poured a little milk into a bowl, then sat back on her heels, watching the cat lap it up.

'Trouble,' she said, grinning in spite of everything that had happened. 'He said I was trouble. Do you know, puss, that's the very first time anyone has ever looked at me and thought "trouble".' The cat looked up, milk clinging to its muzzle, and responded with a purr. 'I know,' Annie said. 'It is immensely cheering. Almost worth wrecking Lydia's car for.' Then, since the cat made a very good listener, 'Tell me, would you describe George Saxon as a likely beach bum?'

The cat, stretching out its tongue to lick the last drop from its whiskers, appeared to shake its head.

'No, I didn't think so, either.'

Surely 'laid-back' was the very definition of beach-bum-hood, while George Saxon was, without doubt, the most intense man she'd ever met.

With Xandra on his case, she suspected, he had quite a lot to be intense about, although if he really was an absentee father he undoubtedly deserved it. And what was all that about closing down the garage? How could he do that while his own father was in hospital? It was utterly appalling—and a private family matter that was absolutely none of her business, she reminded herself.

She just wanted to get the car fixed and get back on the road. Take in the sights, go shopping unrecognised. But, despite Xandra's build-up and her assurance that she wouldn't miss it, she'd be giving the Maybridge Christmas market a wide berth.

Less ho, ho, ho… More no, no, no…

The thought made her feel oddly guilty. As if she'd some-how let the girl down. Which was stupid. If it hadn't been for Xandra, she would have been picked up by some other mechanic who wouldn't have given her nearly as much grief.

A man without the careless arrogance that was guaranteed to rouse any woman with an ounce of spirit to a reckless response. One who wouldn't have held her in a way that made her feel like a woman instead of a piece of porcelain.

Someone polite, who would not have made uncompli-mentary comments about her driving, but would have promised to deliver her car in full working order the next day because that was on the customer relations script he'd learned on his first day on the job.

In other words, all the things that she wanted to get away from.

Whatever else George was, he certainly didn't follow a

script. And locking horns with a man who didn't know he was supposed to show due deference to the nation's sweetheart was a lot more interesting than being holed up in a budget hotel room with only the television remote for company.

For all his faults, George Saxon did have one thing in his favour—he was the complete opposite of Rupert Devenish, a man who had never rated a single 'whew'. Not from her, anyway.

There was nothing textbook about George.

Okay, so he was tall, with shoulders wide enough to fill a doorway—no doubt like the lines carved into his cheeks, around those penetrating grey eyes, they came from hard use.

And he was dark.

But he wasn't, by any stretch of the imagination, classically handsome. On the contrary, his face had a lived-in quality and there was enough stubble on his chin to suggest a certain laissez-faire attitude to his appearance. He certainly wasn't a man to wait for some woman to pluck him off the 'ideal husband' shelf, she thought. More the kind who, when he saw what he wanted, would act like a caveman.

The thought, which was supposed to make her smile, instead prompted the proverbial ripple down her spine. Something which, until today, she'd foolishly imagined to be no more than a figure of speech.

He was, by any standard, anything but ideal and she had the strongest feeling that her wisest course of action would be to make his day and get out of there, fast.

But, then again, why would she when, for the purposes of this adventure, he could almost have been made to order.

Exciting, annoying, disturbing.

She'd wanted to be disturbed, jolted out of her rut. Wanted to be excited and, maybe, just a little bit reckless.

She swallowed as she considered what being reckless with George Saxon would entail.

He was right. She should definitely leave. As soon as possible. Not because the idea appalled her. On the contrary, it was much too excitingly disturbing, recklessly appealing and she'd call a taxi to take her to the motel.

Just as soon as she'd cooked the hot meal she'd promised them.

Her stomach rumbled at the thought. Lunch had been a very long time ago and she'd been too nervous to eat more than a mouthful of that. Not that she'd eaten much of anything lately, a fact that had been picked up by one of the gossip magazines looking for a new angle. An eating disorder was always good copy.

Now, for the first time in months, she felt genuinely hungry and, leaving the cat to its ablutions, she stood up and returned her attention to the fridge.

It was well stocked with the basics, but it wasn't just the bacon, eggs, cheese and vegetables that were making her hungry. She'd already seen the large homemade meat pie sitting on the middle shelf, gravy oozing gently from the slit in the centre, just waiting to be slipped into the oven.

Presumably it had been made by George's mother before she'd left to visit her husband in the hospital. That Xandra knew it was there was obvious from her earlier performance but, anxious to keep her grandfather's garage functioning, desperate, maybe, to prove herself to her father, she was prepared to take any chance that came her way and she'd grabbed her offer to make dinner for them all with both hands.

Good for her, she thought. If you had a dream you shouldn't let anyone talk you out of it, or stand in your way. You should go for it with all your heart.

Annie put the pie in the oven, then set about the task of peeling potatoes and carrots. It took her a minute or two to get the hang of the peeler, then, as she bent to her task, the annoying glasses slid down her nose and fell into the sink.

She picked them out of the peelings and left them on the draining board while she finished.

Her only problem then was the vexed question of how long it took potatoes to boil. She'd left her handbag in the car, but she'd put her cellphone in her coat pocket after calling for help. She wiped her hands and dug it out to see what she could find on the Web.

The minute she switched it on she got the 'message waiting' icon.

There was a text from Lydia with just a single code word to reassure her that everything had gone exactly according to plan, that she'd reached the airport without problem—or, as she'd put it, being twigged as a 'ringer'.

Even if they hadn't agreed that contact between them should be on an emergency-only basis—you never knew who was tuned into a cellphone frequency—she'd still be in the air so she couldn't call her and tell her everything that had happened, confess to having cut her hair, wrecking her car. Instead, she keyed in the agreed response, confirmation that she, too, was okay, and hit 'send'.

There was, inevitably, a voicemail from her grandfather asking her to call and let him know when she'd touched down safely. Using any excuse to override her insistence that she wanted to be left completely alone while she was away.

'You'll have to call me at King's Lacey,' he said. 'I'm going there tomorrow to start preparations for Christmas.' Piling on yet more guilt. 'And the Boxing Day shoot.'

As if he didn't have a housekeeper, a gamekeeper, a houseful of staff who were perfectly capable of doing all that without him.

'And of course there's the Memorial Service. It will be twenty years this year and I want it to be special. You will be home for that?'

It was the unexpected touch of uncertainty in his voice that finally got to her.

'I'll be there,' she murmured to herself, holding the phone to her chest long after the voicemail had ended.

It was twenty years since her parents had died in a hail of gunfire in the week before Christmas and every year she'd relived that terrible intermingling of grief and celebration that made the season an annual misery.

And worse, much worse, the centuries-old Boxing Day shoot that nothing was allowed to interfere with. Not even that first year. Cancelling it would have been letting her parents' killers win, her grandfather had said when he'd found her hiding beneath the stairs, hands over her ears in terror as the guns had blasted away.

'God help me,' she said again, 'I'll be there.'

Then she straightened, refusing to waste another minute dwelling on it. Having come so close to losing this little bit of freedom, she was absolutely determined to make the most of every moment. Even something as simple, as unusual for her, as cooking dinner. But as she clicked to the Net to surf for cooking times, the sound of something hitting the floor made her jump practically out of her skin.

She spun round and saw George Saxon in the doorway, her bag at his feet.

How long had he been there? How much had he heard?

George hadn't intended to eavesdrop, but when he'd opened the door Annie had been half turned from him, so tense, the cellphone so tight to her ear that she hadn't noticed him and he'd frozen, unable to advance or retreat.

He'd heard her promise to 'be there', but the 'God help me…' that had followed as she'd clutched the phone to her chest had been so deeply felt that any doubts about the kind of trouble she was in vanished as, for a moment, all control had slipped away and she'd looked simply desolate.

At that moment he'd wanted only to reach out to her, hold her. Which was when he'd dropped her bag at his feet.

And she'd visibly jumped.

'I'm sorry,' he said. 'I didn't mean to startle you.' Just shatter the spell that she seemed to be weaving around him.

'You didn't,' she said, a little too fiercely. Then blushed at the lie. 'Well, maybe just a bit.'

She looked down at the cellphone, then crammed it quickly into the back pocket of her jeans. Unlike her clothes or the holdall he'd just brought in from the car, which was definitely from the cheap-and-cheerful, market-stall end of the spectrum, it was the latest in expensive, top-end technology. He had one exactly like it himself and knew how much it had cost. And he wondered what kind of wardrobe she'd left behind in London, along with her driving licence, when she'd made her bid for freedom.

A woman whose partner could afford to employ a security company to keep an eye on her would be dressed from her skin up in designer labels. Silk, linen, cashmere. Would wear fine jewels.

What had he done to her to make her run? If not physical, then mental cruelty because she was running away from him, not to someone. His hands bunched into fists at the thought.

'I was just catching up on my messages,' she said.

'Nothing you wanted to hear, by the look of you.' For a moment she stared at him as if she wanted to say something, then shook her head. 'You do know that you can be tracked by your phone signal?' he asked.

Not that it was any of his business, he reminded himself, forcing his hands to relax.

'It was only for a minute. I need to know what's happening.'

Long enough. Who was important enough to her that she'd take the risk? Make that kind of promise?

A child?

No. She'd never have left a child behind.

'Use some of that money you've got stashed away to buy the anonymity of a pay-as-you-go,' he advised abruptly.

'I will,' she said, clearly as anxious as he was to change the subject. Then, lifting her chin, managing a smile, 'I found a pie in the fridge so I've put that in the oven. I hope that's all right?'

'A pie?'

'A meat pie.'

'Ah…'

A tiny crease puckered the space between her beautifully arched brows.

'Is that a good "ah" or a bad "ah"?' she asked. Then, raising her hand to her mouth to display a set of perfectly manicured nails, she said, 'Please don't tell me you're a vegetarian.'

'Why?' he demanded. 'Have you got something against vegetarians?'

'No, but…'

'Relax. You're safe. What you've found is the equivalent of the fatted calf…'

'I'm sorry?'

'For the prodigal son.'

'I'm familiar with the metaphor.' She regarded him intently. 'Just how long is it since you've been home?' she asked.

'A while,' he said.

Which was why his mother, even with his father in hospital, had taken the time to make him one of her special steak-and-mushroom pies, just as she'd been doing ever since he'd gone away on his first school trip. More to avoid his own sense of guilt than tease her, he said, 'Judging by your reaction, I suspect we've both had something of a narrow escape.'

'Escape?' Annie, swiftly recovering from whatever had upset her, placed a hand against her breast in a gesture perfectly calculated to mime shocked surprise and said, 'Are you suggesting that I can't cook, Mr Saxon?'

Despite everything, he found himself grinning at her performance. 'I sensed a lack of conviction in your assurance that you could do better than Xandra.'

'That was no more than simple modesty,' she declared.

'You'll forgive me if I reserve judgement until I've tasted your mashed potatoes.'

'Mashed?' The insouciant air vanished as quickly as it had come. 'Is that another favourite?'

'Food for the gods,' he assured her. 'At least it is the way my mother makes it.'

'Well, I'm not your mother, for which I'm deeply grateful since you appear to be as casual a son as you are a father, but I'll do my best not to disappoint.' Then, as he scowled at her, 'I don't suppose you've any idea how long it takes to boil potatoes?'

Which suggested he'd been right about the narrow escape.

'Sorry. That's not my area of expertise.'

'No?' She lifted those expressive brows, inviting him to tell her what he was an expert in, then, when he didn't oblige, she gave a little shrug and said, 'I don't suppose there's a lot of call for potato mashing on the beach.'

'You know how it is with sand,' he replied, wondering what kind of woman didn't know how to cook something as basic as potatoes.

The kind who'd never had to cook, obviously. Or close car doors behind her.

Who the devil *was* she?

'It gets in everything?' she offered. Then, because there really wasn't anything else to say about potatoes, 'Thanks for bringing in my bag.'

'I didn't make a special journey,' he said and, irritated with himself for getting drawn into conversation, he took a glass from the dresser and crossed to the sink to fill it.

'Thirsty work?' she asked, watching him as he drained it.

'No matter how much water I drink on long-haul flights, I still seem to get dehydrated.'

'Excuse me?'

He glanced back at her as he refilled the glass.

'Are you telling me that you flew from California *today*?' she demanded, clearly horrified.

'Overnight. I slept most of the way,' he assured her. The first-class sky-bed he could afford these days was a very different experience from his early cattle-class flights.

'Even so, you shouldn't be working with machinery. What about Health and Safety?'

'Goods and Services, Health and Safety? What are you, Annie? A lawyer?'

'Just a concerned citizen.'

'Is that so? Well, if you don't tell, I won't,' he replied flippantly, refusing to think about how long it had been since anyone, apart from his mother, had been concerned about him. It was his choice, he reminded himself.

'I'm serious,' she said, not in the least bit amused. 'I wouldn't forgive myself if you were hurt fixing my car. It can wait until tomorrow.'

'You're *that* concerned?' Then, because the thought disturbed him more than he liked, 'Don't worry, I'm only there in a supervisory capacity. Xandra's doing all the hard work.'

'Is that supposed to make me feel better?'

'It's supposed to make you feel grateful,' he said, determined to put an end to the conversation and get out of there. 'Since you're so eager to be on your way.' Then, as he noticed her glasses lying on the draining board, he frowned. 'And actually,' he said thoughtfully as he picked them up and, realising that they were wet and muddy, rinsed them under the tap, 'I'm hoping a taste of the real thing will encourage her to reconsider a career as a motor mechanic and finish school.'

'Always a good plan,' Annie agreed. 'How old is she?'

'Sixteen.'

He picked up a dish cloth and, having dried the frames, began to polish the lenses.

'In that case, she doesn't have much choice in the matter. She can't leave school until she's seventeen.'

'I know that. You know that. Which may go some way to explain why she went to so much trouble to get herself suspended from her boarding school.'

Annie frowned. 'She's at boarding school?'

'Dower House.'

'I see.'

She could sympathise with her father's lack of enthusiasm at her career choice after he'd sent her to one of the most expensive boarding schools in the country. The kind that turned out female captains of industry, politicians, women who changed the world. The school where, two years ago, she'd given the end-of-year address to the girls, had presented the prizes.

She clearly hadn't made that much of an impression on young Xandra Saxon. Or maybe the haircut was worse than she thought.

'Obviously she's not happy there.'

'I wanted the best for her. I live in the States and, as you may have gathered, her mother is easily distracted. It seems that she's on honeymoon at the moment.'

'Her third,' Annie said, remembering what Xandra had said.

'Second. We didn't have one. I was a first-year student with a baby on the way when we got married.'

'That must have been tough,' she said.

'It wasn't much fun for either of us,' he admitted. 'Penny went home to her mother before Xandra was due and she never came back. I don't blame her. When I wasn't studying, I was working every hour just to keep us fed and housed. It wasn't what she'd expected from the son of George Saxon.'

'I'm sorry.'

'So am I.'

Then, because he clearly didn't want to talk about it and she didn't much want to hear about a youthful marriage that appeared never to have had a chance, she said, 'So, what did she do? Xandra. To get herself suspended.'

'She borrowed the head's car and took it for a joyride.'

'Ouch.' Sixteen years old, so she wouldn't have a licence or insurance. That explained a lot. 'Attention-seeking?'

'Without much success. Presumably anticipating something of the sort, Penny had the foresight to switch off her cellphone.'

'Then it's just as well Xandra has you.'

His smile was of the wry, self-deprecating kind. 'I'm the last person she'd have called, Annie. Much as I would have wished it otherwise, I'm little more to my daughter than a signature on a cheque.'

'You think so?'

George held the spectacles up to the light to check, amongst other things, that they were smear-free before looking at Annie.

'I know so. I'm only here because my father had a heart attack,' he said, taking a step towards her and, as she looked up, he slipped her spectacles back on her nose, holding them in place for a moment, his thumbs against the cool skin stretched taut over fine cheekbones.

Her lips parted on a tiny gasp but she didn't protest or pull away from him and for what seemed like an eternity he simply cradled her face.

There was no sound. Nothing moved.

Only the dark centre at the heart of eyes that a man might drown in widened to swallow the dazzling blue. He'd have had to be made of ice to resist such a blatant invitation, but then, according to any number of women he'd known, he was ice to the bone…

'The first rule of wearing a disguise, Annie…' he began, touching his lips briefly to hers to prove, if only to himself, that he was immune.

Discovering, too late, that he was not.

CHAPTER FIVE

ANNIE'S lips were soft, yielding, as they parted on a little gasp of surprise. Not the response of a seductress bent on luring a man to his doom, he thought, more the reaction of a girl being kissed for the first time.

Arousing in a way that no practised kiss could ever be.

And when, slightly breathless, he drew back to look at her, her eyes were closed and the mouth that had tempted him to take such outrageous liberties was smiling as if it had discovered something brand-new.

'The first rule of wearing a disguise,' he tried again, his voice barely audible as he struggled not to kiss her again, 'is never to let it slip, even for a moment.'

It took a moment for his words to get past the haze of desire but then her eyes flew open and he felt the heat beneath his fingertips as colour seared her cheekbones. Whether at the way she'd responded to his touch or at being found out in her deception, he'd have been hard put to say.

'H-how did you know?' she asked, making no effort to put distance between them, which appeared to answer that question. The innocent blushes had to be as fake as her glasses.

'Since you weren't wearing them when you checked your messages, it seemed likely that they were purely for decoration,' he said.

'Decoration?' The beginnings of a smile tugged once more at the corners of her mouth. 'Hardly that.'

'I've seen prettier,' he admitted, struggling not to smile back.

'The wretched things fell into the potato peelings. I put them on the draining board and then forgot all about them.'

As clear an admission of guilt as he'd ever heard.

'You should have tossed them into the bin with the peelings.'

'I doubt they'd have added much to the compost heap.'

'Maybe not, but if you're afraid of being recognised, I'd advise getting yourself a pair that fits properly instead of sliding down your nose.' He waited, hoping that she might tell him the truth this time. 'Maybe go for tinted lenses.'

Something to tone down the distracting blue.

'I bought them on the Internet. I had no idea they came in different sizes.' She gave a little shrug. 'Maybe I should get some little sexy ones with lenses that react to the light.'

'Maybe. I have to tell you, though, that if anyone has put together a photofit of you, you can forget the glasses. It's the hairdo that's the dead giveaway.'

'Oh…' she lifted a hand to her hair in a self-conscious gesture '…no. No danger there.' She pulled a face. 'I cut it myself this morning with a pair of nail scissors.'

Well, yes. Obviously. No woman would walk around with hair like that for a minute longer than she had to.

'I'd have bet on the garden shears,' he said, accepting that she wasn't going to trust him with her secret. Or was, perhaps, protecting him from something he was almost certainly better off not knowing?

Just as he'd be wiser not to imagine how her hair might have looked before she'd hacked it off.

Adding long, creamy-coloured silky hair to the image that was building up inside his head was not helping him drop his hands, take the necessary step back.

'I'd better get back,' he said, forcing himself to do just that.

'Before Xandra, in her enthusiasm, strips your car down to the frame.'

He picked up the glass of water he'd abandoned but at the door he stopped, looked back. Despite a natural poise, a look-him-in-the-eye assurance that was so at odds with her innocent blushes, there was a lack of knowingness in the way she'd responded to his kiss that didn't quite fit with the jealous-partner scenario.

But then, presumably, if she was any kind of con woman, she'd have that down pat.

When the silence, the look, had gone on for too long, he said, 'You might find the answer to the vexed question of how to boil a potato in one of my mother's cook books. They're over there, behind the television.' He didn't bother to check that they were still there. Nothing had been changed in this room in his lifetime. 'And, in case you're interested, I'm partial to a touch of garlic in my mash.'

'Garlic?' She pushed the glasses, already sliding down her nose again, back into place. 'Good choice,' she said. 'Very good for the heart, garlic.'

'Are you suggesting that mine needs help?'

'Actually, I was thinking about your father. Isn't heart disease supposed to be hereditary? Although, now you come to mention it, maybe yours could do with some work in other departments.'

'What makes you think that?' He wasn't arguing with her conclusion, merely interested in her reasoning.

'Well, let me see. Could it be because you're the one with your daughter up to her elbows in axle-grease while you stand back telling her what to do?'

The smile that went with this, reassurance that she was teasing, was no mere token but shone out of her, lighting up her face in a way that could make a man forget that she was too thin. Forget the hair. Forget anything…

'I'm not telling her anything. She wasn't exaggerating when she said she knew what she was doing.'

Her smile became a look of sympathy. 'That must be a worry.'

'My father never forgave me for not wanting to follow him into the business. Given a second chance with Xandra, it's clear that he hasn't made the same mistakes with her that he did with me.'

Or maybe, being a girl, she'd had to beg to be allowed to 'play' cars with her granddad.

He wondered if his old man had seen the irony in that. Probably not. He'd doted on Xandra since the moment she'd been born. Indulged her, as he'd never been indulged. Maybe that was the difference between being a father and a grandfather. There was not the same responsibility to be perfect, do everything right. And getting it wrong.

'She might just love it,' Annie pointed out.

'I'm sure she does, but there's a world of difference between doing something for fun in the school holidays and it being your only option.'

'So if she stayed at school, took her exams, went to university and at the end of it all she still wanted to be a garage mechanic?' she asked.

'If only. She wants to drive rally cars too.' He took a deep breath. 'I don't suppose you have a handy Health and Safety regulation you're prepared to quote on the subject of sixteen-year-olds doing dangerous jobs?'

'I don't have one on the tip of my tongue,' she said, 'but, even if I did, I don't think I'd use it.'

'Not even if I promised to fix your car myself?'

'Not even then. This is something she wants, George. Something she can do. That she believed no one would take away from her.'

'That sounded heartfelt.'

'Yes, well, at her age I had a dream of my own, but I allowed myself to be persuaded against it for what at the time seemed sound reasons. Not that I believe Xandra is going to be the walkover I was. She's nowhere near as eager to please.'

'A daddy's girl, were you?'

She paled, shook her head, but before he could take a step back towards her, say sorry even though he didn't know why, she said, 'You do realise that if you close the garage it will make her all the more determined?'

'It's not an option. No matter how much he fights it, the truth is that my father won't be able to carry on.'

'What about you? This is your chance to prove to your daughter that you're more than just a signature on a cheque. That you really care about what she wants. Or is there a Californian beach with a Californian beach girl stretched out in the sun who you can't wait to get back to?' She didn't wait for an answer but, having planted that little bombshell, said, 'I'll give you a call when dinner's ready, shall I?'

'Do that,' he snapped, turning abruptly and leaving her to it.

Annie didn't move until she heard the outside door close. Only then did she raise her hands to her face, run her fingertips over the warm spots where George Saxon had touched her.

He'd been so close as he'd slipped the glasses on her nose, held them in place, his thumbs against her cheek, fingertips supporting her head. There had been an intimacy about the way he'd looked at her that had warmed her, made her pulse leap, stirred something deep inside her so that when his lips had touched hers it had felt like two pieces of a puzzle finding the perfect fit.

And if he could do that with a look, a touch, a tender kiss, what could he do if…?

She whirled around, refusing to go there.

Instead, she crossed to the corner to root through the small collection of old cookery books before pulling out a heavy black bound book that was reassuringly familiar.

She'd kept all her mother's books—medical textbooks, mostly—and a copy of this basic cookery book had been among them, the inscription on the flyleaf from the foster mother who'd taught her to cook and passed on her own cookery book when she'd left for university.

How much strength of will must it have taken her mother to get to medical school? More than she'd had, she thought, swallowing hard as she opened the book to check the index.

Potatoes…

Potatoes, it seemed, took around twenty minutes to boil, depending on whether they were old or new and, once cooked, should be creamed with a little pepper and marga-rine. Clearly post-war austerity had still been part of life when this book had been published. And a sprinkle of parsley was as exotic as it got back in the days when garlic was con-sidered dangerously foreign.

But, despite the fact that Mrs Saxon's cookery book and fridge appeared to be from the same generation, the large bulb of garlic tucked away in the salad crisper suggested that she, at least, had moved with the times. Or had that been bought specially for the prodigal's homecoming too?

She laid the table, put plates to warm and was energeti-cally mashing butter, milk and finely chopped garlic into the potatoes when she heard the kitchen door open.

'Perfect timing,' she said, concentrating on the job in hand. 'Just enough time to scrub up.' Then, when there was no answer, she turned round. 'Oh!' Not George or Xandra, but a slender middle-aged woman who bore a clear resemblance to both of them. 'Mrs Saxon,' she said, wiping her hands on the apron she'd found hanging behind the door and offering her hand. 'I'm Annie Rowland. I hope you don't mind me making free with your kitchen, but George thought you'd be tired when you got back from the hospital. How is your husband?'

'As bad-tempered as any man who's being told to change the habits of a lifetime and give up everything he loves…'

Before she could say any more, Xandra burst through the door and flung her arms around her grandmother.

'Gran! How's Granddad?'

'He'll be fine. He just needs to take more care of himself. But what about you, young lady? What are you doing here? Why aren't you at school?' Then, clearly knowing her granddaughter better than most, 'I suppose it's got something to do with your mother?'

'I don't care about my mother. I just wanted to be here so that I can help Granddad with the garage.'

'Oh, Xandra!' Then, with a sigh, 'What have you done?'

'You didn't know she was here?' George asked, following his daughter into the kitchen and this time he'd been getting his hands dirty—presumably in an effort to get the job done as quickly as possible so that he could get rid of her and close down the garage.

'I would have mentioned it.'

'You've a lot on your plate.' He crossed to the sink and, squishing soap on his hands, began to wash them thoroughly. 'How are things at the hospital?'

'It would help if he wasn't fretting so much. The garage is his life.'

'He's going to have to widen his horizons.' He picked up a towel. 'If it's any help, tell him I'll take care of the Bentley myself,' he said, drying his hands. 'But I'll have to get in touch with the owner of the restoration job in the end bay. The baby Austin. He'll need to start looking for another garage—'

'It's mine,' Xandra cut in with a touch of defiance as she anticipated disapproval.

George frowned. 'Yours?'

'Granddad bought it for my birthday,' she said, swiftly bending to make a fuss of the cat, as if she knew she'd just thrown a hand grenade into the room. 'It's a restoration project. We've been doing it together.'

No one else was looking at George and only she saw the effect that had on him. As if he'd been hit, winded, all the air driven from his body. A big man destroyed by a few words from a slip of a girl.

Love, she thought. Only love could hurt you like that and she ached to go to him, hold him.

'I'll go and give Mike Jackson a call about the Bentley,' his mother said, oblivious to the tension—or perhaps choosing to ignore it. 'He's got a wedding next week and I know how worried he's been.'

'I'll do it,' George said, clearly needing to get out of the room for a moment. 'I need to talk to him.' Then his eyes met hers and in an instant the barriers were back up. Nothing showing on the surface. 'Sorry, Mum, I should have introduced Annie.'

'We've met.' Mrs Saxon turned to her with a smile. 'I'm so sorry, my dear. I didn't thank you for getting on with dinner.' She patted her arm distractedly. 'We'll talk later but right now I really must go and call my sister-in-law, let her know how her brother is. Xandra, come and say hello to Great-Aunt Sarah.'

Annie wanted to say something, talk about Xandra, ask him what had gone wrong, but this didn't come under polite conversation and she had no idea where to begin.

As if sensing the danger, George crossed to the stove, hooked his finger through the mash and tasted it.

'Not bad for a first effort,' he said.

'Not bad? I'll have you know I've eaten in some of the finest restaurants in London and that stands comparison with the best.'

'Which restaurants?'

Annie had reeled off the names of half a dozen of the most expensive restaurants in the capital in her absolute determination to impress him before she realised that she was giving away rather more than she'd ever intended.

He lifted a quizzical brow. 'What was that you were saying about modesty?'

She pulled a face. 'No point in being coy. Of course you'd only get a tiny spoonful.'

'The more you pay, the less you get,' he agreed, taking a second dip in the potato. 'Maybe that's why you're so thin. You'd have been better occupied doing a little home cooking and saving your money for a more roadworthy car for your getaway.'

She rapped his knuckles sharply with a spoon and having scooped the potato into a serving bowl, bent to put it in the warming oven.

George regarded her thoughtfully for a moment before he shrugged and said, 'How long has your friend had that sorry heap?' he asked.

'Are you referring to Lydia's pride and joy? Only a week or two,' she said, concentrating on straining the carrots and peas. Then, realising that it wasn't an idle question, 'You've found something else?'

'I don't suppose there's the faintest chance that she bought it from a garage that offered her some kind of warranty?' he asked.

'No. She bought it from a woman who was going to use the money to take her grandchildren on holiday for Christmas.'

Lydia had been eager to tell her all about the one careful lady owner when she'd offered to lend it to her. Pride of ownership coming through loud and clear as she'd explained that, although her car wasn't new, it had been well cared for.

'She didn't happen to be a vicar's wife too, by any chance?'

'Excuse me?'

He sighed. 'Did she see any documents? Service record, receipt? Did this kindly grandmother invite her into her house for tea and biscuits while they did the deal or did your friend buy it off the side of the road?'

'I don't know about the documents, but I do know that the woman lived on the other side of London so she offered to bring the car to Lydia to save her the journey.'

'How kind of her.' His intonation suggested she had been anything but kind and he underlined it by saying, 'She must have thought it was her birthday and Christmas all rolled into one.'

'I don't understand.'

'Your friend was sold a cut'n'shut, Annie. A car welded together out of two wrecks. The front half of one car and the back half of another.'

She shook her head. 'That can't be right. She'd bought it new—'

'The classic "one careful lady owner".' He shook his head. 'Your sweet little old lady sold your friend a deathtrap, Annie. If that abomination had come apart while you were driving at any speed...'

He left the outcome to her imagination.

Her imagination, in full working order, duly obliged with a rerun of the carefree way she'd driven down the motorway, relishing her freedom as she'd buzzed along in the fast lane, overtaking slower moving traffic.

All it would have taken at that speed would have been a small piece of debris, a bit of a bump and she could have ended up in the path of one of the lorries thundering west...

And if it hadn't been her, it would, sooner or later, have been Lydia.

'Xandra hadn't seen one before but, when she spotted the welding, she asked me to take a look.'

So that was how he'd got his hands dirty.

'You do understand what this means? It'll have to be crushed. I can't be responsible for letting it back on the road.'

'Crushed?' Right now, she would be glad never to see it again but—

'And any documentation that came with it will be fake,'

he added pointedly. 'This would be a good time to come clean if you've been economical with the truth about the car's provenance, since I will have to inform the Driver and Vehicle Licensing Agency.' His look was long and intense, demanding an answer.

'I've got the picture, George.'

'I can leave it a day or two if it's going to be a problem?' he pressed.

It wasn't necessary, but her heart did a little loop the loop that he was prepared to cover for her. Give her getaway time.

'Thanks, but I won't strain your probity, George. The car is properly registered in the name of Lydia Young. She's the only victim here.' Then she groaned. 'Lydia! She's spent all that money on something that's absolutely worthless.' She looked up at him. 'I imagine the question of insurance no longer arises?'

He shook his head and she let slip that new word she was finding all kinds of uses for, but it didn't help. This went far beyond a slightly shocking expletive.

'How could anyone do such a wicked thing?' she asked.

'For money, Annie.' He made a move as if to put his hand on her arm in a gesture of comfort, but instead lifted it to push his fingers through his thick, dark hair. 'This is going to totally screw up your plans, isn't it?'

'I didn't actually have anything as organised as a plan,' she admitted. 'Just a general direction.'

'Running blind is never a good idea.' Then, almost, it seemed, against his will, 'What will you do now?'

She lifted her shoulders in a resigned shrug. 'Call a cab and go to the motel.' She managed a wry smile. 'Spend the evening working on a plan.'

'Have something to eat first,' he said.

'Thank you. Both of you,' she added. 'I mean that. I'm really grateful that you were so thorough.'

'George Saxon and Son might not look much at the

moment, but it was the finest garage in the area for nearly a century.'

'Until it ran out of sons.'

'Until it ran out of sons who wanted to be a replica of their father.'

'It's an equal-opportunities world, George.'

'Actually, when I asked what you're going to do, I meant without a car.'

Then, as Xandra returned, he leaned back against the table and folded his arms, rather like a shield, she thought.

'You'll be stranded on the wrong side of the ring road at the motel,' he said, 'and taxis aren't cheap.'

'Isn't there a bus service?'

'One or two a day, maybe, but it's a motel,' he pointed out. 'A motor hotel. There isn't a lot of demand for public transport.'

'Annie could stay here tonight,' Xandra intervened, in just the same casual manner as she'd handed her the door key and invited her to make herself a cup of tea.

George looked at the girl with something close to exasperation.

'What?' she demanded. 'There's plenty of room and Gran won't mind.'

That he did couldn't have been more obvious.

'I think your grandmother has quite enough to cope with at the moment without taking in a total stranger,' Annie said, rescuing him. 'But thank you for the offer.'

She took her cellphone from her back pocket but, before she could switch it on, he took it from her with a warning look.

'Actually,' he said, 'it would be easier if you stayed here. I'll need you to deal with the paperwork in the morning.' Then, 'I'll have more than enough to do without driving over to the motel.'

She doubted that, but she knew better than to take advantage of a man who'd been put in an impossible position. Even if he had taken advantage of her and kissed her.

'No, really. You've done enough.'

'True,' he said distantly, returning her phone, 'but I've no doubt you'll be the perfect guest and help with the washing-up.'

That really was too much.

'Maybe you should be the perfect son and buy your mother a dishwasher,' she replied, responding in kind.

'Sorry. I flunked that one years ago.' Then, as the door opened behind him, 'You've no objection to Annie staying, have you, Mum?'

'Where else would she go?' Then, as Annie placed the pie and vegetables on the table and she sank wearily into a chair, the phone began to ring.

'I'll go, Gran,' Xandra said, leaping up.

'No… It might be the hospital.'

George followed her from the room but was back in seconds. 'It's one of my mother's friends. She said to start without her.'

'We can wait.'

'The way she's settled herself in the armchair, I suspect it's going to be a long one. No point in letting good food spoil.'

She ducked her head in an attempt to hide the blush that coloured her cheekbones at the simple compliment and, despite everything, he felt an answering warmth as he watched her cut into the pie. She was such a mixture of contradictions.

Assertive, poised, innocent…

She handed him a plate, then, as he helped himself to vegetables, she served Xandra and herself before putting the dishes back in the warming oven for his mother.

Xandra made a deeply appreciative moaning noise. 'Real food. This is worth getting grounded for.'

'It is good,' Annie said swiftly, presumably to stop him

from saying something inflammatory. Then spoiled it all by adding, 'For pastry like this I'd come home every week.'

'Once a year would be nearer the mark,' Xandra said.

'Are you suggesting it's up to the standard of all those smart London restaurants you're used to?' he enquired, pretending he hadn't heard. 'Always assuming they served anything as basic as meat pie and mashed potato.'

'It's absolutely delicious,' she said quickly, in an attempt to rescue the blunder. 'But then I can't actually remember the last time I was this hungry.'

From the way she was tucking in, it was clear that her thinness wasn't the result of a desire to be size zero and he wondered what, exactly, she'd been going through that had driven her to fly from home. And, more to the point, who she'd made that *'I'll be there'* promise to.

The one with the desperate *'God help me'* tag.

He pushed away the thought, not wanting to go there.

For the moment there was colour in her cheeks and, as she laughed out loud at something Xandra had said, her face was animated, alive. Then, as if she could sense his eyes on her, she turned, looked at him over those ridiculous frames.

The impact was almost physical.

Forget the fact that she was too thin, that dark smudges marred the porcelain-fine skin beneath her eyes.

It wasn't that instant belt-in-the-gut sexual attraction that normally grabbed his attention and he was honest enough to admit that if he'd passed her in the street, head down, he probably wouldn't have given her a second glance.

But he didn't believe for a minute that she'd ever walk along a street with her head down.

Despite that oddly disturbing vulnerability, she possessed a rare presence, an ability to look him straight in the eye, hold her own in a confrontation.

Not the kind of woman, he'd have said, to run away from anything.

He pushed back his chair the minute he'd finished eating. 'I'd better go and put Mike Jackson out of his misery,' he said, desperate to get away from Annie's unsettling presence. He made a general gesture that took in the table. 'Thanks for doing this…'

'I was glad to help.' She continued to hold him captive with nothing more than a look for what felt like endless seconds. 'Can I get you anything else?' she asked as he lingered.

What on earth was the matter with him?

Annie was the kind of woman that no man with an atom of sense would get entangled with, especially not one who, having learned his lesson the hard way, could spot trouble a mile off.

'Coffee?' she prompted.

'If I need anything I'll get it myself,' he said, forcing himself to move.

CHAPTER SIX

ANNIE felt the tension evaporate as George left the room, but it felt surprisingly empty too. He was very contained, with a rare stillness. He made no unnecessary movements, had been terse to the point of rudeness throughout supper. And yet his presence still filled the room.

What could have happened to cause such a rift between him and his family? Was it just the garage, or had a teenage wedding that had evidently fallen apart faster than the ink had dried on the marriage certificate been the real cause of family friction?

And what about his daughter who, now that her father had left the room, had slumped down in her chair, all that chippy bravado gone.

It was obvious that she craved his attention. She might take every chance to wound her father, but when he wasn't looking her eyes followed him with a kind of desperation.

'Can I suggest something?'

The only response was a shrug of those narrow shoulders, making her look more like a sulky six-year-old than sixteen.

'Write a note to Mrs Warburton.'

She was instantly back on the defensive. 'I'm not sorry for taking the car.'

'Maybe not, but you're old enough to know that you must have given her a very nasty fright.' She waited a moment but, getting no response, said, 'Why did you do it?'

'Because I could?' she offered, giving her the same barbed I-don't-care-what-you-think-of-me stare that she used to hurt her father and she felt a pang of tenderness for the girl.

'If you wanted to come home to see your father I'm sure she would have understood.'

'I didn't! It's got nothing to do with him!' She glared at her. 'I'll write when I'm ready, okay? If I'd known you were going to nag I wouldn't have asked you to stay.'

'You're right,' she said, standing up, gathering the dishes. 'I've abused your hospitality.' Then, 'Time to wash up, I think.'

'Oh, right. Wash the dishes? Write a letter?' Xandra held out her hands as if balancing the choice. 'Very subtle.'

'The two have a lot in common. They both need doing and neither gets easier for leaving. And I'll bet I'm an amateur in the nagging stakes compared with your gran. As for your father…'

'If he cared what I did he'd be here instead of sending me off to school so that he could live on a beach,' she declared sullenly. 'He might be able to fix it so that they'll take me back, but I won't stay so he might as well save his money.'

'Where do you want to go?'

'Maybridge High School. It was good enough for him. I'll stay here with Gran. She'll need help,' she said. Then, leaping from her chair, she grabbed the bag that George had dropped. 'I'll take this upstairs.'

'Where are you rushing off to?' her grandmother asked as she rushed past her.

'I'm taking Annie's bag up to her room.'

'I've made up the front right bedroom,' she said. 'You'll have to make your own bed.' Then, giving her a quick hug, 'Your granddad will be all right.'

'Of course he will,' she said tightly. 'I'm going to bed.'

'Sleep tight.'

She turned to Annie with a shake of her head. 'I suppose

this is about her mother getting married again. The woman doesn't have a thought in her head for anyone but herself.'

'I'd have said it was more to do with her father. She did know he was coming home?'

'I told her when I rang to let her know that her granddad was in hospital. George has always tried to do his best for Xandra, a fact that her mother has used to her own advantage, but it's never been easy and, since she hit her teens...'

'It's a difficult time.'

'And they are so alike. George has probably told you that he and his father had a difficult relationship. It's like watching history repeat itself.'

'I'm sorry to put you to so much trouble when you've already got so much on your plate,' she said, taking the food from the warming oven and placing it on the table.

'What trouble?' she said with a smile. Then, looking at the food, 'Actually, I think I'll pass on that, if you don't mind. I had a sandwich earlier and there's something about a hospital that seems to take away the appetite.'

'How is your husband?'

'Like most men, he's his own worst enemy, but he got treatment very fast. The doctor said he's been lucky and if he behaves himself he'll be home in a day or two.'

'And then your problems will really begin.' They exchanged a knowing look. Her grandfather had never been seriously ill but he could make a simple cold seem like double pneumonia. 'Could I make you a cup of tea, Mrs Saxon?'

'Hetty, please.' Then, 'Actually, what I really need is a bath and my bed. You must be tired too.' She patted her arm. 'Your room is on the right at the top of the stairs. It's not fancy, but it's comfortable and it has its own bathroom. There's plenty of hot water. Just make yourself at home, dear.'

People kept saying that to her, Annie thought, as Hetty, clearly exhausted by long hours at the hospital, took herself off to bed.

She smiled to herself as she got stuck into the dishes. This wasn't anything like being at home, but that was good. Just what she wanted, in fact. And she was happy to help, to be able to repay in some small way this unlooked for, unexpected kindness, hospitality.

And she could think while she was working.

The loss of Lydia's car had thrown her simple non-plan off the rails and now she needed a new one.

A new plan, a replacement car and a haircut, she decided, pushing her hair back from her face.

She should make a list, she thought, twitching her nose to keep the glasses in place.

Or maybe not.

Her life had been run by her diary secretary for years. A list of monthly, weekly, daily engagements had appeared on her desk, each month, week, morning without fail.

Everything organised down to the last minute. Even her escape had been meticulously planned. The how. The where. The when.

She'd still been doing things by the book until the wheels had come off. Literally.

At the time it had seemed like a disaster. Now it seemed like anything but. Hadn't kicking back, taking whatever life threw at her, been the whole point of this break from reality? Cooking and washing up hadn't figured on any list of things to do, but it certainly came under the heading of 'different'.

George hadn't reappeared by the time she'd finished, put the dishes away, wiped everything down, so, remembering his aversion to instant coffee, she made a pot of tea and then ventured into the main part of the house to find him.

The front hall had that shabby, comfortable look that old houses, occupied by the same family over generations, seemed to acquire. It was large, square, the polished floor covered by an old Turkish rug. There was a scarred oak table along one wall, piled with mail that had been picked up from the mat and left in a heap. Above it hung a painting of an open-topped vintage car, bonnet strapped down, numbered for a race, a leather-helmeted driver at the wheel.

A small brass plate on the frame read: 'George Saxon, 1928'. It was full of life, energy, glamour and she could see how it might have caught the imagination of a teenage girl in much the same way as photographs of her mother working at a clinic in an African village had inspired her to follow in her footsteps.

Despite George's misgivings, she hoped Xandra was more successful in achieving her dreams.

The living room door stood ajar but George wasn't there. The next door opened to reveal the dining room and, after tapping lightly on the remaining door, she opened it.

The study was a man's room. Dark colours, leather furniture.

There was an open Partner's desk against one wall, but George was sitting in a large leather wing chair pulled up to the fireplace, head resting against one of the wings, long legs propped on a highly polished brass fender, cellphone held loosely in his hand, eyes closed.

Fast asleep.

'George?' she murmured.

He didn't stir but the soft cashmere of his sweater was warm to the touch and she left her hand on his broad shoulder long after it became obvious that he wasn't going to wake without more vigorous intervention.

Eventually, though, she took it away, eased the phone from his long fingers and put it, carefully, on the table, then stood watching him for a moment, wondering whether to try harder to rouse him.

He looked exhausted and, instead, she reached out as if to smooth the strain lines from his face. But the intimacy of such a gesture made it unthinkable and she curled her fingers into her palms before they quite touched his skin.

She wouldn't have done that to a man she'd known for years and George Saxon was practically a stranger.

But then that was the difference.

He didn't know who she was. Didn't feel the need to treat her with kid gloves. He'd kissed her because something in her face had told him that was what she wanted, and he'd been right. For the first time in her adult life she didn't have to be guarded, careful about how everything she said, did, would be interpreted. Didn't have to worry about reading 'all about it' in the morning paper.

The sheer dizzying freedom of that hit her in a rush and she knelt at his feet, uncurled her fingers and let them rest lightly against his face.

Fingertips against the smooth skin at his temple, palm against the exciting roughness of a day-old beard. And then she leaned forward and touched her lips to his.

Not a wake-up-and-kiss-me-back kiss, but a promise to herself to be brave enough to embrace life, embrace every new experience that offered itself.

To be wholly and completely herself.

He didn't stir and after a moment she leaned back on her heels, then, leaving him to sleep, stood up and let herself quietly out of the room before taking the stairs that rose through the centre of the house.

She followed Hetty's directions and opened the first door on the right. Her bag was at the foot of an ornate wrought iron bed and, reassured that she was in the right room, she switched on the light and closed the door.

The house was old and the room was large, with high ceilings. The en suite bathroom, a more recent addition, had taken a bite out of the room and the bed was tucked into the larger section of the remaining L.

The walls were decorated with old-fashioned flower-strewn wallpaper that went perfectly with the bed, the patch-work comforter, the dark oak antique furniture. The velvet button-back nursing chair, oval cheval mirror.

A moss-green rug that matched the velvet curtains lay in

front of a dresser on the wide oak boards and she drew them to shut out the winter dark before taking a look at the bathroom.

The huge roll-top claw-footed bath with its brass fittings was, like everything else in the house, gleaming with care.

She turned on the taps and then, leaving the water to run, returned to the bedroom to open her bag, see what Lydia had packed for her.

She'd sent her a cheque to cover the basics. Underwear, a nightdress, toiletries. Just enough to see her through until she could buy what she needed. There was a pink T-shirt nightie, plain white underwear, a couple of brushed cotton shirts, socks.

Basic as you like, she thought with a smile. Perfect.

But, when it came to toiletries, the clean, simple lines of the packaging disguised a world of luxury and she clutched the bag to her, hoping that her lookalike would get as much pleasure from the special treats she'd packed for her.

Smiling, she picked up a towel from a pile on the chair and then returned to the bathroom.

She uncapped a bottle and poured a little oil into the bath and the scent of lime blossom rose with the steam, enveloping her as she stripped off, piling up the cash she'd stowed about her body.

Not just the thousand pounds in her bra, but the rest of her running-away money that, on Lydia's insistence—who seemed to believe she'd be mugged the minute she stepped outside the hotel—she'd tucked around her waist inside her tights. Fortunately, Lydia hadn't felt the need to lose weight to keep the likeness true, so there had been ample room in the baggy jeans she'd been wearing.

Bearing in mind George's reaction to the thousand pounds she'd produced, it was probably a good thing that it had been safely out of reach, she thought as she sank beneath the water and closed her eyes, letting the warmth seep into her bones.

He'd been suspicious enough as it was. If she'd let him
see just how much she was carrying on her, he would have
called the police on the spot. Unless she'd owned up to her
real identity, she'd be languishing in a police cell right now,
up to her neck in hot water, instead of lying back in this deliciously scented bath.

Her mind drifted to the image of how she'd left him, dark
head resting against the leather wing of his chair. The unfamiliar feel of the day-old beard shadowing his chin.

Her smile faded into a sigh of longing as she wondered
how it would feel against her cheek, her neck, the delicate
skin of her breast.

George stirred, opened his eyes, for a moment not sure where
he was, only that something had disturbed him. A touch, a
faint familiar scent. Then, as he focused on the paper and
wood laid in the grate, waiting only for a match to bring the
fire blazing into life, it all came flooding back. Where he was.
And all the rest.

His father was in hospital.

His daughter had been suspended from the school he'd
chosen with such care—a place apart from the pressures of
family, where she could be whoever she wanted to be.

And the scent belonged to Annie Rowland, a woman with
lips like the promise of spring who was on the run from
something. Someone.

He was three times in trouble, he decided as he raised his
hand to his own lips, wiping the back of it hard across them
as if he could erase the disturbing thought that while he'd
been sleeping Annie had been there. Had kissed him.

He shook his head. That had to be a figment of his imagination.

And yet the image of her kneeling at his feet was so vivid
that he stood up abruptly, bumping against the table, sending
a mug flying.

He made a grab for it, swearing as hot liquid slopped over the rim, scalding his fingers. Proof that someone had been there in the last minute or two. Someone who wouldn't have left him sleeping in a chair, but would have put her hand on his shoulder. Brushed her fingers across his cheek.

And, if he'd woken, would he have tumbled her in his lap, taken up where they'd left off? Finished what he'd so nearly started earlier that evening when he'd slipped the fake glasses on her nose? When he'd kissed her, wanting her to know that he wasn't fooled by her disguise, that he'd caught her out, only to discover himself snared by a woman who, just hours earlier, he'd dismissed as not worth a second glance.

Kidding himself.

Not that her first impression of him would have been particularly flattering. He'd been sarcastic, angry, torn. Wanting to be anywhere else in the world. Wanting only to be here.

And yet there had been something. A recognition, a dangerous edge, a challenge that had sparked between them from the moment she'd cannoned into his arms, fitting the empty space like a hand coming into a glove.

Damn Xandra for getting him involved, he thought as he carried the mug through to the kitchen and grabbed his jacket from the hook. A woman was a complication he could do without right now. Any woman.

This one...

He caught his breath as he stepped outside. It was already close to freezing and his breath condensed and glowed in the concealed lights that lit the path to the gate and in the security lights that floodlit the garage. But he didn't hurry.

Cold air was exactly what he needed to clear his head and he took his time about checking that everything was safely locked, the alarms switched on before he fetched his holdall from his car.

He did the same inside, checking windows, sliding home

bolts, setting the alarm, yawning as the warmth of the house stole over him.

He'd been fighting off sleep for hours, but it was long past time to surrender and, as he pushed open the bedroom door, he kicked off his shoes, pulled his shirt and sweater over his head in one move as he reached the bed, clicked on the bedside light.

And saw Annie's bag open at his feet.

What on earth…?

He straightened, half expecting to see her staring up at him from the pillow. But there was only a ridiculously girlish nightdress—pink with a cartoon rabbit that was saying 'Give me a hug'—that she'd thrown on the bed.

On his bed…

And then it hit him.

His mother had walked into her kitchen and found Annie preparing dinner and she'd leapt to the obvious conclusion that she was with him.

That they were an item. Together. Partners. All those ridiculous expressions used these days to describe a couple who were living together without the blessing of church or state.

He stooped to pick up his shirt and sweater, get out of there, but as he straightened he heard the door open behind him and there she was, reflected in the tall cheval mirror, with only a bath towel wrapped around her like a sarong, her arms full of the clothes she'd been wearing.

She dropped her clothes on the chair. Then, catching sight of her reflection, she pulled a face as she lifted her hands to her hair, using her fingers to push the damp strands off her face, tucking it first behind her ears, then pulling it forward, turning her head first one way, then the other, as if trying to decide what kind of style might suit her.

He'd been given a close-up of that fine bone structure earlier but now, without the distraction of badly cut hair, ugly glasses, he knew without doubt that it was a face he'd seen before.

But where?

Tall, skinny, bones that a camera would love, she had to be a model, he decided, but he didn't have time to think about it. Half hidden in the L, she hadn't seen him and, as she pulled free the tail of a towel that she'd tucked between her breasts, he said, 'I wouldn't do that…'

Practically leaping out of her skin, Annie spun round and her mouth went dry.

George Saxon, wrapped up in a soft shirt and cashmere sweater was a man to turn a woman's head. Now, stripped to the waist, his wide golden shoulders and chest were as bone-meltingly beautiful as a fine Greek bronze.

She swallowed. Managed to croak out, 'Your mother said…' before, realising exactly what his mother must have thought, the words died on her lips and she clutched her towel to her breast as she felt herself blush pink from head to toe. 'Oh…'

George watched, fascinated, as a wave of delicate pink enveloped Annie, not just her face, but her smooth, creamy neck and shoulders, to disappear beneath the towel she was clutching to her breast as she quickly cottoned onto exactly what the mix-up had been.

He knew he shouldn't think about that, but whatever she'd used in her bath smelled as inviting as the promise of a warm spring day and the temptation to unwrap her, see just how far that blush had gone, was almost irresistible.

'Oh, indeed,' he replied, his voice thick, his attempt at briskness failing miserably. 'It's entirely my fault,' he said, trying again. 'I should have explained.'

'She had more important things on her mind.'

'Yes.' Then, 'It's not a problem,' he said, moving to pick up his shoes, but Annie reached out and, with her hand on his arm, stopped him.

'Please. Don't go.'

He barely registered what she said, instead staring at her left hand, white, perfectly manicured nails painted a deep shade of pink against the darker skin of his arm and, when he finally looked up, there were only two things moving in the room. His heart as it pounded against the wall of his chest and the slight rise and fall of Annie's breasts as she breathed a little too fast.

And, as her words finally registered, what had been a simple misunderstanding seemed to become something more. Something that was meant.

One move, that was all it would take, and if she was looking for a night of forgetfulness in a stranger's arms, he would have said he was her man.

But, deep in his bones, he knew that, despite the disguise, the deception, Annie was not a one-night-stand kind of woman. He, on the other hand, had never been interested in anything else and, taking her hand in his, he held it for a moment, wanting her to know that he wasn't rejecting her but being a friend and discovered that she was trembling.

'What are you running from?'

Unable to speak, she shook her head and, swearing beneath his breath, he put his arm around her, pulled her against him.

'It'll be all right,' he said, holding her close, intensely aware of her breath against his naked chest. Her skin, warm and scented from the bath, against his.

Meaningless words, but they were all he could think of and, far from steady himself as she looked up at him, he stroked the dark smudge under one of her eyes with the pad of his thumb as if he could wipe the shadow away. Make everything better.

'You'll be safe here.'

Her response was no more than a murmur that whispered across his skin and he had to tear himself away from the temptation to go with the moment.

'Sleep well, Annie,' he said and, dropping a kiss on her poor tortured hair, he stepped back, grabbed his shoes and walked swiftly from the room. Closing the door firmly behind him with a snap before he changed his mind.

CHAPTER SEVEN

ANNIE stared at the closed door. 'I don't want to be safe!' she repeated, louder this time.

All her life she'd been kept safe by a grandfather afraid that he'd lose her, as he'd lost his son. She'd been educated at home by tutors, had very few friends—mothers tended to be nervous about inviting her to play when she arrived with a bodyguard in tow.

And it hadn't got any better as she got older. The only men her grandfather had allowed within touching distance had known better than to take liberties with the nation's sweetheart. And somehow she'd never managed to get beyond that.

She'd been so sure that George was different.

He'd run out on the family business, had at least one ex-wife, a broken relationship with his teenage daughter. She should have been able to rely on a man with a record like that to take advantage of a damsel in distress.

It wasn't as if she'd screamed when she found him in her bedroom. On the contrary, when she'd turned and seen him she'd known exactly why women lost their heads over totally unsuitable men. Had been more than ready to lose hers. In every sense of the word.

Instead, after a promising start and despite the fact that she was a towel drop away from being naked, he'd kissed her on the top of the head as if she was six years old instead of twenty-six.

How lowering was that?

She looked at the hand with which she'd detained him, used it to tug free the towel, standing defiantly naked. Then, catching sight of herself in the mirror—all skin and bones— she didn't blame him. Who on earth would fall in lust with that? she thought, quickly pulling on the pink nightie to cover herself up.

Pink, cute. With a bunny on the front. Just about perfect for a six-year-old, she thought as she climbed into bed.

Or the oldest virgin in the country.

George woke from a dream in which a large, pink, girl rabbit wearing glasses had him pinned down to the bed, furry paws planted firmly on his chest.

Her familiar blue eyes appealed to him to save her while she murmured softly, over and over, 'I don't want to be safe...' And he knew that in some way they were, for her, one and the same thing.

He sat up with a start, certain that he'd seen those eyes somewhere before. Then he scrubbed his hands over his face to wake himself up properly, telling himself that he'd mis-heard her. She couldn't possibly have said what he thought she'd said.

It was still pitch dark outside, barely five o'clock, but he swung his legs over the narrow single bed of his boyhood room, not prepared to risk going back to sleep just in case the bunny was still there, lying in wait in his subconscious.

He dressed quickly and, very quietly so as not to disturb anyone, went downstairs and let himself out of the house.

Hetty glanced up from the kitchen scales where she was carefully weighing out flour as Annie walked into the kitchen.

'I'm so sorry,' she apologised. 'I had no idea it was so late.'

As she'd lain alone in the large comfortable bed, certain that once again sleep would elude her, she'd started to make a shopping list in her head. The first thing she was going to buy, she'd decided, was a slinky, sexy nightdress. The kind made for taking off rather than putting on. The last thing she remembered was trying to decide whether it should be black or red.

'I can't remember the last time I slept like that.'

'Well, you must have been tired after your journey. Can you make yourself breakfast? There are plenty of eggs, bacon...' She made a broad gesture at the collection of ingredients stacked on the kitchen table. 'I find cooking takes my mind off things.'

'A slice of toast will do me,' Annie said. 'And some tea. Can I make a cup for you?'

She smiled. 'That would be lovely. Thank you, dear.'

Annie dropped a couple of slices of bread into the toaster, put on the kettle.

'It's so quiet here,' she said.

'This used to be a farm. Didn't George tell you?' She looked up. 'How did you meet?'

'Actually, Hetty, George and I aren't...' she made a gesture that she hoped would cover the situation '...together.' She swallowed as George's mother, reaching for a bag of sugar, paused, a frown creasing her brow. 'My car broke down yesterday evening and I called the nearest garage. He came and picked me up.'

'George took out the tow-truck?' she asked, astonished.

'Not with any enthusiasm,' she admitted. 'I was going to call a cab to take me to the motel but Xandra asked me to stay.'

'Xandra?' She raised her hand to her mouth. 'You mean...? But I...'

'It's all right. An easy mistake to make and George was

the complete gentleman…' unfortunately '…and retired, leaving me in sole possession of the bedroom. I do hope he wasn't too uncomfortable.'

'He probably used his old bedroom,' she said, pouring the sugar into the scales. 'Pity. It's about time he settled down with a decent woman.'

'I'm sure he'd be much happier with an indecent one.'

His mother laughed. 'No doubt. Maybe that's why he was in such a bad mood when I took him out some tea earlier. I sent Xandra on an errand to keep her out of his way.'

'Oh. I had assumed she was with him. She seems very keen.'

'I know. My husband dotes on her. Let's her do anything she wants.' She sighed. 'Life would have been a great deal easier if George had been a girl. He wouldn't have been so hard. Expected so much…' Hetty sighed, then smiled as Annie handed her a cup of tea. 'Even so, he really shouldn't have let her get so involved with the garage.'

'She would never have stuck at it unless she really wanted to be a motor mechanic,' she said, buttering the toast.

'George told you about that?'

'No, it was Xandra. She's very determined. And I should warn you that she doesn't want to go back to boarding school. She wants to stay here.'

'She already spends most of her holidays with us. Her mother has other interests. Pass me that bowl, will you?'

Annie would have liked to ask about George. What interests kept him away? But that would be invading his privacy and, instead, she handed Hetty a large old-fashioned crockery mixing bowl.

'Are you making a Christmas cake?'

'It's silly really. You can buy such good ones and I don't suppose George—my George—will be able to eat it. The doctor said he needs to lose some weight.'

'Walking is good. For the heart,' she added. Then, sucking melted butter from her thumb, 'Can I do anything to help?'

'You could make a start creaming the sugar and butter, if you like.' She tipped the sugar into the bowl, adding butter she'd already measured and chopped up. 'You'll find a wooden spoon in the drawer.'

There was no fancy electric mixer to make light work of it, but Annie had seen the process often enough as a child to know what she had to do.

'What's the problem with your car?' Hetty asked when she'd spooned the last of the spices into a saucer and everything was measured. 'Will it take long to fix?'

'It's terminal, I'm afraid. George is going to arrange for it to be crushed.'

'But that's—'

Before she could finish, Xandra burst through the door. 'Got them! Oh, hi, Annie.' She dumped the box on one of the chairs. 'I've been up in the attic sorting out the Christmas decs. Now all we need is a tree.'

'Why don't you and Annie take the Land Rover and go and pick one up from the farm?' her grandmother suggested.

'That would be so brilliant.'

Annie blinked at the transformation from last night's moody teen to this childlike enthusiasm.

'But I...'

'What?'

'I really should be going.'

'Where? You're staying for the Christmas market, aren't you? Annie can stay for the weekend, can't she, Gran?'

'It's fine with me.'

'But you don't know me from Adam,' Annie protested. 'Besides, wouldn't you rather go to the farm with your father?'

'You mean the Grinch?'

'That's not fair, Xan,' Hetty said.

'Oh, please. He hates Christmas and we all know why.' Then, 'Come on, Annie, let's go and choose the biggest tree we can find.'

She swallowed. The scent of the newly cut evergreen brought indoors never failed to bring back that terrible Christmas when her parents hadn't come home.

'You will stay?' the girl pressed. 'We could go to the market together. It'll be fun.'

She looked up, ready to explain that she really had to move on, but Hetty, exhaustion in every line of her face, met her gaze with a silent plea that she couldn't ignore.

'Let's go and get the tree and we'll take it from there,' she said.

'Excellent. Can we go now, Gran?'

'I'll be glad to have the place to myself. Not too big,' she called after her, adding a silent, 'Thank you,' to Annie before raising her voice to add, 'We don't want a repeat of last year.' Then, 'Wrap up. It's cold out. There's a scarf on the hook. Gloves in the drawer.'

'What happened last year?' Annie asked Xandra, tucking the ends of her hair into the woolly hat before she hauled herself up behind the wheel of an elderly Land Rover.

'Granddad came home with a ten-foot tree and we couldn't get it through the door. He's really silly about Christmas.'

'Is he? You spend a lot of time with your grandparents?'

She pulled a face. 'We used to have a lovely house with a garden, but my mother took an interior decorating course and caught minimalism, so traded it in for a loft apartment on the Melchester quays. Not the kind of place for a girl with engine oil under her fingernails.'

'There's such a thing as a nail brush,' she pointed out, biting back the *What about your father?* question.

'I suppose, but my mother treats Christmas as a design opportunity. Last year it was silver and white with mauve "accents".' She did the thing with her fingers to indicate the quotes.

'Mauve?' Annie repeated.

'With the tiniest, tiniest white lights.' And, putting on a clipped accent, Xandra said, 'All terribly, terribly tasteful, dahling.' Then, 'Christmas isn't supposed to be tasteful.'

'Isn't it?' Annie asked, sobering as she thought about the Dickens-inspired designer co-ordinated green, red and gold that traditionally decked the halls of King's Lacey for the festive season. 'What is it supposed to be?'

Xandra's response was a broad grin. 'Stick around and see what I've got planned.' Then, with a groan as she saw her father, 'Come on, let's get out of here.'

George had emerged from the workshop and was striding purposefully in their direction and by the time she'd managed to start the cold engine he was at the window and she had no choice but to push it open. He was wearing overalls and there was a smear of grease on his cheek that her fingers itched to wipe away before her lips planted a kiss in that exact spot.

Losing her mind, clearly, she decided, keeping her hands firmly on the steering wheel, her eyes firmly on him, managing a fairly coherent, 'Good morning.' Unable to resist saying, 'I hope you managed to sleep well.'

He lifted an eyebrow, acknowledging the reference to her turning him out of his bed.

'Well enough,' he replied, although he'd apparently had to think about it. 'You?'

'Like a log for the first time in as long as I can remember,' she said gratefully. 'Thank you.'

He nodded. 'You look…rested.' Then, as he wiped his hands on a rag, 'Where are you two off to?'

'We're going to the farm,' she said. 'To buy a tree.'

'Come on, Annie. Let's *go*,' Xandra butted in impatiently.

He put his hand on the open window to keep her where she was. 'Tree?' He frowned.

'A *Christmas* tree? You remember *Christmas*, don't you? Peace on earth, goodwill, tacky decs, bad songs. Terrible presents.'

His jaw tightened. 'I have heard of it.' Then, looking at Annie, 'Have you ever driven a four-wheel drive?'

About to assure him that, despite all evidence to the contrary, she'd not only been taught to drive everything on her grandfather's estate by an ex-police driving instructor, but had been trained in survival driving, she managed to stop herself.

And not simply because mentioning the fact that her grandfather owned an estate seemed like a bad idea.

'Why?' she asked innocently. 'Is it different to driving a car?'

'In other words, no,' he said, opening the door. 'Shift over, I'll take you.'

'Can't you just take me through it?' she suggested. 'I know how busy you are and I've put you to more than enough trouble.'

'You think?' He held her gaze for so long that she was afraid he knew exactly what she was doing. Then, shaking his head, 'It'll be quicker if I run you there.'

'I'm really sorry,' she said as she edged her bottom along the seat. 'It was your mother's idea and she's been so kind. It's the least I can do.'

Xandra was staring straight ahead, rigid with tension.

'Budge up,' she urged.

The girl moved no more than a hand's width and Annie could almost feel the waves of animosity coming off her. Clearly her plan to get father and daughter to bond over the purchase of a Christmas tree wasn't going to be as simple as she'd hoped.

That said, she was a little tense herself as George squashed in beside her, his arm brushing against her as he reached for the gearstick. He glanced at her, asking her with the slightest lift of his eyebrow if she was all right. She gave a barely discernible shrug to indicate that she was fine.

As if.

She was crushed up against the kind of man who would light up any woman's dreams, her cheek against his shoulder, her thigh trembling against the hard muscles of his leg. She could feel every move he made, every breath and even the familiar smell of hot oil from the engine of the aged vehicle couldn't mask the scent of warm male.

It was too noisy to talk but as they came to a halt at a busy roundabout he turned to her.

'You'll have more room if you put your arm on my shoulder,' he said, looking down at her. But for a moment, mesmerised by his sensuous lower lip, close enough to kiss, she didn't, couldn't, move. Then, before she could get a grip, ease her arm free and lay it across those wide shoulders, Xandra abruptly shifted sideways.

'I'm...fine,' she managed as she reluctantly eased herself away from his warmth.

The Christmas tree farm wasn't far and they were soon pulling off the road and into an area cleared for a car park.

Beside it was the seasonal shop in a little chalet decorated with fake snow and strings of fairy lights. In front of it there was a children's ride, a bright red sleigh with Rudolph—complete with flashing nose—and Santa, with his sack of parcels, at the reins.

As soon as they came to a halt, Xandra opened the door and leapt down, not waiting for her or her father, disappearing stiff-legged, stiff-necked into the plantation.

'Are you coming?' Annie paused on the edge of the seat, looking back as she realised that George hadn't moved.

'You know me,' he said, his face expressionless. 'I'm just the driver.'

'I'm sorry.'

'It's not your fault.'

'No. And I am truly grateful to you for stepping in. Xandra wants to decorate the house for your father before he comes home from the hospital.'

Or was it really for him? she wondered.

Despite everything she'd said, he'd said, was Xandra hoping that he'd relent over closing the garage, stay for the holiday? That they'd all have a perfect fairy-tale Christmas together, the kind that proper families had in story books?

Dickens, she thought as she jumped down, had a lot to answer for.

Hitting the uneven ground jarred the ankle she'd wrenched the day before and she gave a little yelp.

And then she moaned.

'What?' George asked.

'Nothing...' She let the word die away as she hung onto the door.

Muttering something that she was clearly not meant to hear, he climbed out and walked round the Land Rover to see for himself.

'It's nothing,' she repeated, letting go of the door with one hand just long enough to wave him away. 'I gave my ankle a bit of a wrench yesterday when I stepped in that pothole and just now, well, the drop was further than I thought...' Enough. Don't overdo it, Annie, she told herself and taking a steadying breath, she straightened herself, touched her toe to the ground. Bravely fought back a wince. 'Give me a minute,' she said with a little gasp. 'I'll be fine.'

'Let me see.'

She didn't have to feign the gasp as he put his hands around her waist and lifted her back up onto the seat, then picked up her left foot, resting her ankle in the palm of his hand.

'It doesn't look swollen,' he said, gently feeling around the bone, the instep and he looked up, slate eyes suddenly filled with suspicion.

'No. I told you. It'll be fine.' She slid down, forcing him back, and began to limp after Xandra.

'Wait!'

'I promised Hetty I'd keep an eye on her,' she said, not looking back. 'Make sure she keeps her ambitions below ceiling height.'

'Oh, for heaven's sake,' he said, closing the door and coming after her. 'Here,' he said, taking her arms and putting them around his neck. She scarcely had time to react to his irritable command before he'd bent and picked her up. 'Hang on.'

He didn't need to tell her twice and she hung on for dear life, arms around his neck, cheek in the crook of his warm neck as he walked across to the wooden chalet, carried her up the steps and set her down on a chair.

'Stay there and try not to get into any more trouble,' he said, picking up her foot and turning another chair for it to rest on. 'Okay?' his said, his face level with hers.

'Okay,' she said a touch breathlessly.

He nodded. 'Right. I'd better go and make sure Xandra doesn't pick out something that would be more at home in Trafalgar Square.'

'Wait!' she said and, before he could straighten, took his chin in her hand as she searched her pockets for a tissue.

He must have shaved last night after he'd left her, she realised, feeling only the slight rasp of morning stubble against her palm as she reached up and gently wiped the grease off his cheek. Then, because he was looking at her in a way that made her insides melt, she said, 'George Saxon and Son has a reputation to maintain.'

She'd meant to sound brisk, businesslike, matter-of-fact but her voice, trained to deliver a speech to the back of a banqueting hall, for once refused to co-operate and it came out as little more than a whisper.

'And what about Annie Rowland?' he asked, his face expressionless.

'What? I haven't got grease on my face, have I?' she asked, instinctively touching the same place on her own cheek.

'Not grease,' he said, lifting her glasses off her nose and slipping them into the top pocket of his overalls. 'Something far worse.'

'Oh, but—'

He stopped her protest by planting a kiss very firmly on her lips. For a moment she tried to talk through it but then, as the warmth of his lips penetrated the outer chill, heating her through to the bone, a tiny shiver of pleasure rippled through her and she forgot what she was trying to say.

Instead, she clutched at his shoulder, closed her eyes and, oblivious to the woman sitting by the till, she kissed him back. Let slip a tiny mew of disappointment as he drew back and the cold rushed back in.

She opened her eyes and for a moment they just looked at each other before, without another word, he turned and walked out of the door.

The woman behind the counter cleared her throat as, slightly dazed, Annie watched George follow the path his daughter had taken between the trees.

'Are you all right?' she asked.

'I'm not sure,' she said, raising cold fingers to hot lips. 'I'm really not at all sure.'

'Only there are signs warning about the uneven paths,' she said defensively.

'Are there?' She watched George until he disappeared from sight and then turned to look at the woman.

'It says we're not responsible—'

'Oh!' Annie said, finally catching onto the fact that she wasn't referring to the hiccup in her heartbeat, her ragged pulse rate. Or the way George had stolen her glasses before kissing her.

The woman was only concerned about the fact that she'd apparently injured her ankle in their car park and might decide to sue the pants off them.

She shook her head. 'Don't worry about it. I hurt it yesterday,' she said, reassuring her. 'Today was no more than a reminder.'

'Well, that's a relief. You wouldn't believe…' She let it go, smiled, then followed her gaze as she looked along the path that George had taken. 'It's good your man is so caring.'

'Oh, but he isn't…'

Her man.

She'd only met him last night. Barely knew him. And he didn't know her at all. No one who knew her would dare to kiss her the way he'd kissed her.

And yet she'd been closer to him in that short time than almost any man she'd ever known. She already cared about him in ways she had only dreamed of. And his daughter.

She'd grown up without a father of her own and if she could heal the breach between them she would go home knowing that she'd done something good.

'Can I get you something while you're waiting? Tea? Coffee? Hot chocolate?'

The little wooden chalet was, it seemed, more than simply a place to pay for the trees, the bundles of mistletoe and holly stacked up outside.

There was a little counter for serving hot drinks, cakes and mince pies and the walls were lined with shelves displaying seasonal decorations made by local craftsmen, although she was the only customer for the moment, despite the cars lined up outside. Obviously everyone else was out in the plantation picking out their trees.

Annie ordered a mince pie and a cup of hot chocolate and then, while she was waiting, instead of ignoring the decorations as she usually did, she looked around her, hoping to find something that would amuse Xandra.

There were beautiful handmade candles, charming wooden decorations. All perfectly lovely. All so wonderfully…tasteful.

Outside, a child climbed in the sleigh alongside Santa. His

mother put a coin in the machine and it began to move in a motion designed to make over-excited children sick, while it played *Rudolph the Red-Nosed Reindeer*.

Not tasteful at all.

'Here you are.' The woman brought her chocolate and mince pie. 'Would you like the paper?' she asked, offering her one of the red tops. 'Something to look at while you're waiting.'

About to refuse, she changed her mind, deciding to check out the kind of coverage she'd got yesterday. Make sure there was nothing that would rouse the slightest suspicion in an eagle-eyed editor or set alarms bells ringing if anyone in her own office took more than the usual cursory glance.

'Thanks. That would be great.'

A picture of Lydia leaving the Pink Ribbon Lunch had made the front page. With rumours of a wedding, that was inevitable, but the hat, a last-minute special from her favourite designer featuring a Pink Ribbon spangled veil, had successfully blurred her features.

She'd seen so many photographs of herself, her head at just that angle as she'd turned to smile for the cameras, that even she found it hard to believe that it wasn't actually her.

And if Lydia had a bloom that she'd been lacking in recent months, the caption writer had put his own spin on that.

Lady Rose was radiant as she left the Pink Ribbon Lunch yesterday before flying to Bab el Sama for a well-earned break before Christmas at King's Lacey, her family home. The question is, will she be on her own? See page five.

She turned to page five, where there was a double-page spread including a recent picture of her, smiling as she left some event with Rupert. Thankful it was over, no doubt.

There was a huge aerial photograph of Bab el Sama, and

another distant shot of the beach taken from the sea, along with many words written by someone who had never been there—no one from the press had ever set foot in the place—speculating on the luxury, the seclusion of a resort that was, apparently, the perfect place for lovers.

Put together the words 'radiant' and 'lovers' and read between the lines…

Yuck.

But, then again, it was only what she'd expected and with luck the possibility would keep the paparazzi fixed to the spot, hoping for a picture that would earn them a fortune.

She smiled. Sorry, chaps, she thought, as she closed the paper, folded it over so that the front page was hidden and put it back on the counter. Then, brimful of goodwill despite rather than because of the season, she said, 'I don't suppose I could persuade you to part with Rudolph, could I?'

'You'd be surprised how many people have asked me that,' she said, 'but we've only got him on hire during December.'

'Pity.'

'Believe me,' she said as the child demanded another ride and the song started up again, 'after the first hundred times, it feels like a lifetime.'

CHAPTER EIGHT

GEORGE followed his daughter down the path to the area where the farmer and his son were harvesting the trees.

The boy, seventeen or eighteen, brawny, good-looking, smiled as he looked up and caught sight of Xandra.

'Can I help?' he asked.

'I need a tree,' she said, with the cool, assessing look that women had been giving men since Adam encountered Eve in the Garden of Eden. 'A big one,' she added, turning away to inspect trees that had already been dug up and netted.

It was a move calculated to draw the boy closer and he followed as if on a string. It was like watching the rerun of an old movie, he thought. She was younger than her mother had been when she'd looked at him like that, but she already had the moves down pat.

'With roots or without?' the boy asked.

'Without,' he replied for her, stepping forward to make his presence felt.

'With,' Xandra countered, not even bothering to look at him. 'I want to plant it in the garden after Christmas.'

'Okay. If you'd like to choose one I'll dig it up for you.'

'What's wrong with those?' George said, nodding at the trees that were ready to go.

'I want to choose my own,' Xandra said.

'And it's best to get it as fresh as possible,' the boy added.

Wanting to flex his muscles for a pretty girl. 'I'll get a decent root ball with it and wrap it in sacking for you. That'll give it a better chance.'

'Thanks,' she said before turning, finally, to acknowledge his presence. 'Where's Annie?' she asked, realising that he was on his own.

'She hurt her ankle getting out of the Land Rover. I left her in the shop with her foot up.' Then, in an effort to move things along, he indicated a nicely shaped tree and said, 'What about that one?'

'It's not tall enough.'

Clearly whichever tree he'd chosen was going to be rejected but he pressed on. 'It'll be at least two feet taller once it's out of the ground and in a pot.'

He looked at the boy, who was smart enough to agree with him. 'It's a lovely tree,' he added, but if he hoped to curry favour he was talking to the wrong man. He'd been eighteen once, and this was his daughter.

Xandra shrugged. 'Okay. But I want one for outside as well. A really *big* one.'

About to ask her who was going to put it up, he stopped himself, aware that the boy, if he had anything about him, would leap in with an offer to do it for her.

She'd had sixteen years without him to put up a tree for her. Maybe one really big one would make a bit of a dent in the overdraft.

'No more than ten feet from the ground,' he told the boy and, when she would have objected, 'I won't be able to carry anything bigger than that on the roof of the Land Rover.' Even that would be a push.

Then, beating down the urge to grab her by the arm, drag her back to the shop where he could keep her within sight, he said, 'Don't take too long about choosing it. I want to get Annie back into the warm,' he said, turning to go back to her.

'Is she badly hurt?' She sounded concerned.

'She's putting a brave face on it,' he said, rubbing the flat of his palm over his jaw, where he could still feel the warm touch of her fingers, despite the chill.

It had been the same last night. After leaving her he'd taken a shower, shaved, anything to distance himself from the touch of her hand that had burned like a brand on his arm. Somehow he doubted that even a cold shower would have saved him from the pink bunny.

Now he'd kissed her again, just to shut her up for a moment, he told himself, but this time she'd kissed him back. Yet still he was left with the extraordinary sense that for her it was all brand-new.

How crazy was that? She had to be in her mid-twenties at least.

Xandra hesitated, but only for a moment, before turning to the boy. 'Okay, I'm going to trust you to choose the big tree—'

'I know just the one,' he said eagerly. 'A real beauty. You'll love it.' And Xandra bestowed a gracious smile on him before, just a touch of colour darkening her cheekbones, she quickly turned away and swept off up the path.

For a moment they both stood and watched her, each lost for a moment in his own thoughts.

The boy was only seeing Christmas coming early.

His thoughts were darker as he remembered the moment when, not much older than the youth at his side, she'd been put in his arms, the realisation that she was his little girl. The shattering need to protect her. Make her life perfect.

Remembering the beautiful little girl with dark curls who'd run not to him, but to his father for hugs. Who had called Penny's second husband—living in the house he'd paid for—'daddy'.

Annie looked up as he followed Xandra into the chalet.

'Did you find what you were looking for?' she asked, her eyes narrowing as she looked at him.

'I think I can safely guarantee that our trees will be the best that money can buy.'

She still had her left foot propped up and, ignoring the empty chairs, he picked it up, sat down and placed it on his knee, leaving his hand on the curve between ankle and foot.

It was a slender foot, a slender ankle and there wasn't the slightest sign of a swelling.

'Trees?' she asked.

'A six-footer for inside the house. Something rather more stately for outside.'

'Oh, trees *plural*. You're going to need a ton of tinsel, Xandra,' she said, watching her as she wandered around the shop, checking out what they had to offer.

'I'm working on it,' she said, picking up one of the decorations, then putting it back.

'How's your ankle?' George asked, reclaiming Annie's attention.

'Fine, really,' she assured him, not quite meeting his gaze, adding to his certainty that she had faked the injury. But why?

Could it be that she saw the garage as a sanctuary? Wanted to stay on?

'It was nothing that hot chocolate and a mince pie couldn't cure,' she assured him, making a move to put it down, but he kept his hand firmly in place.

'Best to keep it up for as long as possible,' he said.

She took her time about answering him, dabbing at the crumbs on the plate in front of her and sucking them off her finger before, finally, lifting her lashes with a look that went straight to his gut.

Was it deliberate? Did she know what she was doing?

Usually, when he looked at a woman, when she looked back, they both knew exactly what they wanted, but Annie wasn't like any woman he'd ever met.

She left him floundering.

'So,' he said quickly, glad he was wearing loose overalls over his trousers so that she couldn't see the disturbing effect she had on him, 'what's your plan for today?'

Her lips parted over perfect teeth but, before she could tell him, Xandra said, 'She's staying with us until after the weekend. Gran asked her,' she added, glaring at him, daring him to offer an argument.

But if his mother had already asked her to stay, why would she—?

Oh. Right.

She'd seen an opportunity to throw him and Xandra together and, instead of seizing the moment, he'd gone in with both feet and made a complete cobblers of it.

'Not that she'd be able to go gallivanting all over the place sightseeing with a dodgy ankle,' she added.

'Honestly,' Annie said, looking at him, her eyes offering him her assurance that if he was unhappy she'd make her excuses and leave, 'it's not that bad.'

'Best not take any chances,' he said, attempting to unravel the curious mixture of elation and dismay he felt at the prospect of her staying on for several more days.

Relief that she wasn't going to walk away, disappear. That he'd never know what happened to her. Who she really was.

Dismay because he wanted to protect her from whatever was out there, threatening her. And that unnerved him.

'I'm having some water,' Xandra said, examining the contents of a glass-fronted fridge. She turned to him. 'Do you want anything?'

To be back at his beach house with nothing on his mind more important than the design of a multi-million-pound software program, a mild flirtation with a pretty woman, he thought, as he reached for his wallet. One with curves and curls and an uncomplicated smile that let you know exactly what was on her mind.

Since that wasn't an option, he said, 'Coffee and—'

'I don't need your money,' she snapped as he offered her a note. Then, perhaps remembering where the money in her own purse had come from, quickly said, 'Black with too much sugar, right?'

'Thanks.'

He'd been about to tell her to buy the angel she'd looked at, but decided against it. She wasn't a little girl he could buy with a doll.

'And?' she added. He must have looked puzzled because she said, 'You said "and".'

'And if you could run to a couple of those mince pies,' he said, 'it would fill a gap. I seem to have missed breakfast.'

'Sugar, fat and caffeine?' She shook her head. 'Tut, tut, tut.' But she turned to the woman behind the counter and said, 'The water for me, a heart attack for George… And what's that, Annie? Hot chocolate? Do you want a top-up?'

'No, I'm good, thanks.'

'Hot chocolate and a mince pie? Have a care, Annie,' he warned her with a grin. 'The food police will be after you too.'

'At least I had a slice of toast before I left the house this morning.'

'Buttered, of course. My father isn't a man to have anything as new-fangled as low-fat spread in the house.'

'Buttered,' she admitted, smiling as she conceded the point. 'But it was unsalted butter.'

'Honestly. What are you two like?' Xandra said disapprovingly. 'You're supposed to be mature adults. I'd get the "breakfast is the most important meal of the day" lecture if I ate like that.'

'Not from me,' he assured her.

'Well, no. Obviously. You'd have to be there.'

'I was,' he reminded her. 'Out of interest, what did you have for breakfast?'

'Gran made us both porridge. I sliced an apple over mine and added a drizzle of maple syrup.'

'Organic, of course.'

'Of course.'

'Well, good for you.' Annie, he noticed, lips pressed together to keep a smile in check, was being very careful to avoid eye contact, this time for all the right reasons. 'Actually,' he continued, 'you seem to have overlooked the fact that there's fruit in the mincemeat.'

Xandra snorted, unimpressed, but she turned away quickly. He was hoping it was so that he wouldn't see that, like Annie, she was trying not to laugh.

He was probably fooling himself, he thought, reaching for the paper lying on the counter to distract himself with the sports headlines on the back page so he wouldn't dwell on how much that hurt.

'Here you are.' Xandra put his coffee and pastries in front of him, then, sipping from the bottle she was holding, wandered over to the window to watch for the arrival of the trees. Or possibly the young man who'd be bringing them.

'It'll take him a while to dig up two big trees,' he warned her.

'Well, I'm sorry to take up so much of your time.' She took the paper from him, pulled out a chair and turned it over and, having glanced at the front page, opened it up. She was using it as a barrier rather than because she was interested in world news, he thought, but after a moment she looked up, stared at Annie, then looked at the paper again.

'Has anyone ever told you how much you look like Lady Rose, Annie?' she asked.

'Who?' she asked, reaching for the paper, but he beat her to it.

'You know.' She made a pair of those irritating quote marks with her fingers. 'The "people's virgin".'

'Who?' he asked.

Xandra leaned over and pointed to a picture of a man and a woman. 'Lady Rose Napier. The nation's sweetheart. She came to Dower House a couple of years ago for prize-giving day. Chauffeur, bodyguards, the Warthog genuflecting all over the place.'

Since George paid the school fees, he received invitations to all school events as a matter of courtesy. Did his best to make all of them.

'I must have missed that one,' he said, realising that Lady Rose was the pampered 'princess' whose wedding plans were the talk of the tabloids.

He looked up from the paper to check the likeness for himself. 'Xandra's right,' he said. 'You do look like her.' Which perhaps explained why she'd seemed vaguely familiar.

'I wish,' Annie said with a slightly shaky laugh. 'I was just reading about her. She's holed up in luxurious seclusion in a palace owned by the Ramal Hamrahn royal family. I could do with some of that.'

'According to this, she's with that old bloke she's going to marry.' Xandra pulled a face. 'I'd rather stay a virgin.'

'I'd rather you did too,' George said.

She glanced at him. 'You're a fine one to talk.'

'Your mother was eighteen,' he protested, then stopped. This was not a conversation he wanted to have with his sixteen-year-old daughter. 'Did you meet her? Lady Rose?'

'In other words, did I win a prize? Sorry, they don't give one for car maintenance.' Then, since that didn't get the intended laugh, 'Lady Rose is nearly as old as Annie. I suppose she must be getting desperate.'

He looked at the picture of the man beside her. 'He's not that old,' he protested.

'He's thirty-nine. It says so right there.'

With his own thirty-sixth birthday in sight, that didn't seem old to him, but when he'd been sixteen it would probably have seemed ancient.

'It also says he's rich. Owns a castle in Scotland, estates in Norfolk and Somerset and is heir to an earldom.'

'I think that cancels out "old",' he countered, looking up from the photograph of the two of them leaving some function together to compare her with Annie.

If you ignored the clothes, the woolly hat pulled down to hide not just her hair but most of her forehead, the likeness was striking.

And Annie had admitted to cutting her hair, borrowing the clothes she was wearing. She'd even talked about security men watching her night and day.

If the evidence that she'd flown to some place called Bab el Sama hadn't been right in front of him, it might have crossed his mind that Annie was Lady Rose Napier.

Assuming, of course, that she really had gone there. But why wouldn't she? It was the ultimate getaway destination. Luxury, privacy.

Why would she swap that for this?

'Rich, smitch,' Xandra said dismissively. 'Lady Rose doesn't need the money. Her father was the Marquess of St Ives and he left her a fortune. And her grandfather is a duke.'

'How do you know all this?'

'Everything she does is news. She's the virgin princess with a heart of gold. An example to us all.'

She clutched at her throat to mime throwing up.

'I'd have thought a woman like that would be fighting off suitors.'

'Yes, well, she's been surrounded by bodyguards all her life, has a posse of photographers in her face wherever she goes and she has a whiter than white image to maintain. She can never let her hair down, kick off and have fun like everyone else, can she?' She thought about it for a moment. 'Actually, you've got to feel just a bit sorry for her.'

'Have you?' he asked, thinking about the way Annie had reached out to him last night. Her whispered 'I don't want to be safe'. 'What about you, Annie?'

'Do I feel sorry for her?' she asked, looking at the picture.

That was what he'd meant, but there was something about the way she was avoiding his eyes that bothered him.

'Would you marry the old guy in the picture?' he pressed.

She looked up then. Straight, direct. 'Not unless I was in love with him.'

'Oh, puh-lease,' Xandra said. Then, taking back the paper, she compared the two pictures and shrugged. 'Maybe she is in love. There was a rumour going around that she was anorexic, but she looks a lot better here. It's a pity, really.'

'What is?' he asked, never taking his eyes off Annie.

It all fitted, he thought.

The timing was right. The poise. He'd even thought that she was acting as if she were royalty when she'd left him to close the tow-truck door behind her. He doubted that Lady Rose Napier, with a chauffeur and bodyguards in attendance, had ever had to do that in her life.

But it had to be coincidence. There was a likeness, it was true, but wasn't everyone supposed to have a double somewhere? And why on earth would a woman with a fortune at her command take off in a rattle bucket car when she could be going first-class all the way to paradise with Mr Big?

'What's a pity?' he repeated sharply.

Xandra gave an awkward little shrug, shook her head, clearly embarrassed, which had to be a first.

'Nothing. It's just that in the earlier picture the likeness is more pronounced.'

When she was thinner? A little less attractive? Was that what his tactless daughter had stopped herself from saying?

'But if Annie worked at it a bit, grew her hair, had the right clothes, make-up, I bet one of those lookalike agencies would snap her up.'

Annie opened her mouth, presumably to protest, but Xandra wasn't finished.

'You'd have to wear high heels,' she went on, getting

carried away in her enthusiasm. 'She's really tall. But I bet that if you put on a pound or two you could do it.'

'What about the eyes?' George said, trying to see her not in baggy jeans, a chain store fleece jacket with a woolly hat pulled down to cover her hair, but a designer gown cut low to reveal creamy shoulders, long hair swept up. Her face transformed with make-up. Jewels at her throat. He seemed to get stuck on the shoulders… 'Aren't they the big give-away?'

'What?' she said, her attention shifting to the sound of a tractor pulling into the car park. She dropped the paper, more interested in what was happening outside. 'Oh, that's not a problem. She could use contacts.'

'Of course she could,' he said, his own attention focused firmly on the woman sitting on the far side of the table. 'So does that appeal as a career move?'

The corner of Annie's mouth lifted in a wry smile. 'You mean if I were a little younger, a little taller, wore a wig, contacts and plenty of make-up?'

'And if you put on a few pounds,' he reminded her. A little weight to fill out the hollows beneath her collarbone. Hollows that matched those of Lady Rose Napier in her evening gown.

'Much more of your mother's meat pie and buttered toast and that won't be a problem,' she replied, the smile a little deeper, but still wry.

'As good a reason to stay as any other,' he suggested. 'As long as you remember to add garlic to the mash.'

'Are you suggesting that I'm scrawny?'

'The trees are here, George.' His daughter impatiently demanded his attention and he pushed back his chair, got to his feet, never taking his eyes off Annie.

'Not if I have any sense,' he replied. 'And you can save the expense of contact lenses. Your eye colour is more than a match for the people's virgin.'

He took her glasses from his pocket and, taking her hand,

placed them in her palm, closing her fingers over them, holding them in place as he was held by Annie's vivid gaze.

'They look an awful lot bigger on the trailer than they did growing,' Xandra said, breaking the spell. 'Will they be safe on the roof?'

'Don't worry about it,' he said, telling himself that he was glad of the distraction. 'If it's going to be a problem I'm sure your lovelorn swain will be happy to offer a personal delivery service.'

'My what? Oh, for goodness' sake,' she said, rolling her eyes at him before stomping down the steps and striding across the car park.

'I'd better go and find some rope,' he said, still not moving.

'Is there anything I can do to help?' Annie asked, the glasses still clutched in her hand.

'I think you've done more than enough for one day, Annie. If you don't fancy lookalike work, you could always take up acting.'

'Acting?'

He noted the nervous swallow, the heightened colour that flushed across her cheekbones with relief. Despite his earlier suspicion that she might be a practised con woman, it was clear that, whatever she was hiding, she wasn't a practised liar.

'I don't understand.'

'There's nothing wrong with your ankle,' he said bluntly.

'Oh.' The colour deepened. 'How did you guess?'

'I've rarely encountered one in less perfect condition,' he said, reliving the feel of it beneath his palm. 'In fact, I'm seriously hoping that you'll take Xandra's advice to heart about wearing high heels.'

'I didn't pack any.'

'No? Well, you can't run in high heels, can you?'

'If you hadn't gone all macho over the car—'

'Oh, right. Blame the sucker.'

'It wasn't like that,' she protested. 'I just thought—'

'I know what you thought,' he said curtly, before she could say the words out loud. Determined to crush any foolish notion that throwing him into close proximity with Xandra would produce a cosy father-daughter bond. 'I have no doubt you imagined you were helping, but some relationships can't be fixed.'

No matter how much you might regret that.

'Not without putting a little effort into it,' she came right back at him, her eyes flashing with more than a touch of anger as if he'd lit some personal touchpaper. The air seemed to fizzle with it and he wondered what would have happened if, instead of listening to his head last night and walking away, he'd listened to her.

I don't want to be safe...

He took a step back, needing to put some space between them, but she wasn't done.

'Don't give up on her, George,' she said, leaning towards him, appealing to him. 'Don't give up on yourself.'

'I'm sure you mean well, Annie, but don't waste your time playing Santa Claus. It's not going to happen.' He pushed the paper towards her. 'You'd be better occupied thinking about your own future than worrying about mine. What you're going to do next week. The money you've got stashed in your underwear isn't going to last very long when you're out there on your own.'

Reminding her that she might have found a temporary sanctuary, but that was all it was.

Reminding himself.

Annie let out a long silent breath as he walked away, but it had more to do with the anger, the pain that had come off him like a blast of ice than fear that he'd seen through her disguise.

Although maybe, she thought, looking down at the glasses in her hand, maybe she should be worrying about that.

She'd assumed that he'd pushed the paper at her so that she could check out her 'double'. Think about the career opportunities it offered. But he hadn't actually said that.

Even with the evidence that she wasn't the 'people's virgin'—and could it be any more lowering than to have her lack of sexual experience pitied by a sixteen-year-old?—on the table in front of her.

She was in Bab el Sama. It said so right there for the whole world to see, yet still he'd handed her back her disguise as if he thought she needed it.

Too late for that, she thought, dropping the glasses into her bag and switching on her cellphone to thumb in a quick text to Lydia.

Tomorrow there would have to be pictures to prove she was there.

'Are you all right, dear?' The woman who'd served them came to clear the table and wipe it down and glanced after George meaningfully.

'I'm fine,' she said, switching off the phone. 'Honestly.'

'Christmas…' she said, sighing as Rudolph started up yet again. 'It's all stress. You wouldn't believe the things I hear. Did you know that there are more marriage break-ups over Christmas than at any other time of year?'

'Really? I'll bear that in mind. Should I ever get married.'

'Oh… You and he aren't…?'

'We only met yesterday, but thank you for caring,' Annie said, stowing her phone and standing up. 'Being ready to listen. That's the true spirit of the season.'

'The Christmas fairy, that's me,' she said with an embarrassed laugh before whisking away the tray.

And nothing wrong with that, Annie thought, before crossing to the window to see how far things had progressed.

One of the trees had already been hoisted onto the roof of the car, but as George and a good-looking boy bent to lift the second, larger tree, Xandra, who had climbed up to lash the first into place, stopped what she was doing and looked down, not at the boy, but at her father.

Full of longing, need, it was a look that she recognised, understood and she forgot her own concerns as her heart went out to the girl.

They'd both lost their parents, but in Xandra's case the situation wasn't irretrievable. Her mother might not be perfect but she'd be home in a few weeks. And George was here right now, bringing the scent of fresh spruce with him as he returned to the chalet to pay for the trees.

For once it didn't bring a lump to her throat, the ache of unbearable memories. This wasn't her Christmas, but Xandra's. A real celebration to share with the grandparents she adored. And with George, if he took his chance and seized the opportunity to change things.

'All done?' she asked.

He gave her a look that suggested she had to be joking. 'This is just the beginning. When we get back I'm going to have to find suitable containers and erect them safely so that they don't topple over if the cat decides to go climbing.'

'Back', not home, she noticed. He never called the house he'd grown up in 'home'.

'Then I'll have to sort out lights and check them to make sure they won't blow all the fuses.'

'Why don't you ask that boy to give you a hand?' she suggested. 'Earn yourself some Brownie points with your daughter.'

'I don't think so,' he said, handing a grubby handwritten docket to the woman behind the till along with some bank-notes.

Protective. A good start, she thought.

'You can't keep her wrapped in cotton wool.' At least not without the kind of money that would make Dower House fees look like chicken feed. 'And, even if you could, she wouldn't thank you for it.'

'Nothing new there, then,' he said, slotting the pound coins the woman gave him as change into a charity box on the counter.

They piled back into the car and this time Xandra gave her more room so she wasn't squashed up against George. Just close enough to be tinglingly aware of every movement. For his hand to brush her thigh each time he changed gear.

'We'll need to stop at the garden centre in Longbourne to pick up some bags of compost,' Xandra said carelessly as he paused at the farm gate. 'If the trees are to have a chance of surviving.'

'I don't think—'

'Granddad always plants out the Christmas trees,' she said stubbornly.

'I remember,' he muttered under his breath so that only she heard. Then, raising his voice above the sound of the engine, 'He won't be fit enough to do it this year, Xandra.'

Her eyes widened a little as the reality of her grandfather's heart attack truly hit home, but then she shrugged. 'It's not a problem. I can do it.'

'Damn you!' George banged the steering wheel with the flat of his hand. 'You are just like him, do you know that? Stubborn, pig-headed, deaf to reason…'

Xandra's only response was to switch on the personal stereo in her jacket pocket and stick in her earplugs.

George didn't say a word and Annie kept her own mouth firmly shut as they pulled into the garden centre car park.

It was one of those out of town places and it had a huge range of house plants that had been forced for the holiday, as well as every kind of seasonal decoration imaginable.

While George disappeared in search of compost, Annie used the time to pick out a dark pink cyclamen for Hetty and Xandra disappeared into the Christmas grotto.

When they met at the till ten minutes later she was half

hidden behind an armful of decorations in just about every colour imaginable—none of that colour co-ordination nonsense for her—and wearing a three-foot-long Santa hat.

CHAPTER NINE

ANNIE, desperate to find some way to make George see beyond the defence mechanism that his daughter was using to save herself from the risk of hurt, was so deep in thought as she pushed open the kitchen door with her shoulder that the spicy scent of the Christmas cake baking took her unawares.

A punch to the heart.

Like the fresh, zingy scent of the trees, it evoked only painful memories and the armful of tinsel she was carrying slithered to the floor as she came to a dead stop.

'What's wrong?' George asked, following her in.

She tried to speak, couldn't. Instead, she shook her head and, giving herself time to recover, she bent to scoop up the glittering strands, only to find herself face to face with George as he joined her down at floor level.

'What is it?' he asked quietly as he took the pot plant from her.

'Nothing. It's nothing.' Dredging up a smile—a lady never showed her feelings—she wound a thick gold strand of tinsel around his neck. 'Just blinded by all this glitter,' she said, clutching it to her as she made a move to stand.

He caught her by the wrist, keeping her where she was.

'G-George...' she begged, her voice hoarse with the effort of keeping up the smile.

'You will tell me,' he warned her, his own smile just as broad, just as false as her own as he took a purple strand of tinsel and slowly wrapped it, once, twice around her throat before, his hand still tightly around her wrist, he drew her to her feet.

'Oh, well, there's a picture,' Hetty said, laughing as she caught sight of them. 'Did you buy up their entire stock, Xan?'

'You can never have too much tinsel,' she said as she trailed in with the rest of it.

'Is that right?' She took her coat from the hook and said, 'I'll be off now, if you don't mind, Annie. The cake should be done by one-thirty. I've set the timer. Just stick a skewer in the centre and if it comes out clean you can take it out.' She put on her gloves, found her car keys and picked up a bag laden with treats for the invalid. 'I've made vegetable soup for lunch. Just help yourself.'

'Can I do something about dinner?' Annie asked.

George, giving her a look that suggested she was kidding herself, said, 'Why don't I get a takeaway?'

'Oh, great!' Xandra said, sorting through the tinsel and finding a heavy strand in shocking pink and throwing it around herself like a boa. 'Can we have Chinese? Please, please, please…'

'Annie?' he asked, turning to her.

'I couldn't think of anything I'd like more,' she said and got a quizzical look for her pains. She ignored it. 'I hope Mr Saxon will be feeling better today, Hetty.'

'Can I come with you?' Xandra asked. 'I could decorate his bed. Cheer him up.'

'I don't think they'll let you do that. Decorations would get in the way if…' Her voice faltered momentarily before she forced a smile. 'And what about this tree you've bought? You can't leave your father to put it up by himself.'

'Trees. We bought two, but they'll wait until the morning.'

'Will they? But if you come with me you'll be stuck in

the hospital all day. And, besides, Granddad will want to know why you're home. I don't think it'll do his heart any good if he finds out you've been suspended from school, young lady.'

'He wouldn't care. He thinks Dower House is a total waste of money.'

'Your grandfather always did believe that education is for wimps,' George said. Then, clearly wishing he'd kept his mouth shut, he said, 'Go with your grandmother—'

'George—'

'I'll pick her up when I've finished the Bentley,' he said, glancing at his watch. 'Three o'clock? Be waiting outside. I'm not coming in to fetch you.'

'Congratulations, George,' Annie said when they'd gone. 'You came within a cat's whisker of behaving like a father for a moment, but you managed to rescue the situation before you could be mistaken for anyone who gives a damn.'

Furious with him for missing such a chance, she crossed to the stove, took the lid off the soup and banged it on the side.

'Pass me a bowl if you want some of this,' she said, sticking out a hand.

He put a bowl in it without a word and she filled the ladle with the thick soup, only to find her hand was shaking so much that she couldn't hold it. She dropped it back in the saucepan and George grabbed the bowl before she dropped that too.

'Damn you,' she said, hanging onto the rail that ran along the front of the oven. 'Would it have hurt you so much to spend a few minutes with your father? Have you any idea how lucky you are to have him? Have a mother who cares enough to make your favourite food?'

She turned to face him. He was still wearing the tinsel and he should have looked ridiculous. The truth was that he could have been wearing a pair of glass tree baubles dangling from his ears and Xandra's Santa hat and he'd still melt her bones.

That didn't lessen her anger.

'What did he do to you?' she asked. 'Why do you hate him so much?'

'It's what he didn't do that's the problem, but this isn't about me, is it?'

He reached out, touched her cheek, then held up his fingers so that she could see that they were wet.

'Why are you crying, Annie?'

'For the waste. The stupid waste…' Then, dragging in a deep, shuddering breath, she shook her head and rubbed her palms over her face to dry tears she hadn't been conscious of shedding. 'I'm sorry. You're right. I've no right to shout at you. I know nothing about what happened between you and your father. It's just this time of year. It's just…'

She stalled, unable to even say the word.

'It's just Christmas,' he said. 'I saw the way you reacted when you walked into the kitchen. As if you'd been struck. Spice, nuts, fruit, brandy. It's the quintessential smell of the season. And scent evokes memory as nothing else can.'

She opened her mouth, closed it. Swallowed.

'You think you're alone in hating it?'

She shook her head. Took a long, shuddering breath. Then, realising what he'd said, she looked up. 'Xandra said you hate Christmas. Said she knew why.'

'I came home for Christmas at the end of my first term at university to be met with the news that Penny was pregnant. My father was delighted, in case you're wondering. He thought I'd have to give up all thought of university and join him in the business. He was going to build us a house in the paddock, give me a partnership—'

'And you turned him down.'

'Penny thought, once we were actually married—and believe me, there's nothing like a shotgun wedding to add a little cheer for Christmas—that she could persuade me to change my mind.' He managed a wry smile. 'I've never eaten Christmas cake since.'

She stared at him, then realised that he was joking. Making light of a desperate memory. She wondered just how much pressure—emotional and financial—he'd endured.

'You didn't have to marry her. People don't these days.'

'It was my responsibility. My baby.'

She reached out to him. Touched his big, capable hand. Afraid for him.

If Xandra had inherited just one tenth of his stubborn determination, she feared they were heading for the kind of confrontation that could shatter any hope of reconciliation.

'What happened to you, Annie?' he asked. 'What are you really running away from?'

'Apart from Christmas?'

'There's no escape from that,' he said, 'unless, like Lady Rose Napier, you can borrow a palace from a friend.'

How ironic was that? She'd sent Lydia to a Christmas free zone, while she'd found herself in tinsel land.

'How is it on a Californian beach?' she asked in an attempt to head off the big question.

'Sunny, but it's not the weather, or the decorations or the carols. The trouble with Christmas is that, no matter how high the presents are piled, it shines a light into the empty spaces. Highlights what's missing from your life.' He curved his palm around her cheek. 'What's missing from yours, Annie?'

His touch was warm, his gentle voice coaxing and somehow the words were out before she could stop them.

'My parents. They were killed a week before the holiday. They were away and I was fizzing with excitement, waiting for them to come home so that we could decorate the tree, but they never came.'

There was an infinitesimal pause as he absorbed this information. 'Was it a road accident?'

They had been on a road. Four innocent people who, in the true spirit of Christmas, had been taking aid to a group of desperate people. Food, medicine, clothes, toys even. She'd sent her favourite doll for them to give to some poor homeless, starving child.

She wanted to tell him all that, but she couldn't because then he'd know who she was and she'd have to leave. And she didn't want to leave.

'They were passengers,' she said. 'Two other people with them died, too.' She never forgot them or their families, who went through this same annual nightmare as she did. 'They were buried on the day before Christmas Eve and then everything went on as if nothing had changed. The tree lights were turned on, there were candles in the church on Christmas morning, presents after tea. It was what they would have expected, I was told. Anything else would be letting them down.'

And then there had been the Boxing Day shoot.

She looked up at George. 'Every year it's as if I'm six years old,' she said, trying to make him understand. 'The tree, church, unwrapping presents. Going through the motions, smiling because it's expected and every year that makes me a little bit more—' she clenched her fists, trying to catch the word, but it spilled over, unstoppable '—angry.'

She didn't know where that had come from, but it was as if at that moment a dam had burst and all the pent-up emotion of the last twenty years burst out.

'I hate it,' she said, banging on his chest with her bunched fists. 'Hate the carols…' Bang… 'Hate the lights…' Bang… 'The falseness…' He caught her wrists.

'Is that what you're really running away from, Annie?' he asked, holding her off.

'Yes.' She pulled back, shaking her head as she crumpled against the stove and slid to the floor. 'No…'

George didn't try to coax her up, but kept hold of her

hands, going down with her, encouraging her to lean against him so that her cheek was against the hard fabric of his overalls.

'No,' he agreed.

He smelled of engine oil, spruce, some warmer scent that was George himself that mingled to make something new, something that held no bad memories for her, and she let her head fall against his chest.

'You can run away from Christmas, Annie, but you can't escape what it is you hate about it. The bad memories.'

'I thought if I could just get away for a while, see things from a different perspective,' she said after a while, 'I might find a way to deal with it. But you're right. It's nothing to do with the season. It simply shines a light on everything that's wrong in our lives.'

George held her, her hair against his cheek, thinking about an unhappy little girl who had spent year after year being brave for the adults who clearly hadn't a clue how to cope with her grief. And he wondered whether his daughter's desperate need to decorate every surface for the holiday exposed the emptiness at the heart of her life too.

'We are what circumstances make us,' he said, leaning back. 'My father used to make me work in the garage. Every day, after school, he set me a task that I had to finish before I was allowed to go and get on with my homework.'

He knew she'd turned to look up at him, but he kept staring ahead, remembering how it had been.

Remembering the weeks, months, years when anger had kept him going.

'I learned fast.' He'd had to if he was to defeat his father. 'He set me ever more complex, time-consuming tasks, reasoning that if I failed at school I would have no choice but to stay here, so that he could be George Saxon and not just the "and Son".'

By the time he'd been old enough to work that out, pity him, the battle lines were drawn and there was no going back.

'If I inherited one thing from my old man it was obstinacy. I got up early, worked late. Learned to manage on the minimum of sleep. And when I left for university I was the best mechanic in the garage, including my father. He never forgave me for that.'

Finally he looked down at her, not quite believing that he was sharing his most painful memories with a woman he'd picked up on the side of the road the evening before.

Could scarcely believe that sitting here, on the floor of his mother's kitchen with his arm around her, was the nearest he'd come to peace for as long as he could remember.

'And you still found time for girls?'

'That last summer, before I went up to university, I found time for a lot of things that I'd missed out on.' Life at home might have been unbearable, but there had been compensations. 'The minute I turned eighteen, I got a job at a garage that paid me what I was actually worth.'

'Your poor mother. It must have been as restful as living with two big cats walking stiff-legged around one another, hackles raised.'

He smiled. 'Don't tell me, you were the fly on the wall?'

'I've spent a lot of my life watching people. I can read body language as well as I read English.'

He must have shown a flicker of dismay because she laughed. 'Most body language. There are gaps in my knowledge.'

'What kind of gaps?'

She shook her head. 'Tell me what you did. After you'd turned your back on the "and Son". What paid for the California beach house? The fees for Dower House?'

'I knew two things—software engineering and cars—so I put them together and developed a software application for the motor industry. My father disapproves of computers on principle. Driving, for him, is a question of man and machine—nothing in between. So he never forgave me for that, either.'

'Maybe you have to forgive yourself first,' she said.

Forgive himself?

For a moment his brain floundered with the concept, but only for a moment. Annie was looking up at him, smiling a little as if she knew something he didn't. The tears she'd shed had added a sparkle to her eyes and as her lips parted to reveal a glimpse of perfect teeth he forgot what she'd said, knew only that he wanted to kiss her, was trembling with the need to kiss her in a way he hadn't since he was eighteen years old and Penny Lomax had made a man of him.

'Who are you?' he demanded, but as she opened her mouth to answer him he covered it with his hand.

'No. Don't tell me. I don't want to know.'

He didn't want her to tell him anything that would stop him from kissing her, from doing what he'd wanted to do ever since she'd stumbled into him and her scent had taken up residence in his head.

Fluent in body language, she knew exactly what he was thinking and didn't wait, but reached up and pulled him down to her, coming up to meet him with a raw to-hell-and-back kiss that said only one thing.

I want you. I need you.

Her other hand, clutching at his shoulder, her nails digging through the heavy material of his overalls, proclaimed the urgency of that need.

The heat of it shuddered through him, igniting a flame that would have taken an ice-cold shower to cool. Sitting by a solid-fuel stove, they didn't stand a chance, even if he'd wanted one, he thought, tugging her shirt free of her jeans and reaching inside it to unhook the fastening of her bra. He half expected a bundle of twenty-pound notes to cascade out of it but, as he slid his hand inside it, it was filled with nothing more than a small, firm breast.

She moaned into his mouth, tearing at the studs on his overalls, her touch electric as she pushed up the T-shirt he was wearing beneath it before drawing back a little to look up at him, her eyes shining like hot sapphires, silently asking permission to touch him.

He shrugged his arms out of his overalls, pulled off the T-shirt he was wearing beneath it and fell back against the thick rag rug that had lain in that spot for as long as he could remember.

'Help yourself,' he said, grinning as he offered himself up to her.

Her fingers stopped a tantalising hair's breadth from his skin.

'What can I do?'

Do?

'Anything...' he began, then caught his breath as her finger-tips made contact with his chest. 'Anything that feels good,' he managed, through a throat apparently stuffed with cobwebs. 'Good for you,' he added and he nearly lost it as they trailed down his chest, her long nails grazing the hollow of his stomach.

For a moment, as she straightened, he thought she'd changed her mind, but she caught the hem of her sweater and pulled it, shirt and bra over her head and discarded them impatiently. Her long body was taut, strong, her breasts were high, firm, beautiful and her eyes widened in shock and a shiver ran through her body as he touched a nipple.

'You like that?' he asked.

She made an unintelligible sound that was pure delight and, seizing her around the waist, he lifted her so that she straddled his body, wanting her to know that he liked it too. To feel his heat, know what she was doing to him. Had been doing to him since the moment she'd pitched into his arms.

For a moment she didn't move, then, with the tiniest of

sighs, she bent to lay her lips against his stomach and this time the moan came from him.

'You like that?' she asked mischievously, looking up with the smile of a child who'd just been given the freedom of a sweet shop. Then he was the one catching his breath as she leaned forward to touch her lips to his, her breasts brushing his chest. He wanted to crush her to him, overwhelm her, cut short the teasing foreplay, but some things were too good to rush and this was going to be very good indeed.

As she took her lips on a slow trail of moist kisses over his chin, down his throat, he held her in the very lightest of touches, his hands doing no more than rest against her ribcage, giving her control, all the time, all the freedom she wanted to explore his body, knowing that his time would come.

Little feathers of silky hair brushed against his skin, a subtle counterpoint to her tongue probing the hollows beneath his shoulders, to the satiny feel of her skin as his hands slid lower over her back, exploring the curve of her waist, learning the shape of her body.

Annie was drowning in pure sensation. The gentle touch of George's hands as he caressed her back, her waist, slipping beneath the loose waist of her jeans to cup her bottom in his hands, holding her close so that she could feel the power of his need as she kissed and licked and nibbled at his chest, the hollow of his stomach. Came against the barrier of clothes.

Her lips were hot, swollen against his skin and every cell in her body was thrumming with power. For the first time in her life she felt totally alive, warm, vital. This ache in her womb, this need was the essence of life, of being a woman and she wanted him. Wanted all of him.

'Touch me,' she whispered as she pulled at the next stud.

Begging or commanding?

It didn't matter. He'd told her she could do anything that felt good. And this felt…

He released the button at the waist of her jeans, pushed jeans, underwear over her hips.

There were no words to describe what this felt like. All she could manage was his name.

'George…'

And then her body shattered.

George caught her, held her as she collapsed against him, kissing her shoulder, nuzzling his chin against her hair as she recovered, trying not to think about the look in her eyes, an appeal for something unknown, in that moment before she'd dissolved into his arms.

Because he knew where he'd see it before.

He murmured her name and when she looked up, her eyes filled with tears, he knew it was true. She was the 'people's virgin'.

'Will I get sent to the Tower for that?' he asked.

'Not by me,' she assured him, laughing shakily.

Damn it, she was crying with gratitude.

She sniffed. Brushed the tears from her cheeks with the palm of her hand, lifted damp lashes and finally realised that he wasn't laughing with her.

'What?' she asked. 'What did I do?'

He didn't answer and he saw the exact moment when she realised that she answered not to the lie she'd told him when she'd sworn that Annie was her real name, but to Lady Rose.

'Rose*anne*,' she said. 'My name is Rose*anne*. I was named for my grandmother but my mother thought I was entitled to a name of my own so she called me Annie.'

Did she think that was all that mattered? That she hadn't actually lied about that.

Then, when he didn't answer, 'Does it matter?'

He picked up the clothes she'd discarded and thrust them at her.

'George?'

For a long moment she didn't take them but continued to look at him, those dangerous eyes pleading with him.

All his senses were vibrating with the feel of her, her touch, the musky scent of her most intimate being. They were urging him to say that it didn't matter a damn before reaching out to take what she was offering him. Pretend that nothing mattered but this moment.

The shattering sound of the timer announcing that the cake was done saved them both.

'Clearly it does,' she said, snatching her clothes from his hand, standing up, turning her back on him as she pulled them on.

'You used me,' he said to her back. 'You're on a quest to lose your virginity before you settle for the guy with the castle.'

'If that's what you think then there's nothing more to say. Pass me the oven gloves,' she said, sticking out a hand as she opened the oven door.

He got up, passed her the thickly padded gloves, then pulled the overalls back on, fastening the studs with shaking fingers while, still with her back to him, she tested the cake.

'Is it done?'

'As if you care,' she replied, still not looking at him but turning the cake out over the rack his mother had left out. When the cake didn't fall out she gave it a shake, catching her breath as the hot tin touched the pale skin of her inner arm.

'You have to leave it to cool for a few minutes,' he said, taking her hand, turning it to look at the red mark.

'I get cookery lessons too?'

'Simple physics,' he said, not bothering to ask her if it hurt, just grabbing her hand and taking her to the sink, where he turned on the cold tap, holding the burn beneath the running water.

It was icy-cold and he knew that would hurt as much as

the burn but she clamped her jaws together. Schooled from the age of six not to show pain, she'd saved her tears for him.

It had taken the new, shocking pleasure of a man's intimate touch to break down that reserve, reduce her to weeping for herself.

'Who is she?' he asked, not wanting to think about how that made him feel. Feeling would destroy him. 'The girl in the photograph.'

'Lydia,' she said.

'The friend who lent you her car? But she—'

'Looks just like me? Type "Lady Rose" and "lookalike" into your search engine and you can book her next time you want "Lady Rose Napier" to grace your party.'

'Why would I want a copy…?'

He managed to stop himself but she finished for him. 'Why would you want a copy when you rejected the real thing?'

She was shaking, he realised. Or maybe it was him.

'She's a professional lookalike?'

'Since she was fifteen years old. Her mother made her a copy of the outfit I was wearing on my sixteenth birthday and someone took a picture and sent it to the local newspaper. It's not a full-time job for her, of course, but the manager of the supermarket where she works is very good about juggling her shifts.'

'You paid a girl who works in a supermarket to take your place?'

'No. She wouldn't take any money. We met by chance one day and there was a connection.'

'I'll bet there was. Do you really trust her not to sell her story to the tabloids the minute she gets home?'

She looked up at him. 'Do you know something, George? I don't really care. I wanted to escape and she was willing to take my place so that I could disappear without raising a hue and cry. Once I go back I don't care who knows.'

'But how on earth will she carry it off? It's one thing turning up at a party where everyone knows you're not the real thing, but something like this...' Words failed him.

'There's no one at Bab el Sama who knows me. I insisted on going there on my own.'

'But if you wanted a break, surely—'

'I wanted a break from being me, George. From my grandfather's unspoken expectations. I wanted to be ordinary. Just be...myself.'

'How is that?' he asked, gently dabbing her arm dry.

'I can't feel a thing.'

He nodded. 'I've got a car to fix,' he said, tossing the towel aside, wishing he could say the same.

He walked from the room while he still could.

CHAPTER TEN

ANNIE, weak to her bones, leaned against the sink. What had she done, said, to give herself away?

A tear trickled onto her cheek and as she palmed it away she knew. He'd responded to her not as a national institution but as a woman and she'd wept with the joy of it. Ironic, really, when she'd spent her entire life keeping her emotions under wraps.

Tears were private things.

Before the cameras you kept your dignity, looked the world in the eye.

But with a lover you could be yourself. Utterly, completely...

A long shivering sigh escaped her but the years of training stood her in good stead. She took a deep breath, straightened, told herself that George had every right to be angry.

What man, on discovering that what he'd imagined was a quick tumble in the metaphorical hay had the potential to make him front-page news, wouldn't be absolutely livid?

She might be inexperienced, but she wasn't naïve.

Sex exposed two people in a way that nothing else could. It wasn't the nakedness, but the stripping away of pretence that took it beyond the purely physical. Without total honesty it was a sham, a lie.

She knew how she'd feel if he'd lied to her about his

identity. But he'd laid it all out while she hadn't even been honest about the way her parents had died.

She had abused his trust in the most fundamental way and now she would have to leave. First, though, she carefully turned out the cake and left it to cool. Washed the cake tin. Put away the soup bowls.

Straightened the rag rug.

When all trace of her presence had been erased, she went upstairs and threw everything into her bag. Then, because she couldn't leave without saying goodbye to Xandra, she walked along the hall, opening doors, searching for her room, and found herself standing in the doorway of the room in which George Saxon had grown up.

The cashmere sweater he'd been wearing the day before was draped over the wooden chair. She touched it, then picked it up, hugging it to her as she looked around at what had been his boyhood room.

It was sparse by modern standards, with none of the high-tech appliances that were the essential requirements of the average teen's life. Just a narrow bed with an old-fashioned quilt, a small scarred table he'd used as a desk and a bookcase. She knelt to run her fingers over the spines of the books he'd held, read. Physics, maths, computer languages.

The car maintenance manuals seemed out of place, but keeping ahead of his father must have required more than manual dexterity, although personally she'd have given him a starred A for that.

She stood up, holding the sweater to her face for a moment, yearning to pull it over her head and walk away with it. Instead, she refolded it and laid it back on the chair before leaving the room, closing the door behind her.

Xandra's room was next door. Large, comfortable, a total contrast to her father's childhood room, it was obvious that she spent a lot of time with her grandparents.

She had a small colour television, an expensive laptop,

although the girlish embroidered bed cover was somewhat at odds with the posters of racing drivers rather than pop stars that decorated the walls.

There was paper and a pen on the writing desk and a note to Mrs Warburton ready for the post.

She picked up the pen, then put it down again. What could she say? She couldn't tell her the truth and she couldn't bear to write a lie. Better to leave George to make whatever excuses he thought best.

Downstairs, she'd looked up the number of a taxi firm and made the call. She'd catch a bus or a train; it didn't matter where to, so long as it was leaving Maybridge.

'It's a busy time of the day,' the dispatcher warned her. 'It'll be half an hour before we can pick you up.'

'That will be fine,' she said. It wasn't, but if it was a busy time she'd get the same response from anyone else. As she replaced the receiver, the cat found her legs and she bent to pick it up, ruffling it behind the ear as she carried it into the study to wait in the chair where George had fallen asleep the night before. Self-indulgently resting her head in the place where his had been.

The cat settled on her lap, purring contentedly and she closed her eyes for a moment, letting herself rerun images of George's body, his face as he'd looked at her, the taste of his skin, his lips, the way he'd touched her. Fixing it like a film in her memory so that she would be able to take it out and run it like a video when she needed to remind herself what it was like to just let go.

'Annie!'

She woke with a start as the cat dug its claws into her legs before fleeing.

It took her a moment for her head to clear, to focus on George standing in the doorway. 'Sorry, I must have fallen asleep. Is my taxi here?'

'Were you going to leave without a word?' he demanded.

'What word did you expect? I can't stay here, George. Not now you know who I am.'

He didn't bother to deny it. 'Where are you going?'

'That's none of your business.'

'You think?' He moved so swiftly that she didn't have time to do more than think about moving before his hands were on either side of her, pinning her in the chair. 'Do you really believe I'm going to let the nation's sweetheart wander off into the wild blue yonder by herself with a fistful of money stuffed down her bra?'

He was close enough that she could see the vein throbbing at his temple, the tiny sparks of hot anger that were firing the lead grey of his eyes, turning it molten.

'I don't think you have a choice.'

'Think again, Your Ladyship. I've got a whole heap of options open to me, while you've got just two. One, you stay here where I know you're safe. Two, I take you home to your grandfather, His Grace the Duke of Oldfield. Take your pick.'

'You've been checking up on me?'

'You're not the only one with a fancy Internet cellphone.'

Obviously he had. Searched for her on the Net instead of asking. Maybe he thought that was the only way to get straight answers. Her fault.

'And if I don't fancy either of those options?' she asked, refusing to be browbeaten into capitulation. 'You said you had a whole heap?'

'I could ring around the tabloids and tell them what you've been doing for the last twenty-four hours.'

'You wouldn't do that.' He'd hesitated for a fraction of a second before he'd spoken and instinctively she lifted her hand to his face. His cold cheek warmed to her touch. His eyes darkened. 'You wouldn't betray me, George.'

'Try me,' he said, abruptly straightening, taking a step back, putting himself out of reach. Pulling the shutters down, just as he had with Xandra. 'Anything could happen to you out there. Use a little of your famous empathy to consider how I'd feel if anything did.'

'I'm not your responsibility.'

'You can't absolve me of that. I know who you are. That changes everything.'

'I'm sorry,' she said.

'Prove it.'

'By going home or staying here until the seventeenth?'

'The seventeenth?' He looked hunted, as if the prospect of a whole week of her company appalled him, but he said, 'If that's your time frame, then yes. Take your pick.'

'It's a long time to put up with a stranger.' And a long time to spend with a man who despised you. 'If you let me go I'll be careful,' she promised.

'Would that be reversing-into-a-farm-gate-in-the-dark careful?'

'I'll use public transport.'

'That's supposed to reassure me? You stay here or you go home,' he said. 'It's not open for discussion.'

'What would you say to your mother if I stayed?'

'She's got more important things to worry about. This is just between us,' he warned. 'As far as Xandra and my mother are concerned, you're Annie Rowland. Is that understood?'

'You guessed who I was,' she pointed out.

'I don't think they're ever going to see you quite the way I did.'

'No?' She felt a tremor deep within her at the memory of just how he'd seen her. Remembered how powerful she'd felt as he'd looked at her, touched her. As she'd touched him. She wanted that again. Wanted him... 'If I stay, George,' she asked softly, 'will you finish what you started?'

He opened his mouth, then shut it again sharply. Shook his head.

No. Faced with her image, he was just like everyone else.

Being the nation's virgin was, apparently, the world's biggest turn-off.

'It's just sex, George,' she said, hoping that she could provoke him, disgust him sufficiently so that he would let her go.

'If it's just sex, Annie, I'm sure Rupert Devenish would be happy to do you the favour. Put it on the top of your Christmas wish list. Or does he have to wait until he puts a ring on your finger? Were you simply looking for something a little more earthy than His Lordship before you settle for the coronet?'

If he'd actually hit her the shock couldn't have been more brutal. It wasn't the suggestion that she was on the loose looking for a bit of rough. It was the fact that he thought she'd marry for position, the castle, the estates, that drove through her heart like a dagger. And maybe the fear that, in desperation, six months, a year from now she might settle for the chance to be a mother.

Picking up the phone, admitting what she'd done and waiting for a car to take her home would, she knew without doubt, be the first step.

It took her a moment to gather herself, find her voice. 'I'd better go and pay the taxi.'

'It's done.'

'What?' Then, realising what he meant, 'You sent it away without waiting for my answer?'

'He's busy. You owe me twenty pounds, by the way.'

'A little more than that, surely? There's the call-out charge, towing me back to the garage, the time you spent on the car.' She looked up enquiringly when he didn't answer. 'Or shall I ask Xandra to prepare the invoice for that?'

'Forget it,' he said. 'The garage is closed. And forget the taxi fare too.'

'What about board and lodging? Or do you expect me to work for my keep?'

'You are my daughter's guest,' he said, glancing at his watch. 'And right now we have to go and pick her up.'

'We?'

'You don't imagine I'm going to leave you here on your own?'

She thought about arguing with him for all of a second before she said, 'I'll get my coat.'

Two minutes later she was wrapped in the soft leather of the sports car that had been parked on the garage forecourt and heading towards Maybridge General.

They exchanged barely two words as the car ate up the miles but, when he pulled into the pick-up bay a couple of minutes before three, Annie said, 'There's a parking space over there.'

'It's nearly three. Xandra will be here any minute.'

She didn't say a word.

'Are you suggesting that she won't?'

'I'm suggesting that she'll make you go and get her, so you might as well make a virtue out of a necessity.'

'I could send you.'

'You could. But then you'd have to come and get me too. Always supposing I don't take the opportunity to leave by another entrance.'

'Without your bag?'

'I could replace everything in it in ten minutes.'

'A thousand pounds won't go far if you're travelling by public transport. Staying at hotels.'

Again she said nothing.

'There's more? How much?'

'You'll have to search me to discover that,' she said, glancing at him. 'I won't resist.'

His hands tightened on the steering wheel, the knuckles turning white.

'Go and visit your father. It would make your mother happy, make Xandra happy. And me. It would make me very happy.'

'And why would I give a damn whether you're happy or not?'

He was so stubborn. He knew it was the right thing to do, wanted to build bridges with his daughter, but pride kept him from taking that first step. She'd just have to give him a little push.

'Because, if you don't, George, I'll be the one calling the tabloids to tell them that Lady Rose isn't in Bab el Sama but holed up at Saxon's Garage. With her lover.'

'Lover!'

'Why spoil a good story by telling the truth?' she said. 'They certainly won't.'

'You wouldn't do that.'

Exactly what she'd said when he'd threatened her.

'Within an hour of our return from the hospital there'll be television crews, photographers and half the press pack on your doorstep.'

'They wouldn't believe you. They've seen you get on a plane.'

'So what? You were bluffing?'

'Of course I was bluffing!'

He cared, she thought. Cared enough.

So did she.

'Take your pick, George. Visit your father or let me go.'

George dragged both hands through his hair. 'I can't. Please, Annie, you must see that. If anything happened to you—'

'You'd never forgive yourself? Oh, dear. That is unfortunate because, you see, I'm not bluffing. And I know those journalists well enough to convince them I'm not some fantasist sending them on a wild-goose chase.' She held her breath. Would he believe her? After what seemed like the longest moment in history, he glared at her, then pulled over into the empty space she'd pointed out. Cut the engine.

'This isn't going to work,' he said, releasing his seat belt, climbing out. 'Whatever it is you think you're doing.' She jumped as he vented his frustration on the car door, but made no move to get out, forcing him to walk around to the passenger door and open it for her.

George watched as she swung her long legs over the sill, stood up and, without a word, walked towards the entrance of the hospital.

'You know that's a dead giveaway too,' he said when he caught up with her. 'Modern independent women can usually manage a car door.'

'If you insist on acting as my bodyguard, George, I'll insist on treating you like one.'

'Remind me why they call you the nation's sweetheart?' he said.

'Sweetheart, angel, virgin.' She stopped without warning and looked at him, a tiny frown wrinkling her smooth forehead. '*Am* I still the people's virgin?' she asked, her clear voice carrying down the corridor. 'Technically?'

'Annie!' He grabbed her elbow in an attempt to hurry her past a couple of nurses who'd turned to stare. 'What the hell do you think you're doing?'

'Behaving badly?' she offered, staying stubbornly put. 'It's a new experience for me and I'm rather enjoying it. But you didn't answer my question. Am I—'

'Don't say another word,' he snapped. He didn't want to talk about it. Or think about it. Fat chance. He hadn't been able to think about anything else all afternoon and while his head was saying no, absolutely no, a thousand times no, his body was refusing to listen. 'It's this way.'

But it wasn't. His father had improved sufficiently to be moved out of the cardiac suite and into a small ward. Xandra was sitting cross-legged on the bed, Santa hat perched on her head, while his father occupied an armchair beside it. He was laughing at something she'd said and it was obvious that they were on the same wavelength, despite the generation gap. That they liked one another. Were friends. Everything that he and his father were not. Everything that he and his daughter were not.

They both froze as they saw him.

'I was just coming,' Xandra said, immediately defensive.

'No problem,' he lied. 'We were a bit early.'

'Is this Annie?' his father asked, looking beyond him. 'Xandra's been telling me all about you.'

'Oh, dear…' she stepped forward, hand extended—a scene reminiscent of every news clip he'd ever seen of a royal hospital visit '…I don't like the sound of that!' Then, 'How d'you do, Mr Saxon?'

'I do very well, thank you,' he said. 'Certainly well enough to get out of here.'

'I'm glad to hear it.'

George wondered how many times she'd done that. Visited a total stranger in hospital, completely at ease, sure of her welcome.

'Xandra is a tonic,' he said. Then, finally turning to grudgingly acknowledge him, 'You've managed to drag yourself into the garage, I see.'

'Mike is picking up the Bentley in an hour.'

The nod his father managed was as close as he'd ever come to a thank you and he thought that was it, but he said, 'We've been looking after his cars ever since he started the business. I'm glad we didn't let him down.' And then he looked up. 'Thanks, son.'

The words were barely audible but he'd said them and it was George's turn to be lost for words.

It was Annie who broke the silence. 'Where's Hetty?'

'She went to the shop to get Granddad an evening paper,' Xandra said, watching them both.

'You could die of boredom in here,' his father said, with considerably more force in his voice than the day before. 'I don't care what that doctor says, I'm going home tomorrow.'

'Dad…' he protested.

'Your mother will take care of me,' he said stubbornly, the brief moment of rapport already history.

Annie's hand grabbed his before he let slip his first response, which was to tell him not to be so selfish.

'We'll all take care of you,' Xandra said quickly, looking at him, her eyes pleading with him to say that it would be all right. As if what he said actually mattered.

They were all taking tiny steps here and for a moment he clung to Annie's hand as if to a lifeline. She squeezed his fingers, encouraging him to take the risk, throw his heart into the ring.

'If that's what you want,' he said, 'I'm sure we'll manage. Especially since Annie is staying on for a while to help out.'

'Really?' Xandra grinned. 'Great. You can help me put up the decorations.'

'Thank you,' Annie said, but she was looking at him. 'I'd like that.' Then, turning to his father, 'But you really must listen to the doctor, Mr Saxon. If you come home too soon, you'll be back in here for Christmas.'

His father regarded her thoughtfully. Then, taking note of the way their hands were interlinked and apparently putting one and one together and making a pair, he smiled with satisfaction. 'Maybe you're right, Annie. I don't suppose another day or two will kill me.'

Setting himself up for yet another disappointment that he'd get the blame for, George thought, and removing his hand from hers, he said, 'We'd better go, Xandra. Mike is coming for the car at four.'

She bounced off the bed, gave her granddad a hug. Then, transferring the Santa hat from her own head to his, she said, 'Behave yourself. And don't let Gran stay so late tonight. She was too tired to eat last night.'

'Really?' He shook his head. 'Silly woman. I'll make sure she leaves early.'

'Thanks for thinking about your gran,' he said as they headed for the car.

'She can't bear to leave him there on his own.' She turned to Annie. 'They absolutely dote on one another, you know. It's really sweet.' Then, taking advantage of his approval, she said, 'Can you drop me off in town? I'll catch the bus home.'

'I thought we'd decided that you're grounded.'

'Oh, absolutely,' she said. 'But this isn't for me. We've only got indoor lights. I'll have to get some new ones for the outside tree.' Then, 'Annie could come with me if you like. Just to make sure I don't have any fun.'

'Actually, I could do with a run at the shops,' Annie said before he could voice his objection to the idea of Lady Roseanne Napier, her underwear stuffed with cash and about as street-smart as a newborn lamb, let loose in the Christmas crowds with only a teenager for protection. 'I came away with the bare minimum.'

Oh, no…

The look in her eye told him she knew exactly what he was thinking.

'I'll do my absolute best to make sure that neither of us have any fun,' she assured him. 'Although I can't positively guarantee it.'

Xandra's face lit up. Annie did that to people, he thought. Lit them up. His mother, his father, his daughter. They all responded to that effortless charm, the natural warmth she exuded, but he'd done a lot more than just light up.

He'd lit up, overloaded, blown every fuse in his brain as he'd surrendered, had let down a barrier he'd been building against the world ever since the day when, years younger than Xandra, he'd understood that he was on his own.

Only now, when he knew that any kind of relationship between them was impossible, did he understand just how exposed he'd left himself.

Keeping his distance emotionally from this woman who

was so far out of his orbit that he might as well be on Mars was now an absolute necessity. As was keeping her safe. But forbidding her to leave the house wasn't an option either.

'It's Friday so the shops will be open late, won't they?' he asked.

'I suppose.'

'In that case, if you're prepared to wait until after Mike's collected the Bentley, I'll take you both into town. We could pick up the takeaway on the way home.'

It sounded reasonable but he wasn't looking at Annie, knowing that she'd have raised that eyebrow a fraction, telling him that she was winning this stand-off hands down, instead concentrating on his daughter, willing her to say yes.

'You want to come shopping with us?' She sounded doubtful.

'Same deal as always,' he replied. 'I drive, you do the hard work.'

'That means you're going to have to carry your own bags to the car,' Annie said. 'Obviously, as a lady of rather more advanced years, I will expect him to carry mine.' She laid the lightest emphasis on the word 'lady'. She tilted an eyebrow at him. Taunting him. No, teasing him. 'Do you have a problem with that, George?'

'I can live with it,' he said, refusing to meet her gaze, afraid he might just break down and laugh. He was too angry with her to laugh. Too angry with himself for wanting to wrap his arms around her, hold her, kiss her, beg her never to leave because most of all he wanted her.

'What a hero,' she said gently. 'And the three of us could put up those trees while we're waiting.'

And right there and then, knowing that Christmas brought her a world of pain, he thought his heart might break that she would do that for his daughter. For him.

CHAPTER ELEVEN

THREE hours later, the car parked, her arm tucked firmly in George's—it was clear he wasn't going to let her stray from his side—Annie stood in the centre of Maybridge. There were lights everywhere and a brass band was playing Christmas carols as crowds of shoppers searched out presents for their loved ones.

Somewhere, in her subconscious, she knew this was how Christmas was meant to be, but now she was touching it, feeling it as she was jostled by shoppers laden with bags, excited children who'd spotted 'Santa' in a mock-up sleigh, collecting for a local charity. Noisy, joyful, it was a world away from Christmas as she knew it.

'What do you need?' George asked.

This. This normality. This man, she thought, as she looked up at him and for a moment the carols, the lights faded.

'Annie?'

This moment, she thought, refusing to think about next week.

'Just a few basic essentials. Underwear, another pair of jeans—these are a bit big,' she said, tugging at the waist. 'Nothing fancy.'

'I know just the place,' Xandra said. She paused at the entrance to a large store, glanced at her father. 'You might want to give this a miss.'

'If you think you can scare me away with threats of female undergarments, think again.'

'You are so embarrassing.'

'I understood it was a parent's duty to embarrass their offspring,' he replied, unmoved.

'Oh, please! I'll wait here,' she said, taking out her cellphone, her thumb already busy texting before she reached the nearest bench.

'I won't be long,' Annie said, then, realising that he wasn't going to let her out of his sight, proceeded to test his assertion. Faced with the choice between six-packs of pants in plain white, mixed colours or patterned, she asked him to choose.

He took all three packs and dropped them in the basket, lips firmly sealed.

She tried on jeans while he stood guard at the changing room door, modelling them for him. By the time they reached the socks he'd had enough and, after looking down at her feet, he gathered up a pair of each before she could tease him further.

'Spoilsport,' she said.

'You'd better believe it,' he said.

She added a sweater and three tops to the basket and then queued up to pay.

'That was fun,' she said, handing the bags to George and waving to Xandra before obediently slipping her hand through the elbow he'd stuck out. 'What now?'

'Food?' he suggested, heading for a van from which the tantalising smell of frying onions was wafting. 'Who fancies a hot dog?'

'Not for me,' Xandra said, backing away. 'I need some shampoo. Can I get you anything, Annie?'

'Please.' By the time she'd given Xandra some money, George had a halfeaten hot dog in one hand. 'Are they good?'

'You've never had one?' He shook his head. 'Stupid question.'

He ordered two. 'I missed lunch,' he said, catching her look as he sucked mustard from his thumb.

'Me too,' she said, holding his gaze as she took one of them from him.

He looked away first, which wasn't as pleasing as it should have been and, taking the only comfort on offer, she bit deep into the bun, reminding herself that she was in search of new experiences.

Who knew when she'd share another hot dog moment with a seriously sexy man?

It must have been the fumes of the mustard hitting the back of her throat that brought tears to her eyes, making her choke.

'Better?' George asked, helpfully thumping her back. Leaving his hand there.

'Not much,' she said, dropping the remains of the hot dog in the bin. 'It's been quite a day for new experiences.'

He removed his hand as if burned. 'What's keeping Xandra?'

She sighed. 'She said she'd meet us by the Christmas tree in the square.'

All the trees that surrounded the square had white lights threaded through their bare branches, creating a fairyland arena for the seasonal ice rink that had been created in the central plaza and throwing the huge Christmas tree, ablaze with colour, into vivid contrast.

But it wasn't the figures on the ice or the lights that brought George to an abrupt halt. It was the sight of his daughter, sitting on a bench, much too close to the boy from the Christmas tree farm.

'The damned lights were just an excuse to come into town and meet him,' he declared but, as he surged forward, Annie stepped in front of him, a hand on his chest.

'They could have met by chance.'

He looked at her. 'Do you really believe that?'

'Does it matter? She chose to wait and come into town with you.'

'She wanted to come on her own.'

'Oh, for heaven's sake, I could shake you!' She took a deep breath, then, slowly, talking to him as if he were a child, she said, 'Don't you understand? Xandra got herself suspended from school deliberately. Mrs Warburton would have let her go and visit her grandfather in hospital, but she didn't want an afternoon off school. She wanted to be with you.'

'That's ridiculous,' he said. He took another step but Annie didn't budge. 'I tried,' he said. 'It's not easy from the other side of the Atlantic, but I've tried and tried to be a father—I even applied for joint custody.'

'The Family Court turned you down?'

'Penny told them that she would be confused. She was already that. Calling her new husband Daddy, ignoring me. Wouldn't come and see me in London when I was here on business. Wouldn't come to the States, even when I offered the theme park incentive.'

'She doesn't want theme parks,' she said. 'She wants you.'

'But—'

'Not in America, not in London, but here.'

He spread his arms, indicating that she'd got what she wanted.

'That's just the beginning. She's not going to make it easy for you. She'll test you and test you. Keep pushing you away to see how resilient you are. Whether you love her enough to stay.'

'She knows I love her,' he protested. 'I've given her everything she's ever wanted. Ever asked for.'

'Except yourself. She wants you, here, in her life. Not some Santa figure with a bottomless cheque book, but a father. She's afraid that you've only come to close down the garage, tidy up the loose ends, and she's desperately afraid that this time when you leave you'll never come back.'

'How can you know that?' he demanded, not wanting to believe it.

'Because I tested everyone. Not with tears or tantrums, I just withheld myself. Made nannies, governesses, teachers, even my grandfather prove that they weren't going to go away and never come back, the way my parents had.'

'I came back.'

'How often? Once a year? Twice?' She put her hands on his shoulders, forced him to look at her. 'How much do you want to be a father?' she demanded. 'Final answer.'

'Enough not to turn a blind eye to hot-wiring cars or making secret plans to meet up with boys.'

'Right answer,' she said, with a smile that made the lights seem dim. 'Come on, let's go and say hello.'

'Hello?' he said, staying put. 'That's it?'

'It's a start.'

'But—'

Annie felt for him. She could see that he wanted to go over there and grab that boy by the throat, demand that he never come near his precious little girl.

'Open your eyes, open your ears, George. Listen to what she's telling you. She wants you to be part of her life but you're going to have to accept that she's a young woman.'

George tore his gaze from his daughter and looked at her advocate. Passionate. Caring.

'You're not talking about her,' he said. 'You're talking about yourself.'

She didn't answer. She didn't have to. It was obvious. When she was six years old her life had changed for ever. At sixteen she'd become a national icon and had never had the freedom to meet a boy in town. Test herself. Make mistakes.

She knew everything. And nothing. But it was the everything that was important.

'Okay,' he said, 'let's go and say hello.'

'And?' she said, still pushing him.

'And what?'

'And ask him if he likes Chinese food,' she said.

He took a deep breath. 'Let's go and say hello. And ask him if he likes Chinese food.'

'You ask him while I get the skates,' she said, straightening, taking a step back. 'What size do you take?'

'Skates?' He groaned. 'Please tell me you're kidding.'

'I've only got a week. Less. I'm not missing out on a single opportunity.'

'Couldn't you just wait until you go home?' he asked. 'Get your personal assistant to call some Olympic champion to give you a twirl around the ice?'

'I could,' she agreed, 'but I wouldn't be that self-indulgent.' He was being facetious, she knew. He'd briefly let down his guard and now he was using sarcasm to keep her at a distance. No deal. If he wanted her distant, he was going to have to let her go. 'And, anyway, where would the fun be in that?'

'You're saying that you'd rather go out there and be pushed, shoved, fall over, make a fool of yourself in public?'

'Exactly like everyone else,' she said, 'but I don't need you to hold my hand. If you'd rather watch from the sidelines I'd quite understand.'

George growled with frustration.

She was an enigma. A woman of supreme confidence who was at home with the powerful and the most vulnerable. Touchingly innocent and yet old beyond her years. Clear-sighted when it came to other people's problems, but lost in the maze of her own confusion.

On the surface she had everything. She had only to express a wish for it to be granted. Any wish except one. The privacy to be herself.

He regarded her—her eyes were shining with a look of anticipation that he'd seen before—and for a moment he forgot to breathe as he revised the number of impossible items on her wish list to two.

The second should have been tailor-made for a man who

had made a life's work of the no-strings-attached, mutually enjoyable sexual encounter. It was the perfect scenario. A beautiful woman who would, in the reverse of the Cinderella story, on the seventeenth of December change back into a princess.

But Annie had, from the first moment she'd turned that penetrating gaze full on him, set about turning his life upside down.

Within twenty-four hours of meeting her he was beginning to forge a shaky relationship with his daughter, was talking to his father and found himself thinking all kinds of impossible things both before and after breakfast.

And accepting one irrefutable truth.

If he made love to Annie, he would never be able to let her go.

But she wasn't Annie Rowland. She was Lady Roseanne Napier and, no matter what her eyes were telling him, they both knew that she could never stay.

'Well?' she demanded impatiently.

'Have you ever been on ice skates?' he asked.

'No, but they're all doing it,' she said, turning to look at the figures moving with varying stages of competence across the ice. 'How hard can it be?'

'They all had someone to hold their hand when they did it for the first time.'

Skating he could do. Holding her hand, knowing that he would have to let go, would be harder, but a few days of being ordinary would be his gift to her. Something for her to look back on with pleasure. For him to remember for ever.

She looked back at him, hesitated.

'What are you waiting for?' he asked. 'Let's go and get those boots. Just don't complain to me when you can't move in the morning.'

'What about Xandra?' she asked. 'That boy?'

He glanced at them, sitting on the bench talking, laughing.

'They can take care of the bags.'

* * *

Annie felt the pain a lot sooner than the next morning. She'd spent more time in close contact with the ice than gliding across it—would have spent more but for George—and had been laughing too much to waste time or breath complaining about it.

George was laughing too as he lifted her back onto her feet for the umpteenth time. 'Hold onto my shoulders,' he said as he steadied her, hands on her waist, then grabbed her more tightly as her feet began to slide from beneath her again. Too late. They both went down.

'Have you had enough of this?' he asked, his smile fading as, ignoring the skaters swirling around them, he focused his entire attention on giving her exactly what she wanted. 'Or do you want to give it one more try?'

One more, a hundred times more wouldn't be enough, Annie knew. She wanted a lifetime of George Saxon's strong arms about her, holding her, supporting her. A lifetime of him laughing at her, with her.

'Aren't we supposed to be shopping for lights?' she said, looking away.

Xandra and her new boyfriend were leaning on the rail watching them. 'Pathetic,' she called out, laughing at the pair of them. 'Give it up.'

'She might have a point,' Annie said, turning back to George.

'She hasn't the first idea,' he said, his expression intent, his lips kissing close. And neither of them were talking about ice skating.

While the skaters whirled around them, in their small space on the ice the world seemed to stand still as they drank in each other. Every moment.

'Come on,' Xandra called. 'Dan knows a great place to buy lights.'

Annie scrambled to her feet and, for the first time since she'd stepped onto the ice, her feet were doing what they were supposed to as she glided gracefully to the edge of the rink with George a heartbeat behind her.

'Dan?' he said.

'Dan Cartwright.' The boy stuck out his hand. 'We met this morning, sir. At the farm.'

'I remember,' George said, taking it.

The boy didn't actually wince but he swallowed hard.

'I'm Annie,' she said, holding out her own hand so that George was forced to relinquish his grip. 'Shall we go and look at these lights?'

The tree lights were just the start. They piled icicle lights for the eaves, curtain lights for the walls, rope lights for the fence into their trolley. And then Annie spotted a life-size reindeer-driven sleigh with Santa himself at the reins and refused to leave without it.

'We won't be able to get it into the car,' George protested.

'Dan's got a motorbike,' Xandra said. 'He's got a spare helmet so I could go home on the back of that.'

'No,' he replied without hesitation. 'You can't.'

'In fact,' she said, carrying on as if he hadn't spoken, 'when I go to Maybridge High I'll need some transport. You had a motorbike, didn't you?'

Yes, he'd had a bike, but that was different. She was a... 'If you want to go to Maybridge High I'll drive you there myself,' he snapped back.

There was a pause, no longer than a heartbeat, while the reality of what he'd said sank in.

He would drive her. Be here. Change his life for her...

'Oh, *please*!' She rolled her eyes. 'How pathetic would I look? Besides, Dan said he'd teach me to ride.'

'I've never been on a motorbike,' Annie cut in before he could respond. 'Why don't I go with Dan?' Then, 'Actually, I'd love a lesson too.'

'No one is going on the back of Dan's bike!' he exploded. 'And if anyone is going to teach anyone to ride anything, it will be me!'

'Brilliant,' Xandra said, then, just as he realised that he'd been stitched up like a kipper, she nudged him with her shoulder and said, 'Thanks, Dad.'

Dad...

He looked at Annie. She had her hand to her mouth, confirmation that he hadn't misheard, hadn't got it wrong, but something amazing had just happened and he had to swallow twice before he could manage, 'We could come and pick up the sleigh tomorrow in the four-wheel drive.'

'Great. I can get my hair cut at the same time.'

'Whatever you want, Annie,' he replied, and meant it. 'Now, shall we get out of here and pick up some food? Dan? Chinese?'

'Well?' Annie asked, giving a twirl so that George, who'd been waiting for her in a coffee shop opposite the hairdresser, could fully appreciate the stylish elfin cut that now framed her face. 'What do you think?'

'It doesn't matter what I think,' he replied. 'The question is, are you happy?'

'Absolutely,' she said. 'I love it. Even better, no one in there even suggested I looked like...anyone else.'

'A result, then. Although when you reappear in public sporting your new look, they might just wonder.'

'They might wonder, but I've got the pictures to prove I'm in Bab el Sama,' she said, indicating a newspaper left by one of the café's patrons. 'Actually, that's the one downside. Poor Lydia doesn't get a choice in the matter. She's going to have to have her hair cut whether she wants to or not.'

'It goes with the job, but if it worries you buy her a wig for Christmas,' he suggested.

'You're not just a pretty face,' she said, slipping her arm in his. 'Now, let's take a look at this Christmas market.'

'Really? What happened to hating Christmas?'

'Not this Christmas,' she said as they wandered amongst

the little stalls decorated with lights and fake snow, admiring the handmade gifts and decorations. 'The new memories I've made will make this a Christmas I will always cherish.'

'That makes two of us,' he said.

They drank gingerbread lattes to warm themselves, tasted tiny samples of every kind of food, bought some of it, then stopped at a stall selling silly seasonal headgear.

'I have to have one of those,' Annie said and George picked up an angel headband which he settled carefully on her head.

'Uh-uh. The angel is on holiday.' She pulled it off and replaced it with one bearing sprigs of mistletoe that lit up and flashed enticingly. 'Let's give this one a test run,' she teased, closing her eyes and tilting her face to invite a kiss.

His cold lips barely brushed her cheek and, about to pull it off, ask the stallholder if he had something a little more effective, something in George's eyes stopped her. Not the warning to behave that she anticipated, but the mute appeal of a man for whom one more kiss would be one too many. An admission that while he'd walked away from temptation it had not been easy. That he was on a knife-edge.

'Perfect!' she exclaimed brightly as she turned swiftly away to check the rest of the stall. 'This for you, I think,' she said, choosing a Santa hat. She wanted to put it on him, just as he'd put on the angel headband. Pull it down over his ears, cradle his dear face, kiss him so thoroughly that he'd fall.

Yesterday she might have done. Yesterday he'd been this sexy, gorgeous man who'd turned her on, lit her up like the Christmas tree in the square. Today, with one look, she knew that one kiss was never going to be enough. Understood what he'd known instinctively. That walking away after anything more would tear her in two.

So she simply handed him the hat and left him to pay for it, stepping quickly away to look at a stall selling handmade jewellery. Giving them both space to take a breath, put back the smiles, continue as if the world hadn't just shifted on its axis.

She chose a pair of pretty snowman earrings for Xandra, a snowflake brooch for Hetty, a holly tie-tack for George's father and had them put in little gift bags. Just something to thank them for accepting her as she was—no trappings, just ordinary Annie.

She didn't buy anything for George.

She'd already given him her heart.

'All done?' he asked, joining her, and she nodded but, as they were leaving, she spotted the same angels that had been on sale at the Christmas tree farm and stopped. 'I have to have one of those,' she said.

'You're really getting into the Christmas thing,' he said, taking the bag while she paid for the angel.

She shook her head. 'It's for the tree at King's Lacey. A discordant note of simplicity amongst the ornate designer perfection to remind me…' She faltered and, when he didn't press her, she said, 'Let's go home.'

George gave the reindeer a final tug to test the fixing, making sure that it was secure.

'Switch it on,' he called down. 'Let's see if it works.' He was leaving it as long as possible before he was forced to climb down. He felt safer up here on the roof, as far from Annie as he could get.

He'd known a week would be hard, he just hadn't realised how hard. How hard he'd fallen.

He'd never believed in love at first sight and yet from the first moment he'd set eyes on her it had been there, a magnetic pull. Each day, hour, minute he spent in her company was drawing him closer to her. And the nearer he got, the harder it was going to be to break away.

She understood, he knew. Had been careful to keep her distance since that moment at the market when she'd lifted her face for a kiss—he'd kissed her before without invitation, after all—and he hadn't been able to do it. Not kiss her and let her go.

She'd urged him to get involved with the renovation of Xandra's car, build on the new start they'd made—not that he'd needed much encouragement. The moment when she'd called him 'Dad' had been a turning point. There was a long way to go, but he was here for the long haul and he'd spent a lot of time on the phone to Chicago, reorganising his life. But that had still left a lot of time to be together.

Time when she got into trouble trying to cook and needed a taster and he'd stayed to help.

Time around the table when, even when they weren't alone, somehow there was a silent connection, something that grew stronger each day.

Time for quiet moments by the fire when his mother and Xandra were at the hospital. Not saying much. Not touching. Just looking up and seeing her curled up in the chair opposite. Being together.

Perfect moments that had felt like coming home.

'Xandra should do the official switch on,' she called back. 'It was all her idea.'

'This is just a test run. She can do it properly later, when it's dark.'

'Okay…' She put her hand on the switch, then said, 'It gives me great pleasure to light up the Saxon family home this Christmas. God bless it and all who live in it.'

She threw the switch and the lights came on, twinkling faintly in the bright winter sunlight.

'It's going to look fabulous when it gets dark,' Annie said, shading her eyes as she looked up at him. 'You've done an amazing job with Santa. He looks as if he's just touched down on the roof.'

There was no putting it off and he climbed down the scaffold tower. 'I suspect I've broken at least half a dozen town planning laws,' he said. 'It'll be a distraction for passing motorists and in all probability an air traffic hazard. And, as for cheering up my father when he gets home, he'll undoubtedly have a relapse at the prospect of the electricity bill when he sees it.'

'Phooey.'

He looked at her. 'Phooey? What kind of language is that for the daughter of a marquess?'

'Completely inappropriate,' she admitted, looking right back at him, and they both knew that he was reminding her that time was running out. 'Annie Rowland, on the other hand, can say phooey as much as she wants. So... Phooey,' she said, clinging to these final hours. Then, turning back to the house, 'Besides, you won't be able to see it from the road. Well, apart from Santa up there on the roof. And the rest of the lights are energy efficient, so a very merry eco-friendly Christmas to you.'

'I'll bet you don't have one of those on the roof of your stately home,' he said a touch desperately. Reminding himself that she wasn't Annie Rowland, that this was a little fantasy she was living. When the metaphorical clock struck midnight she would turn back into Lady Rose and drive off in a limo with chauffeur and bodyguard in attendance, return to the waiting Viscount and the life she was born to.

'They did have another one in the shop,' she said, turning those stunning blue eyes on him. 'Do you think they'd deliver it to King's Lacey?'

'If you were prepared to pay the carriage, I imagine they'd deliver it to the moon, but what would your grandfather say?'

'I've no idea, but the estate children would love it. In fact, I might see if I can hire a Rudolph the Red-Nosed Reindeer sleigh ride for the Christmas party.'

'You have a party?'

'Of course. It's expected. A party for the local children, with Santa in attendance with presents for everyone. The tenant farmers in for drinks on Christmas Eve and then, on Christmas Day, my grandfather and I sit in state in the dining room for lunch before exchanging perfectly wrapped gifts. The only thing that's missing is conversation because, rather than say the wrong thing, we say nothing at all.'

'I find it hard to imagine you tiptoeing around anyone's feelings. You certainly don't tiptoe around mine.'

'I know.' She smiled at him. 'You can't imagine how relaxing that is.'

'So why do you put up with it year after year?' he demanded, suddenly angry, not with her grandfather but with her for enduring it rather than changing it.

'Duty?' she said. 'And my grandfather is all the family I have.' Then, in a clear attempt to change the subject, 'What about you, George? Are you really going to stay on?'

'You suspect I might be pining for my beach bum existence?'

'That would be George Saxon, the beach bum who designed a series of computer programs that helps to reduce wear and tear on combustion engines?' He waited, knowing that she had something on her mind. 'Who's since designed a dozen applications that have made him so much money he never has to work again?'

'Does Rupert Devenish work for a living?' he asked.

'Rupert runs his estates. Holds directorships in numerous companies. Works for charity. He's not idle.'

'It's no wonder the press are so excited,' he said, wishing he hadn't started this. 'You sound like the perfect match.'

The colour drained from her face but, without missing a beat, she said, 'Don't we?' Then, briskly, 'Okay. The lights are done and we've just got time for that motorcycle lesson you promised me before your father gets home from the hospital.'

'For that we'd need a motorcycle,' he pointed out thankfully. 'I thought perhaps, this year, I might break with tradition and, instead of a bank transfer, I'd let Xandra choose her own present. No prizes for guessing what she'll choose.'

It was meant to distract her and it did.

'It'll be a cheap Christmas, then. The only bike she wants is yours.'

'Mine?'

'The one in the barn?'

George glanced at the stone long-barn, all that remained of the original farm buildings. Over the years it had served as a stable, a depository for tack, garden tools and every item of transportation he'd ever owned since his first trike, then crossed to the door and pushed it open.

'What is it?' she asked as he stared at a familiar tarpaulin.

'Nothing,' he said. 'History. A heap of rust.' But, unable to help himself, he pulled back the tarpaulin to reveal the motorbike he'd bought on his sixteenth birthday.

It wasn't a classic. Nothing like the high-powered one he rode in California, but he'd saved every last penny of money he'd earned or been given for birthdays, Christmas, to buy it and it had represented freedom, independence. He'd ridden it home from Cambridge that first Christmas, high on his new life, full of everything he'd done and seen.

Four weeks later, when it was time to return to his studies, Penny had refused to ride on the back because of the baby and they'd taken the train.

CHAPTER TWELVE

'I DON'T see any rust,' Annie said.

'No.'

The bike had been sitting in the barn for fifteen years and for fifteen years someone had lavished care on it, keeping it polished, oiled, ready to kick-start and go.

There was only one someone who could have done that—his father—and he slammed his fist against the leather saddle, understanding exactly how angry, how *helpless* Annie had felt as she'd lashed out at him.

He wanted to smash something. Roar at the waste of it, the stupidity.

'Why didn't he say? Why didn't he tell me?'

'That he loved you? Missed you?'

Annie reached out for him and, wrapping her arms around him, she held him as he'd held her. And he clung to her because she understood as no one else could. Clung to her, wanting never to let her go.

In the end it was Annie who made the move, leaning back a little, laying warm lips against his cold cheek for just a moment, before turning to the bike.

'Will it start?' she asked.

He didn't care about the damn bike. He only cared about her but, just as he'd kept his distance in the last few days, protecting himself as much as her, now she was the one wearing an aura of untouchability.

Standing a little straighter, a little taller, even wearing a woolly hat and gloves, he had no doubt he was looking not at Annie Rowland, but Lady Rose.

And still he wanted to crush her to him, kiss her, do what she'd asked of him and make her so entirely his that she could never go back.

And that, he discovered, was the difference between lust and love.

When you loved someone your heart overrode desire.

'There's only one way to find out,' he said, unhooking a helmet from the wall. He wiped off a layer of dust with his sleeve and handed it to her, unhooked a second one for himself, then pulled the bike off its stand and wheeled it out into the yard.

It felt smaller than he remembered as he slung a leg over the saddle, kicked it into life, but his hands fitted the worn places on the handlebars and the familiar throb of the engine as he sat astride the bike seemed to jump-start something inside him.

Or maybe it was Annie, grinning at him in pure delight. Somehow the two seemed inextricably connected. Part of each other, part of him. Pulling on the helmet, he grinned back and said, 'Well, what are you waiting for? Let's go for a ride.'

She didn't need a second invitation, but climbed on behind him.

'Hold tight,' he warned and, as he took off, she hung on for dear life, her arms around his waist, her body glued to his.

It was beyond exhilarating. The nearness to everything, the road racing beneath them, the closeness, the trust, their two bodies working as one as they leaned into the bends of the winding country roads. It was as if they were one and when, far too soon, they raced back into the garage forecourt, he seemed to know instinctively the exact moment to ease back, turn, put out his foot as they came to a halt in front of the barn door.

Coming home, exactly as he had done countless times in the past.

For a moment the engine continued to throb, then everything went quiet. It was only then, when she tried to move, dismount, that Annie realised that she was not just breathless, light-headed but apparently boneless.

'Oh,' she said stupidly, clinging to George as he helped her off the bike and her legs buckled beneath her. He removed her helmet as if she were a child. 'Oh, good grief, that was—'

George didn't wait to hear what she thought—he knew. Despite the fact that she was so far out of his reach that she might as well be on Mars, that in a few days she would walk away, taking his heart with her, and he would have to smile and pretend he didn't care. Knowing that each touch, each kiss, would intensify the pain of losing her, he kissed her anyway.

He kissed her not to test her probity, not as a prelude to the kind of intimacy that had overtaken them in the kitchen.

It was a kiss without an agenda, one that would endure in his memory and maybe, on the days when Annie felt alone, in hers. A kiss given with a whole heart.

And that was as new for him as it was for her.

That she responded with all the passion of a woman who knew it would be their last made it all the more heartbreaking. Finally, breathlessly, she broke away.

'No,' she said, backing rapidly away, tears streaming down her face. 'I can't do this to you.' Then she turned and ran into the house.

'Annie!'

George's desperate cry still ringing in her ears, Annie raced up the stairs and by the time he caught up with her she had her cellphone in one hand, calling up the taxi firm while she emptied a drawer. She'd never wear any of the clothes again, but she'd bought them with George and they held precious memories.

She'd crammed a lifetime of ordinary experiences into a

few days. She'd laughed more than she had in her entire life. She'd loved more. And been loved by Hetty, Xandra, called 'lass' by George senior, which she recognised as a mark of acceptance. While George...

George had made it his purpose in life to give her what she most wanted—to be ordinary—even while taking the utmost care to keep a physical distance between them.

And then he'd found the bike and, overwhelmed by what that meant, for a precious moment he'd let down his guard. It was then, when he'd kissed her in a way that made her feel like the woman she wanted to be, when tearing herself away from him had been beyond bearing—

'What the hell are you doing?' he demanded, bursting into the room, taking the cellphone from her and breaking the connection.

'Leaving,' she said, taking it from him and hitting Redial, throwing the clothes into her bag. 'Now. I should never have stayed.'

George Saxon had a real life, a family who wanted him and nothing on earth would allow her to inflict even the smallest part of her life on them. Somewhere, deep down, she'd hoped that they would be able to remain friends. That she could, once in a while, call him, talk to him. But, if she'd learned one thing this week, it was that for someone you truly loved you would sacrifice anything, even love itself.

Forget Thursday. She couldn't wait until then. She had to leave now. Tonight. Never look back.

George stood there, watching her fling her clothes into a bag and feeling more helpless than he had in his entire life. He said her name, as if that would somehow keep her from leaving. 'Annie.'

She looked up.

'I love you.'

The hand holding the phone fell to her side. She opened her mouth, took a breath, shook her head. 'You don't know me.'

'I know what makes you laugh,' he said, lifting a hand to her face, wiping his fingers across the tears that were running unchecked down her face. 'I know what makes you cry.'

She didn't deny it, just shivered as he put his arms around her, drew her close, resting his own cheek against her pale hair.

'I know how your skin feels beneath my hands,' he continued, more to himself than to her. 'The taste of your mouth. The way your eyes look when I touch you. I know that you're kind, generous, caring, intuitive, smart.' He looked down at her. 'I know that, no matter what I say, you'll go home. What I'm asking is—will you come back?'

'This isn't a fairy-tale, George. Will you call me a taxi? Please?'

There was a note of desperation in that final please, but she'd given him his answer and there didn't seem a lot to say after that.

His mother and Xandra had gone shopping before going to the hospital to collect his father and he left a note on the kitchen table, explaining that a family emergency had called Annie home.

'How long will it be?' she asked when she followed him downstairs. 'The taxi.'

'There's no taxi. The deal was always that I'd take you home.'

She didn't argue, just surrendered her bag, got into his car. Neither of them said another word until they reached the motorway, when she looked at him.

'What?' he asked.

'No…'

'Spit it out.'

'It's Lydia's car. Could you… Would you find a replacement?' She took a paper bag out of the big shoulder bag she carried everywhere, placed it in the glove compartment. 'There should be enough.'

'Just how much money were you carrying around with you?' he demanded.

'Don't you mean where did I have it all stashed?'

His knuckles whitened as his hands tightened on the steering wheel.

'Will you do it?'

'Don't you have some little man who does that kind of thing for you?' Then, 'Oh, no. My mistake. You can't ask anyone at home. You wouldn't be allowed out on your own for the rest of your life if your grandfather found out what you did.'

'Red would be good, if you could manage it,' she said, her voice even, controlled. Holding everything in. 'I've left her address with the money.'

'Roadworthy. Red. Is that it?'

'I'd like her to have it before Christmas.'

'Do you want me to put on the Santa hat, climb on her roof and push it down the chimney?' He banged the flat of his hand against the steering wheel. 'I could start hating Christmas all over again.'

Annie could understand why he was angry. There were a thousand things she wanted to say, but nothing that would help either of them.

'If there's any money left, will you give it to some local charity?'

'Anonymously, of course. That's it? All debts paid?'

No. Not by a long shot but there was one thing she could do. 'Would you like me to speak to Mrs Warburton? At Dower House. In case Xandra changes her mind about going back.'

'She won't be returning to boarding school.'

'Her mother might not take the same view,' she pointed out.

'Her mother lost her vote when she switched off her cellphone.'

'Yes, well, I'm sure she'll be happier living with you and her grandparents.'

He shook his head. 'I left home when I was eighteen, Annie. I'm not about to move back in with my parents. What about you?'

'What about me?'

'Are you going to go home and grovel to your grandfather for being a bad girl?' he asked, driven by helpless anger into goading her. 'Beg his forgiveness and promise never to do it again?'

'George—'

'Go on playing the part that he wrote for you when you were six years old?'

'Wrote for me?'

'Isn't that what he did?' He'd read her story on the Net, wanting to know everything about her. 'From the moment you stepped into the limelight. Isn't he the one pushing the wedding bells story?'

She didn't answer.

'I saw that photograph of the two of you together on the day it was first published. Your mouth was smiling, but your eyes... You looked hunted.'

He saw the slip road for a motorway service station and took it. Pulling into the car park, he turned on her. 'You told Xandra that you'd only marry Rupert Devenish if you loved him. Do you?'

'George... Don't do this.'

'Do you?'

'No...' The word was hoarse, barely audible. 'Before I met you...'

'Before you met me—what?'

'I might have been that desperate.'

She was no more than a dark shape against the lights. He couldn't see her face or read her expression and that made it easier. One look from those tender blue eyes and he'd be lost.

'What do you want, Annie?' he asked, fighting the urge
to just take her in his arms, tell her that it would be all right,
that he would make it so. But he knew that this was something she had to do for herself.

She opened her mouth. Closed it again.

'Don't think about it,' he said a touch desperately, wanting
to shake her. 'Just speak. Say the first thing that comes into
your head. What do you really want?'

'I want to be the person I would have been if my parents
had lived,' she blurted out. Then gave a little gasp, as if she
hadn't known what she was going to say. 'A doctor,' she
said. 'I was going to be a doctor, like my mother.'

That was it? Something so simple?

'So what stopped you?' he asked.

'It was impossible. You must see that.'

'I see only a woman who had a dream but not the courage
to fight for it. A quitter.'

'You don't understand—'

'Oh, I understand.' He understood that if she went back
like this, afraid to admit even to herself what she wanted,
she'd never break free. She'd forced him to take a look at his
life, to straighten it out, and now, because he loved her, he
was going to fight for her whether she liked it or not. 'I
understand that you were enjoying being the nation's sweetheart a little bit too much to give it up,' he said, twisting the
knife, goading her, wanting her to kick out, fight back. 'Being
on the front page all the time. Everyone telling you how
wonderful you were, how brave…'

Her eyes flared in the lights of a passing car and he knew
he'd done it. That if she'd had the room to swing her arm she
might have slapped him and he'd have welcomed it, but he
didn't let up.

'If you'd wanted to be a doctor, Annie, you'd have been
one. I'm not saying it would have been easy, but you're not

short of determination. What you wanted was your mother,' he said, 'and being her was the closest you could get.'

'No!' There was the longest pause. 'Yes…' And then, with something that was almost a laugh, 'Instead, I became my father. Good works, duty. Everything by the book.' She looked at him. 'Until he met my mother.'

'She was a bad influence?'

'That depends on your point of view. Without her, he'd have been like my grandfather, like Rupert. But my mother came from another world and she stirred his social conscience. Together they used his money, his contacts, his influence to help change the world.' In the darkness he heard her swallow. 'That's why they were targeted, killed. Because they were the kind of people whose death mattered enough to make headlines.'

She didn't say that her grandfather had blamed her mother for that. She didn't have to. But it explained why he'd kept her so close, so protected. Not just from unnamed threats, but so that she wouldn't meet someone like him. Someone who would take her away, as her mother had taken his son, and, from disliking the man on principle, he found himself pitying him.

But it was Annie who mattered.

'You're not a copy of anyone,' he told her fiercely. 'You encompass the best of both of them. Your father's *noblesse oblige*, your mother's special ability to reach out to those in need, her genuine empathy for people in trouble. You make the front page so often because people reach for it. Your smile lights up their day.'

As it lit up his life.

'But—'

'I've seen you in action. You're not acting. That's all you, straight from the heart, but you have to take charge of your life. Hold onto what's good. Walk away from the rest.'

'You make it sound so easy.'

'Nothing worthwhile is ever easy. I've no doubt you'll meet resistance. The "just leave it to us" response. Like punching marshmallow. It's easy to get sucked in. I'm a designer, so I hire the best in the business to run my company.' He smiled, even though she couldn't see his face. 'The difference between us is that I can fire anyone who doesn't do it the way I want it done.'

'I can't fire my grandfather.'

'No. Family you have for life. You told me to talk to my father—actually, you blackmailed me into it. Now I'm going to return the favour. Talk to him, tell him what you want.'

'Or?'

He shrugged, knowing that he didn't need to say the words.

'You're bluffing again.'

'You want to bet?'

There was the briefest pause before she said, 'No.'

'Good call.'

'Hungry?' he asked.

'Surprisingly, yes,' she said.

'Then here comes another new experience for you. The motorway service station.'

'You're going to keep the garage open to specialise in vintage cars?' Annie asked once they were seated with their trays containing pre-wrapped sandwiches and coffee and, because he'd made his point, he was filling her in on his own plans. 'Will Xandra go for that?'

'I mentioned it when we were working on the Austin yesterday.' George stirred sugar into his coffee, smiling at the memory of Xandra forgetting herself enough to fling her arms around him. 'She knows it's a good niche market. I'll start looking for a manager, staff, in the New Year.'

'So, if you're not going to live with your parents, where will you live?'

'I'm not going to move. They are. I'll buy the farm—'

'Farm?'

'There are just over five hundred acres still let to tenants. Not quite an estate, no park gates, but it's good arable land. I'm going to build a bungalow in the paddock for my parents, something easy to manage.'

'And you'll live in the house.'

The way she said that made him look up. 'It needs some work and I'll have to find a housekeeper, but that's the plan.'

'What about your business?'

'I'll have to make regular trips to Chicago, but I'll turn the barn into an office. Anything I could do in California, I can do here.'

'Everything in one place. The work-life balance achieved. Your extended family around you.'

'You like the idea?'

Annie sighed. 'I'm deeply envious. I totally fell in love with the farmhouse. But won't you miss your place on the beach?'

'There'll be time for that too. Maybe next time you want a break you should give me a call. We could catch up on those motorbike lessons.'

She shook her head. 'I'm not going to run away again, George.'

'No?'

She swallowed. 'No. Open, upfront. The trouble is that when you've used publicity you can't just turn it off, expect the media to back off just because it's no longer convenient. I come with a lot of baggage.'

He heard what she said. Something more. It was the sound of a woman taking a tentative step away from the past. Coming towards him.

'You'll just have to keep your top on when we're on the beach then,' he replied casually.

For a moment the world seemed to hold its breath.

Then she replied, 'And keep the curtains drawn when we're inside.'

'Actually, taking photographs through the window would be an invasion of privacy.'

'You think they'd care?' she said, faltering.

'If we were married it wouldn't be a story.'

'I never thought of that.'

And suddenly they were talking about a life. The possibility of a future.

'What about Xandra? You've just got your life together.'

'Nothing worthwhile is ever easy, Annie. I've fought for everything I've got. Worked hours that would have raised the eyebrows of a Victorian mill owner. Say the word and I'd fight the world for you.'

'I have to learn to fight my own battles, George.'

His only answer was to take a little white box from his pocket.

'I was going to give you this before you left. A conversation starter at the Christmas dinner table. Something to make you smile.' He handed it to her. 'When you're ready to try life on Mars, wear them to some dress-up gala and I'll come and spring you.'

She looked up at him, then opened the box. Nestling in cotton wool were a pair of earrings that matched the mistletoe headband. She removed the studs from her ears and replaced them with the earrings. Clicked the tiny switch to set the lights twinkling.

'Are they working?' she asked.

By way of reply, he leaned forward, took her chin in his hand and kissed her, hard. Then he switched them off.

'That's it,' he said. 'Next time I do that it's for keeps.'

He drove, without haste but sooner, rather than the later he would have wished for, they reached the village of

Lacey Parva. Annie directed him to the entrance to her grandfather's estate but as they cleared a bend there were dozens of cars, vans, even a TV truck parked along the side of the road.

'Don't stop,' she said, ducking down as he slowed in the narrow lane and everyone turned to look. 'Drive on,' she muttered, scrabbling in her bag for her cellphone.

She switched it on, scrolled the news channels. Used that word she'd learned.

'What?' he asked.

'Lydia's missing,' she said, desperately checking her texts. Her voicemail. 'The world thinks I've been kidnapped.'

'Have you?'

She shook her head. 'No. She's left a message to say that there's nothing to worry about.'

'I'm glad to hear it. So, is there another way into the estate?'

'A dozen, but they'll have them all staked out. Just keep going. I'll show you where you can drop me off. I'll walk to the house.'

'Drop… You expect me to leave you by the side of the road?'

'It's all going to come out, George. If I can get to the house, the PR team can cobble together some story. There's no need for you to be involved.'

'That's it? One setback and you're going to run for cover?'

'You don't understand—'

'I understand,' he replied, his jaw so rigid that he thought it might break. Mars? Who did he think he'd been kidding? He was so far out on a limb here that Pluto was out of sight. 'But you don't actually have a say in the matter. I'm taking you home through the front gates,' he said, swinging into a lay-by and turning back in the direction of the house. 'It's not open to negotiation, so if being seen with me is going to be difficult, then buckle up. It's going to be a bumpy ride.'

'Stop!' she demanded. 'Stop right here.'

And that, apparently, was all it took. 'Damn you, Annie,' he said as he brought the car to a halt, eyes front, his hands gripping the steering wheel. 'I thought for a minute that we had something. A future.'

'So did I. So what just happened?' she demanded.

She was angry with him?

He risked a glance at her, felt a surge of hope, but this wasn't the time to pussyfoot around, it was time for plain speaking.

'Reality? Life?' he offered. 'I'm an ordinary man, Annie, from ordinary people. Yeoman stock. Farmers. Mechanics. Why would you want a Saxon when you should have a prince?'

'Ordinary,' she repeated. 'It wasn't dukes or barons that made this country great. It was hard-working, purposeful, good people like your family. *Extraordinary*, every one of you.'

She reached out, took his hand from the wheel, held it in hers.

'I love you, George Saxon, and I would be the proudest woman in Britain to be seen on every front page in the world with you, but this is going to be a media feeding frenzy. I simply wanted to protect you, protect your family from the fallout of my pathetic lack of courage. I should have talked to my grandfather years ago. I won't let another night pass without telling him what I want.'

'What do you want, Annie?'

'You. A house filled with little Saxons. Xandra. Your parents. You…'

'You've got me, angel. The rest comes included.' And he lifted the hand holding his, kissed it. 'As for the hounds at the gate, maybe the answer is to give them a bigger story than you disappearing for a week.'

'Oh? What story did you have in mind?'

He smiled. 'Switch those earrings on and I'll show you.'

* * *

They could have spent the entire evening parked up in the wood but there were people to call, explanations to be made and they spent the next fifteen minutes making phone calls.

'What did your family say?' Annie asked.

'My mother is thrilled. My father said I don't deserve you. Xandra said, "Cool". Yours?'

'My grandfather is so relieved that I could have announced I was marrying a Martian,' she said.

'Then all we have to do is tell the world. Ready?'

'Ready.'

He kissed her once more, then drove slowly up to the gates of King's Lacey.

Cameramen surged forward as a policeman came to the window.

'Lady Roseanne Napier,' he said. 'George Saxon. We're expected.'

He peered in. 'Lady Rose! You're a sight for sore eyes. We've all been worried sick.'

'Just a misunderstanding, Michael. We'll make a statement for the press and then, hopefully, you can go home.'

'No rush, madam,' he said, opening the door for her, waving the press back. 'The overtime comes in handy at this time of year.'

There was a volley of flashes as she stepped from the car. 'Lady Rose! Who was the man in Bab el Sama, Lady Rose?'

'I'm afraid I've no idea,' she said, holding out a hand as George joined her. 'I haven't left England all week. And this is the only man in my life,' she said, turning to him. Smiling only for him. 'George Saxon. The man I love. The man I'm going to marry.'

For a moment they could have heard a pin drop. Then they lit up the night with their cameras as George lifted her hand to kiss it.

It was a photograph that went around the world.

Daily Chronicle, 10th June

FAMILY WEDDING FOR LADY ROSE

Lady Roseanne Napier was married yesterday to billionaire businessman, Mr George Saxon, in the private chapel on her grandfather's estate at King's Lacey.

Miss Alexandra Saxon, the groom's daughter by an earlier marriage, attended the bride, along with children from her grandfather's estate.

The wedding and reception were a quiet family affair, despite a bidding war from gossip magazines who offered a million pounds to charity for the privilege of covering the affair.

The groom made a counter bid, pledging five million to charity if the media left them in peace to enjoy their special day with their family and friends, something we were happy to do.

This photograph of the couple, released to the press by the happy couple, is copyrighted to Susanne House and that charity will benefit from its publication.

We understand that the couple will honeymoon in the United States.

* * * * *

A CHRISTMAS TRADITION

Some years ago, when I'd taken my Christmas cards to the post and felt slightly sick when I realised just how much money I'd spent mailing greetings to every corner of the world, I made a decision that in the future I would send my greetings via the Internet and give the money saved to charity; a far greener, and much more lasting way of wishing the world a Merry Christmas and Happy New Year.

Since then, Third World communities have benefited from, amongst other things, a camel, a trained midwife and a goat, but cards are a hard habit to give up. There are always some truly special people you want to reach out to. Some very senior aunts. Faraway friends. People who have done something special for you during the year whom you want to thank with a special wish. For those two or three dozen people we make our own cards.

This isn't one of those 'craft' things. We don't sit down with paper and ribbons and glue—no one would thank me for anything I made like that. Instead my husband and I go through the photographs taken on trips throughout the year and pick out some moment we really want to share with friends and family.

A mist-shrouded castle, autumn woods, a favourite beach.

Last year we went to Bruges, and whilst there John took a photograph of Michelangelo's beautiful 'Madonna and Child' in the Church of Our Lady. As we looked through the photographs we'd taken through the year the image leapt out as the perfect subject for our card.

It's not just a question of printing a few cards, though. We spend a lot of time together choosing a card that works best with the image—gloss, silk, matt. Then there's the font style and colour, the words. It's truly a joint effort until that point, but once all the details have been decided I leave it to John to work his magic with the computer. My job is to write the envelopes, stick on the stamps, walk across to the box to post them.

It has, in a very short time, become a special Christmas tradition. One that sits happily alongside the cards I post on my website and blog. And beside the Oxfam catalogue from which I choose my Christmas card to the world.

A joyful Christmas and a peaceful New Year to you all.

Liz

HIS VIENNA
CHRISTMAS BRIDE
JAN COLLEY

Jan Colley lives in Christchurch, New Zealand, with Les and a couple of cats. She has travelled extensively, is jack of all trades and master of none, and still doesn't know what she wants to be when she grows up—as long as it's a writer. She loves rugby, family and friends, writing, sunshine, talking about writing and cats, although not necessarily in that order. E-mail her at vagabond232@yahoo.com or check out her website at www.jancolley.com.

I dedicate this book to the music of Johann Strauss II. May you leave me in peace now that I have written the books!

One

Well, well, Adam Thorne thought as he lounged in his chair, staring at the woman who had just entered his office. Mohammed had come to the mountain.

Satisfaction plumped up his chest. The rugby ball he'd been tossing up and down stilled in his hands. She might have shown him the door last month after a magical night of passion, but here she was, standing in the doorway of his London office, in the flesh. He tamped down the urge to smile. She'd better be prepared to grovel, or stump up with the goods. He wasn't a man used to slights and empty promises.

"Hallo, Adam."

Taking his time, he gave the ball one last toss,

caught it, then slid his feet off the desk. "Shouldn't you be twelve thousand miles away, hard at work for my big brother?"

Jasmine Cooper, personal assistant to his brother, Nick, English but presently living in Wellington, New Zealand. Cool, composed and without doubt the most fascinating female in Adam's considerable catalogue.

"I had some leave owing."

Adam unwound his long frame, stood and skirted the desk, tossing the rugby ball into a nearby open box.

She walked toward his desk, unbuttoning her long black woolen coat, and he let his eyes have at her. She was, as usual, impeccably dressed in a navy wool trouser suit, saved from severity with a bright-yellow sweater and those four-inch spiky heels she liked. His eyes were drawn to her heels like a magnet. Years of ballroom dancing had given her the most sensational, mile-high legs. A savage bolt of desire rushed through him and his fingers twitched, recalling never-ending silky smooth skin, firm and strong as they locked around his waist, as he molded them with his hands….

"May I take your coat?"

He held out his hand while she slipped out of her coat, glancing around curiously. His office resembled a bomb site, littered with boxes. Adam was enjoying a leisurely last day as junior partner in Croft, Croft and Bayley stockbrokers. In the new year, he would be opening his own premises in the Docklands for a markedly different venture.

He slid the garment on to a hanger and turned back to her, indicating she sit. "To what do I owe this very unexpected pleasure?"

She lifted a graceful hand and patted at her long dark hair, tied back, as usual. Adam preferred it out, remembering how it tickled his chest as she straddled him, kissing his mouth. Her almond-shaped eyes, he'd discovered, interchanged between smoky gray and blue, depending on her level of arousal.

Today, she was poised and elegant, lightly made-up, the perfect milk and roses of a true English beauty with a warm, rich shade on her lovely lips. As if he hadn't been assaulted by the same sights and sounds dozens of times over the past weeks, he again recalled those eyes hazed with passion, her short, well-kept nails digging into his hips, urging him on. The desperate little panting noises that escaped her throat at the onset of orgasm, and which he just bet prim and proper Ms. Cooper was mortified about later.

Pity she'd blotted her copy book. Adam was still mightily displeased at the way she'd treated him afterward. It had taken six dates to charm her into bed, spurred on by her quietly confident decree that she would not be another notch on his crowded bedpost. He'd persevered because he was on holiday, his time was more or less his own and he'd enjoyed her company more than expected, considering she was nothing like the women he usually dated. If people had a type, Jasmine Cooper was nothing like his.

Hell, he'd persevered because she'd told him no.

"I just spoke to Nick last week," he mused. "He didn't mention you were coming over."

He'd also courted the displeasure of his brother, who seemed to take a personal interest in keeping him away from his P.A., going so far as to tell him that a woman like Jasmine wouldn't give him the time of day.

Adam never could resist a challenge, but his brother had been partly right, as it turned out. After an incredible night of unbridled passion, he'd been shown the door. She couldn't wait to be rid of him. Perhaps she considered him a lapse of her impeccable judgment, or thought he might be less than discreet and tell her boss. One moment, she'd been all over him—literally—the next, it was here's your hat, what's your hurry?

Adam was a master of keeping things casual but at least he did so with charm and good manners. This elegant woman in front of him may look genteel, with her cultured accent that would be at home in Windsor Castle, but she'd dented his normally robust esteem and he didn't like that one bit.

Now she sat in front of him, her hands clasped tightly in her lap. A second glance showed him how tightly. Her knuckles were white. An interesting show of nerves.

"I usually come home at Christmas."

Logical. It was Christmas Eve and she was English and presumably had family here. But why bother coming to see him when a few short weeks ago she couldn't wait to be rid of him?

"And you just happened to be passing?" he said dryly.

Her lips softened. "Not exactly."

Jasmine was a woman of few words. Well-educated, classy, she would never run away with her mouth—although he recalled one or two things she had done with her mouth that had caused him all sorts of pleasure. Adam put his desk between them, feeling as horny as a school kid. He'd been working twenty hours a day since returning from New Zealand, winding up his affairs here, hunting out investors, organizing new premises. He hadn't had a date since he got back. The London debutantes that usually peppered his crowd had had short shrift from him of late—and that, he told himself firmly, had nothing to do with the trouble he was having dislodging the thought of one particular woman from his mind. He only gave Jasmine Cooper a second thought because she'd pissed him off!

"I need to ask a favor," she said, her gaze steady on his face.

Adam raised a brow. That was rich. He'd asked her a favor, one that could make a huge difference to the success of his new entrepreneurial start-up business. She had promised to help and yet every time he'd called from London, she had frozen him out, told him she was too busy to talk.

What could she want? His body? That tantalizing thought flirted with his mind. He'd gladly oblige, but first he'd teach her some morning-after etiquette. One does not hand one's lover his pants and usher him out the door before he's even had his coffee. "I see. Is it just me, or do you see the irony in that?"

For the first time, she had the grace to look a little discomfited. Not much, just a brief shift in her gaze, a tiny clearing of the throat. His brother, Nick, liked to boast that he had the best P.A. in the country: scarily efficient, über-professional, absolutely composed. But Adam possessed the secret to unlocking that composure. All he had to do was get close to see the way he affected her.

He stood and perched on the edge of his desk right in front of her.

"If I acted a little distant after…" she began.

He kept his brow arched and his eyes on her face. He wanted that apology. "After our unforgettable night together?"

Adam smiled when she swallowed, noting the faint tinge of pink on her cheeks.

"I apologize," she said gravely. "I'm afraid I'm not very experienced in these matters."

"Which was one of the most charming and unforgettable things about that night," Adam told her. And he meant it. For a woman in her midtwenties, she was beguilingly shy and inexperienced. "Was it not to your satisfaction?" he asked, knowing the question would discomfit her, and that she had been satisfied several times over.

Her skin pinked even more and he could tell she'd embedded her teeth into the inside of her cheek.

"I'm very sorry, Adam," she told him earnestly. "It was a special night, one I'll never forget."

Adam held her eyes for a few seconds more, then nodded. He deserved no less, but the apology seemed to be from the heart and his anger dissolved. Besides, having her grovel put the ball firmly in his court. She had come to him. He wanted what only she could give him.

And presumably, she wanted him, or else why was she here? "What can I do for you, Jasmine?" he asked, settling back on the desk to give her a modicum more breathing space. He folded his arms, intrigued now that his pride had been restored.

Jasmine swallowed again and looked him directly in the eye. "I want you to spend Christmas with me at my family's estate in Lincolnshire," she said. "As my fiancé."

In the shocking silence that followed, Jasmine forced herself to keep her eyes on his handsome face. She must stay calm and controlled, act as if this was just an everyday request and not the most preposterous thing she'd ever done in her life.

Under his short, razor-textured dark hair, his forehead creased in surprise. His toffee-colored eyes

were wide with astonishment. Designer stubble and
sideburns normally turned her right off but the moment she'd met Adam Thorne, playboy, high-flyer,
and—according to his brother—a shameless flirt and
womanizer, she was mesmerized. Model good looks,
a tall, lean build that looked oh-so-good in his designer suits and trendy open-necked shirts.

Now all traces of his heart-stopping smile had
vanished, his full lips pursed as he stared at her intently. Lord, why had she come out with it just like
that? She should have worked up to it.

Jasmine bit her lip, cursing the long flight that
seemed to have loaded her brain with cotton wool
and feeling less than her best physically. For some
reason, a few weeks ago, this interesting and very
sexy man had found her attractive. Today, she felt as
dull and dowdy as the winter's day outside.

"Perhaps I should expand a little."

She never volunteered details about her family,
not to Adam, Nick or anyone. It was easier that way,
to shun relationships, not get close to people. She'd
fled England five years ago to get away from her col-
orful past.

On the morning after they'd finally slept together,
Adam had asked her about a magazine article she'd
cut out and left on her coffee table. At the time, Jasmine was distracted, admiring his naked chest, the
long line of his spine, the length and sheer fluid
beauty of his legs as he walked around her lounge.

Distracted mostly by the utter novelty of having a gorgeous naked man walking around her lounge.

"That's my uncle," she'd responded to his question before realizing the danger. Adam lived in London. He might have heard something. He might mention it to Nick. She couldn't bear it if her few New Zealand friends and colleagues found out about the complicated circumstances that had dogged her all her life.

Jasmine had panicked, barely hearing him as he told her he'd been trying to get hold of the great Stewart Cooper—the subject of the article—for two months, and maybe she could get him an introduction. "Yes, probably," she'd told him, thrusting his shirt and trousers at him, making excuses that she was late for something, sorry, have a good trip back to London, thanks for everything. She had practically closed the door on his goodbye kiss, full of regrets because it had been the best night of her life and now it was spoiled.

But she hadn't worried about it for too long. Adam Thorne was hardly likely to remember her. That was one of the reasons she'd indulged herself, that and the fact he was heading back to London in the next couple of days.

He had called, as it happened, several times. She'd managed to stay cool and vague and after a couple more calls, he stopped asking how her garden was looking, had she been dancing lately and was Nick working her too hard. He only asked about her uncle.

She'd stammered that she was too busy to talk, she hadn't been able to contact him. Jasmine felt terrible, but what could she do? She'd never met her uncle. Never wanted to because of the bad blood between him and her father. And according to her father, he'd never wanted to meet her. Really, she'd done Adam a favor. Stewart Cooper, the reclusive billionaire, might never agree to see him if he knew Jasmine was a friend.

Now, she cautioned herself against telling him more than he needed to know. "Firstly, my name isn't Jasmine. It's Jane."

Adam frowned, pursing his lips, and she nearly smiled when he softly formed the word a couple of times, *Jane,* as if testing it on his lips.

Then he shook his head. "Doesn't do it for me, sorry."

"I haven't changed it officially," she told him, digging her fat traveling wallet out of her bag. She slid her passport from its compartment, opened it and showed him. "My passport and official documents are still Jane."

"Jasmine suits you better," he insisted, glancing at the passport.

She wondered with trepidation if her next words would get a reaction. "My father is a retired barrister, Sir Nigel Cooper?" She raised her brows in query.

Adam shook his head again.

She took a breath, maintaining eye contact while relief coursed through her. He hadn't heard of her father or her. She could scarcely believe it. But then, he'd only been in London four years, arriving more than a year after the scandal that caused Jane Cooper to become almost as prominent a household name as Princess Di—and not for the first time in her life. "He and my stepmother live at Pembleton Estate. It's a two-thousand acre estate in Lincolnshire. A stately home, part of which is open to the public." Again, Adam looked nonplussed, but she wouldn't expect him to be interested in English stately homes.

Now for the difficult part. "My father needs a male heir, a son or grandson to be able to keep the estate. Since my older brother died as a toddler, Father has always been very keen to see me married."

"You mean, like an arranged marriage?" Adam asked, leaning back and crossing his legs. "Do people still do that?"

"I expect he thought I'd take care of things myself," Jasmine said dryly. "Anyway, he's recently been di-agnosed with a brain tumor. I'm afraid it's very ad-vanced." The tumor was slow-growing, but her father had apparently ignored the signs for much too long. Jasmine was haunted by the thought that if she had been here, she may have seen the signs or persuaded him to be vigilant about medical appointments.

Adam made the usual platitudes of regret.

Jasmine continued, telling him her father even had a suitor for her in mind. "Our neighbor. He's an old school friend of mine."

"The wicked prince," Adam murmured.

Jasmine smiled. "He's not. He is a nice man, but I have no intention of marrying him."

She knew this must sound strange to someone who hadn't grown up in the rarefied atmosphere of English gentry, with all the tradition and history that was still alive and well in the country estates.

Jasmine looked down at her hands. "This is going to be a rather fraught visit. It's almost certainly Father's last Christmas. I…" She exhaled, feeling childish. Get it over with, she urged herself. Who knows? Adam may find the whole thing a lark.

But it wasn't. She had been a disappointment to her father all her life. She just wanted to please him, once, and have the memory that she'd done so. "I'm afraid I told an untruth a couple of months ago. I told him I was already engaged."

"And that's where I come in." He suddenly leaned forward quickly, fixing her with an intense look. "Why me, by the way?"

Because you are unaware of my past, she thought. *Because I felt guilty about the way I treated you. Because I wanted to see you again…* "I don't know very many men," she said truthfully. At least, not many that didn't pity her or think she was a laughingstock.

"And when your father asks about the wedding… where we're going to live…the pitter-patter of tiny feet?"

"We'll be suitably vague," she answered with confidence. "My father and I don't see eye to eye about some things." Most things, she thought. "Our relationship is quite distant. I am close to my stepmother, Gill. She may ask questions but probably not in front of him, and she's very discreet."

Adam's eyes never left her face. Jasmine mentally crossed her fingers and toes, knowing it was a lot to ask at such short notice. He was bound to have plans. She had thought about calling but hoped a surprise attack might have better results.

Still unsmiling, his eyes assessed her. If only she could turn the clock back and play that last morning again, or the phone calls afterward. Adam used to look at her with such regard.

He hadn't lost the habit, however, of maneuvering himself too close to her. Jasmine wished he'd sit at his desk rather than on it because he was too close for comfort. He always had been.

As if he read her mind, he suddenly sat up a little straighter. "And will your uncle be present at this family Christmas?"

She had expected him to ask. And in the scheme of things, this was the most important point of all. She kept her reply crisp. "No. He and my father have had a small falling out and it would be best not to mention him." Illness or not, the whole of Lincolnshire would hear Sir Nigel's roars if anyone mentioned his nemesis's name.

She softened her voice, plumping for sympathy.

"Since this may well be his last Christmas, I'd hate to upset him."

Adam's sharp eyes searched her face. She held his gaze steadily, waiting for his reply.

"For a favor of this magnitude," he said slowly, "and considering I have plans for Christmas…"

"Do you?"

"I *always* have plans, Jasmine." Adam smiled but there was little warmth in it. "Is there any good reason I should put myself out for you when you virtually ran me out of your house a few weeks ago?"

Friends were not a commodity Jasmine was flush with, but she had enjoyed every minute of their dates, of doing things she hadn't done before, the parry and thrust of his attempts to charm her into bed. "I thought we were friends."

She reminded herself that friends don't, as a rule, have hot, sweaty, plentiful sex in nearly every room in her house. Incredibly though, the experience had left her with such good—no, great—memories, it wouldn't worry her if Adam Thorne was her last lover ever. Who else could possibly measure up?

A shiver went through her and judging by the sudden flare of attention in his eyes, he'd noticed. She swallowed quickly. He couldn't know what steamy recollections had just filled her mind. Or how, all of a sudden, she could identify mint and orange blossom in his cologne. Or was so attuned to his breathing, her own emulated it. Nor how bloody attractive she found the way his fierce brows feathered a little on either side of the bridge of his nose.

"Friends help each other out," he murmured.

She closed her eyes and began to despair. Adam used the same voice as he had the night he finally persuaded her that she wanted him as much as he did her. Why deny each other, he'd said, when sex was such a natural and pleasurable way to show appreciation? That voice was her downfall; sultry, suggestive and warm, it coated the senses like honey on ham. Erotic images of their night together, his whispers inciting her to do things she'd never dreamed she could do, had her toes curling in latent pleasure.

For the first time—unless in her overheated state, she was imagining it—his eyes warmed a little—a lot. Adam Thorne knew exactly what she was thinking.

"Oh, I'm not discounting *that,* lovely Jasmine," he confirmed a second later, his deep, soft voice raising the hairs on the back of her neck. "Believe me, I remember every spectacular, soft, passionate inch of you."

She sucked in a breath to try to contain a pulse gone mad. Heat bloomed on her cheeks and all the way down her body. How did he do it, send her senses wild without even a touch? He used to toy with her at work, sitting on her desk, talking of nothing very much in that velvety voice of his, watching her with eyes that would tempt a saint. She'd thought it was about needling his brother or shattering her good-girl reputation. His effect on her was powerful and he knew it.

"That's not on the agenda this trip," she said, not as firmly as she would have liked. Which of them was she trying to convince?

She had to shoot him down. There were more important priorities than her own selfish desires. "I slept with you in a moment of weakness, not expecting to see you again. I wasn't looking for anything more."

Adam chuckled. "Well, I'm certainly not in the market for a relationship. But back to your 'agenda—'" he held up his index finger to indicate quote marks "—there doesn't seem to be an equitable balance of mutual reward between friends here."

Jasmine's desire seeped away. She knew what he wanted, but if he discovered the full extent of the hatred between her father and uncle, she would cease to be of use to him. She had to gloss over the family feud, at least until he was there at the estate, accepting their hospitality. Hopefully his good manners and charm would do the rest.

"All I want," Adam prompted, "is the introduction. The rest is up to me."

Seeing the determination on his face, Jasmine realized glossing over it wouldn't be enough. This man preferred something a little more concrete.

With six months to a year left to live, her father's happiness was her first priority. With no idea how she would go about it, Jasmine summoned up a self-assurance she didn't feel. "If you do this for me, I give you my word I will set it up—" She hesitated and then said firmly, "—after Christmas."

"Good." Adam got up and went back to his side of the desk. "Now that's settled, there is one more thing…"

Jasmine was already half way to her feet, preparing to depart.

"It's the annual company Christmas bash tonight. I've been too busy to find a date. Come with me."

Even as she reluctantly agreed, Jasmine had a sinking feeling about this. The more time she spent in Adam Thorne's company, the more she wanted to spend. Hopefully her good intentions wouldn't get her into trouble.

Then again, she'd had few enough opportunities to feel like a woman over the last few years.

Adam Thorne made her feel all woman.

Two

Adam picked her up in a silver Mercedes cabriolet that smelled brand-new, and took her to a trendy club only a short drive from her hotel.

"What name are we going by tonight?" he asked as they waited to be checked off the guest list.

"Just Jasmine," she said firmly, and it suddenly occurred to her she may be recognized. This was the kind of place some of her friends from five years ago might have frequented. She looked around warily, hoping that her long dark hair was different enough from the shaggy, lighter style she went with back then.

They made their way to a mezzanine, where about a hundred VIP guests of Croft, Croft and Bayley milled about. Almost immediately, well-wishers swamped them and she learned that tonight doubled as the annual corporate Christmas function, as well as Adam's farewell from the company. She looked around in amazement at the incredible interior. Every wall depicted what appeared to be a blue waterfall of vertical lines of numbers.

"Very high-tech, isn't it?" Adam smiled at her open-mouthed wonder. "Corporate clients can digitally design their own colors and atmosphere—or their brand, if they want to be boring—onto computers and have that imagery projected onto the walls for their event." He explained that Croft, Croft and Bayley had gone for a stock-exchange depiction tonight, but he'd been here when heaving blue seas seemed to crash against the walls. He'd seen panoramic landscapes of canyons that almost echoed, and meadows filled with nodding wildflowers in a gentle breeze. "You could come here every night of the week and feel you're somewhere different." He shook his head. "I liked the idea so much, I bought into it."

"You own this club?"

Adam shook his head. "Just a percentage of the multimedia company that came up with the concept."

Jasmine knew that innovative and daring ideas intrigued Adam. That was the catalyst for his start-up business, to give talented people with big ideas the means and expertise to go global.

She accepted a glass of champagne from a Santahatted waitress and was introduced to too many people to count. While Adam chatted, one of the senior partners extolled her escort's virtues. "I first saw him on the floor of the exchange four years ago, making money hand over fist as a day trader. A successful trader should be passionate about markets, rather than trading. While everyone else ran around in a panic, Adam just sat there, watching, sticking to his plan. I knew we had to have him."

As the night progressed, she heard much more of Adam's ambition, how hard he'd worked to attain his high level of success.

"The youngest-ever partner in this company," another partner confided. Croft, Croft and Bayley wasn't the biggest stockbrokerage in the city, but it was one of the oldest and most venerated. "We'll miss him but we're too small to contain his ambition." Another of his colleagues told her that the new business was risky but if anyone could pull it off, Adam could.

All this left Jasmine a little confused and a lot impressed. Until today, her preconception of Adam Thorne, based on their half-dozen outings in New Zealand, had been of a fun-loving, sexy and rich young man, an opinion reinforced by his brother's declaration that he wasn't to be taken seriously. Nick loved his brother, she knew that, but looking around at the army of admirers, the breathtaking backdrop of moving numbers, the copious bottles of French champagne and decadent hors d'oeuvres, she couldn't help feeling Nick hadn't given enough credit to Adam's work ethic.

The formalities of the evening commenced as the partners wished their staff a happy Christmas and then made a special presentation to bid Adam farewell and wish him good luck for what was sure to be a stellar future. Jasmine watched the proceedings from well back in the crowd, feeling sorry for every other man in the place. It was unfair that one man should be so overendowed, not only with good looks and vitality, but success, too. Not so long ago, she'd thought Nick Thorne the most handsome man she knew. He was bigger than Adam but similar enough in coloring, athleticism and those hypnotic eyes, so she'd been as surprised as anyone when it came out recently that Nick was adopted.

But they were as different as night and day. Nick was straight-A all the way, a brilliant but conservative businessman in his expensive suits and neatly cropped hair. Jasmine tried and failed to imagine him tossing an old rugby ball around his office, or even with his feet up on the desk. Never in a million years.

Adam Thorne probably didn't even know how to knot a tie. Certainly she'd never seen him in one, not even the night last month he'd escorted her to the Royal New Zealand Ballet. Style oozed devilishly from every pore. His fierce brows and the stubble shadowing his jawline and full sexy lips lent him a bad-boy demeanor, even though his smile was a lot more ready than Nick's.

While she'd been busy daydreaming, another half hour had passed and the formalities wound up. Adam returned from the front of the room and drew her into his side.

"Very nice," he said in that low, sultry voice, leaning so close his lips almost touched her earlobe.

Jasmine shivered, knowing that he felt it since he'd placed one hand lightly on the small of her back. If that hadn't alerted her, his self-satisfied smile when he drew back did.

"What?" she asked casually. Adam Thorne was too discerning for his own good.

"Being the object of your avid attention."

So she'd been staring. "I believe it's polite, when listening to a speech, to pay attention to the speaker."

Adam's grin only widened. "You can be very *English* sometimes, Ms. Cooper."

He was playing with her. He knew the effect he had on her and was using her gratitude to his full advantage. But Jasmine had her pride and after all, he wanted something from her, too.

Aside from sex...she resisted the urge to fan her hot face and thought it best to change the tone of the conversation. "I think Nick would have been very proud of you tonight."

His surprise at her comment showed in the slight arch of one dark brow. Jasmine wasn't sure if it was the subject matter or just the change of direction but when he pursed his lips a second later, she saw that he was pleased. And that, funnily enough, pleased her.

"You'll never guess!" A young colleague of Adam's joined their small group, brimming with a sly kind of excitement that Jasmine recognized as typical of a gossip. "Which esteemed royal is in the gents', popping party pills right this minute?"

"Vincent de Burgh," someone said quickly.

"Not again!" Another member of their party rolled his eyes.

Jasmine's heart plummeted and she almost swayed on her feet. Vincent de Burgh, notorious playboy, tenth in line to the British throne, and the man whose betrayal five years ago sent her packing to the other side of the world.

Careful not to turn her head, she looked for the bathrooms, which she located on the first level. She then scrutinized the messenger's face, wondering if he was telling her in a roundabout way that he knew she had once been engaged to the very same royal louse fittingly off his face in a toilet.

The young executives compared recent stories about the troublesome royal, not giving her any particular interest. Satisfied it was just idle celebrity gossip, Jasmine relaxed slightly. Nonetheless, she couldn't afford to stay here and risk being recognized.

That Vincent was still behaving badly didn't surprise her. She'd heard he recently divorced the woman he ditched her for—her ex-best friend—and no doubt was drowning his sorrows and searching for some other rich, deluded female. The unfathomable thing was that he always succeeded, as her father had repeatedly warned her.

She turned to Adam, her mind racing. If he found out about her high-profile engagement, it would take just one Google hit to find out the rest. All she needed was tomorrow, one day, to play happy couples at the estate. Then Adam could leave "on business" and she could continue her holiday and spend some quality time with her father before she had to get back to work. She didn't expect to have to keep the pretense up for too long. Her father was getting weaker and more forgetful by the day, according to Gill. In two or three months, he might not comprehend anything, and if he did, then she would tell him that sadly, she and Adam hadn't worked out.

But if Adam discovered before tomorrow how acrimonious the relations were between her father and Stewart, she could kiss her Christmas Day goodwill mission goodbye.

Adam's eyes were on her face and she realized she'd been staring again. He had his back to the conveniences on the ground floor and she flicked a glance to the door of the men's toilets, just in time to see an older, but by the look of him, most un-wiser, Vincent lurch out.

Jasmine froze. He seemed to be looking directly up

at her but it was hard to tell with the lighting in here. After a moment, he turned toward the bar, stripping off his jacket as he did. While breathing out relief, she relished the rather nasty thought that her ex had not weathered the passing of years well. Too much good living showed in his paunch and the way his thick neck battled to be reined in by his tie. It may have been the lighting but his previously thick, sandy hair looked wispy from her vantage point on the mezzanine.

She watched as he joined a small group of men at the bar. The private function on the mezzanine had waiter service so he was obviously not part of the Croft, Croft and Bayley group. Jasmine began to breathe again.

Adam touched her arm and she brought her eyes back to his face.

"I'd like you to meet someone."

She shook hands with John Hadlow, Adam's new business partner, and his wife, Sherrilyn.

"I see why you've stood us up for Christmas, old boy," John said jovially.

Jasmine bit back a smile and glanced at Adam's face. Had he deliberately given her the impression his plans were more romantic than Christmas dinner with this pleasant couple? She apologized for upsetting everyone's schedule.

Half an hour later, she had almost forgotten about Vincent when a break in the music exposed an altercation by the stairs. She glanced over to see her ex-fiancé arguing loudly with a security man, who blocked his entrance into the private function. She spun around quickly, looking for Adam and hearing Vincent's voice clearly over the myriad conversations surrounding her. "Do you know who I am?"

Adam was a couple of feet away, talking to an attractive blonde. What to do? She could hole up in the ladies', or just pray the security guard remained aloof about Vincent's lineage. There were two stairways on either side of the mezzanine leading down. Jasmine contemplated making a dash for it down the left-hand side while Vincent was engaged with the bouncer on the right.

Her heart pounded in near panic. If he accosted her, she could claim not to know him—or she could just come clean and tell Adam the truth; that she was persona non grata to her uncle and didn't have the tiniest chance of setting up a meeting between them.

"But I just want to say a quick hallo to someone," Vincent insisted loudly to the staunch security man.

Making a decision, and hoping she wouldn't live to regret it, Jasmine walked up to stand beside Adam and slid her arm around his waist, inside his jacket. Sucked in a breath against the impact of lean, muscled torso, a very appealing male cologne and the peculiar pheromones or hormones that always had her off-kilter with this particular man. Absorbing the jolt to her senses, she bravely waited as he slowly turned his head to her. Yes, cool blonde or not, she had his full attention.

"Sorry," she said apologetically to his companion. Lifting up on tiptoe, and without removing her hand from his body, she put her lips directly onto his ear. "I think the jet lag has just caught up with me," she whispered, ensuring her lips caressed his ear with each syllable.

Adam had bowed his head in deference to his greater height. Now he turned his face and looked down into hers. His eyes burned gold, interest and wariness flickering.

Jasmine reached up toward his ear again but because he had turned his head, her cheek brushed his, thrilling her with the contact. "That," she whispered seductively, "or the champagne."

He moved as she withdrew, so that his cheek blocked hers from retreat. Triumph, query and a wolfish sort of warning blazed out from the golden depths of his eyes. If there wasn't so much at stake, she would have run to save herself. The message was clear: *Don't play with me.* Or maybe that was just her guilty conscience.

After a second's hesitation, he became all concern and solitude, making his excuses to the blonde, saying goodbye to John, shaking hands with people as they prepared to go.

And moving toward the wrong staircase. Vincent was still there, of course. She'd learned during their engagement that when he didn't get his own way, the arguments lasted for days.

"This way." She tugged on his arm, nodding at the other staircase. "I need to visit the ladies'."

They veered to the right. "You don't have to come," she told him rather half-heartedly once they were at the bottom of the stairs, glancing around fearfully in case His Royal Highness emerged from the sea of people celebrating Christmas Eve. "It's your big night, I feel guilty."

She did feel guilty about spoiling his big night, but not too guilty. And she would prefer he didn't hang around without her in case Vincent bailed him up and asked about her.

No sign of him, though, and no sign that Adam was disposed to let her disappear into the night. There was a nasty moment on the way to the exit when a photographer came from nowhere, his camera up. "The man of the hour. Quick photo for the *Out and About* magazine?"

Luckily Jasmine was able to melt judiciously into the ladies' directly beside her, hoping it would not seem ungracious.

Nothing eventuated and soon they were at Adam's car. "Feeling better?" he asked as she strapped herself in. He started the car but made no effort to put it into gear.

"Much." She allowed herself to relax a little. It was a close call but the ends justified the means and now they were safe. "I'm sorry about this. I could just take a cab…"

Adam reached over and picked up her hand. "What sort of fiancé would I be if I didn't look after you?"

He lifted her hand to his mouth and pressed his lips to the pulse point on her wrist. Her bones melted as he nibbled and sucked at the sensitive point. Suddenly, Jasmine was in real danger of keeling over and it had nothing to do with jet lag. A warm flush bathed her as she imagined a thousand arrows of fire wove a prickly scarf on the back of her neck. Her skin felt tight and stretched, her insides jumped about nervously while her mouth was as arid as the desert. "Wha-what are you doing?" she asked.

The big motor purred. Adam didn't answer right away, engrossed in driving her mad with equal parts delight and trepidation. Then he lowered her hand and spoke with the honeyed, seductive tone he'd used before. "Let's just say I'm getting into character for tomorrow." He brought her hand to his mouth again, kissing each fingertip.

Just for a moment more she wanted to enjoy this, the desire that raced through her veins, her heart beating a tattoo on her rib cage. Maybe it was jet lag, because Jasmine was a sensible woman. Why else would she seriously consider succumbing to the incredible pull to move closer, drink in the heat coming off him in waves of male scented sensuality? It wasn't right that this man should have such a monopoly on her innermost desires and be able to exploit them at will.

Summoning every ounce of concentration and willpower, Jasmine stiffened her fingers and tugged until he let go. For good measure, she turned her face to the front, knowing that his strong-boned face, those wicked lips branding her flesh, turned her on unbearably. She'd never missed sex until she'd tasted it with him.

Adam's laugh was almost inaudible in the hum of the car, but decadently amused. "I enjoy watching you squirm, Jasmine, if only because it's out of character."

She huffed out a breath, her cheeks burning. "I don't know what you mean."

She didn't look at him again until they'd pulled up outside her hotel. The moment the car stopped, she released the seat belt and opened the door, welcoming the freezing blast of air on her hot face.

Adam's eyes were still amused. "About nine?"

Jasmine nodded and closed the door.

A couple of minutes later, she swept back the curtains in her deluxe room, sank down onto a chair and looked out over Trafalgar Square and the world's most famous Christmas tree. Her stepmother, Gill, had first brought her to see the tree when she was only six or seven and she'd been many times since. Strings of vertical lights draped the huge Norwegian spruce, picking out the snowflakes as they fell. It was a magical sight, one that should have felt familiar and soothing.

She wasn't soothed. Her nerves felt chafed raw.

In the last five years she thought she'd found peace, if not happiness. From the way Adam had been talking, it wouldn't be long before he was back in New Zealand, probably Wellington, laughing and teasing and driving her mad with lust. Why had she slept with him? Far from satisfying her sexual curiosity, it had only served to make her want him more.

Three

The drive from London took longer than expected because of a thick snow flurry, but finally they arrived at the estate just in time for lunch. Jasmine's apprehension and excitement built as they passed through the heavy wrought-iron gates. She loved the drive up to the house. Fallow deer grazed in the wooded parkland. She pointed out the stud farm her father established a decade ago. Snow dusted the reeds around the lake fronting the house.

Pembleton, originally a large Georgian house, had been greatly added to in the years before the First World War and now lent itself more to the Edwardian era.

Even Adam expressed his admiration as they slowly approached the great dun-colored house, whose dimensions more resembled a terraced street than one residence. Jasmine sighed with pride. She might have grown up here and certainly had her share of bad memories of the place, but the house and setting still took her breath away.

"How many rooms?" Adam asked as they pulled up in front of the massive porticoed entrance.

"Over a hundred, though half of it is closed up."

Her stepmother, Gill, burst out of the door and raced down the steps. Sixty years young, a petite, iron-gray-haired bundle of energy and efficiency, she greeted them with a volley of warm squeals.

"Your father is having a good day," she told them, "and is quite excited about meeting Adam, even if he probably won't show it."

Jasmine didn't take offense that her father was more excited about meeting Adam than seeing his daughter. She had always been a disappointment to him, first by being born a girl, and then when she became the willful teenager who defied his wishes.

But in his distant manner, Sir Nigel did seem pleased to see her. He sat in his comfortable chair by the fireplace and inspected her for a minute or more while clasping one of her hands with both of his. Jasmine—Jane, to them—tried to conceal her shock at his frail appearance. He'd always been a burly man—that's where she got her height from, since her mother had apparently been tiny. His most notable feature had always been his booming voice but there was little evidence of it today, except occasionally when addressing Adam. He was a shadow of his former self.

Jasmine grappled with guilt. She should be here to take care of him instead of leaving everything to Gill. She'd been with the family since Jasmine was ten years old. Gill was the warmest thing about her childhood and beyond.

They ate Christmas lunch in the formal dining room, a room that had, in the past, hosted banquets for heads of state. Among many great portraits on the walls there was a Madonna and child painted by Murillo hanging over the antique fireplace. They sat at one end of the massive table for "One's table should never exceed the nine muses," Gill liked to say.

As usual there was a daunting array of food— quail; turkey, roast beef; a whole salmon, pink and delicious; vegetables of every variety and then Christmas steamed pudding and brandy sauce with Gill's folly, ancient threepences hidden within. Jasmine had pre-warned Adam of this eccentricity to avoid breaking a tooth.

Afterward, her father insisted Gill take the seal off an old bottle of port and they adjourned to the more informal drawing room.

"So you're engaged at last," her father said croakily,

settling into his chair. Adam and Jasmine sat on an overstuffed antique couch opposite her father while Gill served the drinks.

This would be the awkward part but she didn't expect there would be many questions. Her father would not care who she married, as long as his estate was looked after. "Yes, we are," she replied, trying to sound excited.

"When is the wedding? Will it be here?"

Adam's arm slipped around her shoulder and she tried not to flinch. "As soon as possible," he murmured, "as far as I'm concerned."

Jasmine's smile didn't slip but every muscle in her body tensed up and her mind raced. "We haven't had time to discuss it," she said, before burying her nose in her port.

Her father's head raised. "Well, six months, a year?"

Her heart went out to him. With a death sentence hanging over his head, of course he wanted a date to grasp on to. "We'll discuss it while we're on holiday and let you know."

"Hmph." Her father subsided back into the seat, picking at the rug Gill had put over his knees. "I'll have to announce it."

"No!"

Jasmine's sharp response had all eyes swiveling to her face. She swallowed down the panic that comment had instigated. "I'd really prefer to keep this just within the family, if possible."

Her father gave her a spiteful look. "My daughter, the procrastinator," he muttered.

She heard Adam's quick indrawn breath and couldn't look at him.

"That's understandable, dear," Gill said sympathetically.

Adam's hand slid around and surreptitiously tugged on her ponytail. "I'm all for shouting it from the rooftops," he said in a low voice that only she could hear.

Jasmine resisted the shiver of awareness that generated and kept her eyes on her father, amazed he would even suggest a public announcement after what happened with Vincent nearly six years ago. When the story broke that her fiancé and her best friend had run off into the sunset together just a month before her wedding, she hadn't been able to leave the house without paparazzi on her tail. That was when she realized she could never escape her past. All her hopes and dreams crashed in spectacular style, played out in the media, and she decided to move as far away as she could get. Somewhere where no one knew of her infamous past, and hopefully never would.

"Have you spoken to Ian recently?" her father asked, his stern gaze losing none of its sharpness despite the ravages of age and illness.

"No." Jasmine sighed. "Should I have?"

"Who's Ian?" Adam leaned forward to set his port

glass down. His brows were raised and his knee pressed against hers.

She gave him a cool glance. If you asked her, he was playing the amorous fiancé just a little too well for her liking. "A friend. Our neighbor." She had told him about Ian—the little she wanted him to know at this point.

"A little more than a friend I think," her father murmured.

Ian had been there all her life. They were the same age, had played together as children. He was her friend—until her father decided he would make an ideal husband. "He's steady, a hard worker, and boys run in that family," he declared. "Plus he will inherit the adjoining thousand acres. That gives us options to expand the estate and generate more income."

From the time she was eighteen, her father never let up but Jasmine gave no serious consideration to a union. When her past and present collided with vivid impact, Ian was there to pick up the pieces. Because he was the only one in the world who didn't look at her as if she had two heads, and because her father did all in his power to push them together, she went out with him for a couple of months and tried to think of him as more than a friend. She even slept with him, but there was no chemistry there for her.

They usually got together for a coffee or a meal on her annual trips home but she hadn't felt obliged to let him know she was coming. Besides, she knew he was in Switzerland for Christmas.

Now everyone, Adam included, was looking at her as if she was a jezebel. "He's a friend," she repeated firmly, sipping her port.

"Hmph." Her father glared at her hands. "No ring?"

"We plan to remedy that on this visit, don't we, darling?" Adam took her free hand and squeezed it. "Antwerp or Amsterdam?"

Jasmine smiled faintly and forced herself to relax her fingers, one by one, while thinking of ways to kill him.

Thankfully the excitement and port had worn her father out and he retired shortly afterward for a nap. The blazing fire and overstuffed bellies had everyone yawning. Gill rose, saying she had made up Jasmine's room. "You are staying? And for the party tomorrow?"

Jasmine prepared to say that she would stay but not Adam, and then Gill's words filtered into her brain, setting up a wave of temptation to batter her defenses. *Her* room, she'd said. Not two rooms…

Her room where she'd played with dolls, swooned over the Backstreet Boys, experimented with clothes and makeup, fantasized over real boys, sneaked Vincent into…and then howled her anguish into her pillow when he broke her heart. What was a girl's bedroom but a catalogue of the most intimate experiences of one's life?

It couldn't get any more intimate than having Adam Thorne in her room, in amongst her personal things. Heat that had little to do with the fire and more to do with that *blasted* man caressing her fingers spread through her, dampening her forehead.

And then there was the annual Boxing Day party tomorrow that the estate put on for the locals in the district. An afternoon tea and free tour for the villagers and later, cocktails and a dinner party for closer friends and the village dignitaries. The chances of getting through the whole thing without Adam discovering the depth of hatred between her father and his brother were slim. The locals loved to gossip about the inhabitants of the estate. The family feud and her personal shame were bound to arise at some point.

"Sorry," she managed at last. "I can, but Adam has some business in town."

Her "fiancé" lifted her hand to his mouth and pressed his lips to her palm. "Nonsense. It's Christmas. We'd love to stay."

Oh, she really would have to kill him. Refusing to look at him, she gave Gill a rather strained smile and shrug.

Adam was clearly trying to embarrass and discomfit her. She set her mouth. It wouldn't work. Pembleton wasn't short on bedrooms and Jasmine knew where the bedding was kept.

Gill gave her a curious glance. Her stepmother was pretty intuitive. What was Adam playing at? She'd have thought he'd be pleased to get away from the ancient old house and her overbearing father. This just didn't seem his scene.

"I think I'll show Adam part of the house," she said, rising. "And walk off some of that wonderful dinner."

Gill nodded. "If you get hungry later, there are plenty of leftovers in the kitchen. Just help yourselves. Your father usually has his tea in his room but he might come down later."

As soon as she'd gone, Jasmine turned back to Adam and kept her voice low. "Did you have to say you'd stay?"

He remained seated, looking up at her thoughtfully. "I've never stayed in a stately home before... tell me about Ian."

She missed a beat. "What about him?"

"Have you slept together?"

Jasmine pressed her lips together to stop the hot retort that sprang to mind. Something in the way his sharp gaze focused so intently on her stopped her. After a long pause, she nodded.

"I see."

What did he see? That she'd slept with him, therefore she was obliged to marry him? A smile nearly slipped out when she thought of the dent that would put in Adam Thorne's womanizing ways.

Yet she felt compelled to justify herself. "It was comfort sex. And my father has his own acquisitive reasons for wanting me to marry Ian."

"Do I need to dust off my dueling swords?"

She let another heartbeat go by, squashing down, as she often did, all the clever things she'd wish she'd said later, when she was alone. "Would you like to see the house or not?"

Adam got up, looming tall over her. She turned toward the door but he caught her arm and turned her back. "Why did you need his comfort?"

Jasmine blinked, needing to think. Overfull, overheated, overwhelmed by him...how much did he deserve to know? She couldn't bear it if all the salacious stories got back to his brother and her colleagues. Of course she missed home, this house mostly, Gill, and sometimes her cantankerous father. But New Zealand was her haven. Her comfortable art deco house in the eastern suburbs was a far cry from the luxury and tradition of Pembleton, but she felt safe there. With one careless word, Adam could whip that safety net out from under her.

From the determined gleam in his eye, she deduced the lesser of two evils would be her failed love affair, the incident that sparked the return of all the unwelcome publicity from years before. The most important thing was to keep the feud from him, for now at least.

Jasmine looked pointedly at his hand on her arm. "A broken heart, reasonably common when you're twenty."

Adam merely raised his brows.

She sighed. "Against my father's wishes, I fell in love with the man who is tenth in line for the throne. It didn't last. He preferred my best friend. They recently divorced, but the point is, for a few months, I was a lamb to the slaughter for the press. An engagement announcement—" she gave him a scathing look "—for our *pretend* engagement might bring it all up again."

Adam's face cleared. "Vincent de Burgh. That's why you were in such a hurry to leave last night—and you didn't want your photo taken."

Jasmine nodded, not realizing he'd picked up on that.

His eyes searched her face for so long she began to fidget. Finally he nodded. "Okay. That wasn't so hard, was it?"

"What?"

"To bring me up to speed. I'm beginning to think there are more secrets hoarded up in that lovely head—" he tapped her temple with his index finger "—than currently floating around the Secret service."

Adam was enjoying himself. Despite Jasmine's stuffy father, who seemed to regard her achievements and wishes as an afterthought, her stepmother was great and the house was out of this world.

The best part was making her squirm, because as he'd pointed out last night, she didn't like it one bit. Playing her fiancé gave him carte blanche to touch, to be suggestive, to tease. He almost forgot why he was here. Oh, he wanted Jasmine—or Jane, as he had to keep reminding himself—more with each passing minute but his main goal was the opportunity to meet her uncle.

The touching, being suggestive and teasing just made it all the more enjoyable—for him.

The private apartments were bright and light, showcasing plenty of marble, plasterwork, windows and gilded furnishings. It was a different story "below stairs", as the basement was known. This is where the twenty or so servants in the early nineteen-hundreds had worked, Jasmine explained. "And that doesn't count the gardeners, farmhands, garage or stable hands. Or, would you believe, the night watchmen."

History wasn't his thing, but as they slowly wandered the areas open to the public, Adam was transported back to another time. She astounded him with her knowledge. It seemed she had a story about every nook and cranny, every priceless heirloom, every brick in the house! It was all so fascinating.

"The hall of summons," she announced, pointing out the labels where forty bells hung high on faded plaster walls, some sporting the names of some of her ancestors. She showed him the cavernous kitchen, with its incredibly high ceiling, "to dissipate the heat and steam from the coal-powered range, which could eat up to a hundredweight of coal in a day."

"How do you know all this stuff?" he marveled, declining her invitation to walk up the ninety stone stairs to the maids' quarters in the attic.

"I grew up here." She ran her hand over some ancient books in the butler's rooms—*Burke's Peerage, Baronetage and Knightage* was one tome that caught Adam's eye. "And I have a degree in English history."

He straightened, surprised. "You do?"

"Uh-huh. I got interested in history when we started a family tree at school," she explained. "It took me years to finish, even though our family has only been here for a couple of hundred years." They walked up the basement stairs into the entranceway, blinking at the strong light after the gloominess below. "I enjoyed it so much, I decided I wanted to work in a museum one day."

"And yet now you reside in one of the youngest countries in the world and work as a personal assistant in a financial organization."

Jasmine laughed. "Ironic, isn't it? Maybe Te Papa would have me."

She referred to New Zealand's national museum in Wellington. Adam's interest in Jasmine doubled. She was well-educated, cultured, elegant. She oozed class, spades of it—and it wasn't something she'd learned. Rather, she was born to it, to this grand house with hundreds of years under its belt.

As she uncovered history for him, he so wanted to uncover her many layers, to know her secrets and desires and fears and dreams. Despite her culture and poise and obvious smarts, she was vulnerable, softer than the socialites or corporate sharks he normally dated.

But Adam had a feeling unraveling Jasmine's mysteries would take a lifetime.

"Don't you miss it here, all the history, the house and the countryside?"

"Sometimes."

"Will you stay in New Zealand?" he asked.

"For now," she said pensively, neither her tone nor the brief reply a confirmation.

"What do you like about it?"

She thought for a moment. "The laid-back, fair-dues character of it. The small population. A lot of things. It just seems a more open and fair society."

Adam nodded. He missed his country often— when he wasn't working fifteen-hour days or squiring some gorgeous woman around London—and was looking forward to returning, probably within the next year, and showing his brother and father that he'd risen to the top.

They'd eat his dust. So he was an irresponsible lightweight who could not sustain his incredible success. He'd show them and raise them some. And when he'd set up in Australia and expanded into the States, perhaps by the time he was forty, he'd choose a mate and start a family. And his family would come first. Adam would not emulate his parents, who had worked six days a week for most of his childhood.

Not that he was complaining. He liked his particular set of familial individuals. He'd just come out of the womb always wanting to do better…at everything. What was wrong with that?

That night, they said their good-nights to Gill and he followed Jasmine up the incredible silver stairway, which apparently took three men three days to polish in its day. They hadn't discussed sleeping arrangements but she wasn't at ease. The stiffness of her back as she showed him the way corroborated that. After several fruitless dates in New Zealand, he was conversant with her resolve.

His desire for her had only increased since their passionate encounter last month. Far from slaking his thirst, he was parched to the bone. She'd been very proper throughout the day, even when he pushed the boundaries a little, touching her, whispering in her ear, all the little nuances that hopefully had her father and stepmother believing they were a couple.

She hadn't cracked. He admired her composure but it only made him more determined to break it. He thought back to some of the dark rooms "below stairs" and imagined there was a ghost or two clanking around this mausoleum—perhaps he could play the "afraid of the dark card"…

She opened a door and showed him into a bedroom that would fit most of his town house inside. The room and salon were tastefully decorated in sage green, overlooking an Italian fountain in the lily pond, and with the ubiquitous fire crackling in the antique fireplace. This house must be hellish cold, he thought, with the number of fireplaces throughout.

"Don't tell me this was your actual room?" He touched the four-poster bed that looked the size of an Olympic swimming pool. He was amazed anyone could sleep here. The furniture and decor belonged in a palace.

"Mmm." She walked over to their bags, which the housekeeper had brought up from the entrance. Watching her, it suddenly hit Adam that she'd grown up here, this was a slice of her life, with all its pomp and ceremony and tradition.

And yet it just didn't mesh with the shy woman he knew in Wellington. Her home was comfortable, small, with a bright garden full of camellias and rhododendrons, but not luxurious by any means.

Adam blew out a long breath, it suddenly occurring to him that Jasmine was serious money. Not that he cared about having money half as much as the making of it. But with her obvious love of history, her family so ancient and well-connected, how could she turn her back on this and expect to find happiness in a country where only the odd tree dated back more than a couple of centuries?

She belonged here, couldn't she see that?

Jasmine picked up her bag and headed for the door. Adam leaned on the fireplace, knowing she was too well-mannered to leave without saying good-night.

She turned at the door, gifting him a small smile. "Sleep well."

"That's a fine way to say good-night to your fiancé," he said in a low, teasing voice.

She shifted the overnight bag into her other hand. Her eyes were wary but not hostile. "You're enjoying this, I believe."

Adam's head went up, his smile ready. He always enjoyed the chase. She should know that! "I am, I admit it."

And he wasn't just teasing. He enjoyed seeing her in her natural environment. "It's like a different world."

"Good night, Adam," she said quietly, looking into his face, and as always happened when they looked at each other, the overpowering attraction leaped to life between them, boosting his anticipation.

Then she blinked rapidly and began to back away toward the door. Adam spoke quickly. "And now you're going to leave me to the mercy of the resident ghosts and go off to some crypt somewhere, because you don't trust yourself in the same room with me."

Yes, he was disappointed. The desire he felt for her was much too intense for a woman he had already slept with. What was this hold she had over him?

Jasmine smiled gently. "The ghosts are friendly and I'll pass on the crypt, but I should be safe in the maids' quarters in the attic."

Adam nodded. "Ninety stairs should render you relatively safe, yes."

Again she turned to go, then stopped. "Thank you for this."

Simply said, classy. He *really* liked this woman—but he had to remember what his purpose here was. His whole life stretched out in front of him, time enough for distractions. But for now, he had a new business to contend with, people who depended on him.

He shrugged carelessly. "You want something. I want something."

Often he'd thought Jasmine's eyes looked sad. If not sad, then as if they were expecting something to make them sad in the very near future. Now she stood in the doorway, both hands grasping the strap on her holdall, her chin tucked into her chest, and her eyes almost silver in the firelight, filled with sadness and secrets.

"Of course," she said, and left the room.

Four

A weak sun came out on Boxing Day, so Jasmine decided to show Adam the grounds of the estate. They took her father's four-wheel drive and motored slowly around the two-thousand acres. There were a couple of hundred acres of woodland and grazing for fallow deer, the thoroughbred stud, stables and track and expansive but basically disused parklands, backed by rocky, heather-covered hills behind the house.

"Father always said he'd like to develop a golf course here. I don't know why he hasn't."

"How many staff look after all this?" Adam asked. She told him that the estate retained only a small staff of a live-in housekeeper, part-time cleaners and kitchen hands, cook, tour guide and gardener. "Plus the stud manager," Jasmine finished. "It's not nearly enough. We need an agricultural specialist, first and foremost. Gill still handles most of the administrative tasks, but she hasn't kept up with learning new techniques and technology." She turned her face to the house in the distance. "And I doubt she'll have time for the next few months."

Jasmine had many ideas for improving the estate, although her personal choice would be to concentrate on the house and heirlooms first.

"All those empty rooms could be put to such good use," she mused, her mind clicking into second gear. "An antiques center, private exhibitions, niche weekends for small groups like writers and such, small conferences, weddings…" There were endless possibilities that excited her but not, sadly, her more conservative father. "Father doesn't hold with the modern trend of opening up stately homes to the public. He's had to, to some extent, to keep up with the maintenance costs, but it's a struggle getting him to listen to any new ideas."

"With you in charge," Adam commented, "Pembleton could be a world-class venue."

She smiled at him and gazed around at the snow-dusted landscape. Perhaps absence did make the heart fonder. Or the reality of her father's mortality brought it all closer to home. She had loved the house and the land, would always love it, but the memories

that remained at the edges of her mind were of distance, of being let down. She'd always been convinced that the events in her early life colored how
her father saw her, ultimately as a burden and a disappointment. She had long accepted that they would
never be close, and that that wasn't her fault. But after
Vincent, the place became a prison. And if she'd
gone along with her father's wishes to marry Ian, it
would be her prison now.

They drove into the village and stopped for a pint
at the local pub. She acknowledged the curious stares
of the locals, a few of whom she remembered vaguely.
Suddenly she was glad she lived in New Zealand.
Just something so small as to be able to drink a coffee
or a beer in public, without everyone speculating on
your love life or your parents' tragedy of a marriage,
was worth the pangs of regret she sometimes suffered
when thinking about home.

"Is that little Jane Cooper?" the barmaid asked.

Jasmine trawled her memory banks. "How are
you, Mrs. Dainty?"

They chatted for a minute or two about the sad
state of her father's health. "Some families have their
share of tragedy," the pleasant woman said, shaking
her head, "but yours has had more than most."

"What did she mean?" Adam asked as they took
a table by the fireplace.

Jasmine had spent a good part of the night, bedded
down in a room four doors away from Adam, think-

ing about him. Wishing that she could separate sex from emotion, because her emotions were going haywire with him around.

She didn't regret that she'd slept with him a few weeks ago, but involving him in her family affairs could turn out to be the biggest regret of all, because despite his arrogance and his teasing, he was dangerously likeable.

She looked at him over the rim of her beer, felt the kick in the pit of her stomach whenever their eyes met. If only she could accept, as he did, that sex was the only thing between them, the only thing that would ever be between them.

She remembered what he'd said the day before about her secrets. She was full of them and experience had taught her not to confide in people.

Since she'd been here, she'd had one fright on Christmas Eve with Vincent, and now faced the prospect of Adam hearing about her past tonight at the party. She didn't think for a moment he would be unsympathetic about the rest of it, but the killer would be her non-contact with her uncle.

Jasmine decided he should know the details—with the exception of the insurmountable rift between her father and uncle. She crossed her fingers and hoped he'd feel so sorry for "poor little Jane Cooper" that he'd forget about Stewart Cooper.

Adam waved his hand in front of her face. "Are you still with me?" That wicked, expressive mouth curved. She warmed to the crinkles in the corners of his eyes.

It would be a relief to share, after so many years hiding it away as if it never happened. Even as her fingers tapped the side of her pint glass, as she inhaled in preparation of laying her life bare to a virtual stranger, she wondered, why take the risk when there was no future for them? What if he misused the information?

What if he didn't and it brought them closer?

Jasmine swallowed and looked at him steadily. "My mother died when I was fourteen, after spending ten years in a psychiatric institution. She—she never got over the fact that she was driving when my brother was killed in a car accident, not long after I was born."

Adam had been holding his pint to his mouth. Now he set it down slowly, his eyes focusing intently on her face, and put his elbows on the table. She imagined this was what he looked like when chasing a financial deal.

Or a woman... She looked away.

"They said she was suffering from post-natal depression after having me." Jasmine shrugged, her eyes flitting in an ordered way to each object on the wall behind his head, from the stag's head to the rusty old scythe to an ancient photo of Pembleton, which she must remember to have a closer look at. "Anyway, she bore it for a few years but when I was three years old, while my father was away on business, she took me on the ferry to Paris and left me there."

Adam exhaled carefully. "Left you where, exactly?"

"On the Montmartre carousel, actually." Jasmine smiled ruefully. "Going around in circles."

Thankfully, she'd been too young to remember. It hadn't dimmed her love of the horses on the estate, and she had only nice thoughts of France the couple of times she'd visited. "She came home without me. Father came back to Britain two days later and saw the news, saw me—" she cleared her throat "—on the news, and called the police."

Being only three, the media frenzy had gone over her head, but it must have been terrible for her parents. Every European country published pictures of the "poor abandoned soul" and in Britain, her parents—especially her mother—were vilified as monsters. Her father kept the details from her over the years but Jasmine picked up a fair amount from the playground at school. Her mother struggled on for another year after "the incident," heavily medicated and supervised, but continued to deteriorate. Another furor in the papers erupted when she was finally committed to the psychiatric facility, and again when she died and Sir Nigel married Gill a few years later. Every time the Cooper family name came up, the whole sad story was rehashed, most spectacularly of all when her engagement to Vincent failed. "That was when I realized that I couldn't escape my past and moved to New Zealand," she finished matter-of-factly.

Adam eyes were warm, soothing, full of compassion, but all he said was, "Wow."

"I didn't tell you this to get sympathy but you're probably going to hear bits and pieces tonight."

"Did you see your mother after that?" Adam asked.

Jasmine shook her head. "After an argument with Gill one day when I was about thirteen, I told her I wanted to see my real mother. Later, when I'd calmed down, she said I could if I wanted to and she would take me. But somehow, we never did."

Her father hadn't been so forbearing. He refused to allow her mother's name to be mentioned. It was Gill who told her that her mother was so ill and so heavily medicated, she wouldn't know her.

"Why New Zealand?" Adam asked.

Her shoulders rose. "Fresh start and about as far away as I could get."

"Does Nick know any of this?"

"No." It was as flat and final as she could make it.

He reached over the table and squeezed her shoulder briefly. "Thanks for telling me. Your secret is safe with me."

Jasmine believed him. Then again, what choice did she have? She picked up her half-full glass and took a mouthful, then pushed it to the center of the table. "Drink up. We'll be late for the meet and greet."

After the locals left the estate, full of ale, cider and the cook's excellent afternoon tea, Adam dressed for the dinner party, wandering around Jasmine's room as he did. Although it was furnished fit for a princess, and obviously hadn't been used as a regular bedroom for years, it retained some little touches of her. A stuffed toy or two, a collection of boy band CDs, a cluster of framed photos that had pride of place on an armoire that belonged in a museum, like nearly everything in this house.

One photo showed her in front of a huge Christmas tree in Trafalgar Square, if he wasn't mistaken, dated 1994; she must have been about eleven years old. Another in a silver ball gown that still hung in her closet. He knew she was a member of one of his mother's dancing clubs for a number of years.

Adam understood better now her fiercely guarded personality. She didn't let people close because those close to her had let her down, abandoned her. Those she should have been able to trust—her mother, her lover— had, for whatever reason, turned their backs on her.

There was another photo of her with a handsome, thick-set young man in muddy boots and oilskins, leaning on a rifle. Jasmine looked about eighteen and wore a smile as fresh and open as a child's. He wondered if that was the neighbor or a young Vincent de Burgh, the louse who had broken her heart.

He checked his watch and straightened his jacket, thinking at least he'd brightened up her sad eyes a bit last month. They'd gone clubbing, sailing and once for a wild motorcycle ride around the bays of Wellington.

She'd lost her breath and laughed, saying she'd never done anything like that before. She took him to the ballet and cooked for him one night at her home. And the last night, when he'd finally got her into bed, there was no sadness or tight control, only passion.

And that, he supposed, opening the door and stepping out into the hallway, was why she had chosen him for this well-intentioned scheme to convince her father they were engaged. She didn't know many people because she liked to keep to herself and with her backstory, who could blame her? Adam had made an effort, which was nothing unusual for him, but he suspected not many people in her life did that for her. Certainly not her father....

He would keep her secrets and keep her old man sweet for tonight but he wanted something, too, and he wasn't her savior. Once she had helped to bring her uncle to the negotiating table, they would go their separate ways, hopefully after a last sensational night together. After what she'd been through, he doubted she had any illusions left about love and forever, and Adam had no time in the foreseeable future to take a woman seriously.

Jasmine came out of the room down the hall and waited when she saw him. She inspected him as he approached and nodded approvingly. He hadn't expected to be hobnobbing with the gentry and had only brought a leather jacket, but Gill had come up with a smart sports jacket that fit perfectly.

"You look nice," she said, and tucked her arm through his.

"And you are ravishing, as always," he said. She wore her rich dark hair swept back in a loose French twist, long wisps trailing her shoulders. He liked the softer, less restrained look. Her trouser suit was platinum-gray, with a lacy cami underneath the open jacket and a dark green chiffon scarf looped simply around her neck and hanging down to her waist. Emerald and diamond studs glinted at her ears, her only jewelry. Simple, elegant, classy. "Very country," he murmured as he escorted her proudly into the formal dining room. And from nowhere came the fleeting thought that if he ever was to take a woman seriously, it would be this woman....

The English gentry knew how to eat. It seemed compulsory to showcase every meat known to mankind on the same groaning table. The old historical dramas that showed Vikings and warriors at table, gnawing on a massive hock, were not so far removed from today, cutlery and table manners notwithstanding.

Jasmine's father sat at the head of the long table of thirty guests. Most were older, all of them local, but there were a couple of people around Jasmine's age that he learned had attended the same schools. She stayed close to him during the dinner and they were both relieved that her father did not mention the engagement. Adam was introduced as "Jane's friend."

As dinner was cleared away by the attentive staff,

everyone adjourned to the large room called the orangery, a kind of insulated and robust conservatory, with underfloor heating, impressive sculptures, exotic plants and lots of glass. In the less formal situation, Jasmine's attention was avidly sought. Everyone wanted to know how she liked New Zealand and when she was coming home. Left to his own devices for the first time, Adam engaged in conversation with a blustery gentleman whose brick-colored complexion increased alarmingly with every glass of port he was able to snag from the circling waiters.

"Oh, yes, I've known the family all my life," the man said, his eagle eyes already scoping the progress of the next waiter. "Tragic story, Sir Nigel's wife and all."

Adam nodded absently, his eyes searching for Jasmine, bored by the man's inebriated waffle. He prepared to make his excuses when he suddenly heard the name Stewart Cooper. He raised one eyebrow, signaling his interest.

"Both brothers loved the same woman, you know," the man confided while Adam braced himself against the alcoholic fumes wafting from his companion's mouth. He waved a meaty hand in Jasmine's general direction. "Her daughter takes after her in looks. One only hopes not in morals or mental health."

Adam turned to face the man and stepped forward, backing him up against the wall a little. He wanted to hear more but didn't necessarily want the rest of the room to hear. "Really?"

The man needed no more encouragement. By the time he was finished, Adam knew every detail of the troubled marriage of his pretend fiancée's parents. Every twisted betrayal and tragedy, and the aftermath of bitterness that lived on today.

She'd duped him. He set his glass on a passing waiter's tray and went looking for her, his mood black. He'd been set up. Jasmine—or Jane—had no intention of helping him with his goal. How could she, when there was such a bitter rift between her family and her uncle that he would probably rather do business with a badger than any friend of hers?

The English rose had some major explaining to do. He found her coming back to the orangery, having just said good-night to her father. He waited until Gill led the frail man away, then turned on Jasmine, his anger close to the surface.

"What is it?" she asked, her brows knitting together.

Adam grasped her arm firmly. "I need to talk to you, *darling*," he gritted, walking her away from the party. "Somewhere private, I think."

She led him into a nearby room that must have been an office or library, as there were wall-to-wall books. The drapes were open and the bright lights of the party across the courtyard lit up the falling snow in friendly sparkles.

Adam didn't feel friendly at all. "How long did you think you could go on playing me for a fool?"

Jasmine drew the drapes and switched one small

lamp on by the desk, but the cavernous room was still dim. She turned to face him, a resigned look in her face. "What did you hear?"

She wasn't surprised, probably why she'd clamped herself to his side all night, he thought angrily. "That your mother was sleeping with both brothers, but when she got pregnant, she chose your father because he inherited the estate and Stewart got nothing. That the baby—your brother—was your uncle's child, not your father's. That she was so unhappy with your father, she was running away to Stewart on the night of the accident that killed his son."

Jasmine held his gaze for a long moment, then swallowed and looked away. "I don't know for sure that any of that is true," she said quietly.

"You've never met him, have you?" That realization only angered him more. "I bet he doesn't want anything to do with you. Why would he? Yet still, you promised me you'd set up a meeting."

"And I will try, as I promised, after Christmas."

Adam gave a derisive bark of laughter. "Don't do me any favors, sweetheart. If he knows I'm at all connected with you, he'll probably laugh me off the planet."

Jasmine brushed her hands over her face and rubbed her arms. Her face radiated guilt. "I'm sorry."

"You're sorry." He reached out and grasped both ends of the scarf she wore, watching her eyes widen.

"Not good enough, I'm afraid." He tugged on the scarf until Jasmine had no option but to take a step forward, and another.

"I'll get what I need, with or without you," he growled, referring to Stewart Cooper, "and I'll take what I want, as well."

She tottered another step forward, her mouth rounded and surprised and infinitely appealing. "What you want?" she whispered breathlessly.

Adam's anger sizzled under his skin, aggravating him to a fever pitch of desire. He tugged her relentlessly forward, his eyes lighting hungrily on the delicate line of her shoulder exposed by the scarf as he seesawed it over her skin. Her pulse pumped and jerked in the hollow of her throat, mirroring his, he'd wager. The tip of her tongue shot out quickly to moisten her lips, capturing his avid attention. He had no idea where the hell they were, but he wasn't averse to taking her right here, against the towering dusty bookcases, not twenty feet from where her peers partied on, oblivious.

"*You,* lovely Jasmine." Adam bent his head to stop an inch away from her mouth. Her eyes filled his vision, hazed over, too dark to be gray. "As soon as possible," he breathed, watching her beautiful lips part slightly. "As often as possible." He closed that last inch, his tongue flicking out to sweep her lower lip. "You owe me that, at least."

She shivered. Her front bumped up against his,

ratcheting up the tension a little. Her breath escaped in a rush and she immediately gasped in another. From past experience, he'd say Ms. Cool, Calm and Collected was about to lose it, and he remembered every thrilling erotic detail of the last time she'd lost her composure.

Nothing wrong in helping her along. Adam let go of the scarf and put one finger in the waistband of her trousers. Her front bumped him again, all knobs and bone, soft and hard, bumping together, burning for more. His other hand circled the back of her neck as he tilted her face up and finally crushed his lips down on hers.

She opened for him immediately. He pulled her hard against him, dipping into her mouth with a hunger that blasted away any finesse he might normally employ, or that she might expect. Her scent was rich in subtle passion; the warmth and smoothness of her skin incited him to go deeper, push more insistently. Adam considered himself an experienced lover who always had his partner's needs in mind, but with this woman, all bets were off. He wanted more fiercely, needed more of everything she could offer.

And he wasn't the only one. Her tongue delved in and out of his mouth, maddening him. Her hands clutched and kneaded his shirt and she strained against him, her sighs loud in the dim room. Just as hungry, just as needy as he.

He maneuvered his hand inside the camisole and

slid up toward her breasts. Jasmine's spine tensed like steel and she pushed her front out hard against him. Her head fell back, breaking the kiss, and she moaned softly as his fingers caressed the underside of her firm globe. Heaven help him, she was so sweet, tasted so sweet.

And then a harsh white light flooded the room. Her eyes snapped open and locked on his, full of alarm. Adam cursed under his breath and looked toward the door. A man he didn't recall seeing at the dinner party tonight stood there, framed in the light from the hallway.

They stared at each other, or more correctly, Adam glared at him, he stared at Jasmine and Jasmine—after a quick glance at the intruder—stared at Adam's throat, her lips moving in soundless surprise.

"Can I help you?" Adam asked, the warning in his voice implying he'd like to help him into next week through the closed windows, if necessary. He took his hand out from under Jasmine's top reluctantly, away from her glorious breasts that still rose and fell robustly.

It was an older version of the man in the photo in her room. Adam studied his pale and surprised face, impatiently waiting for his explanation. What, did he want to watch?

"I'm not sure," the man said, his voice infuriatingly vague. "I thought I'd found my fiancée but it can't be her, because you have your mouth and hands all over her."

Five

Jasmine's eyes closed in distress. Ian! What on earth next? And why did he have to say *that,* of all things?

Her hands dropped from Adam's shirt, trembling with interrupted passion, shock and now shame. She began to straighten her clothing, not sure which of the two of them she most did not want to look at. She felt, rather than saw Adam's head slowly turning her way, and licked her chafed and sensitive lips nervously.

"What did he say?" he asked her softly.

Jasmine covered her mouth with her palm, exhaling. Excuses clamored to be let out: He didn't mean it, it's a joke, I was going to tell you… She took a step back from him, looking over at Ian, who looked as confused and embarrassed as she felt. Her heart clenched in sympathy. She walked quickly to him, put her hands on his shoulders and kissed his cheek. "Why aren't you in Switzerland?"

Ian studied her face, looking somewhat relieved. "My father called to tell me you were back. You might have warned me. It was no mean task, getting flights at this time of year."

She stepped back from him and glanced at Adam. His eyes bored into her face, one dark brow raised. He looked ready to explode.

Jasmine exhaled, agitated. She hated being agitated. "I'm not engaged," she said to the room in general, not looking at either of them.

"To me or him?"

Oh, the softness of his voice, like a velvet noose...

"Well, technically—" Ian ventured.

She shot him a venomous look, willing him to shut up, then turned back to the smoldering man a few feet away. "It's not what you think."

"Oh, you don't want to know what I think."

Scathing, angry, disgusted. Arrows of displeasure pummeled her. Coming on top of learning about her family history, this could be the last straw for them.

Jasmine couldn't bear not to see him again, not to be held or kissed by him again....

With a last hard look at her, he stepped forward. "I'll be off, since I'm surplus to requirements."

"Adam, I can explain."

"I've had enough of your explanations." He brushed past her, pausing to look into Ian's face. "You're welcome to her, mate. I've even warmed her up for you."

Shame coursed through her and she hurried after him. Ian grabbed at her arm as she passed and she spun on him. "Why did you have to say *that?*"

"We need to talk. Your father's dying. You can't keep putting it off."

Jasmine shook him off, her eyes on the tall, angry figure striding away down the hallway.

"Talk to me, Jane."

The agitation in Ian's voice stopped her at the door but she didn't turn around. "I have to go after him. Please, Ian, just wait for me here."

He let out a petulant sigh. "I've been waiting all my life. When is it going to end?"

"A few more minutes," she said with her back to him. "I promise."

She found Adam in her room, tossing clothing and toiletries into his small overnight bag. If only he'd left this morning, as she'd intended. His face was closed and angry. She could barely believe he was the same man who had kissed her so passionately just a few minutes ago, as if he'd die if he hadn't.

"Please don't go." She stood in the doorway, twisting the ends of her scarf in her hands. "It's all a mistake."

"It sure is." He took off the borrowed jacket and laid it on the bed. "Thank Gill and your father for their hospitality."

"Listen—" she said hurriedly; his bag was already packed and he'd picked up his leather jacket— "what he said…it's not really true. It was just a silly pact we made five years ago before I left to live in New Zealand."

"Jasmine—*Jane*—get this through your lovely head: I don't care. I've had enough of your silly games and your secrets and your lies. I have wasted all the time I'm going to."

"You have every right to be angry, but—" she walked to him swiftly and took his hand in hers "—please let me explain."

With his dark glower and black leather jacket, he looked dangerous, unapproachable, but she had to try. She thought too much of him to just let him walk out, maybe forever.

Besides, she had to think of her job should his displeasure get back to Nick. Suddenly Jasmine was tired, mentally. So many revelations today after years of holding it all in.

With a deep breath, she started at the beginning. "My father has always wanted Ian's family land adjoining the estate, mostly because he's worried about developers getting their hands on it. Ian is a farmer; he wants to farm the estate. Anyway, as I told you in your office, my father needs a male heir to keep the estate after he's gone."

"Or what?" Adam interrupted brusquely.

At least he wasn't leaving. "Or it passes to Stewart." There was a long silence while he digested that. This was the tricky part, because now he knew how irreconcilable the differences between the brothers were. What use would she be to him?

In front of her, Adam shifted impatiently. She'd lose him if she didn't get on with it. "When I met Vincent, my father strenuously disapproved. His connections aside, he thought he was a money-grabbing opportunist." Sage words as it turned out a short time later.

"Because of his high profile in the tabloids, I came in for a lot of interest but it wasn't until he ran off with my best friend that…" Jasmine closed her eyes to blot out the headlines. "Everything you heard tonight about Uncle Stewart and the love triangle, my mother abandoning me and going mad. Poor little Jane, everybody leaves her, they said. I was a national joke."

She gulped in air, reliving the horror of the paparazzi at the gate, being followed everywhere. "My father was beside himself with shame." It had taken her years to forgive him for his cruelty in those dark days. "He said the only thing I could do to make it better was to marry Ian. The press would lose interest and we'd all be left alone. And the estate would be safe from Stewart."

But there must have been a bit more life in her. She

couldn't bear the thought of staying and being at the mercy of the press all her life. And she couldn't bear the thought of waking next to a man she didn't love every day. Jasmine had been hurt badly by the actions of her mother and lover, but something inside her wouldn't let her give up on life and love just yet.

"I tried to love Ian, I really did, but I just couldn't make myself go through with a wedding. I had finished my degree but had plans to work in the history field or at least do some more study, but the publicity didn't let up. In the end, I took the coward's way out. I ran away."

Was she imagining it or had Adam's hand, sandwiched between hers, softened and warmed? "When I left, Ian and I made a silly promise that if neither of us was married by the time we were twenty-five, we'd marry each other." Twenty-five had seemed a lifetime away when she was twenty. Jasmine knew Ian felt more for her than she did him, but he didn't love her, either, not the way she wanted to be loved. They were friends and he wanted the estate. "I honestly thought he'd find someone else in my absence."

"But he didn't."

She looked up and saw that Adam's expression wasn't any friendlier than before.

"It was a stupid agreement, entered into at a time when I was overemotional and just wanted to be away." She squeezed his hand between hers, imploring him with her eyes to believe her.

Unmoved, Adam retrieved his hand from hers. "He seems to be taking it seriously enough."

Jasmine swallowed, feeling him cool and close up. "I'll talk to him tonight."

Adam gave her another hard look, then walked away from her toward the window. He pulled the drapery back. The snow was still falling. She clutched at the hope that he wouldn't be able to leave because of the weather.

"You're full of surprises, aren't you, *Jane?*"

"The only lie I told was assuring you I could set up a meeting with my uncle."

"Oh, but you've been very economical with the truth." He turned, his gaze dark as night. "These little games, playing hard to get a few weeks ago, making promises you have no way of keeping, telling me half truths—I didn't expect it of you."

Jasmine's heart fell. His attention, his admiration had surprised her from the first. It was a nice feeling, and it saddened her to lose it. "I've been such a disappointment to my father," she said quietly. "I wanted to please him just once before he died."

Adam shrugged and turned back to the window. "I don't particularly like the way he treats you, but the ultimate way to please him, if you want to throw your life away, is to marry Ian." He paused. She saw him tilt his head at the reflection, knew he was watching her in it.

"As you know," he continued conversationally,

"I'm not in the market for marriage. I certainly won't stop you."

She shook her head miserably. It wouldn't be fair, to herself or to Ian.

Adam's disappointment in her lanced her heart. Right from the start she'd been determined not to get involved with him. He hadn't seemed to mind her reticence; he'd just set about seducing her over a period of weeks. She loved the attention—and the company. Even while fending him off as nicely as she could, she dreamed of him, vivid, addictive dreams that left her hot, turned on and uncomfortably aware of her loneliness. The reality, when finally she couldn't bear to push him away, was so much better than her dreams.

Adam might be a career womanizer but he'd always made her feel special, as if she was worth the wait. However, she had no hold on him now; he'd sampled the goods, and because of her actions, he was disappointed in her.

The fight left her. Jasmine hung her head, the design on the carpet blurring as she studied the floor. "I'm so sorry, Adam. And grateful, for everything." Her shoulders rose and fell helplessly. "I wish I could make it up to you."

Two large black shoes appeared in front of her feet. She looked up in surprise, not hearing his approach.

His eyes were cool, his lips set in a thin line.

"Oh, you'll make it up to me, all right," Adam said

softly. "I want you, God help me." His thumb brushed the corner of her mouth and continued slowly on along her bottom lip. "Don't bother adding to your litany of lies by denying that you want me, too."

She took a deep, shuddering breath in, hoarding it. Excitement gripped her in hot, sharp claws.

"And I intend to collect," Adam continued, his finger tracing her chin, down over the edge, and kept going to the hollow in her throat.

Jasmine's head rolled back a little, all her senses focused on his stern, searing eyes, his wicked mouth and the finger burning a path down her front.

His eyes never left her face, watching her struggle to breathe, to contain the soaring desire that only he could invoke. He brought his hand back to her chin, cupping it, studying her like an exhibit. His voice became businesslike. "I'll send a car for you on Thursday, at noon. Bring your passport and pack enough for a couple of days."

She blinked, her mind a flurry of nerves, desire and confusion. Maybe a little relief that he still wanted her. "Where…?"

Adam smiled grimly. "I have no idea yet." His fingers on her chin firmed and his smile became a scowl. He bent his head so that his mouth was very close to hers. "But make no mistake, wherever it is, we will be together." His fingers gentled and then he released her. "Don't even think of letting me down."

Jasmine tried to formulate a reply but her mind

was in a spin. The most galling thing to accept was the excitement dulling her senses, thickening her tongue, sending that howl of triumph through her blood. Not indignation, defiance, or even fear. And that was not a good sign.

With one last hard look, Adam turned to go. But at the door, he swung back to her. "There is no question you have suffered in your life. No one could blame you for having abandonment issues." He paused, his eyes pitiless. "But for God's sake, if you don't intend to marry him, put that poor sap out of his misery."

Six

Three days later, she found herself on a private executive jet, wondering what on earth she was doing. Where was Adam? The car had arrived at noon, driven her to an airstrip just outside London, and a flight attendant had bustled her up the steps and into a seat and taken her passport away for checking. Now the engines began to roar, and there was still no sign of him.

This wasn't her intention. After he'd left the party, Jasmine realized Adam was right. She'd been keeping Ian hanging, giving him hope. Afraid that she'd lose the only friend she had if she stripped him of that. After all, hadn't everyone else let her down?

Her heart-rending talk with Ian had convinced her that she was about to be humiliated again. He'd checked Adam out, said his playboy status was on a par with Vincent's. Adam himself had told her he wasn't in the market for a relationship.

Jasmine recognized the danger of losing her head and her heart to Adam Thorne. This madness must be nipped in the bud before someone—she—got really hurt. So yesterday she had taken the bull by the horns and gone to see her uncle, telling only Gill what she was up to.

The flight attendant returned with her passport and checked that her seat belt was buckled.

"Is Mr. Thorne here yet?" Jasmine asked.

The woman shook her head. "You are our only passenger today."

"But—" Jasmine's mouth fell open. "Where are we going?"

"Vienna," came the reply.

Vienna? In one second flat, she forgot her resolution and soared with excitement. She'd never visited the city before and yet felt she knew it intimately. Courtesy of her love of ballroom dancing, especially the waltz, she had dreamed for years of attending a ball in the Austrian capital. Each year, Vienna staged around three hundred balls, and tonight—New Year's Eve—was the opening ball of the season, the Kaiser-ball, the greatest of them all. Jasmine nearly passed out with excitement and recalled telling Adam on one of their dates that it was a lifelong ambition to attend this particular ball.

He'd remembered. Her throat closed up. Emotions she didn't want to acknowledge rose up and begged to be acknowledged.

But she'd only come to tell him about her uncle. She had fulfilled her part of the bargain and when the car had arrived at Pembleton, she'd gotten into it with no intention of going away for a dirty weekend. Determined not to be tempted, she hadn't even packed a bag. She didn't expect a fight about it. After all, it was what he'd wanted all along. She was only the consolation prize.

The reception she'd gotten from Stewart Cooper had overwhelmed her. Far from being spiteful or angry at her unannounced visit, he seemed hungry for her company. Hungry for some connection to her mother. He had never loved another soul.

Jasmine liked him. For all his money, he cut a sad and lonely figure. He told her he'd visited her mother every single week in the ten years she'd been in the psychiatric institution.

"I would sit and hold her hand," he said sadly, "looking at her face while she stared out of the window. She never looked at me and never spoke. I think she was so wracked by guilt—the car accident, abandoning you, hurting Nigel—that she couldn't bear to see me. But I couldn't bear not to see her."

Jasmine had wept, haunted by the thought of it.

She hadn't known her mother well and had good reason to despise her. But the thought of this kind, sad-eyed old gentleman holding her mother's hand, week after week, year after year, when she wouldn't look at him or speak to him…it was so terribly sad.

Her uncle hoped to see Jasmine again. He also promised to check out Adam's business. If his advisors were in favor, he would contact him directly.

Jasmine sat back in her seat as the plane took off, her mind racing with excitement and confusion. Was Adam already there? Please God it was the Kaiserball she was going to. If so, how could she resist anything he asked of her?

And what was she going to do for clothes?

"Danke schoen."

Adam left the boutique having purchased the gown and arranged for it to be delivered to the hotel. He checked his watch. She would be landing in an hour. He had time to shower, dress and leave her a note. And the gown.

He hadn't been able to resist. He'd intended to take her shopping since she'd have no idea of the event they were attending. Luckily he knew a savvy travel agent who'd not only managed to find tickets to the coveted event but also, through a late cancellation, to get him a suite at *the* hotel in Vienna. Considering it was New Year's Eve, the man deserved a medal.

Quite by chance, he'd seen a creation in the window of a boutique that took his breath away—at least, when he imagined Jasmine Cooper's curves poured into it. God knows she didn't deserve it, but after all, it was for his pleasure, not hers.

She'd made him crazy with all her heartbreaking secrets. Maybe—just maybe—he felt a tiny bit guilty about the sex-as-payment thing. Not too guilty, but once he started on the arrangements, the whole thing took on a mind of its own. He was setting the scene for sex, that's all, and he would give her a night to remember.

He couldn't wait to see how she looked in her finery. His step was light, his smile ready as he entered the opulent Hotel Imperial and headed for the elevators. On impulse, he doubled back and with his rudimentary German, asked the clerk to order a horse-drawn carriage for tonight. The princess was going to the ball in style.

Jasmine stood outside the fabled Hotel Imperial, her mouth hanging open. This was supposedly one of the most romantic hotels in the world. Her day just got better and better.

The flight was uneventful and speedy—or that might have been her mind racing. The only hitch came as she walked uncertainly into the airport, wondering where Adam was. Wondering if there was some cruel joke afoot.

But there was a man with a sign: *Fräulein* Cooper.

And a short drive later, here she was, so excited she could barely contain it.

She checked in, her heart soaring when told they were expecting her, and asked for a map and a directory of clothing stores. Her head told her to entertain the possibility that she wasn't going to the ball—she'd find out in a few minutes—but she needed underwear, toiletries, something to wear tomorrow.

She followed a personal butler to the suite booked in Adam's name. He opened the door with a flourish and left her alone.

Jasmine was too awestruck to wonder where Adam was. She shed her coat, handbag and shoes where she stood, walked out into the middle of a star-patterned parquet floor, and just stood for long minutes, taking it all in. It was too much! If she expired right this minute, she could not be happier.

Opulence of a degree she'd never encountered transported her back to another age. Crystal chandeliers glittered from the high ceiling. Rich silk covered the walls behind gilded frames holding precious nineteenth-century oil paintings. Antique chaise lounges, bowls of flowers and fruit—she nearly cried out when she saw the perfect Biedermeier armoire. Everywhere she looked, a new treasure delighted her.

After an age, she walked into the bedroom with some trepidation. Surely such perfection could not be improved upon. She was wrong. The huge canopied bed somehow didn't dwarf the room, perhaps because of the impressive height of the ceilings or the massive Baroque-framed mirror opposite. Elegant casement windows flooded the room with light and looked out over the Musikverein, one of the finest concert halls in the world and home to the Vienna Philharmonic.

By the time she got to the bathroom, Jasmine's senses were exhausted but it boasted every conceivable luxury, she was sure. Plus a sign that Adam had been here, a damp towel on the rail and his toiletries on the double vanity. Further checks revealed clothes in the closet, a used cup in the sink and an English newspaper open on a sofa.

She sat on a plush chaise lounge and took out her phone, assuming he would have the same number he'd used in New Zealand. But on a whim, she called Gill instead of Adam.

"You'll never guess where I am."

Gill squealed when she heard. Jasmine floated around the suite again, trying to describe it. Finally, she remembered to ask after her father.

There was an ominous pause. "He's not having a good day. He talked to Ian who painted a rather grim picture of Adam's character and also said you've given him no hope of you two marrying someday."

Jasmine sighed. She knew her father would be upset to know there was no hope of her and Ian marrying. Why couldn't he see how unreasonable it was to try to force her in this day and age?

She snorted and looked around. What day and age was she in again?

A knock at the door sounded. "Gill? I have to go. I think Adam's just arrived back." She told her stepmother she would be back in a couple of days and opened the door to find the butler holding a very large flat box.

"Fräulein Cooper?"

"*Ja?*"

She took the box and he waved away her tip. Jasmine pulled off the ribbon and tissue paper, humming with excitement. Her breath caught in her throat when she saw the color of the gown. She'd describe it as thistle, a pale purple but with a depth that surpassed lilac. It was strapless with two ruched panels in the front, so that the full overskirt raised up, revealing lilac gauze underneath. The bodice sparkled with Swarovski crystals. It was the most beautiful thing Jasmine had ever seen. She lifted it carefully, noting the handwrought hanger, and rushed to the bedroom mirror, holding it up against her.

In the image, her average gray eyes were shining and looked almost indigo. One hand held the dress against her front while she hurriedly scooped her hair up with the other. Her happiness knew no bounds. Adam had bought her a gown. What else was she to think but that Cinderella *would* go to the ball!

But where was her prince? She remembered her

phone and regretfully hung the gown in the wardrobe. She had just walked out of the bedroom when another knock sounded. The butler with another box. Jasmine just stood there, looking at him stupidly, and the poor man had to walk past her, place the box on the table and close the door behind him.

A white fur cape. Correction, faux fur. And not quite white, a smoky pale gray. The perfect accessory for the gown.

Accessories. She'd need gloves, shoes, a strapless bra. Maybe some earrings…how much time did she have? It was then that she noticed the envelope on the exceptional Baroque writing desk. Of course, he would think with her love of antiques that she would have looked there first, but the whole suite was full of such treasures. She slid a single heavy page from the envelope. Handwritten, brief:

> Your carriage will be waiting downstairs at 7:00 p.m. I'll see you by the Grand Staircase. A.

Jasmine checked her watch and got moving.

A couple of hours later, she staggered into the suite, laden with bags. Shower, makeup, hair…no time for an appointment with a *ballfrisuren,* the hotel hairdresser specializing in ball hairdos.

She'd have to make do herself. Humming *Die Fledermaus,* she threw herself into her preparations.

At five minutes before seven she left the suite,

walked out of the hotel and was guided into a horse-drawn carriage. Of course...

They moved slowly down the Ringstrasse toward the Hofburg Palace. A light snow fell, and the city glittered. Everything was so perfect, Jasmine felt she might die with happiness. And the first nerves were starting to bite at the thought of seeing him again. He had been so angry with her.

She hadn't expected him to be so thoughtful. Or generous. She'd heard Adam was well off, but this excursion must have cost a small fortune. How could she ever repay him?

Unease slipped below the mantle of joy cloaking her, just for a moment. She knew exactly what he expected for payment. But surely he knew that all this trouble and expense wasn't necessary. Her acquiescence to Adam Thorne came as cheap as one touch, one look into his eyes.

Then the lights of the palace showed through the snow and her nerves evaporated. The fairy tale continued. They slowly approached the great palace, from which it seemed a thousand windows glowed. Jasmine floated toward the entrance, along with hundreds of others in their beautiful clothes, and finally she was inside.

Lord, how would she ever find him? There must have been a couple of thousand people milling around, all craning their necks, waiting with a muted air of expectancy.

She looked for the staircase and took stock. The men were all in black or white tails or dinner suits. Jasmine moved in the direction of the great marble staircase and then, wonder of wonders, there he was, head and shoulders above everyone else, even though he leaned against a wall. His dark good looks magnetized her eyes. Perfect—except there were still about a thousand bodies between them.

Luckily the Imperial Guards chose that moment to conduct their changing of the guard ceremony and the crowd mostly stilled so she was able to push her way through, looking up every so often to check on his location. Her apprehension grew as she neared. Would he like the gown on her? Was he still angry? But she couldn't believe he would go to all this trouble and expense if he did not intend her to enjoy it.

She paused about ten feet away to admire him. The elegant black dinner suit draped his tall, lean body, caressing his broad shoulders and slim hips. With his trendy haircut and trademark stubble, he hardly fit the mold of one of the imperial family, but he stood out like an emperor with his presence and vitality. A perfectly tied bow tie completed the package. She drank the sight in and tucked it away to last her the rest of her life.

As if on cue, he half turned. His head raised, as if scenting the air, and then his eyes found hers and sucked the breath from her lungs. He straightened but did not walk forward to meet her. A commanding

presence in a sea of people. The crowds and the
opulence, even the orchestra faded away and to
Jasmine, they were the only two people here. Holding his gaze, her confidence surging, she moved
toward her prince as if in a dream. They stared at each
other, his stern demeanor softening into admiration.
Finally Jasmine could breathe again.

She felt more beautiful than she had ever felt in
her life. In that one long look, he'd given her back
her pride, her self-confidence, her belief in herself as
a desirable woman. All the things she'd lost years
ago. He took both her gloved hands and just looked
at her as if seeing her for the first time.

A fanfare rang out and there was a hush while
everyone waited for the official welcome by the
actors playing Emperor Franz Josef and Empress
Sisi. The spell was broken. Adam inclined his head
and offered her his arm. They made their way up the
marble staircase to the state chambers, Jasmine's
eyes devouring every detail: myriad twinkling
lights, beautifully set tables, huge urns of carnations
everywhere. A silk-liveried waiter showed them to
their table and finally, she could sit, take off her
cape and say hello to the man who had made this
all possible.

He passed her a glass of champagne.

"I'm—speechless," she said, and then, because
she wanted to clear the air so they could enjoy themselves, she asked if he was still angry.

He shook his head, his eyes on her face. "It's your night, for now."

The implication was clear but Jasmine didn't mind. She was too happy to mind that she was here because she owed him. "Don't worry," she smiled. "I promise not to turn into a pumpkin at the stroke of midnight."

He gazed at her, his eyes rich with approval.

"Adam, all of this—" she raised her gloved hand, indicating the sumptuous surroundings "—it's too much. This—" her hand swept down the front of her, and his eyes followed "—and the hotel. It's like a dream. I can't believe I'm here."

He turned in his seat to face her, his hands clasped in front of him. "Tonight we're going to indulge our every whim."

A bubble of desire popped in her veins. Every muscle tightened and warmed. Adam noticed, she knew, because his eyes sharpened and again roamed slowly down her body. Her arms ached to wrap around him, to feel the burn of his beard on her face, the strength of his arms around her.

"Don't think about it," he said softly. "Just enjoy."

"It's perfect, Adam." She leaned close and touched her lips to his. "Thank you."

He gave a short laugh. "You won't thank me when I step on your toes."

They served themselves from the sumptuous buffet and watched the opening polonaise where beautiful girls in white gowns and boys in tails strutted and stepped expertly in formation. "It's a sort of debutantes' dance," she explained to Adam. "I was reading about this ritual before the major balls in Vienna that turned me on to ballroom, when my friends were all into pop or sports. Now it's my only social life."

"Poor lonely little dancer." He smiled. "Perhaps you should take up surfing or watching rugby."

"Typical Kiwi bloke. I don't dance to meet men. It just gets me out of the house."

"Perhaps you haven't danced with the right men," Adam said enigmatically.

As she wondered what he meant, the dance master called out the words that everyone was waiting for—
"Alles Waltzer!"

Adam stood and offered his hand. "Shall we?"

Jasmine's smile stretched wide. "I would be honored, sir."

In between courses, they danced to Strauss and Mozart in each of the seven ballrooms. A Viennese waltz was much faster than other waltzes, and once it was learned, every other waltz seemed pedestrian.

From the moment Adam took her into his arms, Jasmine realized that this would be a dance like no other. He wasn't quite the best dance partner she'd ever had, and anyway, the finer points of the waltz were somewhat lost in the crush of people. But dancing with him was like making love with him. He was all she could see and feel. His eyes never left her face, bathing her in such intensity that she moved on autopilot, which, thankfully, she was proficient enough to do. She forgot about her feet and concentrated on feeling the music on the inside and absorbing his presence on the outside. His hands under her palm and on the small of her back were warm and dry and as they moved together, so did his hands, causing starbursts of delicious friction on her skin that effervesced to every nerve ending.

She remembered how she felt after they'd made love for the first time. Sensitized, energized, pulsing in small bursts of sensation that she never wanted to end. She felt his breath on her face, his muscles bunched under her fingertips and the length of his legs when they brushed hers occasionally. Her body became his instrument, to lead and spin and twirl at will, an extension of his own.

Her anticipation grew as one dance flowed into another and another. Adam Thorne exuded sexuality and could turn her on even in the midst of thousands of people. And if that was his intention, he was exacting his payment early in the evening but strangely enough, it wasn't more than she wanted to give.

Seven

Adam could not take his eyes off her. The pleasure he took from her enjoyment of the evening was unsurpassed by anything he had known, which perplexed him because of his selfish reasons for doing it. He crushed it down in case the feeling became addictive, and then where would it all end?

Her enchantment was to be expected. What was unexpected was how enthralled he was watching her eyes sparkle—no sign of sadness now—her lovely mouth curve in yet another delighted smile as each new image or dance or bar of music registered and gave her joy.

His instincts about the color and style of the gown were spot-on. Her pale skin and dark hair and brows

lent the delicate shade of fabric a richness that anyone else would have overpowered. Dusky gray eyes
and her hair pulled back in a classic, elegant chignon
completed a picture that would stay with him for a
long time.

And yet what arrogance he'd displayed to choose
her clothes. What vanity to set the scene as he had.
But what pleasure to see her happiness, especially
knowing that this woman did not usually allow herself to get carried away.

What anticipation he had of the night to come…she
looked amazing in that dress, but he wanted her out
of it more with every minute that passed. His body had
been reminding him of that all night.

Just before midnight, the orchestras faded away
to the chimes of the giant bell of St. Stephen's as
it rang the old year away. Adam stood behind her
at the stroke of twelve and as the crowd erupted
into applause, his hands dropped onto her bare
shoulders and Jasmine turned and smiled at him.
Everyone was smiling, some were kissing and hugging and shaking hands, some had moved between
the tables and began to dance to the first strains of
The Blue Danube waltz, heralding the New Year in.

He and Jasmine stared at each other and he saw
his desire glow in her eyes, darkening them to a shade
deeper than her gown. He knew now why he'd
bought it. He stepped closer and bent his head, keeping his eyes open.

"Happy New Year, Jasmine."

She raised up to meet him, whispering something, her lips soft and fragrant and perfect. He tasted her upper lip with the tip of his tongue, tracing the outline of her mouth, and she leaned even closer, sighing, her mouth moving under his. His hand on the small of her back tightened, drawing her close, and they kissed until they were breathless.

When Adam drew back, he felt on a more even keel, even though his breath was ragged and he was as hard as rock. Normal service had been resumed. She wanted him. He wanted her. She would go where he led, just like on the dance floor.

They stayed to watch the New Year operetta and the Fledermaus Quadrille, a highlight for Jasmine. It was late and the ball would go on for hours yet, but Adam was suddenly tired of people. They left the Imperial Palace. The night was cold but clear and they decided to walk along the busy Ringstrasse back to the hotel.

Jasmine was hungry since she'd professed to be too excited to eat much of the buffet at the ball, so they stopped at a *Wurstelstand* for the Viennese equivalent of hot dogs. The streets were packed with party hounds. She almost skipped along, tipsy on champagne and excitement, humming at patchy intervals. Adam held her arm tightly, mindful of the earlier snow, the uneven paving stones and the spiky high heels she insisted on wearing.

The drinking establishments were mostly over-flowing but not far from the hotel, they were drawn by a beautiful voice. Jasmine headed down a cobbled alleyway and they stopped by a tiny bar where inside, a black woman crooned a Tina Turner ballad very credibly.

Jasmine pulled on his arm, facing him. "Let's go in,"

"With that smudge of mustard on your mouth?" He reached his thumb out, but thinking better of it, bent his head and licked the spot with the tip of his tongue.

In the freezing chill under a rusting old street lamp, Jasmine shifted restlessly, inhaled a ragged breath, and magic of a new kind entered her face.

Adam stilled, instantly, viciously aroused by the sudden flood of awareness darkening her eyes. All his senses clamored for more and he bent his head again, caging her face with both hands, sipping now at her lips. He tasted the piquant mustard she'd eaten, garlic and spices from the sausage, a crisp fruity hit of champagne. It all fed his hunger and he deepened the kiss.

Jasmine's eyes closed while her lips parted. She was still now, but he sensed her blood, her muscles, her very cells reaching for him, as palpable as if she'd raised her arms and pulled him close. He thrust his tongue into her mouth, holding her cheeks firmly, exulting at her response as the tip of her tongue played with his.

"Let's not." His eventual response to her question about going inside the club sounded hoarse and raw.

A desperate need swamped him and he couldn't wait another minute. He pressed against her, his thighs bumping hers as he turned and pushed her toward the hotel.

Another couple entered the Hotel Imperial's elevator with them and they exchanged New Year wishes. Adam's eyes bored into her as he discreetly tugged at the fingers of one of her gloves, easing it all the way off. Jasmine leaned against the wall, unable to look away and shivering with anticipation and nerves.

For a moment on the street, she'd wished they didn't have to go back to the hotel. Not because she didn't want him—she did, desperately. But that meant the fairy tale was over. They were now leading up to the real reason they were here. Payback. She had done a deal with the king of deals.

She knew she'd be compensated handsomely. She'd already enjoyed his prowess in the bedroom, her body's response to him. But for a few hours, she'd chosen to believe she was living this dream because he really felt something for her, rather than collecting on a contract she had failed to honor.

She hid a smile behind her hand when he wrapped the glove around his neck; the spoils of war. She was really in trouble here. She liked him, enjoyed him so much. The anticipation when he looked at her, held her face in his hands...payback never felt so good, even though she should be running for her life.

He opened the suite door and stood back while she entered, stiff-backed, her stomach tight with nerves. Adam cast an interested glance at the bags from her shopping expedition still strewn around. Flustered, she began scooping them up, but he caught her hand and the bags stayed where they were.

He lifted her hand by the finger of her glove and without breaking eye contact, he tugged until the silk slid smoothly down her forearm, making her tingle.

"Shall I call the butler to help you off with your gown?" he asked, his eyes glinting.

"I think we can manage." And then she smiled sweetly. "Did he help with your tie?"

Adam bared his white teeth and hooked a finger in her cape, tugging until she bumped against his front. "My lips are sealed, but I gave him a very good tip."

He cupped her face and bent his head to feather her lips with kisses, undoing the clasp of her cape as he did. He slid his hands inside the fur and skimmed up her back, stroking over her shoulder blades. Then he settled in for a deeper, soul-touching kiss she felt all the way to her toes.

Jasmine loved the way he kissed. A complex mix of tease and command. Of pleasing himself and invitation. His kiss invited her to be passive, free to enjoy and be taken. But it also incited her to hum blissfully in her throat, to allow her impatience to come to the fore, tearing off the cape and tossing it blindly at a sofa a few feet away. She would shudder about that tomorrow but right now, she just wanted one less obstruction between them.

Again he used his thighs to walk her backward toward the bedroom, still with his mouth locked on hers. His fingers ran down her bare arm and clasped hers and he danced her into the room, spinning her once, twice, three times, closer to the bed every time. The ball continued, only to a much more private composition than Herr Strauss ever devised.

When the backs of her legs bumped the edge of the bed, Adam drew back and switched one bedside lamp on. His face fell, he sighed, looking at her hair, and then he began to take down her hair, pin by pin.

A guilty laugh escaped her. "Sorry." Why hadn't she left it down? Thank heaven the dress had a zipper and not a hundred buttons!

He smiled distractedly, intent on his work. "Don't ever apologize for making an effort to please me."

Ditto, she wanted to say, but she reached for him instead, knowing she, too, had her work cut out. Black tie involved far too many clothes—and buttons. The tie was easy but there was still the waistcoat, braces and the stiff-fronted white shirt whose buttons were not cooperative with her fumbling fingers. His hands left her hair and landed on hers to assist in guiding the buttons through the damnably unyielding holes, while he somehow managed to shrug out of his jacket and take the waistcoat with it.

He finished with her hair. It spilled around his

hands and he ran his fingers through it, smoothing
it down over her neck and shoulders and cleavage.
Her skin burned wherever he touched. She sucked
in a breath and tried to ground herself, feeling her
knees dangerously close to buckling. Not only that,
but her tight breasts were dangerously close to
pushing out the bodice of the dress. It didn't help
when he bent his head and took her mouth again in
a deep, carnal kiss, igniting a storm inside. And when
he moved his mouth lower, nuzzling her earlobe,
down the slope of her shoulder and across the front
of her cleavage, she swayed a little, almost afraid to
breathe.

"Breathe," he commanded softly.

She sucked in a breath obediently and her head
cleared a little.

Adam straightened, his hands on his shoulders. "I
can honestly say," he murmured, sliding his hands
around to her back, "I have never wanted anything
as much as I want to see you out of this dress." He
found the fastening on the zipper that ran the length
of her back. Slowly, slowly, he pulled the fastener
down, his knuckles grazing her back, his body siz-
zling her front. She had time again to think about
touching him, in between congratulating herself for
the new lingerie. Good move, she thought, her hands
slipping inside his open shirt to skim across the
smooth, warm skin of his chest and abdomen. She
leaned forward and pressed her lips to his sternum,

running her hands over long, curved pectoral muscle, using the edges of her teeth on his nipple.

The gown swished down to her feet with a pretty rustle. Jasmine stepped daintily out of it, still in her heels, and it occurred to her she should never have walked across the parquet floor in heels. She eased them off now and started to bend to pick up the dress but Adam had hold of both her hands and kept her upright. She stilled as he stepped back, his eyes sweeping her body, ablaze with stark hunger. Down over the ivory front-clasp bra, to the matching panties and the thigh-high shimmering stockings that had—as the saleslady promised—actually stayed up with their silicone grippers, even after dancing the night away.

His head moved in a half shake, his tongue swept his bottom lip and there was a crease between his eyes that looked like a frown of concentration rather than displeasure. Jasmine raised her head, about to ask what was wrong. But when he lifted his eyes to hers, she felt again as she had at the Palace. Beautiful. Desirable. His.

He shucked off his shirt and undid the fastening of his dress trousers. Without the braces to hold them up, they fell to the floor in a pile and he added to the mess by kicking off his footwear. Jasmine bit back a smile at the snug-fitting gray hipsters, all out of shape and probably stretched way past the manufacturer's most stringent seam tests. The sight distracted her so that she didn't even worry about the expensive clothing scattered drunkenly around the antique carpet. When Adam crushed her to him, his hands molding her body against him, she forgot everything except the burn of his skin, his hard planes against her soft curves and the texture of his tongue as she eagerly drew it deep into her mouth.

His hands stroked over her, cupping the back of her neck, spreading the pleasure down the middle of her back, over the curve of her behind and down the back of her thigh. She shifted restlessly, needing more, needing everything. He raised his head, his eyes hooded and dark, leaving her mouth wet and feeling puffy. He cupped her breasts, weighing and squeezing until her world shrank to focus solely on the soft slope of her breast, the way each tiny bump around her nipple seemed to raise and pulse, begging for touch. Oh, sweet heaven, when his mouth finally closed over one taut bud, when he drew her into his mouth and sucked. The sensation was so primal, so deeply wrenching inside, her mind screamed "more!" It wasn't possible to be this close to release when he hadn't touched her intimately, when he hadn't even touched her breasts except through the silky bra she wore.

Suddenly, he bent her over the crook of his arm so she lay back against him, her legs stretched out, the backs of her heels on the floor. One arm was trapped by his side, the other clutched ineffectually at the muscles of his upper arm. But he held her so easily and his dark smile was all reassurance. "Relax," he ordered in response to her sharp intake of breath.

He pinged the front-clasp bra with one touch and it slid apart. *Now,* she thought, *please now, touch me...* His hand swept down her body in one stroke, taking her panties on the downward sweep, leaving her naked except for the stockings. Stroking unhurriedly, he kissed her mouth and throat, turning his head often to look down her body, laid out before him, trembling for him. Her breathing came in gasps. He held her helpless in one arm like the dip of a tango. She ordered her limbs to relax but her whole insides clenched like a vise, even more so when he began to lavish his mouth on her breasts. And all the while, his hands worked magic from her knees up to her inside upper thighs, firm, sweat-inducing strokes that reminded her he knew exactly how to play a woman.

Her eyes were open, staring at the impressive arched ceiling, wondering if this was the famous former chapel. A smile surprised her; the imperial family that may have worshipped here would not be amused at the way Adam was worshipping her. Perhaps they'd answer her prayer for release, for his touch *there* where she needed it as he circled and stroked and drove her mad. Helpless to touch him back, her head lolled over his arm, his bunched muscles her pillow. Helpless to do anything but try to absorb the millions of sensations he evoked.

A strangled pant erupted from her throat when finally he cupped her, his palm pressing firmly on her pubic bone, his fingertips teasing. The more he pressed down, the more tension built inside. She squirmed uneasily, almost afraid of the storm of sensation, the lurking torment that awaited her. Scrabbling back the fragments of her mind, she remembered her precarious position, her heels having little purchase on the floor and her mind in splinters on the ceiling. His fingers glided over her most intimate flesh, unerring, unhurried, firm yet tender, expertly applying pressure where she needed it most. And someone heard her prayer.

Her legs clenched, her throat constricted. Her breath stopped altogether. As she hovered at the edge of release, his clever fingers and his clever mouth intensified and tipped her over. The climax crashed into her, squeezing her eyes shut, emblazoning every cell in her body with streaks of ecstasy, holding her taut and shaking for brilliant eternity.

He continued to ply her with such exquisite touch until the blood cleared from her brain and she gradually became conscious of the coolness of her wet nipples, the aftershocks still rippling through her and her deadweight on his arm.

She opened her eyes and Adam was watching her, his eyes filled with dark purpose. He lifted her, his arm tensing so that her grasping hand nearly slid off. He straightened, bringing her upright. Boneless, liquid, she could only hope her legs would hold her up.

* * *

That her legs held her up surprised him. Then again, she had seriously beautiful legs, long, strongly muscled, smooth as satin. And those stockings were the sexiest thing he'd seen. Her sigh resonated with satisfaction and he couldn't help but mentally beat his chest with pride. He'd done that, put that smile there, stolen her breath and her mind for moments that stretched into the stratosphere.

He wanted more of her satisfaction, he wanted those legs around him. He needed to be inside her, all over her, to see and feel her response again and again. Her dancer stamina would be put to good use tonight.

He hurriedly shucked off his underwear and reached down to grab a fistful of condoms where he'd stashed them earlier in the bedside table. Her eyes lit up when he tossed them on the bed. She reached up and looped her arms around his neck, pressing her body along the whole length of his. She smelled amazing, her elegant but subtle fragrance mingled with sex, the sharp drugging scent of her own climax on his fingers.

Without preamble he tipped her onto the bed and rolled to his side next to her. He raised up on an elbow and fed his eyes, his senses with her. She was sensational, a vision of pale marbled skin, well-proportioned, glorious breasts, her tiny waist and flared hips giving her a feminine delicacy for all that strength. Her flawless skin glowed and was so smooth, he couldn't keep his eyes, hands, lips off her. How his blockhead brother failed to properly appreciate the sexy beauty right outside his office for five years was beyond Adam. He'd known from the moment he saw her that under the crisp business suits and severely tied-back hair, there was great beauty, a lush-for-loving body, and a response to him that drove him wild.

She smiled, a slow curve of her lips, her eyes bright with anticipation and a playfulness he hadn't associated with her before. She'd told him he was only her third lover and he'd believed it because she'd been shy and unsure, unused to showing her body or touching a man.

While he was still thinking about that, he suddenly found himself flat on his back. She rose up, a sexy phoenix, her long dark hair falling over her shoulders, her perfect breasts jutting out above him, begging for his touch, and those damn naughty stockings with their thick band of lace at the top now straddling his waist.

"You want to play, beautiful?" he murmured, sliding his hands up over her hips and settling on her waist.

"A little." She took his hands off her and arranged them by his sides.

Whatever the lady wants, he thought, narrowing his eyes. She began to run her efficient, questing hands over him and within an embarrassingly short time, he was squirming impatiently, feeling his excitement build fast, too fast. He began to count as a distraction. One elegant fingertip circling his nipples, ten nails scraping over his stomach. One lush pair of lips sipping at his mouth, the tip of her tongue delving and teasing, while he shifted, bringing his straining erection into contact with her shapely backside. He put his hands on her hips, pressing her back.

Her mouth moved all over his body, starting fires everywhere. He let his head loll back, not too far. He was enjoying the show too much not to watch, but the strain of holding back was immense. Her hair tickled his chest as she dragged her head down, bending from the waist, going lower while he went higher. His hand scrabbled around on the bed for a condom, finding one and tearing it open with his teeth.

Jasmine raised her head, distracted by the noise.

"Put it on," he said hoarsely, holding it out to her. He couldn't wait a moment more. They could take it slow next time....

She straightened and took the pack from him, slowly extracted the contents and held it up daintily between index finger and thumb. Adam closed his eyes. She was killing him in tiny, torturous increments.

She rose up on her knees and wriggled down a little so his jutting erection was between them, then tossing the condom onto his stomach, she began to fondle, light, teasing caresses interspersed with slow, firm, two-handed strokes. His mind blanked. The air punched out from his lungs and he began to sweat.

Sweet torture, he couldn't take much more, but on she went until he thought he'd explode in her hands.

He grabbed the condom and held it up to her. "Put it on," he growled. Then he grasped her thighs, prising them apart, and exacted his own punishment, dipping his fingers inside her heat, feeling her clench around him, her thigh muscles tight and hard. Good. That got her attention. Adam liked to play as much as anyone but he was wound too tight, had wanted her for so long. They had all night to indulge her playful side.

He ground his teeth as she smoothed the condom over his flesh with such painstaking care. Finally she scooted forward and raised up over him. He thought he'd expire as she eased him into her hot body to the hilt. She stilled, settled, stretched while he filled his hands with her breasts. There was something just so damn right about this, the way she looked, felt, responded to him.

She began to move her lower body in a torturously slow circular motion, her waist twisting, her breasts firm, her body gloving him tightly.

It was bliss but the need to thrust, to take, to plunge overwhelmed him. He reared up and flipped her onto her back, swallowing her squeak of surprise with his lips. He thrust his tongue into her mouth at the same time he thrust into her body. She arched up as he filled her, panting his name, matching him stroke for stroke, lifting those lovely legs to wrap around his waist. All playfulness melted from her eyes and they filled with a steely resolve as intense as his. Release became the only goal for both of them. He tried to hold on for a few moments more, wasn't confident as his own release clawed at him, gripped him hard.

He grabbed a nearby pillow and pulled her up, shoving it under her hips. The different angle was electric, deep, amazing. Her eyes shot open; she gasped and tightened her legs around him. He thrust again, taking them to another level, higher and hotter and more consuming than anything he'd ever experienced. He felt her walls, gloving him so snugly, begin to ripple. He tore his mouth from hers and watched her shatter, sob her pleasure and relief, and followed her into endless pleasure.

Eight

Adam sat on a chair a few feet away from the bed, watching Jasmine sleep. It was after ten. He'd pulled the drapes to find the quiet streets looked clean with crusted snow at the edges, and sun shone down from a blue sky.

He'd been woken by a text from John, his friend and business partner in London. There had been a phone call for Adam from a man claiming to be an advisor of Stewart Cooper's. When told Adam was away for a couple of days, the man said he'd call back.

Adam looked over at Jasmine's sleeping face. Over the past couple of months, he'd left several messages and e-mails, but hadn't been able to breach the eccentric recluse's inner circle. He didn't want to wake her; they hadn't gotten to sleep until well after four. But it was driving him crazy, wondering if she had anything to do with the billionaire's sudden change of heart.

Not that he could tire of looking at that face. Adam doubted he'd ever forget the way she looked last night in the lovely gown, or out of it, for that matter. Now her warm, walnut-colored hair spilled over her face and the pillow, the ends twirling like gift-wrap ribbon.

He tilted his head, listing the many faces of Jasmine Cooper. So far in their brief acquaintance, he'd seen her mussed from a motorcycle ride, all conservative glamour for the ballet, crisp and tailored at work, elegant and regal last night, and hot, naked and very discomposed a few hours ago.

Jasmine Cooper with her different faces, her secrets and her very sexy body, was one interesting lady. Who would have thought that Nick's bookish personal assistant would burrow her way under his skin so completely? Too completely, perhaps. Adam could not afford the distraction of secrets, different faces and sexy bodies right now, sexy bodies excepted. For the next few months, it was nose to the grindstone all the way.

Thankfully she'd be returning to New Zealand soon. What with the fake engagement, her uncle and her working for Nick, it seemed he was becoming inextricably entwined in her life.

Which should worry him more than it did….

His cell phone beeped and he swore softly and flipped it open. It was John wanting an ETA tomorrow.

"Business on New Year's Day?" Jasmine asked sleepily.

Adam's head snapped up. She'd lifted her head up off the pillow and looked fresh and pink-cheeked. He finished his text and closed the phone. Picking up the cooling cup of coffee he'd poured from the breakfast tray the butler had delivered, he walked over to the bed and offered her the cup. "Did you contact your uncle about me?" He sat on the edge of the bed and restrained himself from brushing a wisp of hair from her face.

Jasmine blinked rapidly. "Umm." She slurped at the coffee, made a face and handed it back, then struggled into a sitting position, dragging the sheet up over her. "Why?"

Adam watched her, amused at the secretive face she wore. "Apparently he phoned, wanting to talk to me."

She nodded, her eyes wary. "That's good, isn't it?"

"That's very good." He caught her chin in his fingers. "You did that for me?"

She nodded and looked away. "I owed you."

He stilled, hearing his words, his demand on her lips, devaluing the night they'd just shared. "And yet you still came."

The tip of her tongue appeared and she moistened her lips. "I—didn't intend to. I didn't bring anything except what I was wearing and a handbag."

Hence the shopping spree, the bags he'd noticed spread all over the suite.

"You were going to stand me up?" His brows lifted. "Mind telling me why?"

She raised her eyes to his for a long moment and then shook her head.

Adam breathed out, strangely relieved. Something in her troubled eyes told him he didn't want to know why. Not now, when he had to keep this casual. "What changed your mind?"

She looked down at her hands, breathing out carefully. "I asked the flight attendant where we were going." The milk-and-roses complexion leaned heavily in favor of the roses. "It was New Year's Eve…"

Adam nearly smiled. "So you arrived at the airstrip—"

"I expected you to be there," she interjected.

"—at the airstrip," he continued, "intending to tell me where I could stick my weekend away because you'd done what I asked."

Her pink and guilty countenance confirmed it.

"But when you discovered it was Vienna…"

She gazed around at the opulent suite, chewing on her bottom lip. "I hoped…I remembered telling you in New Zealand that I'd always wanted to go to the Kaiserball."

"And you couldn't resist?"

She shook her head.

Adam stared at her, unsmiling, for a few moments longer, enjoying her guilty discomfort. Then he began to chuckle. "And here was me thinking it was my irresistible sex appeal and scintillating charm."

Jasmine's shoulders dropped, her eyes meeting his at last. Her lips twitched. "I'm not sure about the charm, but maybe the sex appeal…."

They smiled at each other. Then he reached out and caught her chin again. "Thank you." He knew how worried she was about her father's declining health. Risking his displeasure wasn't something someone like Jasmine would take lightly. "Going to see your uncle can't have been easy."

Her smile faded a little. "It wasn't so bad. I liked him."

"I appreciate it." He brushed her mouth with his. "Get dressed. It's your day for sightseeing. Anything you like."

Several hours later, they left the world-famous Kunsthistoriches Museum.

"Another lifelong ambition achieved." Jasmine sighed happily. "This is the best New Year ever!"

She hadn't stopped prattling for hours, showing off her knowledge of Austrian Baroque art and sculptures and the many other treasures in this massive museum. Poor Adam. She gave him a sidelong glance. He would probably much prefer a bar or the

Lipizzaner horses. Or, her heart skipped a beat, being holed up at the hotel with her.

"I'm sorry if I bored you." She took her gloves from her pocket and began to put them on. "I guess museums aren't your thing."

No, from what she knew and had heard of Adam, culture, history and tradition would not be his first choice of entertainment. But he'd borne their woefully quick trip to this great museum with good humor.

"Not at all," he said loftily. "Seeing it through your eyes has been a revelation. Your knowledge amazes me."

Jasmine preened a little. She really must do something to add to her degree, a postgrad art course or something.

"Like I said over Christmas," Adam said, turning his collar up against the crisp late-afternoon air. "You have all this passion for history and yet you work for a financial company, typing letters and picking up my brother's dry cleaning."

She slipped her arm through his as they walked out onto Maria-Theresien-Platz, trying not to be miffed by his summation of her job. She did more than type letters and run errands. Nick and his father traveled a lot, there were always flights and hotels to book, conferences to register for, soirées and functions to organize...and she realized that it may have been challenging for the first year but she could manage all of that now standing on her head.

"I enjoy my job," she insisted. "I like being organized. Nick pays well and the staff are nice."

The staff kept to themselves and that was the most important thing. As personal assistant to the boss, she was treated with respect and held at arm's length and that suited her fine. No embarrassing family secrets slipping out over social occasions.

Adam squeezed her arm. "I'm not knocking the job, I'm just interested in your reasons."

Her reasons were completely justifiable and she didn't feel the need to explain. She'd endured scandal and pity and finger-pointing all her life. She wanted privacy. It wasn't hard to understand.

"I think maybe you're running away," he continued after giving her plenty of time to answer him. "Burying yourself in an unsatisfactory career to escape a bit of bad publicity."

"What's the alternative?" she demanded, trying not to sound testy. "Stay in England and be subjected to a media frenzy every time I step outdoors?"

He squeezed her arm. "You're exaggerating."

She booted at the snow crunching underfoot. Then she sighed noisily. "You're right, of course."

What happened last time seemed a million miles away, and it was stupid to let the past intrude on their winter wonderland now. Jasmine put it out of her mind. She pulled him over to admire the statue of Maria Theresa, the Holy Roman Empress of the Habsburg dynasty, and mother of Marie Antoinette.

"Did you know," Jasmine said, her enthusiasm for history drowning out any residual pique, "she had sixteen children?"

Adam grunted, craning his neck to look up the tall edifice.

"Rumor has it," she lowered her voice conspiratorially, "she asked her physician to stop her falling pregnant and he told her to take an apple. 'Before or after?' she asked, and he said, 'instead of.'"

Adam chuckled and patted the stone pillars that surrounded the statue. "*She's* not running away from a bit of gossip, is she?"

Jasmine laughed. Their eyes met, held and heated while insane thoughts of reproduction and birth control and Adam, naked and holding an apple, careened through her mind. Freud would have approved of the analogy: Adam, apple, sin...

Something in her face must have offered an inkling of her thoughts because his eyes darkened to a luscious molten caramel and filled with awareness. Her smile faded as an all-consuming deluge of desire buffeted her, turning her bones to water. They stood in the middle of the plaza, staring at each other as people walked around them, uncomprehending of the desire that pulsed between them.

She turned her head, looking in the direction of the hotel. They were only three or four blocks away. The back of her neck dampened with the need to get her hands on him.

Adam tightened his grip on her arm. "Hotel," he muttered. "Now."

They ran the relatively short journey without another word. The moment the elevator doors closed, Adam pulled her into his arms and kissed her hungrily. Even last night, she'd never known such burning need.

"Hurry, hurry," she whispered against his mouth as they watched the floors slowly pass. Finally they spilled out into the passageway and rushed to their room, only to find their way blocked by the service trolley. They hadn't left the suite until after midday, so the housemaid was still in attendance.

They looked at each other, panting as if they'd just run a marathon, while the woman, wide-eyed, waited for instruction. The polite thing to do would be to go downstairs, have a drink on the turn-of-the-century sofas in the secluded bar and let the woman finish her task. Jasmine couldn't wait and by the look of impatient anguish in Adam's eyes, neither could he. She flicked a glance through the suite to the bedroom— the bed had been made, at least.

He produced a handful of euros and thrust them into the woman's hand. She nodded and pushed her heavy trolley into the passage, turning to shove a bundle of towels into Adam's hands as he shut the door.

Alone at last, and Jasmine's mirth erupted in a snort. "Poor woman. She was speechless."

"I gave her a good tip," he muttered, backing her

against the wall, seemingly more interested in getting her out of her abundant clothes. He yanked at her scarf until it slid off and was halfway through the buttons on her overcoat by the time she stopped laughing.

They tore into each other, even while she wondered why this urgency, this overpowering need? After the hours spent making love every which way last night, her desperation now stunned her.

She shivered as he roughly stripped her of each outer garment, leaving her in panties and her ankle boots. With every success, as he threw the offending article aside, he captured her mouth in a hungry, lustful kiss that shook her to her marrow. A whirlwind of activity, he tugged at her braided hair, using both hands to free it.

"Bed," he ordered, turning her with his hands on her shoulders and propelling her ahead of him, stripping off his own coat as he went. He didn't stop when they got to the bed and tumbled her down in front of him. Jasmine scrambled onto her hands and knees and began to move up toward the head, but suddenly his fingers closed around her ankle. She twisted her head around and her heart went into overdrive when she saw the fierce need on his face, his lips parted, breathing heavily. A touch of apprehension fluttered through her. This was dark and edgy, not the polished seduction she'd come to expect. She fleetingly thought of how she must look from where he stood, her backside waving in the air, her silly

ankle boots with the high heels probably in danger
of ruining the antique bedspread.

Adam's fingers tightened around her ankle while
with his other hand, he unzipped his trousers. And
then he began to pull her slowly back toward him.

The sight of her nearly naked on her hands and
knees and still in those boots nearly undid him. Her
hair spilled over her shoulders in a riot of waves,
kinked up by the braid she'd worn. When she twisted
her head around to look at him, her eyes were huge
with desire and apprehension. He sucked in air and
called on all his powers of control to calm his breathing, needing to slow this down, reassure her. But
dear God, he was riding a savage hunger.

Holding her gaze—and her foot—he drew his
zipper down then used the same hand to extract his
wallet and take out a condom. He let go of her foot
for a moment to slip on protection but kept his eyes
on her face. Then he pulled, dragging her inch by
inch back to the edge of the bed to where he waited,
still in his shirt with his trousers around his ankles.

Her back arched, her hands flat on the bed. He let
go of her foot, leaned right over her back and slid his
cold hands under her body. She gasped and tensed,
sucking her stomach in and thrusting her breasts right
into his hands.

Adam's body settled on hers, his legs taking most
of his weight. Calling on all his shredded control, he
buried his face in the fragrance of her hair and nuz-

zled and nipped her neck. She shuddered under him as he caressed her, her bottom pushing up against him, driving him to distraction. Somehow he slowed things down to a simmer, stroking and kneading her breasts until she was like a sea beneath him, a writhing, moaning sea. He moved one hand down her body and stroked her leg, from calf to buttock and back, paying particular attention to the back of her knee, an exceptionally sensitive area for her, he'd learned last night.

She moaned his name, and his control shattered. Nothing else mattered, his goals, his business, only this, taking her, making her his, surrendering to mindless passion and taking her with him. He nudged her legs apart and stroked her intimately, swearing when he felt her scalding heat.

She heard the muttered oath torn from his throat, felt his fingers on her, in her, and lost it. From the very deepest part of her, something broke, something that walled in her reason, her dignity, and she cried out and it was guttural and hoarse and long. Her body arched up like a bow, gripped in such an intense rush of sensation, she couldn't contain it. Oh, and he knew just how to prolong it, how to nurture the ecstasy, wring out every drop for what might have been a minute or ten. When she finally floated back to something resembling consciousness, she trembled inside and out with sweet release.

He slid his hands up her arms and linked his fingers with hers and made love to her from behind. She purred and pressed back into him, depleted but eager to please. The slide of him in the unfamiliar angle, the thud-thud of his heart beating on her back, the speed with which her own excitement ignited again and surged to equal his all collided in an apex of wonder when he suddenly withdrew and turned her.

"I want to see," he groaned, plunging his hands into her hair, holding her face still. Jasmine welcomed him in again, looking up into his eyes, and then felt her heart stutter, slide, leave her adrift for a few seconds. Something nagged at her, something was wrong inside, and yet he felt so right. She pushed the niggling feeling away, rising to meet every thrust, feeling her climax rushing upon her, wanting it so desperately. But his eyes stared down and it seemed to her she could see too far in, see his soul or hers or both, and they were melding together, becoming one. With dizzying certainty, Jasmine knew she had fallen in love.

The jagged edges of her pre-orgasmic mind filled her with hope but also foreboding. But her body surrendered to a flood of aching pleasure, wiping her mind blissfully clear of anything else.

Above her, Adam became one large, rigid muscle, burying himself one last time with something between a howl and a bellow. He collapsed, breaking eye contact at last, and after a minute, she gingerly removed her fingernails from his bicep.

He wrapped her up and held her close and they waited for their breathing to return to normal. But try as she might, Jasmine could not stop the errant notion of love from invading her thoughts. To distract herself, she made a list: where they would go for dinner; whether they'd have time to visit the Liechtenstein Museum before the flight tomorrow…but it was no good.

What was wrong with her that she couldn't separate sex and emotion? The whole male population managed that standing on their heads. Anyway, it wasn't love. It was lust. People thought and said things of no consequences in the throes of passion.

She couldn't be falling in love with Adam Thorne. She just couldn't.

He shifted a little, turning his face toward her. She concentrated on the row of half-moons indented into the smooth flesh of his bicep and ran her fingertip over them. "Sorry," she whispered. "I scratched."

Adam grinned. "Always happy to sustain a wound in the pursuit of a good time."

She didn't smile. She was thinking how relaxed he seemed, how she liked that. How she must not go there.

Adam's finger tipped her chin up. "What's up?"

"Nothing." She pretended to concentrate on his arm, licking her fingertip and rubbing it over the tiny marks. "Everything's perfect."

He exhaled noisily, a sound of satisfaction, contentment. He began playing with her hair, twisting a long strand around his finger. She sensed he was leading up to something.

"Have you and Nick ever...?"

Her head jerked up and she stared at him in astonishment. "Why would you ask that?"

Adam kept his eyes on his fingers combing through her hair. "You have to admit, you two seem tailor-made for each other."

Jasmine's indignation spilled over. "Perhaps his fiancée would disagree."

If he noticed her cool tone, he didn't defer to it. "Jordan's sensational, but on the surface, she doesn't seem his type."

That hurt. "She's more *your* type, you mean." Which was a pretty clear indication that she, Jasmine, wasn't Adam's type. Jordan was beautiful, stylish, loved clubbing and didn't seem to mind her every move being courted by the press.

Adam's smile only made her heart sink lower. "Perhaps, if one can have a 'type.' You didn't answer my question."

Jasmine exhaled, knowing her indignation was justified, but a fragment of guilt rose to the surface. She thought hard before answering. What good would it do to tell him that indeed she had believed herself in love with Nick for about three years? She had prayed that one day, he would look up and see her as more than his personal assistant. But she'd never have acted on it unsolicited.

That state of affairs changed the second Adam Thorne walked into the offices of Thorne Financial Enterprises about two months ago. The heartbeat gone mad, sweaty palms and neck and complete incapability of stringing a sentence together, convinced her that what she'd been feeling for Nick was friendship, affection, gratitude for being a great boss. She'd only felt that way about him because he was very much her "type"—conservative, solid, a constant presence in that she saw him every day. And there was no question she was lonely. There were few people she counted as friends in Wellington and none as lovers.

No point divulging that former affection now, when he was happily engaged and she was sleeping with his brother.

"I think a lot of Nick," she said rather stiffly, "and I hope he counts me as a friend, but neither of us would take our professional relationship lightly."

"He needs his head read, having you there every day and not acting on it."

Her heart skipped a beat while she wondered if he'd seen right through her. He continued. "But I'm glad, because I wouldn't like it."

"Can't stand the comparison?" she asked a little snidely.

"Oh, I think—" his voice warmed "—I know who'd win that one." His finger unraveled the long strand of hair and then landed in the dip between her breasts. Despite the instant, piercing arousal as he ran

his finger slowly down between her breasts, it ran-
kled to be considered a pawn in the competition that
was the largest component in the relationship between the two brothers. The anger was good because
there was no way she could be in love with such
arrogance.

"He has set the bar quite high with Jordan, hasn't
he?" she asked sweetly, then immediately lost track
when his fingertip circled her nipple. Her very hard
nipple.

Adam licked his lips, eyeing up her breast hungrily. "I don't mind losing out to him in the marriage
stakes," he murmured. "At least for the next ten years
or so."

His dark head bent lower. Jasmine closed her eyes,
accepting it. He'd given her no reason to expect more
than a temporary fling.

His tongue swiped across one nipple and despite
the leaden weight she felt on her heart, she shivered
with delight.

"I'll tell you what's perfect," Adam said, matter-
of-factly, cupping her breasts. "*These* are perfect.
Feel free to scratch."

Later that night, Jasmine persuaded Adam to take
a cab out to Grinzing, the wine suburb of Vienna. "I
want to go to an *Heuriger,* a sort of wine tavern with
a cellar. They sell their new harvest."

"So long as there is food."

They walked into a rustic tavern with a green branch tacked to the door, sniffing appreciatively as they entered. The room was rich with the aromas of roast pork, pasta and paprika-flavored goulashe-soup. The menu was buffet, the tables unadorned wooden benches—a far cry from the sumptuously furnished Hotel Imperial, but she liked the disparity—and an old man played *The Blue Danube* on an accordion in the darkest corner.

They ate a leisurely meal, followed by the ubiquitous *apfelstrudel*. Jasmine was determined no rogue feelings would spoil their last night together. They were still on fairy-tale time.

"The flight's at midday tomorrow. Is that all right?"

No. She nodded.

"I need to go in to the new office, but why don't you stay with me tomorrow night?"

Her heart leaped. Don't get excited. He just wants more of that crazy sex….

Adam had spent the afternoon teasing her. Miss Prim and Proper Cooper, kneeling on a bed that belonged in a museum, wearing nothing but high-heeled boots. He told her it was the sexiest thing he'd ever seen.

"Okay," she replied, hoping he couldn't see her blush in the dim room. "If my father is all right."

They talked of how long she was staying in England and when his next trip home might be.

"Will you come home for Nick's wedding?"

He nodded. "Of course. April, isn't it?"

He sat back in his seat, his healthy tan showcased by his open shirt collar, the sort of man who turned heads wherever he went. Jasmine felt blessed that for a couple of short days, he'd only had eyes for her. "You'll be best man, I suppose."

He grinned. "I always am."

Jasmine shook her head with a wry smile. "You're very competitive, you and Nick, aren't you?"

"Dad always set us against each other. Everything was a competition. He'd actually pay us to win—the most tries at rugby, the best grades." He grinned. "The most broken bones, girls… Not that we needed much encouragement. That's what boys do when left to their own devices."

She raised an interested brow. "Left to your own devices?"

He shrugged. "My parents were hardly ever there. We had live-in nannies or caregivers. Dad traveled a lot, setting up the bank in the major centers. Mum was doing the same, building her chain of dancing clubs. We saw nothing of them through the week and even on weekends, after rugby or whatever, we'd be dragged around their respective empires to amuse ourselves while they worked."

Jasmine had no idea his home life was like that. She knew Randall, his father, quite well and liked him, for all that he roared like a bear when anything went wrong.

Adam must have seen the concern in her face. "Don't get me wrong, we had a good life. We wanted for nothing and we pretty much knew our parents loved us. We just didn't share things as a family."

Jasmine knew all about that. Being an only child—especially a female—meant her father tended to overlook her existence, although once Gill came along, she had no complaints.

Adam looked around the tavern and pointed out two tables with children in attendance. "Parenting has changed a lot since then. I'm sure our generation—or the next—will do much better."

And he'll probably never know, she thought sadly, gazing at him. Not if he didn't intend on marrying for the next decade.

Adam scratched his head, looking perplexed. "I wonder if Nick decided to settle down and have a family because of the adoption thing."

It was only a month ago that Nick had discovered he had been "adopted" by his parents when they believed they could not have children of their own. Adam had later come along to disprove the diagnosis.

"Are you so against marriage you can't believe that other people actually want to do it?" Jasmine countered. "To share their lives with one special person and want to have children with that person?"

When he shot an interested, considering look at her, she really wished she hadn't started this.

"I'm not against marriage and kids at all," he said

slowly. "But I'm going to make a hell of a lot better job of it than my folks. I won't even consider it until I'm financially secure enough not to have to work all the time. *My* family will come first."

Jasmine moistened suddenly dry lips. Since this was probably the end of the line for them anyway, she may as well ask. "And ten years is the benchmark?"

"I'm going global. Even if that only means say, five more countries after England, it's still a year or two scoping each one out, setting up, tracking growth. There is no way I'd consider marriage while all that's going on."

Jasmine had her answer and told herself it was no more than she'd expected.

Nine

Jasmine stared out at the dull shade of gray as they landed, remembering the gorgeous sunny day they had woken to in Vienna a few hours earlier. She tried to be happy, knowing this magical weekend was etched on her heart forever.

Adam had sent for a car and as the driver loaded the bags and they settled in the back, his cell phone rang. "Holiday over." He sighed. "Welcome home."

His expression lightened considerably a minute later when his business partner told him Stewart Cooper wanted to see him at his house at four o'clock.

"He wouldn't want to see you unless his advisors

had checked you out and he was interested," Jasmine enthused.

Adam leaned forward and conversed with the driver. "I'll drop you at my house." He handed her a key. "I have a good feeling about this, and I want you there to celebrate."

The car dropped her at his town house. "I'll keep my fingers firmly crossed for you," she told him as they kissed goodbye.

She let herself in and set her bag on the floor. Now she was alone, she indulged a girlish sort of high, waltzing around his lounge, reliving the wonderful memories of Vienna. The hotel. The ball. The music.

Adam.

She hoped his meeting went well and suspected he didn't need her prayers. He would succeed in his endeavors, she had no doubt. He was so determined with all his goals mapped out and she knew he would reach every single one, even if just to rub his brother's nose in it.

The music in her mind faded away and her steps slowed. He still had all his boxes to tick and no time for love. Could she handle this as a temporary relationship, feeling the way she did about him?

She wandered around the living room of his stylish three-bedroom town house in West Greenwich. She hadn't expected the city playboy to have a garden and backyard. Then again, he was a Kiwi and if he was anything like the New Zealanders she

knew, he'd have spent most of his childhood outdoors. Most Kiwi men were sports mad. Sure
enough, when she peered down the length of his
neatly cut lawn, she spied a set of cricket wickets
jammed in the ground.

A city playboy. Hadn't she been here before with
Vincent? Light years apart in character but the lesson had been drummed into her. One woman was
not enough.

She checked out his fridge. Adam obviously wasn't
a cook; it was a desert in there, although there was an
open bottle of New Zealand chardonnay. Why not?
She found a glass and poured, her organized mind listing the pros and cons of sleeping with Adam Thorne.

Sex. Wow. Double wow.

His generosity, vis-à-vis Vienna. The fun they had,
a commodity sorely lacking in her life. He knew
pretty much all of the bad stuff now, the sticky stuff
that she never talked about to anyone. He was a great
listener. Quick to make her feel special and admired.
Pretty good dancer—and sexy with it. He would be
returning to his home country in the not too distant
future. And she liked his family.

She only had so many fingers, so turned her mind
to the cons, but was interrupted by her phone.

It was Gill and she sounded stressed. "No, no,
he's fine," she answered Jasmine's worried inquiry
after Nigel. "Well, not fine. Agitated. He wants to
speak with you."

Jasmine heaved a sigh of relief.

"I'm sorry, love, I've put my foot in it," Gill continued in a low voice.

Apparently Stewart had called the estate, looking for her. In one of those quirks of fate, because he hardly ever answered the phone, Sir Nigel had today and learned that she'd gone to see her uncle. To him, it was a betrayal. To calm him down, Gill told him the purpose of Jane's visit wasn't to reunite the family or to go behind his back. It was about Adam's business. "Now he's worried that if you marry Adam, and Stewart goes into business with him, he will somehow manipulate Adam into handing over the estate to him one day."

Jasmine pressed her fingers to her temple. Her plan to please her father before he passed away had backfired. Why had she lied? She sat down on the sofa and waited tensely for Gill to put her father on the phone.

A couple of hours later, she sat in the same chair. The house was in darkness and it was cool enough to make her shiver. She got stiffly to her feet, wrestling with remorse, longing, regrets.

"I'm dying," her father had reminded her needlessly, several times. "It won't be long now, less than a year."

That "bastard"—his brother, Stewart—had taken his wife. He'd ruined all their lives. He'd get his hands on the estate via Adam and once he did, she and Gill would be tossed out like yesterday's rubbish. "Beware his tentacles," her father warned, when

Jasmine murmured she was sure her uncle wouldn't do that. "He wraps them around lovingly then he squeezes and never lets go. Look at your mother."

Jasmine promised her father she wouldn't contact her uncle again. At least, she thought, until after he'd passed away.

He then started on Adam's womanizing ways, alluding to what he called "frequent" snippets in the papers about his conquests. He'd obviously been talking to Ian. "He'll humiliate you just like Vincent did."

Yes, she thought. He would. He was dangerous because of her escalating feelings for him. She'd already told him more about her life than she'd ever told anyone. She'd also given him more of her body than anyone else and had a feeling she was about to wrap up her heart and hand it to him in a beribboned box.

Her father had finished by declaring that cancer or not, he would burn the estate to the ground before he'd let his brother get his hands on it.

Jasmine's misery and guilt went bone-deep. She should have told her father the truth about the sham engagement. She'd so wanted him to be proud of her for once. But something stopped her, some stupid naïve little part of her held on to the hope that Adam would realize he loved her, too.

Two hours sitting in the dark, mulling it all over had clarified things. Who was she kidding? Her father was right, she would get hurt. Adam Thorne was not permanent. She wasn't the one to turn his head, make him reevaluate his life. He loved his life as it was, the challenge of business, the fun, the competition. He would smash her heart into little pieces, and after the battering it had taken in her life, she didn't think she could take any more.

Jasmine drained her glass and went to the writing desk in the corner of his living room. She switched the lamp on and found some writing paper. She would leave a note; it wasn't as if he'd care. And then she'd go home and somehow find the courage to tell her father the truth about the fake engagement.

Adam tucked the bottle and his briefcase under his arm and put his key in the lock just as the door opened from the inside. Jasmine stood on the other side, her overcoat buttoned, a mustard-colored scarf coiled around her neck, one glove on. Her eyes were wide and surprised.

"Sorry I'm late, it went on longer than I expected, but—" he raised the bottle "—I'm hoping that champagne will get me off the hook."

She lagged behind, saying nothing as he moved into the kitchen. Maybe she was just going out to get something to eat. Adam was tired but exhilarated and he couldn't think of anyone he would rather celebrate with. "It's freezing in here. Aren't you going to ask me how it went?"

"How did it go?" she asked dutifully from halfway across the room.

"It's a deal!" he declared, setting the bottle down on the bench.

Jasmine did smile, eventually, but it didn't exactly light up the sky. "He's with you then? That's wonderful, Adam."

He frowned. *"That's wonderful, Adam?"* She wasn't exactly jumping for joy. "I think we can do better than that, can't we?" he chided, taking off his coat and tossing it over a bar stool. "You were the one who set things in motion, weren't you?" Her uncle had been amiable but had gotten straight down to business and they didn't discuss Jasmine. "Champagne?"

He noticed a piece of paper folded in half lying on the bench, but was distracted by the obvious effort Jasmine was making to widen her smile.

Something was off. He frowned down at the piece of paper. "What's this?" he asked, turning to scoop two flutes from the cocktail shelf behind him. By the time he'd turned back, she'd sidled around to his side of the bench, her eyes on the paper.

Adam was closer. He set the two flutes and the bottle on top of the paper, then unhurriedly went about opening and pouring, wondering about the troubled expression on her face. He'd expected more excitement from her. Surely she knew how much having Stewart Cooper on board meant to him.

Keeping his eyes on her face, he handed her a

glass and saluted her with his. "To the launch of Thorne-Hadlow Investments in the very near future," he announced.

Jasmine raised her glass and touched it to his.

"First thing tomorrow, I'm going to start organizing the launch party. This show is on the road!"

Her eyes slid off his. Something was very definitely wrong. She hadn't removed her coat. "Where were you off to just now?"

She swallowed. "I was— I have to get home."

He thought of her father, his failing health. "Home the estate or home New Zealand?"

"Pembleton," she replied listlessly. "My father found out I went to see Stewart. He is furious with me."

Adam was instantly concerned. "I'm sorry. I'll come with you, tell him it was all my fault."

Jasmine gave a bleak smile. "He won't listen, I'm afraid. He thinks if you go into business with Stewart, he'll use you to get his hands on Pembleton after Father passes away."

Now he was confused. "How would I do that?" He was obviously missing the big picture.

She studied the bubbles in her untouched glass. "After we're married…"

Concerned, confused and now confounded. "*After* we're married…?"

She didn't seriously harbor hopes that this engagement would morph into a real one any time soon, did she? Adam thought she was fantastic. He'd enjoyed their weekend as much as she had and was already planning another, but marriage?

Her lips tightened. "That's why I'm going. I have to put his mind at rest, come clean about the engagement."

He relaxed a little. "You had me worried there for a moment." He tugged on her scarf. "You can do that tomorrow."

This was supposed to be a celebration and Adam had spent the last hour since leaving the meeting thinking of just how he wanted to celebrate. He knew one thing, he couldn't get enough of this woman. "Take off your coat," he ordered, "have some bubbles and let's celebrate." He leaned toward her and nuzzled at the side of her mouth.

Jasmine huffed out a breath and turned her head away. "No, I— Don't, Adam."

He was barely listening, intent on tasting her lips again. She smelled amazing, looked amazing. Being close to her put more bubbles in his blood than the very best French champagne. "I bet I could persuade you…"

Jasmine stepped back like a scalded cat, raising her palms at chest height between them. "No!"

The sharpness of her voice surprised both of them. Adam realized this went deeper than guilt about lying to her father.

He put his own glass down and noticed the piece of paper again, still under the bottle. "What's this?" he asked, tapping it with his index finger.

Jasmine inhaled and held out her hand. "May I have it, please?"

Holding her gaze, he lifted the bottle and picked up the single sheet of paper. "Why?"

"It doesn't matter. You're here now." She made a half-hearted grab for the paper but he moved it out of her reach.

"Let's see…what sweet nothings…?" He opened the paper, an ominous feeling darkening his mood, and cleared his throat. "'Adam,'" he read aloud, "'Thank you for spending Christmas with me and for an unforgettable weekend. I loved every moment. No doubt I will see you in New Zealand from time to time.'" He sent a scathing look to her pink face. "'*Best*, Jasmine.'"

Best? That was low. They'd spent the last two days being as intimate as two people could be, and he only warranted a "Best"?

She said nothing, her face a picture of guilt.

"Dumped by note," he murmured, his quiet tone belying the anger starting to sizzle in his blood. "That's classy."

The expensive wine left a vinegary aftertaste. His satisfaction in landing the biggest defining achievement of his career ebbed away.

"I'm sorry," Jasmine said quietly. "I had no idea what time you'd be back."

"So you thought you'd just sneak away like a common thief."

Being dumped was a novel experience for Adam. It stung, he decided. He didn't like it. He thought he'd done everything to ensure she had a good time and this is how she repaid him. Worse, he was being dumped on what should have been one of the most satisfying nights of his life. "You're really something, you know that?"

"You got what you wanted, didn't you?"

Adam's head went up and he glared at her. Maybe he deserved that at the start, the old "you owe me" flung back in his face. But what about Vienna? Not that he begrudged a single penny, but he'd paid handsomely for his demand. Her lack of appreciation angered him.

He inclined his head stiffly, his eyes sweeping her body. "On all fronts, yes." He'd never had better. The sex was off-the-planet sublime.

Jasmine sighed heavily. "Well, they were your words. You said you'd take what you wanted, and you did and it was—" her voice hitched and her eyes were strangely brilliant but Adam was wound too tight to care "—wonderful," she continued. "Really wonderful."

"I aim to please," he bit out while at the same time, images of how she'd looked at the ball, in the gown he'd bought her, pummeled him. Especially the laughter and excitement and magic in her eyes.

Those eyes watched him now as if waiting for something. Did she think he was going to make her feel better about giving him the heave-ho, offer some platitude or other like, *Hey, don't worry about it, it was only sex, right?*

She looked away and began to pull her gloves back on. "Adam, I hope we—you—"

"Can still be friends?" he asked with a lightness he didn't feel. He raised his glass and tossed the contents back in one. "Sure, baby."

His tone, the careless response to her question, the unintended sharp report of the base of the flute banging down on the bench between them, made her flinch. What did he care? It was a relief, really. Now that New Year was over, his focus needed to be on the business.

A good five seconds passed before she spoke again. "Please don't tell Nick—everything."

Her words slashed at his pride. So that was her primary concern, after her father. She didn't want Nick to know his chaste personal assistant had gotten down and dirty with his disreputable brother. As if he'd want Nick, of all people, to know he'd been tossed aside by her. His brother had warned him repeatedly not to mess about with her feelings.

Who cared? He was off the hook. "Consider your debt paid in full."

So much for celebrations. Adam topped his glass up as she closed the door behind her.

Ten

Adam, his partner, John, and their new reception-
ist sat in his corner office on the prestigious Docklands site. They were open for business but, far from
being excited, Adam stifled a yawn. He'd been working twenty-hour days to get to this point, as well as
organizing the launch party next week, unpacking
here at the new offices, hiring staff and fielding calls.

Lots of calls. The word had gotten out that Stewart
Cooper was the principal investor in Thorne-Hadlow
Investments. That started an avalanche of interest
from some of the country's wealthiest business icons,
clamoring to be included. The fledgling company's
projected equity would far surpass their initial esti-

mates at this rate, proving Adam's instincts about how vital Stewart's credentials would be correct.

"Promotion for the launch…" John said, rifling through his notes. "Everything is in hand, thanks to Lettie here." He indicated the bespectacled young lady beside him. "You're going down to sign the contract and pay the deposit on the venue today, aren't you?"

She nodded. "As soon as we're finished here. Have you finalized the guest list numbers?"

This would be a smallish but classy event at one of London's most prestigious clubs. Adam guessed that many of those who'd accepted personal invites to the launch were only coming in the hope of catching a glimpse of the notorious Stewart Cooper. They would be disappointed. The former pop-star manager hadn't been seen in public for a decade or more and Adam was fairly sure he wouldn't make an exception for Thorne-Hadlow.

He'd also invited Jasmine—a gesture of apology for his churlishness a week ago. Of thanks for her intervention with her uncle.

Of just plain wanting to see her face, hear her voice. Touch her, anywhere and everywhere.

"I have the reporter from the *Mail* here any minute for a bit of promo. Be prepared to have your photo taken."

Adam grimaced. "The offices are a mess." There were furniture boxes everywhere, his people sat at desks with wiring all over the place and no phones, and the entrance on the ground floor was wide-open. "Where is that security company?"

"I'll call them before I go," Lettie said, rising.

"Rome wasn't built in a day." John grinned at him. "Things will fall into place. They always do, with you on the job."

Adam grunted and watched his friend leave. It was nice to be given credit but it was primarily John's belief in Adam's ability to attract investment that had got them this far. Just a few short months ago, a lot of the big players they approached had run the other way. He owed John for keeping the faith.

He owed Jasmine, too. Without her, he doubted her uncle would have been interested. Once the launch was over and things started to settle down a little, he would give her a call. He'd hate her to return to New Zealand thinking badly of him.

He stood at his office window, looking out over the white disc of the O2 Dome in the distance, and finally allowed himself to acknowledge that he missed her. He'd lashed out because she hurt his pride and he wasn't used to that from anyone. Subsequently, he'd taken her slight far more seriously than it warranted.

A deep, booming voice broke into his thoughts, followed by John's voice, surprised and inquiring. Adam turned just as Stewart Cooper himself marched into his office with John on his heels.

The man who never left his house in the Lake

District, a virtual recluse, shunned by his family and denied his birthright, stood framed in Adam's doorway. And he did not look pleased to be here.

Adam moved to meet him but didn't smile. He was obviously in no mood for pleasantries. Adam thought again how frail Jasmine's younger, taller father looked in comparison to the physically powerful man approaching him now.

Stewart stopped at the desk, his legs braced like a fighter, and fixed Adam with a glower. "I came to tell you that if you marry my niece before her father dies, the deal is off."

Adam's vision deserted him for a second. He bit down on a howl of protest that lodged in his throat, and then unclenched his fists. Who the hell did this bloke think he was to demand whom he could or could not marry? If he thought that was the way Adam did business, he had another think coming.

Behind the big man, John's mouth dropped open. Adam ignored him, fuming inwardly. Damn, but this woman and her secrets were proving to be a monumental pain in the rear. He'd like to go just half a day without thinking about her.

"Well?"

Adam forced his mind on the facts and away from Jasmine's face. He recalled her saying her father needed a male heir to pass the estate on to. If that didn't eventuate, presumably the estate would go to Stewart, the next of kin. Bloody family feuds! His own family had just been through the wringer in New Zealand because of a stupid historical feud. Didn't people have anything better to do with their time?

Stewart Cooper and John still waited expectantly. Adam's good business sense kicked in. The word *no* was his least favorite word in the world but Stewart was a vital link to their success. Without his money, and more importantly, his involvement, Thorne-Hadlow would be just one more angel investment company. John and Adam weren't interested in small businesses; they were playing with millions of pounds to start up innovative companies that were going global. And marketing and management for global IT and technology required massive investment—and massive risk.

The big Englishman watched him through cold gray eyes that had similar color to his niece's but none of the life. "I'm waiting for an assurance from you that this engagement won't proceed."

How had he found out? Surely Jasmine had told her father by now it was all an act.

John moved into view behind the bulk of their visitor. Adam squared up to his task. If he ordered him out, he'd be wasting five years of planning and hard work, not to mention the fortune that he personally had sunk into this project. He had John to consider, one of life's good blokes with two young kids and a large mortgage. And for what? A pretend engagement that she—Jasmine—had instigated?

Besides which, hadn't she dumped him last week?

Adam cleared his throat. "The engagement is off, Stewart. I won't be marrying your niece."

Stewart's piercing eyes bored into him for a few seconds more then he snapped off a nod. "Good man. Nothing personal, you understand."

His entire demeanor changed in an instant and he became the affable man Adam had met at his home last week on his return from Vienna. "My lawyer will be in touch in the next day or so." He shook hands heartily with both of them. "Boys." And was gone, as unexpectedly as he had come.

"You were engaged?" John turned to him, looking mystified.

"Long story," Adam said, shaking his head.

He told himself he had done the only thing he could have under the circumstances, but a hollow feeling of distaste perplexed him. It was as if he'd dishonored her by going along with her uncle's preposterous demand. Which was ridiculous. Jasmine would not want his business undermined. And there was no engagement. It wasn't as if they'd announced the union anyway. Only her father and Gill knew about it, and maybe Ian. Anyway, she would have set them all right by now, and Stewart was certainly not going to open his mouth about this conversation.

Realizing he wasn't going to get an explanation from his partner, John looked at his watch, frowning. "Where's that bloody reporter?"

Left alone, Adam ordered himself to stop worrying about Jasmine and get back to trying to track down the phone people.

The phone began to ring at seven in the morning. Jasmine jerked awake as her father's booming displeasure seemed to reach every corner of the house, taking her back to the Vincent debacle before his illness. The return of his voice at top notch was not a good sign.

She hurried into the small yellow drawing room where her father spent most of his days, wrinkling her nose against the smell of sickness that was beginning to pervade the room.

Her father was agitatedly pushing newspapers all over the table when he looked up and saw her. "Here she is," he erupted. "My *infamous* daughter."

Jasmine's heart plummeted. What had she done to disappoint him now?

His anger at her for approaching his most hated enemy had abated only slightly since she'd told him the engagement between her and Adam was off. He behaved exactly as she'd expected and spent every minute lauding Ian's virtues.

Now, he tossed one of the newspapers across the table to where she stood. Jasmine looked down. "Poor Jane Dumped—Again!"

"Try another," her father said acidly, tossing more papers. "And another."

She closed her eyes briefly, her shoulders slumping. *My worst nightmare...*

Taking a shaky breath, she forced herself to open her eyes.

"The Heiress and the Playboy—History Repeats." She winced at the next one—"Poor Little Jane—Abandoned Again" while Gill shushed her father at the other end of the table.

Trembling, she sank into the nearest chair as the words on the newsprint swam in front of her eyes. Her father vigorously filled her in, saying that Adam had indeed humiliated her, humiliated all of them. Her uncle had threatened to ditch his investment if Adam didn't ditch her. And ditch her he had in double-quick time.

She barely heard her father's "I told you so"s as her mind sank into anguish and her heart with it. It was happening again. She didn't know if she could bear it. She'd angered Adam with her clumsy farewell and shouldn't have been surprised by any callous disregard for her feelings. But why choose the public arena? He must have known how scarred she was by her past, the lengths she'd gone to to get away from all this.

I think you're running away, he'd said in Vienna.

"When will you learn," her father lamented, "that love is for fools? Anyone with half a brain knows that."

Predictably, he started up about Ian again as she sat numb with shock. How Ian would never let her down, he would protect her from all of this. Finally, her stepmother persuaded him to subside and he left the room, muttering that Jasmine was as bad as her mother.

Gill sat down beside her and flicked her fingers over the papers. "Take this with a grain of salt, love. It states 'unnamed sources.' I bet no one even spoke to Adam, or they misheard or misunderstood and didn't bother to confirm it with him."

She nodded slowly, thinking that cautious hope was better than no hope, even if it wouldn't change the outcome. Perhaps he hadn't knowingly humiliated her. He could be hard, but cruel? She refused to believe she could have lost her heart to a cruel man.

Remember Vincent, her memory taunted her...

She leaned her head back on the chair and stared, unseeing, out the window, waiting for the pain to come and clamp her insides with rusty jaws. "I suppose you think I should marry Ian, too," she whispered.

Gill squeezed her arm, kept her hands there. "There's a lot to be said for compatibility, security."

Jasmine stared at her for seconds, finally seeing what she'd been blind to all these years. She grabbed on to it—anything to sway her mind from her own humiliation. "You don't love my father, do you?"

Sir Nigel never displayed affection, except perhaps to his horses, and she'd wondered if he was even capable of love. But she'd always assumed Gill saw something in him to admire. Surely they must share some kind of bond to stay together all these years.

Gill's eyes showed gentle understanding. "I married for love first time around. He left me. When I came here, I recognized that Nigel and I could be of use to each other. I could bring you up properly and manage some of the workload around here. In return, he would give me security, prestige, a little luxury." She smiled, and Jasmine's heart squeezed. "And I got to have you, honey, to watch you grow. That alone was worth the price of admission."

A tear rolled down Jasmine's cheek and Gill, wonderful comforting Gill, reached out and wiped it away. "He's not a bad man. He was terribly hurt by your mother and in his way, he doesn't want to see you hurt."

Too late, Jasmine thought. Still, there was no need to worry anymore. Her heart was dead to the possibility of love now.

All through that long day, unable to stop herself, she tracked the progress of the story on Internet sites and TV. On signing into her work e-mail address, she was dismayed to find the story breaking on the main New Zealand news page because of her Kiwi connection. It was the middle of the night there but she imagined her boss, her work colleagues, the one or two friends she had warmed enough toward to share a coffee with occasionally, all waking up to the news that she was not who she purported to be. The real Jane Cooper was so much more interesting than the efficient, reserved Jasmine.

It was all laid out in grotesque clarity: her mother's affair with Stewart, the questions around her dead brother's paternity, the car accident, abandonment and her later broken engagement. "Misplacing one fiancé was unlucky," one scribe gleefully proclaimed. "Losing two is careless."

Whatever Adam's part in the story, her uncle's actions had wounded her. She thought they'd connected in some way, felt he wanted to expand on that. But it appeared Stewart was just after the estate and his revenge.

Ian came around, but she did not want to see him and Gill sent him away. The phone didn't stop ringing. The story, even with no fresh legs to run with, seemed to stutter on: inane comments from anyone who might have known her at school, staff at her mother's psychiatric facility, even a couple of locals that had attended the Boxing Day party and who looked thrilled to find themselves being interviewed on television.

Jasmine knew one thing. She couldn't go back to New Zealand and face Nick and her colleagues. With a heavy heart, she composed and sent e-mails to him and to an international moving company to pack up her house.

Gill showed Adam into one of the unused rooms, where he found Jasmine unpacking some of the estate's forgotten antiques. From the look on her stepmother's face, he wasn't the most popular man in Britain at the moment. The atmosphere in the house was ghost-cold.

He found Jasmine sitting in the middle of a ring

of chests and boxes, with piles of packing foam and wood chips scattered around. She held a small, square silver object in her hands and was carefully turning it this way and that. She wore a black cowl-necked jumper over gray pants and both garments were liberally spotted with packing debris and dust.

When she heard his approach, she looked straight at him, her sharp inhalation straightening her back. Adam stood still, stunned at the pain reflected in her eyes. Hating the knowledge that he'd put it there.

She finally looked back at her prize. "Solid silver card case, Victorian, early eighteen-fifties. Made by Alfred Taylor, a silversmith of Birmingham."

She carefully put the case into an open box.

Adam stepped forward quickly. "What can I do?"

Her blink of surprise at his concern shamed him. Did she really think he was that callous?

"You shouldn't be here," she said quietly. "It will be worse if anyone sees you."

There was no censure in her voice or her eyes, but Adam needed to tell her it wasn't intentional, he hadn't seen it coming. "We had a reporter coming to the offices for some promo for the launch. I suspect he saw Stewart coming in, decided to eavesdrop, and then disappeared."

With the reception area in a state and Lettie out anyway, no one had noticed anyone lurking outside Adam's office while the conversation with Stewart took place. There were so many publications doing the rounds, they couldn't be sure of the original source. The fact that the reporter supposedly covering the launch hadn't shown for his appointment suggested he was the culprit, but there was no way the editor was admitting to anything. "I knew nothing about it until I saw it in the papers."

The guarded acceptance in her eyes made him feel worse, if that was possible. The weight of culpability with each new publication or Internet site or TV broadcast was heavy indeed. How could he have exposed her to this? He knew what it had cost her in the past. No matter how miffed he was at her dumping him, he wouldn't have wished this particular personal nightmare on her if she was his worst enemy, because he knew how far she'd run to put it behind her last time.

Jasmine picked up a lumpy object and began peeling back layers of Bubble Wrap. Adam paced, not looking at her, but so aware of every move she made, the way she bent her head to study the object—some sort of bronze cannon—her concentration so intense, he knew she wasn't seeing it at all. All her senses were on him.

Suddenly he whirled and squatted down in front of her. He rested his hands on her knees. "Marry me."

Jasmine nearly dropped the cannon. "Wh-what?"

"I can't change what's happened but I can make things better."

Her gray-blue eyes had a rosy tinge in the dimly lit room, suggesting recent tears.

"How?" she asked. "How could marrying you make it better?"

Adam sighed. Maybe it couldn't, but he felt so useless. "I wouldn't be abandoning you." He squeezed her thighs, not sure which of them he was trying to convince more.

"You've been talking to Nick." There was an accusatory tone in her voice.

Adam didn't deny it. Both his brother and father had called to castigate him as soon as the story broke over there. They'd taken turns to berate him for his lack of responsibility, his carelessness in hurting a fine woman like Jasmine. When would he learn he couldn't just continue to sail through life, letting people down, never thinking of consequences? Adam had been lucky to escape with his hearing.

They had some valid points. He should have taken more care with Jasmine's particular set of circumstances. His brother would never have gotten into this situation, but if he had, he would take full responsibility.

"We might be all right. We're friends, aren't we?"

They were. Not only that, but the sex was amazing. Many marriages survived on less.

"And when my uncle finds out you've gone back on your word? Your business?"

A muscle twitched in his cheek. That had kept him awake all night, but he'd contributed to this mess. He had to clean it up. "I don't think it will come to that, but that's my problem."

"Why, Adam?"

Her quiet question reminded him of all the things that had gone through his mind when Stewart made the demand. Watching the news break yesterday illustrated that he was no better than her mother or her ex. The publicity may not have been intentional but still, he'd hung her out to dry as nonchalantly and effortlessly as they had done before him.

"Because I hate that it's made things worse for you. I hate that I've made you sad. You've suffered enough."

Jasmine smiled. He warmed to see it. "Thank you, Adam," she said quietly. "That's very kind, but it won't be necessary."

Despite his earnest desire to help, relief washed through him—followed by a sharp jet of green suspicion. "You're not going to do anything stupid, are you? I won't let you marry Ian…"

Her nostrils flared. "That's not for you to say," she said sharply.

She had told him that after what happened last time, the pressure her father put on her to marry the neighbor drove her away. No way would Adam let that happen.

"But, no," Jasmine said in a more reasonable tone. "I'm not marrying anyone." She looked down at his hands, still on her knees. "You owe me nothing, Adam. The engagement was my misguided attempt to give my father some pleasure before he died."

Adam wondered how the old man had taken this.

As if she'd read his mind, Jasmine smiled ruefully. "And you can imagine the pleasure he is feeling today."

"I bet," he said feelingly. In his limited acquaintance with Sir Nigel, he could almost feel the wind of disapproval and censure from here.

"We're even," she continued. "I did you a favor, you did me one. It was my stupid idea that caused all this trouble. My fault, not yours. You did everything I asked of you—" she covered one of his hands with hers "—and more. You gave me Vienna."

She lifted her hand from the all too brief caress and brushed at her top. With her pale face and hair tightly tied back, the shadows under her eyes, she looked so much less, somehow, than the night of the ball. Not less beautiful, just faded and smaller than before. Adam's heart squeezed in his chest. He would make this up to her, he promised himself. Somehow…

He rose to his feet, for once in his life unsure of what to say, to do. "Nick said you'd resigned," he said to the crown of her head.

Jasmine merely nodded.

"Why, Jasmine? You love that job and you love New Zealand."

She exhaled and looked out the window. A minute ticked by before she answered. "I do. But the Jasmine over there is not the real me. She was just a front, born to hide my problems." She looked at him, her eyes clear. "I haven't got it all worked out yet, but I need to be here for my father. It would be a mistake to leave England at the moment. There are things I started here that I never got around to finishing." She paused, choosing her words carefully. "In fact, there is a lot of unfinished business in my life. I think it's time I faced up to it."

Eleven

Adam checked his watch for the tenth time. Where were they? His most important guests had flown halfway across the world to be here tonight, and yet the party had been going for an hour and there was no sign of them. John and the events manager of the Café de Paris kept shooting him raised-brow looks, reminding him that the venue was booked for another event in an hour.

No one was more pleased than Adam when Nick said they were coming. He'd made a flip comment like he was just keeping an eye on his investment, but Adam knew his brother was behind him all the way. It hadn't been as difficult as he'd imagined, going cap in hand to Thorne Financial Enterprises and asking them to underwrite the new company's debt, should some or all of his big investors pull out.

"Why would they do that?" Nick had asked.

"Because I'm going to tell Stewart Cooper that he can stick his investment where the sun doesn't shine," Adam had replied.

After leaving Jasmine last week, he knew he'd missed a golden opportunity. He'd needed a little more time to get used to the idea that he loved her. Some last-gasp vestige of confirmed bachelorhood had its claws into him still. She'd have been nuts to accept his pathetic proposal.

"The natives are getting restless," John said at his elbow.

With a last look around, Adam followed his friend to the front of the gathering. Sure, he was disappointed Nick hadn't made it but that was nothing compared to his disappointment that Jasmine hadn't showed. Hardly surprising, given the media contingent here.

As he stepped up onto the small stage, he ran his fingers over the tiny box in his pocket. Before the night was out, he'd have a private audience with her, and the second chance he hoped her generous nature would allow him.

Someone handed him a microphone and he called for quiet.

"I'm Adam Thorne, and this—" Adam clapped a hand on his partner's shoulder "—is John Hadlow.

We are pleased to welcome you all to the international launch of Thorne-Hadlow Investments."

He looked out over the sea of heads at the business icons, friends and invited media, and launched into his well-rehearsed speech. He was midway through when he caught sight of his brother and father right at the back and breathed a sigh of relief.

"There are many people to thank. It's been a long road, but without my family's support, and that of a few select friends, we wouldn't be here today."

He finished his short speech and stepped back so John could say a few words. His former mentor, Derek Bayley of Croft, Croft and Bayley, was next and that concluded the formalities. The hundred guests continued to graze on the food and drink provided and Adam began to work his way through the crowd of well-wishers to the back of the room, simmering with impatience. He'd say a quick hello and then flag the family meal he'd arranged downstairs in favor of a couple of hours' drive and some unfinished business at Pembleton Estate. This time he would do it properly, give her reasons she could live with.

A plethora of camera flashes lit up the back of the room. Adam craned his neck and saw the tall figures of Nick and his father, head and shoulders above the throng of people. A swish of gold fabric and blond ringlets by Nick's shoulder confirmed the photographic interest. Nick's fiancée, Jordan Lake, stopped traffic wherever she went.

Adam stopped abruptly, his eyes snagged on a deep-red off-the-shoulder dress, close to his father. He stretched tall, but with half the crowd turning and moving to see what the fuss was about, he could only pick out parts—long, blood-red baubles at her ears, a flash of white teeth, glossy dark hair pulled back in a stylish twist. The cameras flashed again and Adam's heart gave him a kick.

Jasmine. A strong impulse to melt into the crowd and escape gripped him. Was he ready for this? Matrimony? Love? It went totally against his life plan, the goals he'd set, his vision of his future. All the valid reasons why not had hammered through his brain at regular intervals for days.

The crowd noise around him hushed and the people in front stepped aside, their eyes moving between him and Jasmine with fascinated expressions. Adam stood as if in the spotlight, wishing he were anywhere else in the world, until she half turned and saw him.

A small, uncertain smile played across her face. Adam's heart slowed and swelled and for the first time since the day he met her, he felt at peace.

It was hard not to make a dramatic entrance at the Café de Paris; the opulent decor, impressive staircases and air of grandeur demanded it. Jasmine forced herself to hold her head high but in reality, if she wasn't firmly supported by Randall on one side and Nick and Jordan on the other, she would have bolted at the first camera flash. As it was, she sagged at the second.

"I'm right here, girl," Randall rumbled in her ear, holding her arm firmly. On the other side, Jordan's eye-catching beauty and vivacity pulled a few of the cameras off her face, for which Jasmine was grateful.

They were late. That was her fault. She'd argued loud and long against going, but her surprise visitors to Pembleton wouldn't take no for an answer. They'd caught most of Adam's speech but she barely heard a word. The pain was too raw, her nerves stretched to breaking at the prospect of more denigrating publicity in tomorrow's press.

She had spent the last week keeping busy to take her mind off Adam and his kind-hearted marriage proposal. This afternoon, Nick had looked over the business plan she'd put together for the bank and pronounced it excellent. She'd spent hours working on her lists, talking to her father and Gill and prioritizing the multiple ways to best drag Pembleton into the twenty-first century.

As Adam stepped down from the dais and headed in their direction, she thought how ironic that he had offered the thing she wanted most—marriage to him—and she had turned him down. Accepting his proposal, born of guilt and pity, would be as bad as accepting Ian, who only wanted her for the estate. Jasmine vowed to forget about love, marriage and children and concentrate on her father in the short term and Pembleton in the long.

Suddenly the crowd parted and Adam walked toward them, tall, confident, larger than life, and his eyes on her face. She forced herself to breathe, told herself over and over that she could do this, she could be friends with him on this auspicious occasion. But oh, it would be so much easier in a less public forum, without oafish reporters loudly querying the current status of their relationship and cameras going off left, right and center.

In the interests of public relations, she offered him a smile and he smiled back and ran his hand down her arm. "I'm glad you came," he murmured in her ear, leaning close.

"Shall we go?" Adam turned to the others. "I've booked a table downstairs." He glanced at Jasmine. "It will be quieter down there."

They ate a relatively private dinner with a couple of Adam's friends and the family. Randall was, as usual, the loudest and best company. Jasmine warmed to see how he had taken to his daughter-in-law-to-be. After all the angst between Randall and Jordan's father, Syrius, she could scarcely believe how close they'd become in such a short time.

But as soon as dessert was cleared away, Nick began yawning and making jet lag excuses, belaboring the point so much that Jasmine quickly saw through his act; her boss was determined that she and Adam be left alone. Maybe he hoped Adam could talk her into coming back to work.

The Thornes and entourage left. Adam put her coat around her shoulders and suggested a walk. The night was crisp and cold, with no wind.

"Uncle Stewart didn't come?" she asked, pulling her gloves on as they began to walk slowly toward nearby Trafalgar Square.

Adam shook his head. "I didn't expect him to."

A phone call from her uncle a couple of days ago had thrown Jasmine into a quandary. She had made a promise to her father, but Stewart begged her to come. The old man felt terrible about the publicity he'd unwittingly sparked.

While speaking to him, she realized that he was lonely and wanted nothing more than to belong to a family. Now she told Adam a little of Stewart's history. "His father kicked him out of home very young because he wanted a career in the music industry, not the done thing for an English country gentleman."

Her uncle had discovered and managed what became one of the world's biggest glam rock bands in the seventies. The predecessors of punk, glam rock bands were the outcasts of the music industry with their makeup and glitter and rocky ballads, but a handful of artists had huge success. "He met my mother in the mid-seventies when he was riding high," she continued. "Naturally her parents hated her going out with someone so anti-establishment, so they had to sneak around and she pretended to be going out with my father instead. And then she got pregnant and my father married her."

"Did he know who the father was?"

"I've never had the nerve to ask him," Jasmine said quietly. Talking about personal matters was not the done thing around her father. "Stewart lost everything, his own family, the love of his life, his son. I'm not surprised he's bitter. He's so alone."

"Are you going to keep in touch?"

Jasmine nodded. "Yes, but I'll have to be discreet. I don't want to upset my father. He'll never make his peace with Stewart now."

"You don't know that. By all accounts, Dad and Syrius are making an effort for Nick and Jordan's sake. Enough, at least, to sit down together at a family engagement dinner."

Jordan had told her as much. Syrius and Randall had been close friends before the accident that had put Syrius's wife in a wheelchair and robbed him of his son.

They walked onto Trafalgar Square, her eyes automatically gravitating to where the Christmas tree had been until a few days ago. She sighed. Another year older, but wiser? She didn't think so.

She clapped her cold hands together. "I've broached the possibility of Stewart coming to live at Pembleton when Father passes away—provided Gill agrees, of course. I feel disloyal but…it was Stewart's home, too, you know? I feel he has as much right to be there as I do."

Her uncle had no intention of kicking her and Gill out after her father died, even though she had failed to marry and provide a male heir. She glanced sideways at Adam. Best not to mention the word *marriage* in present company.

Adam pursed his lips thoughtfully. "What did he say?"

Jasmine's eyes misted with emotion. Stewart had nearly wept when she'd asked him. "He would dearly love to see Pembleton again. I think he would enjoy being involved and I could certainly use the help."

She'd told Adam over dinner about the improvements she'd instigated in the redevelopment of Pembleton Estate. She had already hired the contractors to develop the golf course. The events program could wait for now while she concentrated on setting up the new Antiques Center.

"I've asked him to tell me about my mother, let me get to know her through his eyes, because I never really knew her at all."

Stewart had said he would gladly oblige in return for having the pleasure of watching Jasmine's children grow, but she decided Adam didn't need to know that.

"And is he going to tell you about your mother?" he asked.

She nodded. "Maybe it will fill a hole in both our lives."

Jasmine recognized that she'd closed herself off from the world, afraid of reaching out to people. Perhaps that stemmed from her mother's abandonment, perhaps not, but she knew she had some growing to do.

Adam stopped and leaned against one of the famous lion bronzes, flanking Nelson's Column. "I think you'll be very happy there, amongst all your old relics."

"I'm going to try," Jasmine said.

He was right about her passion for history. Pembleton could be her museum. It would take years to unpack, catalogue and restore the treasures packed away. Now that she'd resigned and made arrangements to pack up her Wellington house and put it on the market, she needed to keep busy and to heal her heart. That particular relic would be packed away safely, perhaps never to be exhibited again.

Given her love for the man watching her right now, that was a bleak prospect. Feeling the need to lighten the mood, she craned her neck and peered up the length of Nelson's Column.

"Do you know why some rum is called Nelson's Blood?"

Adam shook his head, looking interested. Jasmine admired his tolerance for her historical prattling.

"When Admiral Nelson was killed," she began, "the ship's officers preserved the body in the crew's vat of rum and halted their rations. But when they got to England, they found the body well preserved but the vat empty. Unbeknown to the officers, the crew hadn't liked giving up their daily tot and so had drilled holes in the vat to get at their rum."

Adam pulled a face. "Well, that's certainly set the scene for romance."

Jasmine tilted her head but her query died on her lips when his eyes locked onto hers and became serious.

Her heartbeat began to rattle. Oh, please, not another of those great, addictive surges of longing. She'd tried sleeping with him without losing her heart. It hadn't worked.

Adam reached out and took her hand in his. "Marry me, Jasmine," he said simply.

Jasmine closed her eyes, cherishing the words but wishing that they came from his heart and not some warped sense of responsibility.

"We've been here before." She sighed.

"No," he murmured. "We haven't."

When she opened her eyes, Adam stood in front of her, holding a tiny red box. Her mind howled foul—it was unfair of him to tempt her so much when she was at her weakest. Inhaling, she called on all of her composure to crush the surge of hope that burst within her. With more poise than she knew she possessed, Jasmine raised her eyes to his, but could do nothing about the hitch in her breathing.

"Adam, we discussed this. I won't marry for the wrong reasons. Otherwise why not just marry Ian and be done with it?"

Adam squeezed her gloved hand. "What about

the right reasons?" He paused and then inhaled deeply, working up to something. The pressure on her hand increased. "Such as love?"

Jasmine blinked and felt frozen in time. Was he saying that he loved her?

He held out the box. "Open it."

She eyed it almost fearfully, then shook her head. There was too much longing, too much dashed hope for her to take that step.

He opened it. She tried, she really did, not to look at it. Instead, she searched his face, looking in vain for sympathy, the anguish and guilt she'd seen a few days ago. There was only strain etched around his mouth and his serious, waiting eyes.

She looked down and blinked several times. The stone was huge, a perfect cushion-cut diamond surrounded by smaller round diamonds. The band was handcrafted platinum, delicately millegrained around the square shoulders. It was a true Edwardian antique or at least, manufactured to a very high standard of reproduction. Either way, it was the most beautiful ring she'd ever seen.

She ghosted a step closer, unable to take her eyes off it.

Adam cleared his throat. "Jasmine, last week I couldn't say the right words. I would never marry anyone I wasn't head over heels about. But I made a real mess of it and you were quite right to turn me down."

She looked into his eyes and saw that he was completely serious. The tension overwhelmed her; the desire to believe him was immense. After all the secrets and games between them, could it be true that Adam Thorne wanted her for no other reason than love?

Adam lowered his arm and as he did, the ring box snapped shut. Jasmine couldn't help the tiny moan of protest and longing that slipped out.

He noticed. Smiling, he lifted her hand and wrapped her fingers around the box, covering both with his hand. She looked up at him and opened her mouth to speak, but he put his index finger on her lips. "Just let me get this out."

He was nervous, she realized incredulously. She had to bite her lip not to smile, not to pat his arm and tell him he was doing fine. Amazingly, wonderfully fine.

"I wanted you at first because you were so—cool and unattainable. And because Nick said I couldn't." A quick smile flashed over his face. "I like needling Nick. But then I got to know you, all your secrets and intrigues, all the sadness and disappointments. And then, Vienna."

"Vienna." Jasmine sighed against his finger. Where she had free-fallen into orgasm and the explosive knowledge that she loved him desperately at the very same instant.

"I agreed to Stewart's demand because my pride was hurt," Adam continued, "knowing deep down that it was wrong, it wasn't what I wanted to do. But I couldn't get my head around it. I mean, what engagement? It was a sham, and anyway, you'd finished with me. There were other valid reasons but I knew—I knew I'd let you down just like your mother and just like your ex. And I knew it would come back to haunt me."

Jasmine's heart went out to him, humbled that he, too, had suffered so much.

"After the publicity hit, I felt that marriage was the right—the only—thing to offer, but still I couldn't admit to myself, let alone you, that I loved you. I'm so sorry for that."

"I so very nearly said yes." Jasmine exhaled sadly and reached up to place her hand on his cheek. The leather glove against his stubble scraped dully. "It's not like I have high expectations. But I love you so much, I couldn't stand to tie you into a marriage because you pitied me."

There was no guilt or pity in his eyes now. He turned his head and pressed his lips against her fingers. "Then say yes, because love is the right reason, the only reason."

His hand squeezed hers around the jewelry box, reminding her of its presence. Joy and hope, waiting in the wings for so long, began to fill and warm her from top to toe. Yet, caution—an innate part of her nature these last few years—still whispered questions in her mind. "And Stewart? Maybe I can talk to him?"

"I've talked to him already, told him that's not the way I do business. He's thinking about it. In the meantime, I've asked Nick to underwrite the debt if the other investors pull out. It's a risk I'm prepared—and equipped—to take."

Jasmine's mouth dropped open. "You asked Nick for help?"

"He didn't mention it?"

She shook her head, full of wonder.

"Probably still in shock," Adam said, smiling.

For Adam Thorne to ask his brother for help was unbelievable. Nick was the very last person in the world Adam would admit to that maybe, just maybe, he didn't have the deck stacked. "That must have cost you."

"You have no idea." He ran a hand along his brow.

Jasmine liked his family so much. When she'd refused point-blank to go to the launch tonight, Nick had pulled rank quite forcefully.

"You haven't worked out your notice," he'd warned. "That still makes me your boss. Now, get dressed!"

Now she smiled at his brother. "I get the impression Nick wants me back at work."

"Nick will like the idea of you as his sister-in-law better, trust me," Adam told her confidently.

Nick's sister-in-law. It sounded wonderful.

Just one more thing stopped her from giving in to the impulse to jump on him and scream her delight, and get that gorgeous ring on her finger before he changed his mind—or they were mugged. "Where would we live?"

"There is room at that dusty old manor for me, isn't there?"

"Of course." She blinked. "But you always intended on going home, setting up there."

He nodded. "There will be some teething problems, especially initially. I know I said I wanted everything perfect before I married, but we can work out these things over time." He took both her hands. "All I know is, you need to be at Pembleton for now, and I need to be with you."

"It's not like we don't have support, good support, here and in New Zealand," she agreed. Gill was very capable if given direction and when her father passed, there would be Stewart. "I think a wedding will perk Father up, give him something extra to mutter about."

Adam pulled her into his front, their hands in between them. "As soon as you like," he said solemnly. "Sooner."

Then he bent close. "I think it's customary in deals of this nature to seal the contract with a kiss."

They kissed, a long sweet kiss, full of friendship and forgiveness, hope and love. Jasmine felt the remnants of her reserve and caution melt away.

"Just one thing worries me."

He pulled back, putting on a long-suffering look.

"You like excitement. Fast cars. Clubs and fine food. Travel and stock-market drama." She cocked her head. "Isn't playing an English gentleman in the countryside going to be rather tame?"

Adam all but rolled his eyes at her. In reply, he pulled her glove off and she watched, thrilled to bits as he slid the beautiful ring onto her finger.

"Let's see," Adam murmured, holding her hand up and bending each finger closed as he ticked off his points. "Fake engagements. Royal fiancé's. A scandalous past. An eccentric billionaire." He paused, but Jasmine was too caught up in the glitter of the diamond on her hand to notice.

"The sight of you in nothing but ankle boots on an antique canopied bed…"

She glanced up at his face, his wonderful, loving smile, and matched it with one of her own.

Adam squeezed her fingers. "Jasmine Cooper, if you promise to try and make life marginally less frenetic, I promise to love, cherish and try my best to keep up with you."

* * * * *

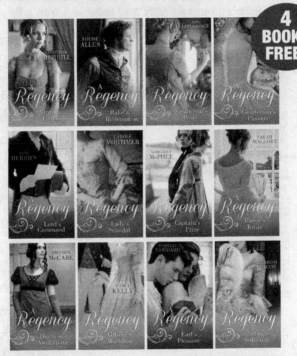

  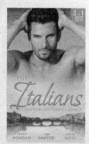